www.facebook.com/EloisaJamesFans
www.twitter.com/EloisaJames

Praise for Eloisa James:

'Sexual tension, upper-class etiquette and a dollop of wit make this another hit from *New York Times* bestseller Eloisa James'
Image Magazine Ireland

'She is one of the brightest lights ... Her writing is truly scrumptious'
Teresa Medeiros

'[This] delightful tale is as smart, sassy and sexy as any of her other novels, but here James displays her deliciously wicked sense of humour'
Romantic Times BookClub

'Graced with sly humour, addictive dialogue, elegant prose, and a skillfully woven subtext, this smart, deliciously sensual twist on a fairy tale classic is a breathtaking addition to James's series of reimagined fairy tales'
Library Journal

Duchess in Love

Eloisa James

piatkus

PIATKUS

First published in the US in 2002 by Avon Books,
An imprint of HarperCollins Publishers, New York
First published in Great Britain in 2013 by Piatkus
by arrangement with Avon

Copyright © 2002 by Eloisa James

The moral right of the author has been asserted.

A CIP catalogue record for this book
is available from the British Library.

ISBN 978-0-7499-5949-4

An Hachette UK Company
www.hachette.co.uk

www.piatkus.co.uk

Duchess in Love

Chapter One

A Brief Conversation
The Duchess of Girton's Bedchamber

Lady Troubridge's House Party
East Cliff

"Well, what does he look like?"

There was a pause. "He has black hair, I remember that," Gina said dubiously. She was sitting at her dressing table and tying a hair ribbon into small knots. Ambrogina, Duchess of Girton, rarely fidgeted. *Duchess is as duchess does,* one of her governesses had insisted. But Gina was panicking. Even duchesses panic, on occasion.

Esme Rawlings burst into laughter. "You don't know what your own husband looks like?"

Gina scowled. "It's easy for you to laugh. Your husband isn't returning from the continent to find you in the midst of a scandal. I've been insisting that Cam annul our marriage so that I can marry Sebastian. After he reads that dreadful bit of gossip in *The Tatler,* he'll think I'm a loose woman."

"Not if he knows you," Esme chortled.

"That's just it! He *doesn't* know me. What if he believes the talk about Mr. Wapping?"

"Fire your tutor and it'll blow over in a week."

"I won't fire poor Mr. Wapping. He came all the way from Greece to be my tutor, and the poor man doesn't have anywhere to go. Besides, he hasn't done anything wrong, and neither have I, so why should I act as if I had?"

"Being seen with your tutor at two in the morning by Willoughby Broke and his wife was not the soundest policy."

"You know we were simply observing the meteor shower. At any rate, you're not answering me. What if I don't recognize my own husband?" Gina turned around on her stool and fixed her eyes on Esme. "It will be the most humiliating moment of my life!"

"For goodness' sake, you sound like a bad actress in a melodrama. He'll be announced by the butler, won't he? So you'll have time to collect yourself. *Oh my dearest husband,*" Esme said, casting Gina a melting look of welcome. "*What a terrible, terrible sorrow your absence has been to me!*" She began fanning herself languidly.

Gina grimaced at her. "I suppose you employ that sentence frequently?"

"Naturally. Miles and I are always polite, whenever we meet. Which is rare, thank goodness."

Gina put down the ribbon, now knotted in fifty places. "Look at this—my hands are shaking. I don't know anyone who has experienced such a horrendous meeting."

"You're exaggerating. Think how poor Caroline Pratt felt when she had to tell her husband she was pregnant—and he away in the Low Countries all the previous year!"

"That must have been difficult."

"Although she really did him a favor. What in God's name would have happened to the estate if she hadn't managed to produce an heir? They have been married over ten years, after all. Pratt should have thanked her very nicely, although I have no doubt but what he didn't, men being the boors they are."

"My point is that meeting Cam is going to be prodigiously difficult," Gina said. "I'm not sure I will know him from Adam."

"I thought you spent your childhood in his pocket."

"That's not the same as meeting him as a grown man. He was just a boy when we married."

"There are plenty of women who would love to see their husbands move to the continent," Esme pointed out.

"Cam is not really my husband. For goodness' sake, I was raised to think he was my first cousin, until the very day we married."

"I don't see how that changes things. There are plenty of married first cousins, more's the pity. And you are not truly first cousins, given that your mother merely raised you, as opposed to giving birth to you."

"Just as my husband is not truly my husband," Gina added promptly. "Cam jumped out the window within fifteen minutes of his father forcing him to say the vows. It has simply taken him twelve years to return and annul the marriage."

"At least *my* husband left through the front door like a civilized man."

"Cam was hardly a man. He turned eighteen only a few days earlier."

"Well, you look glorious in that rose gown," Esme said, smiling at Gina. "He'll weep to think that he ever leaped out your bedchamber window."

"Nonsense. I'm not beautiful. I'm too thin and my hair resembles nothing so much as a carrot." She peered at herself in the mirror. "I wish I had your eyes, Esme. Mine are the color of mud."

"Your eyes are not muddy, they're green," Esme corrected her. "And as for not being beautiful—look at you! You look like a Renaissance Madonna today, all slender and composed and a bit teary. Except for your hair, of course. Do you think you inherited all that red hair from your scandalous French *maman*?"

3

"How should I know? My father refused to describe my real mother."

"Actually, a Madonna is a perfect description," Esme continued with a wicked twinkle. "Poor dear . . . yet another married virgin!"

There was a knock at the door, and Annie, the duchess's maid, answered it. "Lady Perwinkle would like to visit for a moment, Your Grace."

"Do ask her to come in," Gina replied.

Carola Perwinkle was small and deliciously rounded, with curls that bounced around her heart-shaped little face. She let out a squeal of delight at the sight of Esme.

"Darlings! I had to come even though it's past time to dress because Lady Troubridge told me the most astounding tale about Gina's husband—"

"It's true," Gina put in. "My husband is returning to England."

Carola clasped her hands together. "How romantic!"

"How so? I see nothing romantic about my husband annulling our marriage."

"All the way from Greece, simply to free you, to allow you to marry the man you love? I've no doubt but that his heart is secretly broken at the thought."

Esme looked faintly nauseated. "Sometimes I can't imagine why I'm friends with you, Carola. My guess is that Gina's husband is outrageously pleased to be getting her off his hands. Your husband and my husband would jump at such a chance of annulment, wouldn't they? Why should Gina's husband be any different?"

"I prefer not to think of it that way," Carola said, turning her little nose in the air. "My husband and I may not agree, but he would never annul our marriage."

"Well, mine would," Esme said. "He's simply too good-natured to say so. After we first separated, I tried my damnedest

4

to make him angry enough to divorce me, but he was too much of a gentleman. But if annulment were an option, he'd leap at it."

"You *are* a fool," Gina said, looking at her affectionately. "You destroyed your reputation just to get Miles's attention?"

Esme smiled ruefully. "Close enough. I can't imagine why you're friends with me, proper duchess that you are."

"Because I'm getting married, naturally. Whom should I come to for marital advice but you?" Gina had a wicked twinkle in her eye.

"Better Esme than me," Carola put in, with a little giggle. "My husband and I parted ways after only a month or so. Whereas Esme didn't separate from hers for over a year."

"The truth is, you're the one who should be doling out advice, Gina," Esme said. "Carola and I shucked off our spouses and have spent a good deal of time since blowing up scandals. But you have always behaved like an exemplary married duchess!"

"You make me sound so boring," Gina protested.

"Well, in comparison to *our* tarnished reputations . . ."

"Speak for yourself," Carola said. "My reputation may be marred but not yet tarnished."

"Oh well, mine is black enough for all three of us," Esme said lightly.

Carola was at the door. "I'd best be off if I don't wish to look a proper hag tonight." She slipped out the door.

Esme jumped from her chair. "I had better fly. Jeannie is planning to dress my hair à la grecque, and I don't wish to be late. Bernie might despair of my arrival."

"Bernie Burdett? I thought you said that he was a flat bore," Gina said.

Esme smiled impishly. "I'm not interested in his brain, my dear."

"You do remember that Lady Troubridge said your husband is arriving today?"

Her response was a shrug. "Of course Miles is coming. Lady Randolph Childe is already here, isn't she?"

Gina bit her lip. "That's only a rumor. Perhaps he wishes to see you."

Esme's eyes were a blue that had been likened to sapphires by many a young man. They were often just as brilliant and as hard as precious gems. But they softened looking at Gina's face. "You are a truly sweet person, Your Grace." She stooped and kissed her cheek. "I must go make myself into a femme fatale. It would be hideously uncomfortable if Lady Childe looked better than I."

"*That* is not possible," Gina said with utter conviction.

"You're simply fishing for a compliment." Esme's silky black curls, provocative mouth, and delicious curves had forced comparison with the most beautiful courtesans in London, since her very first season. And generally speaking, she was considered to leave her competition in the dust.

"Weren't *you* fishing for a compliment when you moaned about your muddy-colored eyes?"

Gina flipped her hand at her. "Not the same. Every gentleman I know would grovel to enter your bedroom door. Whereas they just think of me as a straitlaced, skinny duchess."

Esme snorted. "You're cracked. Try telling Sebastian how homely you are. I'm sure he can wax eloquent about your alabaster brow, etcetera, but I must dress." Blowing a kiss, she left.

Annie answered Gina's sigh, not the silence. "It's a shame, that's what it is," she said, picking up a hairbrush. "There's

Lady Rawlings, one of the most beautiful women in the whole of London, and her husband makes no pretense of his relationship with Lady Childe. A shame, that's what."

Gina nodded.

"You know, her husband requested a room adjoining Lady Childe's," Annie added.

Gina met her eyes in the mirror, startled. "Really?"

"It's not all that uncommon. More the opposite. Now that I'm an upper servant, Mrs. Massey talks freely before me. And the trouble she and Lady Troubridge have had to go to during this house party, shifting the rooms around, well, you wouldn't believe."

"Goodness," Gina said lamely. At least she and Sebastian wouldn't be that kind of couple once they were married. Poor Esme.

Chapter Two

An Encounter Between a Duke, a Piglet, and a Solicitor

There was no ignoring the fact that he had landed in England, Camden Serrard thought gloomily as he shook rainwater from the brim of his hat. His Italian boots squelched through rivers of mud. The rain was coming down so hard that the air had turned white, and he couldn't see the end of the track leading from the dock.

"Look out, sir!"

He swung about, but not in time to avoid a pig eagerly bolting for freedom. Sharp little hooves trotted across his mudsplattered boots faster than he would have thought possible.

Cam continued walking grimly toward lights that indicated some sort of hostelry. Why the hell they had to land here, in a godforsaken dock on the far side of *Riddlesgate,* he didn't know. The captain of *The Rose* had blithely announced that he'd made a small error in navigation, excusing himself with the claim that London was a mere hour by coach. From Cam's point of view, London might be in the next continent, given the muddy salt flats that stretched in every direction as far as the eye could see.

He ducked his head as he entered and was rather dismayed to realize that while his man Phillipos had arrived before him and presumably bespoke a room, the pig had also joined the company and was rooting around a chair. Other than Phillipos, the pig, and the innkeeper, the room held only one customer, a fair-headed man who was reading by the fire and barely looked up when Cam entered.

John Mumby, the innkeeper, rushed forward when he saw the broad-shouldered aristocrat standing in his doorway. "Good afternoon, Your Grace! It is an honor—a true honor—to welcome Your Grace to my humble inn, the *Queen's Smile*. May I serve you some refreshment?"

Cam slung his cloak over Phillipos's waiting arm. "Whatever you've got," he said flatly. "And don't address me as Your Grace, if you please."

Mumby blinked but quickly recovered. "Of course, my lord," he said, beaming. "Yes, sir. Coming right up, sir. Lord Perwinkle, I'll have to ask you to remove that pig. We don't allow livestock in the public room."

The fair-haired man looked up, aggrieved. "Damn it, Mumby, you just told me to leave the beast where it was. You know the blighted animal doesn't belong to me."

"Your coachman paid for him," the innkeeper said with irrefutable logic, "and I've no doubt but what he'll come back for him as soon as your axle is fixed. If it's quite all right with you, sir, the boy will put him in the back shed."

Perwinkle nodded, and a boy tucked the piglet under his arm and headed into the rain.

Cam threw himself down in a comfortable chair before the fire. It did feel good to be back in England. Last time he'd been in the country he'd been as raw as a rag, eighteen years old and full of rage . . . but even so he remembered with deep affection the smoky, wheatish smell of an English pub. Nothing like it, he thought as Mumby put a foaming mug of ale in his hand.

"Or would you prefer a spot of brandy?" the innkeeper asked. "I admit, sir, that a friend of mine drops off a bottle now and again . . . through the back door. Nice stuff, even if it is French. Goes down a fair treat."

Likely the captain, Cam thought idly. Smuggling brandy, the impudent sod. No wonder we landed at the back of beyond. He took a deep draught of ale. Superb ale, and a smuggled brandy. Life was improving.

"I was thinking of roast pheasant to start," Mumby said anxiously, "and perhaps a little fresh pork to follow."

"How fresh?" Cam asked. He didn't necessarily wish to see Perwinkle's piglet served up for dinner.

"Killed just last week," Mumby affirmed. "Been hanging, it has, and it's just reached perfection. My wife cooks a sweet pig, sir. You can depend on that."

"Right. And the brandy when you have a moment."

"Yes, *sir*!" Mumby chorused, seeing a shiny pile of coins growing in his mind's eye.

One thing led to another, one of which was the discovery that the inn had a dartboard. As the evening wore on, it turned out that Lord Perwinkle was not only an expert with a dart, but he had a veritable passion for fishing, a passion shared by Cam. And by the time it transpired that Tuppy Perwinkle and Cam had attended the same school, separated by a mere five years, the two had achieved a state of intimacy found only among those raised in the same nursery or pickled in the same French brandy.

In fact, when Mumby inquired whether Cam wished to hire a coach at first light, the duke refused. It had been a weary journey from Greece, all of forty-five days and a storm around the Bay of Biscay. There was plenty of time to meet his ball and chain, and he didn't feel any need to rush to London.

Tuppy agreed with that, having misplaced his own wife a few years before. "She left in a huff for her mother's and never returned. Having tired of her complaints, I did not retrieve her. And so it's been ever since."

"Tell my solicitor to come to me," Cam told Phillipos. "I pay the man enough. He can join me for breakfast."

Phillipos never ceased to admire his employer's ability to put away the best and show no effect the next day. Even so, he doubted whether the duke would really wish to see a solicitor at first light, given that a third bottle of brandy stood uncorked and waiting. But he bowed and sent off an urgent message to the metropolis, requesting the presence of Mr. Rounton, Esq., of Rounton & Rounton at a breakfast meeting with his esteemed client, Camden Serrard, the Duke of Girton.

As a matter of fact, Phillipos had no cause for alarm.

Edmund Rounton, the Duke of Girton's solicitor, was not a foolish man. He had had abundant—far too abundant—acquaintance with the duke's late father. And on the off chance that the present duke was anything like his forebearer, Rounton had no intention of arriving until the early afternoon, when the man was as mellowed by food as possible.

Around two o'clock a starched and gleaming Rounton descended from a coach, uncomfortably aware of a flutter of nervousness in his stomach. Interviews with the duke's father had been a trial, to put it mildly. In a nutshell, the old duke seemed to specialize in projects that wandered from allegiance to the rule of law, and he would explode with rage on hearing the slightest disagreement.

On the surface of it, the present duke seemed a different kettle of fish from his sire. "Good afternoon, Mr. Rounton," he said, bounding out of his chair. He had the same dark eyes as his late father, although they were rather more cheerful. The old duke looked like Beelzebub, what with his nasty, sooty eyes and white complexion.

11

Rounton bowed. "Your Grace, it is indeed a pleasure to see you in such fine health and returned to your native land."

"Yes, well," Girton replied, waving at a chair. "I won't be in England for long, and I need your help."

"If there is anything I can do, of course, I am more than willing, Your Grace."

"Do stop 'your gracing' me, then," his client said. "I can't stand formality."

"Of course, Your—of course." He eyed the duke's casual attire. No coat! And his shirtsleeves rolled up, showing muscled forearms. In all truth, Rounton found such informality quite unattractive.

"I mean to annul my marriage," Girton began. "I shouldn't think it will take too long, under the circumstances. Everyone knows that it wasn't a real marriage, and never has been. How long do you think it will take to draw up the papers?"

Rounton blinked. The duke continued blithely, "And I might as well see Bicksfiddle while I'm there. Not that I plan to make any changes to his management. He has been making a surprising amount of money. But I do want to ensure that it's all in fine fettle for Stephen."

At that the solicitor's mouth fell open.

"I shall settle a good amount on my wife, of course," Girton added. "She's been remarkably nice about the whole thing."

Mr. Rounton shook himself. "You wish to annul your marriage, Your Grace?"

"Exactly."

"And did I understand that you wish to transfer your estate to your cousin . . . the Earl of Splade?" The man looked perfectly sane, if a bit unconventional. He was downright messy, the way his hair bristled up in that queer way, but he didn't appear drunk.

"The estate and the title will ultimately be Stephen's or his son's, at some point. I make no use of it. Swore to my father my word that I wouldn't touch his estate, and I've never taken a penny from it."

"But . . . what—your heir—your wife—" Rounton spluttered.

"I have no heir other than Stephen," Girton pointed out. "And I don't have a wife in more than name. Given that I have no intention of marrying again, I would like to dispense with the estate as soon as possible."

"You wish to annul your marriage, but you do not have another wife in mind."

The duke began to show signs of impatience. "As I said."

"Preparing the annulment papers is a relatively easy task, Your Grace. But such a process takes a great deal of time to effect. Much longer than a week."

"Even in our situation? After all, I haven't seen my wife since she was, what—eleven or twelve years old? There can't be anyone foolish enough to think the fiasco was ever consummated."

"I doubt that will present a problem given that your wife was so young," Rounton replied. "However, the process requires the confirmation of Parliament *and* of the Regent. It could not happen readily. I am afraid that you must consider a longer stay in this country."

"Can't do it," Girton returned promptly. "I have work to do in Greece."

"Surely—" Rounton put in, desperately.

"No." And the solicitor could see he meant it. "I go into a frenzy if I'm away from my studio too long. You wouldn't want a mad duke roaming the English countryside, would you?" Girton stood up. The interview was clearly over. "Why don't you see how far you can get in the next few days? If I sign the papers, surely you could take care of it on your own."

Rounton rose slowly, his mind dancing over the thousands of legal obstacles that lay ahead of him. "I shall need to speak to you frequently before you leave the country," he said, rather anxiously.

"I believe I'll stay in this inn for a night or two," the duke said. "I hear there's some very good fishing just to the north. Why don't you investigate the process, and return here tomorrow?"

"I will do my best," Rounton replied. The young duke *was* like his father: they both wanted impossibilities, and wanted them yesterday.

"Then I shall look forward to seeing you for dinner. And thank you very much." The duke bowed.

Back in London, Rounton settled into his comfortable office in the Inns of Court, and thought long and hard about the situation. He could see as clear as day that the duke was going to annul his marriage and then run back to the fleshpots of Greece, or whatever he had been doing over there in the last twelve years. And there would go the dukedom of Girton.

His father and his father's father had served the Dukes of Girton. And Edmund Rounton would be damned if he'd let it be thrown aside by an arrogant young whippersnapper who cared only about shaping bits of marble, and didn't understand the importance of his own title.

"I can't let the boy do it," he muttered, walking around his desk. It was a serious matter, letting an ancient and honored dukedom fall into new hands.

Naturally he could understand why the man went abroad in the first place. Rounton never forgot the dizzy rage in the youngster's face as he muttered his vows, marrying a young girl whom he had thought was his first cousin until that very morning. It didn't surprise him when the bridegroom fled out a window after the ceremony and was never seen in England again. Not even when his own father was dying.

"Godspeed his soul," Rounton said reflexively, and then added, "the old bastard."

Besides, Girton's only heir was the Earl of Splade, although as a Tory representative for the Oxfordshire district, Splade had long refused to use his title. Not that it mattered, because Splade was no better than his cousin. He was never going to get married. Too interested in politics. He was older than Girton anyhow. Must be thirty-six, if he was a day. Splade would fall dead on the floor of the House of Commons; Girton would continue his merry, unmarried debauchery off in Europe; and the dukedom would be gone. Doomed. Dead.

Rounton himself had failed to produce a male heir, and so the equally old and honored firm of Rounton & Rounton was due to fall into strangers' hands as soon as he retired. At the thought a stab of pain shot through his stomach. Rounton sighed. Let Girton do as he wished. Throw away his lineage. The hell with it.

He opened up the newspaper that lay on his desk, neatly ironed and waiting. His doctor had suggested that calm activities such as reading would soothe his recurrent bouts of dyspepsia. For a few moments he stared listlessly at "General Observations About the Town," mechanically reading down a list of frivolous activities performed by frivolous persons. Suddenly a passage jumped out at him:

We find ourselves confused by a recent trend amongst the most fashionable: the beauteous young Duchess of G__, who surely can have no complaints of boredom, given that she receives invitations to every amusement in the town, has taken a history tutor with her to Lady Troubridge's famed house party. Rumor has it the tutor is a handsome young man . . . one can only hope that the duke will return from abroad and entertain his wife himself.

15

Rounton's eyes narrowed, and he forgot the burning in his stomach. Energy ran through his limbs. He wouldn't retire until he saved the Girton lineage. It would be his final act of loyalty: the last and best gift to the Dukes of Girton from the loyal Rountons.

At least he himself had made a decent attempt to produce a little solicitor to inherit the firm. He and Mary, bless her heart, had been unable to have youngsters; well, so be it. But the duke had a perfectly good young wife sitting around, and he could damn well try to breed with her before he went back to the continent.

"I'll *make* him do it," Rounton said to himself. His voice had the ring of a man who habitually wrangled the law—and feeble humanity—to suit his clients' interests. "And what's more," he decided, "I'll do it with a bit of finesse. Creativity, that's what is called for." God knows, the old duke had forced him to learn creative ways around the law. It shouldn't be too difficult to make the new duke dance to his piping.

Chapter Three

Family Politics

The Queen's Smile, *Riddlesgate*

The upshot of Mr. Rounton's decision to rescue the Girton lineage from certain oblivion was that three men descended from a carriage in front of the *Queen's Smile,* just around six o'clock the following evening.

It only took a second for Cam to recognize his heir, Stephen Fairfax-Lacy, the Earl of Splade. "Stephen!" he shouted, leaping up from his chair and hauling his cousin into his arms. "How marvelous to see you. It must be eight years since you came to Nissos!"

Stephen extracted himself and sat down, a quiet smile lighting his eyes. "Since when have you taken to hugging? What shall I call you? *Your Grace* would be proper."

"Bollocks to that. I'm still Cam, and you're still Stephen. I've come a long way from all that rotten English formality business that my father so believed in. In Greece, men express themselves as they wish."

Rounton cleared his throat. "Your Grace, I trust you do not mind that I asked the Earl of Splade to accompany me. A subject of the highest importance has arisen."

Cam grinned at Stephen at once. "The pleasure is mine."

"May I introduce my junior partner, Mr. Finkbottle?" Rounton asked, indicating a nervous-looking man in his twenties. "He will act as a liaison between yourself and my office."

"A pleasure to meet you, sir. Shall we all have a seat? There are plenty of chairs here, and the landlord has some excellent brandy."

Stephen sat down and stretched his legs. A man of his height—he was a good six feet four in his stocking feet—found even an hour in a coach to be an uncomfortable endeavor. "You look older, Cam," he said abruptly.

His cousin shrugged. "Age is an infirmity we all share. I've not been living the dandy's life for the past twelve years."

Mr. Rounton cleared his throat and started a fussy sermon about the legal hurdles involved in annulments. Stephen sipped his brandy and stared at his cousin. For a man who lived in Greece, Cam's skin was remarkably white. In fact, in the flickering light of the fire, his eyebrows looked like slashes of charcoal on parchment. His was a face of hard angles and impatient gleams of light. But his hands hadn't changed, Stephen thought with a fuzzy sense of nostalgia. Their childhood had been enlivened by what those long fingers could make from wood—

"Do you still whittle, Cam?" he asked abruptly, jumping into a moment's pause in the conversation.

A fleeting smile crossed his cousin's face. "Look here." He reached down beside his chair and picked up a splinter of wood.

"What's that?"

"It's a dart," Cam said, turning it over. Interest had lit up his eyes. "I had an idea that if I moved the flight up the shaft, the dart would be faster to the target."

Stephen reached out and took the slender piece of wood in his hand. Like everything Cam made, the dart was beautifully shaped, a sleek, dangerous spike with a narrow groove waiting for its feather.

18

"What d'you think?"

"It'll dip when weighted. It may fly faster, but once you put a tip, the feather won't balance." He illustrated with his finger. "See? The dart will spiral down rather than fly straight forward. You might get around it by narrowing the tip."

Cam looked at it broodingly. "Likely you're right," he admitted.

"You always were short on the mechanics," Stephen commented. "Remember all those boats you whittled?"

"Sank, almost every one of them," Cam said, laughing.

"They wouldn't have, if you had shaped them in a normal fashion. You invariably tried to be too clever."

Mr. Rounton judged it time to turn the conversation to a more delicate area, since the duke seemed to be in a reasonable frame of mind. "Your wife is currently at a house party in East Cliff, around an hour's travel from here," he stated.

Cam's deep-set eyes rested on the solicitor's face for a moment and then returned to the dart in his hand. "A pity," he said casually. "I would have liked to meet the chit after all these years. But I haven't time to be jaunting about the country."

Rounton recognized the set to his employer's jaw immediately: he'd seen it often enough in the duke's father. But he had his rejoinder planned.

"It appears to be virtually impossible to prepare annulment papers in a week," he stated.

"May I suggest that you try very, very hard?" The duke's tone was kind.

His father's son, Rounton thought gloomily. "There is another problem, Your Grace."

"Oh?" The duke had taken out a small knife and began whittling the tip of the dart.

"I am prepared to initiate the annulment. However, something has recently happened to your wife which has complicated matters."

He looked up at that. "What about her?"

"The duchess is . . ." Rounton hesitated. "The duchess has found herself in the midst of a scandal."

"A scandal?" The duke sounded only mildly interested. "Gina? What sort of a scandal could Gina make? Likely a storm in a teapot, Rounton. She's a sweet little thing."

"Naturally I agree with you as to the duchess's virtues, my lord. However, she is currently viewed by the *ton* in a less salubrious light."

Cam turned the dart over and over, his long fingers searching for any irregularity in its surface. "Now that I find hard to believe. Every Englishman who has made his way over to Greece—and there've been a surprising number of them, with France in a frenzy—has been keen to applaud my wife's virtues."

Rounton said nothing.

Cam sighed. "I suppose they *would* say that?"

"If you seek to annul the marriage at this particular moment, I have no doubt that you can obtain that annulment, but I am afraid that Her Grace may be barred from society in the aftermath."

"I gather little Gina has been burning the candle at both ends," Cam said. His eyes moved to Stephen. "Well?"

Stephen shrugged. "I don't move in those circles."

Cam waited, long fingers flipping the dangerous little arrow.

"I've heard rumors," his cousin said. "Gina has a rather wild group of acquaintances. Young married women . . ."

"All married?"

"Their reputations are not chaste," Stephen added, rather reluctantly.

Cam's jaw tightened. "In that case, why would annulling the marriage make any difference to Gina's reputation?"

The solicitor opened his mouth but Stephen cut in. "Rounton thinks you should make a show of support. He has asked me to go to this house party as well."

Cam scowled down at the dart in his hands. What the devil was he supposed to say to Gina? If she was gallivanting around with her marquess, well, she meant to marry him, after all. "Once Gina marries Bonnington, won't it all blow over?"

"I doubt it," Rounton said. "That would certainly mitigate matters, but what if the marriage does not occur?"

"Gina is thought to have spent the night not with Marquess Bonnington but with a man named Wapping, a servant of some sort," Stephen put in. "There is now some doubt about whether Bonnington will wish to go through with the marriage."

"That's nonsense," Cam snapped. "Wapping is the tutor that *I* sent her. Found him in Greece and dispatched him over here."

Rounton nodded. "You can see how important your opinion will be in the aftermath of this unfortunate debacle, Your Grace. If you were to spend a few days at the house party, making it clear that Wapping is your employee, it will go a long way to soothing people's suspicions."

Cam's jaw tightened. "Gina has written me letter after driveling letter about Bonnington, telling me how much she wishes to marry him. Someone has made a mistake."

"I have no doubt but that is the truth of it," Rounton said. "And after you make it clear where your opinion lies, Your Grace, society will follow your lead. You are her husband, after all."

"Hardly. A few minutes before the altar twelve years ago doesn't make the title worth much. I dislike even referring to

Gina as my *wife*. She and I are both aware that we are not truly married."

"I suggest we both travel to East Cliff," Stephen put in. "I can spare a night or two. You may not know this, Cam, but Parliament isn't in session until early November."

"Of course I know that, you ass!"

Stephen shrugged. "Given that you have shown no interest in taking up your seat in the House of Lords . . ."

A twisted grin crossed Cam's face. "You may be older, Stephen, but you haven't changed. You were always the one who understood responsibility. And I was always the one who ran from that same admirable trait," he continued. "I see no reason to alter my entirely comfortable habits at this point. I have work to do at home."

"I think you owe it to Gina," his cousin insisted.

"You don't understand. I have *work* to do."

Stephen eyed him. "Why can't you make something over here? We have stone and chisels—and beautiful women to serve as models."

"I'm in the middle of a glorious piece of marble, of the faintest pink. Do you know how much time I've already lost, just by traveling here?"

"Does it matter?" Stephen said with the insolence of a politician convinced of his own usefulness in the grand scheme of things.

"Yes, it bloody well does," Cam snapped. "If I don't work—well, it's the only thing that does matter."

"I saw your Proserpina, the one Sladdington bought from you last year. Quite nice."

"Oh, yes. That was a bit risqué, wasn't it? Now I'm working on a Diana. A prudish one. Modeled on Marissa, of course."

"Of course," Stephen murmured. "I think you owe it to Gina," he repeated. "She's been married to you most of her

22

life. You can't blame her for kicking up a bit of dust with you out of the country. But once she's not a duchess anymore, she's likely to be tossed out of society. I doubt she understands just how brutal the *ton* will be to an ex–duchess with a damaged reputation."

Cam's knife gouged the dart and broke off its tip. "Bloody hell!" He tossed the dart to the floor.

"We'll go together," Stephen said. "I'll find a hunk of marble and you can bring it with you. Make yourself another Proserpina."

Cam's mouth quirked. "Do I detect a snide note, cousin? Don't like Roman goddesses?"

Stephen said nothing.

"Oh, all right," Cam said. "I'll desert my Diana. I just hope that Marissa doesn't gain too much weight while I'm gone. I'll have to starve her back into a goddess shape."

"Marissa is his mistress," Stephen informed Rounton and Finkbottle.

"My muse," Cam corrected. "Gorgeous woman. At the moment I'm sculpting her as Diana rising from the water."

Stephen threw him a darkling look.

"Not to worry. I have put some foam around her hips." He smiled his lopsided, sardonic smile. "Think it's rubbish, do you?"

"Yes, I do," his cousin said bluntly. "Because it *is* rubbish."

"People like it. A beautiful woman can enliven the garden. I'll make you one."

"You don't respect it yourself," Stephen said savagely. "That's what I dislike the most."

"You're wrong there," Cam replied. He stretched out his hands and looked at them. They were broad and powerful, marked by small scars from the slip of a chisel.

"I'm proud of my goddesses. I've made quite a lot of money on them."

"That's not a good enough reason to keep fashioning naked women," Stephen snapped.

"Ah, but that's not the only reason. My talent, such as it is, lies in naked women, Stephen. Not in darts, nor in boats. I can't really fabricate objects worth a damn. But I can fashion the curve of a woman's belly so that it would make you uneasy with desire just to see it."

Stephen raised an eyebrow but held his silence.

Cam shrugged an easy apology to Rounton and Finkbottle. "Please forgive the family squabble, gentlemen. Stephen is our gift to the world, standing up for crippled army veterans and climbing boys—"

"Whereas Cam has made a fortune selling plump naked women fashioned in pink marble to parvenus such as Pendleton Sladdington."

"Marissa is not plump yet," Cam observed mildly. Then he reached over and swatted Stephen on the shoulder. "It feels good to argue with you again. I missed you, old moral sobersides that you are."

Rounton cleared his throat cautiously. "Am I to understand that you will join the earl in a visit to Troubridge Manor, Your Grace?"

Cam nodded. "I just remembered that I have a gift for Gina, sent from her mother's estate. I'll deliver it in person . . . if Stephen arranges for a one-foot cube of marble to be delivered within a day of my arrival."

"If you fashion it into something other than a female body," Stephen snapped back.

"A challenge!" Cam said gleefully.

"No less," his cousin retorted. "I doubt you know how to model anything but life-size female torsos."

"I can hardly make a life-size torso out of a block that size. But promise me you'll display whatever I make in your house and you're on," said Cam.

"Done."

Rounton sighed inwardly. Now he had to depend on the duchess's beauty to win her husband's heart. It was the best he could do, to throw them together for a brief period and let nature take its course. The young duchess was famed for the vivid beauty of her red hair and green eyes; Rounton returned to London, offering a brief prayer to the gods that Girton would find himself unable to resist her hair, if nothing else.

Stephen stayed on at the *Queen's Smile* with his cousin. He sent Cam's man back to London to fetch his own valet, some luggage and one-foot block of marble. It felt oddly comfortable to be sitting in an inn in the back of beyond, drinking brandy and amiably quarreling with his only living relative.

Tuppy Perwinkle joined them as evening wore on. Apparently, the cartwright would not be able to fix his gig's axle until the following day.

"How do you do, sir?" he asked, shaking hands with Stephen.

Stephen immediately warmed to the man's blue eyes. "Very well," he replied. "Are you a resident of these parts?"

"Leave him alone, Stephen," Cam said, looking up from his fifth attempt at making a dart. "Tuppy's house is in Kent, so he's out of your bailiwick. No votes there."

Stephen's mouth tightened. "It was merely a polite question," he snapped. Seeing that Tuppy's eyebrow was raised, he explained, "I'm the MP from Oxfordshire."

Tuppy nodded. "Congratulations."

Stephen bowed slightly and turned to his cousin. "How on earth did you find out that I'd made it into the House, then? Don't tell me the *London Times* makes its way over to Greece!"

"Actually, it does. Not that there's much of interest to read in it," Cam said. "I heard from Gina, of course. She's written me about your campaign. I even got you a vote."

Stephen looked deeply skeptical.

"I did!" Cam protested. "Some old fussbudget named Peter Parkinson ended up at my table. He was from Oxford and he solemnly promised to vote for you."

"Thank you. Are you getting many Englishmen over there?"

"More and more," Cam replied. "Come out of curiosity, I suppose. You don't even have to pay tuppence to see the cracked English duke. What's more, you can take a statue home to plant in your garden, *if* you have the money. I charge absurd amounts these days."

Stephen snorted. "Using your title to get yourself sales?"

"Absolutely. It's useless in every other respect. Only good for handing on to a son, and I've got no wish to acquire one."

"You might well marry once you get this annulment out of the way," Stephen pointed out.

"Not bloody likely," Cam grunted. But when he said nothing further, Stephen changed the subject.

"What are you doing in these parts, Lord Perwinkle?" he asked.

"On my way to visit my aunt. She's a funny old thing, and she always has a house party around now. Wants me to come and show myself as the heir, even though I don't live up to her expectations." He grinned faintly. "She'll shriek herself blue in the face when she sees these clothes, unless my man discovers where I am. He was following with my luggage."

"What the devil's the matter with your clothes?" Cam asked.

Tuppy laughed. "Nothing that's not wrong with yours."

26

Cam wore a shirt of white linen tucked into gray trousers. Neither article of clothing was in the first fashion, nor were they new; instead, they were comfortable and extremely clean.

"Who's your aunt?" Stephen asked.

"Lady Troubridge of East Cliff."

"We'll take you up with us tomorrow, if your gig isn't repaired. That's the house party where you'll find your wife, Cam."

He grunted and didn't look up from his dart.

Tuppy's mouth quirked. "We'll both be seeing our wives, then."

At that, Cam did look up. "I thought you lost yours."

"Doesn't mean I don't see her now and again. Generally only at this house party. I can't miss it since my aunt threatens to disinherit me. I spend most of my time fishing. My aunt has a decent trout stream."

"So what's the house party like, then?" Cam was still whittling away.

"A nuisance. My aunt fancies herself something of a literary hostess. There's a load of bad poets and dissolute actors wandering about. Gawky girls, being polished up for their debuts. And my wife's set, of course. They're usually there as well."

At Stephen's raised eyebrow, he went on. "Young and married, bored to death with their own lives and their own skins, rich enough to flaunt convention and discontented enough to do it."

Cam looked up. "My duchess?"

Tuppy's smile was rueful. "Quite so, Your Grace. I believe she is one of my wife's closest friends."

"Don't call me that," Cam said impatiently. "I can't stand all that folderol. Call me Cam, if you please. Why didn't you tell me yesterday that our wives were friends?"

27

"I didn't think it was particularly relevant," he replied, surprised.

"Gina always was a devilish little thing. Remember when she followed us fishing, Stephen?" Cam turned to Tuppy.

"We wouldn't take her with us because she was a girl, so she snuck after us and while we were fishing she stole our lunch."

Stephen gave a snort of laughter. "I'd forgotten that."

"What'd she do? Throw your food away?" Tuppy asked.

"No, that would be too simple. We'd told her that she couldn't come with us because girls can't handle worms without screaming. So she opened up every pasty and every tart and carefully packed worms inbetween the layers. Cozily lined the basket with worms as well."

"Once we got over the shock," Stephen chimed in, "it was fabulous. We had no lunch, but we had enough worms for a week's worth of fishing."

Cam grinned. "We took her along the next day, of course."

"She got more fish than either of us."

"Now I think about it," Cam said thoughtfully, "it makes absolute sense that Gina would be in a wild set."

"As far as I can tell, she and her friends don't do anything but make scandals," Tuppy said. "Sometimes I think my wife left me merely because it was considered tedious to live with one's husband."

Stephen looked curious. "That is a remarkably frivolous reason to desert the marital bond," he commented. Tuppy shrugged. "None of them have husbands about. Your wife"— he nodded at Cam—"has you, and you live abroad. Esme Rawlings has a husband but they haven't shared a house in ages. Mind you, he makes no secret of his love affairs. And the last is Lady Godwin."

"Oh," Stephen said. "That would be Rees Holland's wife, correct?"

"He has brought an opera singer to live in his house in Mayfair," Tuppy put in. "Or so they say."

Stephen frowned.

"So they are all husbandless and free to do as they wish," Cam said thoughtfully.

Silence fell over the group, broken only by the gentle slide of Cam's knife up and down the dart.

Chapter Four

Domestic Pleasures

Troubridge Manor, East Cliff

Emily Troubridge was a woman who considered herself lucky indeed.

About twenty years previous she had had the good fortune to attract a man whose chief characteristics were years and holdings on the 'Change. In both areas, his possessions were enormous. In fact, as her second cousin had whispered to her on the morning of her marriage, her husband was twice as wrinkled as Methuselah and richer than Midas.

Not that hers was an enforced marriage. After Troubridge had declared himself captivated by the young Miss Emily, who paired docility with likely fertility, Emily's mother had not scrupled to point out the advantages of the match. Troubridge was old; ergo, he would not trouble her for long. He was rich; ergo, she would have a maid in the country and a maid in the town, and more drunken footmen than she knew what to do with.

And sure enough, Lord Troubridge quickly went the way of all flesh. Somewhat to Emily's relief, he suffered a heart spasm after only two months of marital bliss. The funeral was followed by a rather apprehensive fortnight, during which everyone waited to find out whether her presumed fertility was up to task, but after that possibility had been cleared away

Lady Troubridge settled down happily to spend as much of her yearly income as was humanly possible.

Early on she flirted with the idea of remarriage, but quickly realized that she had no interest in a long-term bed partner. Nor, more to the point, did she want a male to hold her purse strings. So she summoned her husband's heir, Lord Peregrine Perwinkle, also known as Tuppy, assured him that she would never marry, and proceeded to spend every penny of her dear, dear husband's money that wasn't entailed.

In the next few years, Emily Troubridge grew into a woman whom her ancient husband would not have recognized. She adopted an air of authority and command. Her dress took on an eccentric sense of fashion only successful among those who were either very beautiful or (as in Emily's case) who paid obscene amounts of money to their modiste. Her face was pale and too long, but it daily became lovely through an exertion of its mistress's strong will combined with her maid's gift for cosmetic application.

With the passing of time, Lady Troubridge's parties—especially those held in the tedious summer months after the close of season and before the return of Parliament—became well known. In fact, invitations were fairly lusted after, given that her gatherings spanned the scandalous and the marriageable. Those seeking to marry and those seeking to undo a marriage could find themselves equally entertained, and since Lady Troubridge had decidedly advanced opinions on horticulture, she dotted the landscape with small Greek temples and circular conservatories, ensuring privacy enough to achieve whatever goal one might wish to advance.

Young men flocked to hunt Troubridge's grouse-rich forests, and to flirt with unprincipled young matrons. Where unmarried men went, there went matchmaking mamas, daughters trotting at their sides like beribboned spaniels.

31

As well as the cream of the *ton,* Lady Troubridge always invited a bevy of performers, musicians, painters, and artists, who attended in the hopes of gaining a patron, and with the certitude that they could live high on the hog for a matter of a month.

Of course, the presence of those with artistic temperaments did not make things easy for Lady Troubridge. But, as she told her friend Mrs. Austerleigh, artists were hardly more trouble than lovers. And lovers she had plenty of, this summer at least.

"For there's Miles Rawlings and Lady Randolph Childe," she said, ticking them off on her fingers. "And I believe Rawlings's wife is setting up Bernie Burdett as her latest flirt, although how she can stand his company, I simply can't say!"

"Well, I can," Mrs. Austerleigh said. "He's terribly beautiful, you know, and Esme Rawlings is partial to beauty."

Lady Troubridge had no such weaknesses. She merely snorted and continued. "Sir Rushwood hemmed and hawed and finally informed me yesterday that he would like to be housed on the same floor as Mrs. Boylen."

"Oh?" Mrs. Austerleigh tittered. "Dear me, I remember when she married Boylen. She rushed all over London declaring that there was no lady happier than she."

"I don't suppose she knew about his fancy bird then, did she? All those children of his—five or six, isn't it?—must have been a terrible shock for the poor girl.

"And there's the dear duchess, of course," Lady Troubridge continued.

But Mrs. Austerleigh broke in. "The Duchess of Girton? Just *who* do you consider her lover? Or should I say, which one?"

"Marquess Bonnington, of course, my dear. You don't believe that taradiddle about the tutor, do you?"

"I don't see why not. Willoughby Broke was quite adamant that he saw the duchess and her tutor in the conservatory in the wee hours of the morning."

"She says they were watching a meteor shower."

"Scandalous, that's what it is," Mrs. Austerleigh remarked, wondering if the haddock served at breakfast could have been off. Her stomach was taking a nasty turn.

"The duchess is no more disreputable than Mrs. Boylen."

"Yes indeed she is. Mrs. Boylen is discreet. But the duchess was seen with the man at night—and he is a *servant*!" It was hard to shock Mrs. Austerleigh, but she looked genuinely shocked at that.

"Well," Lady Troubridge said, "I simply don't believe it. Mr. Wapping is a very odd little man, after all. Have you encountered him?"

"Certainly not." Mrs. Austerleigh tittered. "At my age, I have no occasion to frequent a classroom!"

"*The Tatler* took a great liberty in calling him handsome. He has hair all over his face, which I most dislike. He has a pompous manner as well. Knole complains that he doesn't know his place."

"Butlers always do say that, don't they? Mine is always making a fuss about someone's valet not knowing his place. Meteor shower or not, the duchess ought to be more circumspect. Marquess Bonnington is a very prudish sort, for a man so young."

"Did you hear the rumor that the duchess's husband is returning to England?"

"*No!*"

"Yes indeed. And there can only be one reason for it, in my estimation. Bonnington must have asked for her hand."

"I expect that was before this Wapping business," Mrs. Austerleigh remarked. "I still think it's quite strange that she brought her tutor to your house party, my dear."

"There is something odd about Mr. Wapping in general," Lady Troubridge agreed. "Perhaps he's an impoverished younger son, or some such thing. Because he——"

But whatever insight she was about to deliver was lost when the door burst open. Mrs. Massey, the housekeeper, had just discovered that mice had gotten at the linen over the winter, and what did the mistress care to do about it?"

Mrs. Austerleigh was not the only person in Troubridge Manor who felt that tutors do not belong at house parties.

"I would like you to consider giving up your tutor," Marquess Bonnington told his betrothed, the duchess herself, as he handed her a peeled pear. "It is quite unheard of to bring a history tutor to a house party." Then he added, rather unwisely, "There's nothing more dreary than a bluestocking."

He was answered by soft lips feathering across his cheek. "Am I so dreary, then?" came a seductive voice.

"Don't, Gina."

"Why not?" she coaxed. "Do you know, Sebastian, your hair looks exactly like guinea gold, shining in the sunlight. How annoying to be marrying a man so much more beautiful than oneself. You truly would have made a lovely woman."

"Please do not make funning comments about my person." He pulled away. "Kissing in the open is extremely inadvisable."

"We're picnicking in the country! There isn't a gabster for miles. Hawes is all the way down the road at that inn. No one can possibly see us. Why not kiss me?"

"This picnic is improper," he replied. "I don't care for kissing in the outdoors. It's unsightly behavior at the best of times."

"I'll never understand men," Gina lamented.

"It's not that I don't want to kiss you. You understand that, don't you?"

"There's nothing improper about kissing your betrothed," she pointed out.

"You are *not* my betrothed, given that you are married," he said, frowning. "I should never have agreed to accompany you on this picnic. Imagine if your mother knew where you were."

"Don't fool yourself, Sebastian. She wouldn't give a hang, and you know it."

"Well, she ought to," he said.

"Do you know what they do to adulterous women in China?" Gina asked, braiding three grass strands together.

"No idea."

"They stone them," she said with some relish.

"Well, you may be married, but you're not adulterous."

She giggled. "Thanks to you."

The marquess stiffened. "You don't really mean that, Gina. You're just trying to shock me by talking like your friend Lady Rawlings."

"Please don't criticize Esme. Her bad reputation is vastly exaggerated. You know that all those gabsters watch her like a cat, simply longing for a misstep."

"No doubt. After all, she's provided so many interesting tales in the past."

Gina scowled. "Esme is my very dearest friend, and since you're marrying me, you'll have to start squelching rumors about her, rather than starting new ones."

"That will be difficult," he said. "Don't tell me that she was only exchanging kisses last night—why, she and Burdett were absent from the ballroom for over an hour!"

"I couldn't say what they were doing. But I am quite sure that it was nothing improper," she snapped. "For one thing,

Esme thinks that Burdett is a dead bore. She would never allow him any familiarities."

"He's a handsome bore."

She narrowed her eyes. "You are being quite unfeeling. Esme has suffered a great deal due to her horrible husband—and it's too mean of you to carry tales about her!"

"I never carry tales," he retorted. "I simply don't understand why you can't find friends as virtuous and unblemished as you are!"

"Esme is virtuous," Gina said. "She's also funny and clever and she makes me laugh. Moreover, it doesn't matter what people say about her, she's my *friend*."

A puzzled frown creased Sebastian's forehead.

"Oh, all right, let's leave," Gina said, standing up and shaking out her light muslin gown. "I suppose you're right about the impropriety of our picnic, although everyone knows how it is with Cam."

"The only reason I agreed to accompany you is because you *are* married. I would never accompany an unmarried damsel on a picnic without a chaperone."

"You know, Sebastian," Gina said thoughtfully, slipping the plates back into a basket, "you are beginning to sound just a bit priggish."

"Paying attention to propriety is not priggish," he huffed.

"Ever since you inherited the title," Gina continued.

"Why, when I first met you, years ago, you were far less interested in propriety. Remember when I stole out of the house and you took me to Vauxhall?"

His lips tightened. "Achieving maturity is not the same as being priggish. I do not wish the reputation of my future wife to be slurred by gossip. After all, you will be my marchioness, perhaps as early as the new year."

36

Gina was fast losing her temper; he could tell that by her rising flush and the way she was fairly throwing the silver into the picnic basket. He kept silent and watched as she gathered the sliding strands of her hair and began pinning them to her head.

"I don't wish to brangle with you."

"Nor I with you," she said. "I am sorry, Sebastian. I love you for being so steady and respectable, and then I nag at you for the same reason." She wound her arms around his neck.

But he didn't kiss her. "We are a most appropriate match, except when it comes to your friends. You are a woman of the highest moral fiber. Why do you have such ramshackle acquaintances? I believe not a one of them is living with her husband."

"They are not ramshackle. Esme, Carola, and Helene are unlucky in that they have unsteady husbands. But one could say that it's due to them that we are together. After watching their marriages, I knew exactly what I wanted in a husband—you."

His eyes softened, and he pressed a kiss on her forehead. "I dislike it when we are irritable with each other."

"Yes indeed," Gina said, looking at him with a gleam of mischief in her eyes. "We're already squabbling like an old married couple!"

"Quite so," said the marquess, looking taken aback.

Chapter Five

Troubridge Manor, Crammed with Company and Giddy with Grandees

"Carola!" Gina called, leaning over the banister.

Carola threw her head back and smiled. "I'm afraid the orchestra will begin playing soon, and I should hate to miss the first dance."

Gina walked down the last few stairs. "You look lovely." She took her arm and gave it a little squeeze.

"I'm not certain that this light material is becoming for someone as short as I am."

"Those bosom crosses are the very newest style," Gina said comfortingly. "You look just like an angel, all floaty silk and curls."

"I'm a bit nervous because my husband generally attends the opening assembly," Carola whispered. "Are you certain I don't look plump, Gina?"

"Quite certain." They drifted past Lady Troubridge, greeted with secret smiles that promised intimate discussion at breakfast.

"Why does your husband make you nervous? Granted, I only met him once, but I thought he was very likable."

"He *is* likable," Carola said, rather miserably. "That's the worst of it. I do like him, I do."

"I'm suffering a similar case of nerves," Gina remarked. "My husband may also appear tonight."

Carola raised an eyebrow. "Has he landed, then?"

"I received a note from his solicitor saying he would probably attend the party tonight," Gina explained. "And I don't remember what he looks like."

"I wish I didn't know what my husband looked like. It would make it all so much easier."

"Make what easier?"

"Well, living away from him . . ." They slipped past a cluster of diamond-clad matrons. "When I'm not with Tuppy, I don't think about him all that much. You know I love to dance and shop, and I see my friends."

"Yes?"

"But when I see him, well—I feel guilty!" she finished in a rush.

"Why *did* you leave him?"

"We fought," Carola said. "We fought bitterly, and so I left. I thought he would come to my mother's and beg me to return, but he didn't."

Gina looked at her curiously. "Did that make you sad? I thought you had a perfectly amicable arrangement."

"Oh, I cried endlessly at first," Carola said lightly. "I had high ideas about marriage, in those days."

Gina noticed that her eyes looked a little watery. "But you are very happy without him."

"Yes, of course," Carola replied, giving a wavering smile. "It's vastly more entertaining this way. He is a terrible stick in the mud, Tuppy. Never wanted to go out in the evenings."

"Hmm," Gina said. She had just caught sight of Sebastian talking to Cecilia Deventosh, who had five daughters to marry off. "Look at Lady Deventosh! She's trying to wrap up *my* fiancé and give him to one of her daughters as a present."

"I wouldn't worry. The marquess is devoted to you. Anyone can see that." An impish smile lit up Carola's brown eyes.

"What does he offer as a husband that the duke does not?"

"It's different!" Gina exclaimed. "Camden and I barely know each other, but Sebastian is everything I want in a husband: calm, and steady, and just *good*."

"Yes," Carola said, following her gaze. Marquess Bonnington was undoubtedly one of the handsomest men in England, with high cheekbones, a lean jaw, and deep-set blue eyes. "But do you ever think that marriage with him might be . . . a trifle constraining?"

"Constraining?" Gina looked startled. "No, do you?"

"He's very particular. Look how he's snubbing Lady Deventosh. I gather she offended him in some way."

"Well, she *is* quite pretentious to try to foist one of her daughters onto Sebastian!" Gina exclaimed. "He is a marquess."

"Yes," Carola murmured.

"He may be a little stiff in his manners. But it's just his way. He may be stuffy in public, but not in private. Although I don't think he'll be as easygoing as your husband."

Carola smiled, a little crooked smile. "No indeed, because he loves you. Husbands are only so easy when they feel no love at all."

"Oh dear," Gina said, unsure what to say. Her friend's eyes were bright with tears.

"It's quite all right. I always find the first evening difficult, but after that Tuppy and I shall be quite comfortable in each other's company, I promise you."

Marquess Bonnington came up beside them and bowed. The sounds of tuning violins sounded from the far side of the room.

Carola's face brightened. "I wonder where Neville is?"

"Here he is," Sebastian said, moving to the side as an extravagantly elegant gentleman rushed through the crowd.

He had the penny-bright hair and blue eyes of a dandified cupid.

"You must forgive me!" he cried. "Your Grace, Lord Bonnington, my *dearest* Lady Perwinkle. I had a terrible time dressing this evening. Slapdash, that's what I am!"

Gina smiled. One couldn't not smile at Neville's merry grin.

Carola had tucked her hand under his. "I'm feeling blue. Shall we dance?"

"Your every breath is my command," he exclaimed. "I believe that Lady Troubridge has decided to open the assembly with a polonaise."

"That's splendid," Carola said. Her face was quite happy now.

He bowed. "If you will excuse us, Your Grace, Lord Bonnington. Lady Perwinkle will likely expire if I don't find her a place at the top of the line."

She, Carola, and Esme shared a table for supper, and Gina had to admit that Esme's Bernie Burdett—though boring as a pumpkin—had remarkably good-looking features.

"He has lovely hair, don't you think?" Esme whispered when the gentlemen had gone to fetch something to eat. Her face was alight with wicked laughter. "It's soft as silk!"

"Esme! Don't say that out loud!"

"You should feel his arm," she said irresistibly. "We found ourselves alone earlier in the evening, and he's pure muscle! Although it is truly his profile that excels."

"Beauty is not an important attribute in a man," Gina said primly.

"Your Sebastian is remarkably handsome," Esme pointed out.

Gina couldn't help but smile. "But that's not why I love him."

"No?" Esme had that wicked look again.

"No," she said. "Sebastian will make a wonderful father because of his character, not because of his profile."

Her statement seemed to surprise Esme into a thoughtful silence. But Gina sighed, despite herself. She and Sebastian never found themselves alone . . . he was far too watchful of her reputation to allow such a thing. She had no idea whether he had a muscled arm. She drank some more of her champagne, watching the bubbles moodily. Why didn't her fiancé ever relax his rules a trifle? It wasn't as if she was some green girl, just out of the nursery.

"Yes, I will, thank you," she said to the footman offering another glass of champagne.

Sebastian, who had just returned to the table, frowned. Esme cut in. "Be careful, Gina. Your"—she paused wickedly—"your guardian is watching your every sip."

Sebastian got the pained look with which he invariably responded to Esme. "I was merely going to point out—"

"—that bosky behavior is unbecoming in a lady," she finished, in a perfect imitation of his lofty tones.

Gina picked up her glass, feeling rebellious. "When you are my husband, Lord Bonnington, you may forbid champagne in the house."

Sebastian cast Esme a glare and contented himself with silence.

Gina rose, determined to make her fiancé break a few more of his sainted rules. "Oh my, I think you may have been right," she said sweetly. "I fancy I drank a wee bit too much wine and I need a breath of fresh air. It is so desperately stuffy in here!"

He had risen the moment she did and was already standing at her side. She cast a smile over the table, meeting Esme's eyes. "Do continue without us," Gina said. "I really couldn't say how

42

long we shall be. I feel so dreadfully . . . stuffy!" Carola choked back a giggle and Esme broke into a clear peal of laughter. Bernie looked around, bewildered, and said, "What? What?"

They skirted the tables and walked down the stairs into the long drawing room, and through the open French doors onto the gardens. Sebastian halted as soon as they reached the pavement outside the windows.

Gina pulled on his arm. "Shall we go for a walk, Sebastian?" To her ears, her voice sounded velvety smooth.

He disengaged her hand and looked at her. She was dismayed to find his mouth clamped into a tight line. It was Esme, she knew. For some reason, she drove him to distraction with her teasing.

"I don't know what you're doing," he said frigidly, "but I greatly dislike being an object of amusement."

"We weren't making fun of you," she replied.

"You were," Sebastian retorted. "You and Lady Perwinkle and that trollop, Esme Rawlings!"

"You mustn't call Esme a name like that!"

"Plain speaking is sometimes a virtue, Gina. Your friends are the next best things to *très-coquettes* that are to be found among the gently born."

Gina bit her lip. "Don't you think that you're being a little overly stern?"

"Or do you mean stuffy? You have obviously complained to them about my *stuffiness*! Let me tell you, among those people who value good manners, I am not seen as at all stuffy! Merely intelligent as opposed to debauched."

"I didn't complain about you," she said, ignoring a twinge from her conscience. "It's just that my friends have a lively sense of humor, that's all."

"Lively or loose? Do you know that there are many people who won't even acknowledge Esme Rawlings?"

"Well, that isn't very fair, is it?" she said angrily. "Those same people are no doubt slavering over her horrible husband, whereas Esme is painted far blacker than she is!"

Sebastian's eyes narrowed. "Look me in the face and tell me that she is not intimate with Bernie Burdett."

"She is *not* intimate with Burdett!" Gina cried.

"Not yet perhaps," Sebastian said with a twist of his lips. "But the man doesn't have a chance of escaping."

"Don't, Sebastian, don't—don't talk about Esme this way! You'll say things—"

"That what? That you don't want to hear?"

"Yes," she said defiantly. "That I don't want to hear!"

"Everyone says them," he said flatly. "She's a trollop, and you know it, and the world knows it."

Gina stared at him, her face white.

"Then I'm a trollop as well!" she cried. "Because my husband ran off and left me, just as Esme's did to her. And I've been dallying with you, just as Esme has with Burdett."

Sebastian's lip twisted. "Utterly different. She joins her *friends* in bed, and you, my dear, are an innocent."

"She does not!" Gina flashed back.

He shrugged. "Perhaps she beds them in the garden then."

"Esme doesn't allow any man to . . . to . . ."

Sebastian's eyes met hers with a touch of contempt. "A likely story," he commented.

"Have you ever heard a man say that he visited her bed?" Gina demanded.

"Gentlemen do not boast of the muslin they sleep with!"

Her jaw set. "Stop it! Stop it right now. You have no right to say those things."

He took a deep breath and glanced around. Luckily no one had followed them onto the terrace. "Shall we go back inside, Your Grace?" He held out his arm.

She hesitated and looked up at him. "I hate to feel this angry with you."

What on earth was he supposed to say to that?

Gina drifted closer. "I should like to go for a short stroll."

"I swore I wouldn't take walks with you, after what happened last night," he said slowly.

She held out her hand without speaking, green eyes shining in the moonlight.

"You're a witch," he said, sighing, and took her hand. They strolled just into the line of shadows that marked the beginning of a small copse and stopped.

She put her hands flat against his waistcoat and then let them slide up his chest to his neck.

"Don't do that!" he said sharply. "We should not be so intimate at this stage in our relationship."

"Kiss me," she whispered. "Kiss me, please."

He bent his head and warm lips met hers. But no arms came around her, and when he drew back she saw that his eyes were cool and untouched by desire.

"What's the matter?"

"Where is your sense of propriety?" he asked flatly. "I don't want to kiss you out in the copse. You are my future wife, not my light-o'-love. Furtive gropings in the dark—leave that for all your loose friends!"

Anger rose in the back of her throat again, but Gina choked it down.

"When you behave like this," she said slowly, "I feel as if you don't want *me,* Sebastian. As if you wish to marry Her Grace, the Duchess of Girton, not me, Gina."

"Of course I want to marry you! But you are precious to me, Gina. Not a lightskirt to be treated as such."

"Kiss me," Gina coaxed. "No one lost her chastity kissing."

He sighed and bent his head again. At first the kiss was a mere matter of lips, but then his body woke to the soft body pressing against his, and the eager lips under his, and slowly the kiss deepened, until Gina was being held tightly. Her hands escaped only to smooth the planes of his face, to trace his cheekbones with her fingertips.

His arms fell away. "Is that sufficient?"

"Of course," she agreed. "Shall we return to the house?" For he deserved a reward as well.

He gave her a pleased smile. "Yes!" he said, rather too eagerly, to Gina's mind. Oh well, once they were married, it would all be different. She wouldn't feel so much like a hunter stalking a deer. Once they were married, he would be free to express his love for her—if only in the confines of their bedchamber.

They neared the house when he stopped for a moment. "I just want to make sure that you know that I want to marry *you*," he said, voice low.

"I know."

He cupped her cheek. "Because I do. I want you as my wife. I simply don't want to ruin your reputation, that's all."

She smiled. "I do understand, Sebastian."

There was a country dance just beginning when they walked into the ballroom, so they took their places next to a flushed and laughing Carola. Every time the dance brought Gina back to Sebastian, she smiled at him so deliciously that the tips of his ears began to warm. "Gina!" he hissed as they turned in a circle.

"What is it . . . *love*?" she said, so quietly that no one else could hear it. She leaned back against his arm as he twirled her in a circle, and the way she looked at him! There was naked lust in her eyes, to his mind.

"Gina, what if someone sees you?"

She giggled, and Sebastian realized for the first time that his fiancée had indeed drunk far too much champagne. She stood alone for a moment as he processed in a circle before twirling her one last time and handing her to the next partner.

As he took her in his arms she flung her head back, and smooth red curls fell from their moorings and slid over her bare shoulders and arms.

"Why do you have to look so . . . so seductive?" For some reason her whole demeanor was infuriating him.

She glanced down at her gown, a slim gown of floss silk with a deep rose trim. "The bosom is low, isn't it?" she acknowledged.

"Yes, it is!" Sebastian challenged.

"I feel as if you are always angry at me lately," she replied. "This gown is no more daring than those worn by most women."

She was right. "I apologize. It's just that—you are going to be *my* wife. I would like to be the only one admiring your bosom."

She giggled and moved into his arms for their final twirl. "Silly," she said softly, touching his cheek with one finger. He tightened his grip, and her hair flowed over his black sleeve. "You shall," she whispered, her smile deepening. "I promise you, we will have a private viewing."

Camden William Serrard, the Duke of Girton, walked into the ballroom flanked by Tuppy Perwinkle and his cousin, Stephen Fairfax-Lacy. He looked about impatiently, hoping to see Gina. But there was no sight of her anywhere. A long winding line of dancers was slowly bouncing their way along a diagonal. Just then a gap in the line of dancers widened and he saw a gorgeous woman laughing up at her husband. Her body was so indicative of desire, bending toward the man like a willow toward the sun, that he felt a matching burn in his chest. She shook pale red hair over her shoulder, and it fell like rose silk down her back.

"My God," he said appreciatively, "who is that beautiful woman?"

"Which?"

"The one over there, dancing with her husband."

Stephen leaned to the left so he could see and chuckled.

"Why do you ask?"

"She'd make a lovely Aphrodite," Cam said dreamily.

"She's a scandal, though, isn't she? I think she's going to eat her husband alive, right there on the dance floor." Stephen straightened, and the humor disappeared from his face. "That isn't her husband," he said flatly.

"No?"

"No." He cleared his throat. "*You* are her husband."

Chapter Six

A Meeting of Spouses

Whatever Gina imagined she would feel on meeting her errant husband for the first time in twelve years, she never considered pleasure. None of her despairing fears came true. The moment she glanced up from the dance and glimpsed a man with a mobile, intelligent mouth and great slashes of black eyebrows, she dropped her fiancé's hands and shrieked, "Cam!"

From then it was only a second until she ran across the dance floor, babbling as she went. "You look just the same— no, you're so much bigger. Hello, Cam! It's me, Gina—your wife!"

His smile was exactly the same lopsided, teasing grin she remembered. "Of course it's you, Gina," he said. He bent down and kissed her cheek.

She threw her arms around him, squeezing as hard as she could. "Oh my, but you've grown!" she cried. "I'm so happy to see you! I've missed you so much! Why *didn't* you write more often, you fiendish man?"

"You wrote so many letters I couldn't keep up," he complained.

"You should have tried," Gina accused him.

"I couldn't match your wifely devotion," he drawled. But he took one of her hands in his. "When I first left England, I read your letters over and over. They were my only link to home."

Her face brightened. "How silly I am, Cam! I was so pleased to see you that I forgot to introduce you to my fiancé." She pulled forward the tall man behind her. "Cam, may I introduce Marquess Bonnington? Sebastian, this is my husband, the Duke of Girton."

Cam was surprised to feel a flicker of dislike at the sight of the man. He was infernally handsome, for one thing. Undeniably one of those Englishmen who come to Greece only to complain about the lack of water closets and civilized food.

"I'm honored to meet you," he said, bowing. "Gina has written me many letters about you."

The marquess seemed taken aback by that. He bowed as well. "I hope that Her Grace's indiscretion did not cause you any distress. She should not have addressed such an intimate subject through the post."

Cam eyed him thoughtfully. A prig, that's what the marquess was. But it was none of his business whom Gina wanted to marry. "She only did so because we are childhood friends," he said.

Gina had tucked her hand under Bonnington's arm and was smiling up at him in an irritating way. "You mustn't fuss about Cam. He's quite my oldest friend in the world, and so naturally I write him about everything important, just as I might to a brother. You see," she said, turning back to Cam, "Sebastian is a fierce guardian of my reputation. He dislikes the idea that anyone might draw inferences about our future."

Cam raised an eyebrow. The way she had looked at her marquess on the dance floor, someone would have to be blind not to expect they would marry the moment an annulment was established. "Then stop simpering at him, Gina," he said, surprising himself with the sharpness of his tone. "A person would have to be an oaf not to guess at your intimacy."

At that, the marquess bridled and stiffened his shoulders again. "No such intimacy has occurred between us," he announced. "Nothing has occurred that could cause Your Grace the slightest concern. I have far too much respect for the duchess."

"Hmm," Cam said. Looking at the marquess, he could almost believe that he had stayed out of Gina's bed. How he managed it, Cam didn't care to think. "Well, since we've aired our relations for the whole ballroom with this heartfelt meeting, *wife,* would you care to say hello to Stephen?"

Stephen had backed up a step and was watching with amusement from just behind Cam's shoulder. He stepped forward and bent over Gina's hand with great aplomb. "It's a pleasure to see you again, my dear."

Cam looked around for Tuppy, but he had disappeared. "Surely you know my cousin, Stephen Fairfax-Lacy," he said to the marquess. Bonnington had not lost his rigid stance and was looking more poker-faced than ever.

"I have had the pleasure of working with Mr. Fairfax-Lacy on matters to do with the House," Bonnington replied, bowing even more deeply. "It is always a pleasure to meet a member of the duchess's family."

"Do you address her as the duchess in private?" Cam asked with some curiosity.

Gina laughed. "No, of course he doesn't, you goose. But Sebastian's behavior is always irreproachable in public."

Cam looked over her head at Bonnington. He looked about to explode, poor fellow. It couldn't be easy, being irreproachable *and* engaged to Gina. "Well, I believe Stephen and I will retire to the card room," he said. "I promised him a game of hazard."

"Without dancing even one dance?"

"Not even one." To Cam's mind, it would be better to give the poker-faced bridegroom a chance to recover his composure.

"Very well," Gina said gaily. "But I shall invade the card room and drag you onto the floor if you stay there too long." She leaned close to Cam, and he caught a drift of perfume, faintly flavored with apple blossoms. "I am trying to lure Stephen into marrying," she whispered. "And I think I have found just the right woman."

"Are you going to set me up with a wife, as well?" he asked, with some interest.

Gina looked enormously surprised. "Would you like to remarry, Cam? I thought you disliked the state."

"It hasn't bothered me so far."

She chortled. "Well, of course it hasn't, you stupid man. We live in different countries!"

Cam shut off his answering grin and stepped back. The last thing he wanted was for the marquess to get strange ideas about his friendship with Gina.

He bowed grandly. "What a pleasure it has been to meet my childhood playfellow after such a long parting," he said clearly, allowing his voice to carry. "As soon as certain arrangements are taken care of, I shall look forward to furthering our acquaintance. And yours as well, Lord Bonnington." There—that should put a sock in the gossips' mouths. Now everyone would know why he was in England. And he had made it quite clear that the marquess was welcome to his wife.

He and Stephen retired posthaste to the card room. "What a stick!" he said disgustedly, as they strolled into the smoke-filled chamber.

"Who? Bonnington?"

"Of course."

52

"He didn't show to best advantage tonight," Stephen said thoughtfully, "but actually he's a good man. I've heard that he takes remarkably good care of his tenants, for example. Inherited the title from his uncle. Whenever we're estimating votes in the upper house, I can always count him to be on the right side."

Cam shrugged irritably. "So Bonnington's a bloody saint. He isn't right for Gina, and if you ask me, he knows it. He looks like a sick cow. She's going to drive him around the twig within a month."

"What on earth are you saying?"

"The man's regretting it," Cam stated, flinging himself into a comfortable chair.

"Do you mind if I smoke?" Stephen took out his pipe.

"Yes, I bloody well do." He drummed his fingers on the tabletop. "Anyone could see that he looks hunted. Probably asked her in a rash moment. Fell in love with her beauty— God, who would have thought that little Gina would turn out so well?—but he forgot to consider what she would be like at the breakfast table."

Stephen was stamping down his tobacco. "I think she'd be a fine breakfast companion," he put in.

Cam shuddered. "Too lively by half."

"I disagree about Bonnington as well," Stephen continued, putting a match to his pipe. "From everything I know, he's head over heels in love with your wife, and he considers himself lucky to have her."

"But he's only beginning to realize what he has," Cam put in. "The devil! Didn't I tell you not to smoke?"

"I didn't ask your permission. I only asked if you minded."

"Well, I do mind. I hate that bloody smoke in my face."

"What's put you in such a foul mood, then?"

"Brandy," Cam snapped at a footman. "Foul mood? I'm perfectly cheerful. This is the real me, cousin. You've forgotten."

"I didn't forget anything. I used to have to thrash you once a week after you turned six or so."

"What I remember is trying to beat the tar out of you on your twelfth birthday."

Stephen shuddered. "Do you remember the consequences? God, I thought your father would never let us out of that sanctuary."

Cam's eyes darkened. "He was a nasty piece of work, my father. I'd forgotten about that part. Spent all day in there, didn't we?"

"And half the night. It was dark and cold. I remember getting terribly hungry."

"I just remember being terrified. He'd told me that my mother would haunt me whenever I was naughty. I was frightened by dark places for years."

Stephen put down his pipe and looked across the table. "That was unconscionable, Cam. Did he really make your mother out as a ghost?"

"Unfortunately. Took me years to get over the idea that my mother might jump out of a closet dressed in a white sheet and scare the living daylights out of me." Cam helped himself to a glass of brandy from an offered tray.

"I had no idea. I remember you telling joke after joke to make me stop crying. I felt miserably ashamed because you never shed a tear, even though you were five years younger than I."

"You were visiting for the summer, weren't you?"

Stephen nodded. "My parents went to the continent."

"I was used to it by then. But I still have a horror of the dark. And I still tell jokes to make it palatable."

54

Stephen drew on his pipe, his eyes somber and kind.

Cam shifted his gaze. He hated pity, but he hated a false front even more. In the life he'd carved for himself, there was no place for lies only to protect his consequence. That had been his father's specialty.

"She doesn't blame you for never coming back," Stephen said, after a pause.

"Who? Gina? Why on earth should she?"

"Because you're her husband, you ass. Because you had—have—responsibility for her, and you've neglected it for years."

"What are you talking about? I've never taken a ha'penny from the estate, you know. I swore to the old man in a fit of rage that I wouldn't, and I haven't." He looked across the table with a gleam of mischief deep in his eyes. "Of course, I live off the proceeds of fat pink statues, as you describe them."

Stephen sighed. "She's your *wife*, Cam. Your *wife*. You married her when she was eleven, and didn't come back for twelve years—and you think the extent of your responsibility was turning over your bank account?"

Cam smiled, unruffled. "That's about right. You can try, but you'll never be able to cram that hidebound sense of English responsibility you were born with into my useless soul. The only thing I give a damn about is where my next piece of marble is coming from. Gina and I both know that we're not truly married, so why should I return before she asked me to?" He swallowed some brandy. "At any rate, here I am, ready to hand over my so-called wife to the marquess."

Stephen snorted.

"Do you suppose she's dancing with him again?" Cam asked. For some reason, he didn't feel like sitting around in the comfortable male confines of the card room.

"What do you care? He'll likely throw her over after you annul the marriage. She'll have to go live in a cottage somewhere in the north."

Cam stood up so suddenly that he bumped the table, spilling brandy onto the polished surface. "Any time you decide to stop moralizing long enough to breathe, just let me know, will you, cousin? I've had all the boredom I can take at the moment."

He strode out of the room, conscious of a prick of guilt. He shouldn't have snapped at Stephen like that. But he'd had that lesson drilled into him one too many times—by a master of morality, his own father. His lip twisted. Responsibility! In the name of responsibility his father had locked him in every dark closet in the house, destroyed any reverence he had for the name of his mother, and married him to a woman he had, until the day of his marriage, thought to be his first cousin.

Gina stood out in the ballroom like a lighted torch among a bunch of squibs. As it happened, she wasn't dancing with her marquess. Instead, she was partnered with a stout middle-aged man. He leaned against the wall for a moment and watched. She wasn't strictly beautiful, his wife. Not beautiful the way Marissa was beautiful. Marissa had the deep-set eyes and rounded cheekbones of a Mediterranean goddess. Whereas Gina . . . Gina had a lovely mouth. His fingers itched to shape it in marble. Although coaxing that sweetness into stone would be a tremendous challenge.

Marissa didn't look real in stone. She looked like the embodiment of man's greatest fantasy about women: placid, sensual, gloriously languid, unspeaking. Gina was like a moving flame. Where on earth did she inherit those tip-tilted eyes? Her spirit leaped so clearly from them that they would be almost impossible to reproduce.

56

The dance was drawing to a close and Cam strolled over to the side of the ballroom where she was standing. As he walked up, she turned and smiled.

He almost caught his breath.

My God, but Gina had grown up well! At eleven years old, she'd been a lanky, leggy wisp of a girl with big green eyes and hair that was always falling out of its braids. But here she was wearing a gown that barely covered her curves. In fact, what cloth there was seemed no more than a backdrop to her breasts and those long, long legs. No doubt about it: French gowns were made for figures like Gina's, he thought. Marissa would look positively plump in one of them.

"Hello, Cam," she said. "Have you come to dance with me? Because I'm afraid that I promised this dance to—"

"A husband's privilege," he said smoothly, taking her arm. Some couples were putting themselves into a circle so he towed her forward, enjoying the way she wiggled, trying to pull her elbow from his hand.

"That's enough! That's enough! Three couples only, if you please," an elderly-looking man said fussily. "All right, everyone! We're set for Jenny Pluck Pears—do watch your slide, *if* you please!"

Cam looked down at Gina with laughing eyes. "What the devil is he talking about?" he whispered.

"Dancing, you fool!" she whispered back. "Eight slides, then set left and turn single."

"What?"

The music started.

"Follow me!" she said, taking his hand. *That* Cam liked. He picked up the hand of the portly matron to his right.

"All right, slide left," Gina hissed.

Grinning broadly, Cam slid left. But since Gina hadn't given him a termination point, he slid until he bumped into her hip. He liked that too. Gina had lovely curves for such a slender woman. She gave him a flustered look and pulled him to face her.

"Partners face," she whispered. "No! No, follow me!"

Cam chuckled. "Now what?"

"We skip around the outside next."

"Skip? I don't skip!"

She pulled at him sharply, and he found himself obeying her just for the pleasure of holding hands.

He was looking around laughing, when Gina hissed at him again. "We're supposed to flirt, Cam!"

"What?"

"I know, it's a ridiculous notion, isn't it? But we should speak to each other at this point in the dance."

Flirting with Gina didn't seem ridiculous to Cam, but by then they were back in place and he bowed for what seemed like the tenth time.

"Well, that was amusing," he said as they walked off the dance floor. "English society skipping in a circle."

"Didn't you have a dancing master as a boy?" she asked with some curiosity.

"Sporadically. Father had trouble retaining servants, if you recall."

"And I don't suppose there's much dancing in Greece."

"Oh, but there is! The whole village dances."

"You dance with them?" Gina looked up at her husband in some bewilderment. He was so different from the boy she remembered. She remembered very little of their wedding, so she had always thought of her husband as a bigger version of the lanky, twiglike boy who used to whittle dolls out of wood.

Now here he was, grown broad in the shoulders and big—big all over. He'd grown into his father's frame, she thought. He looked muscled all over, perhaps from the sculpting. She hadn't thought of sculpting as physical labor. He stood out in the elegant ballroom like a sore thumb, with his wild, beguiling smile.

"You used to be quite normal," she said wonderingly.

"But now—"

He waited, eyebrow raised.

"You don't fit in here," she said, hoping that wouldn't offend him.

"Wouldn't want to," he said promptly. "I do remember all the folderol of the ballroom though, Gina. Would you like me to claw my way to the drinks table?"

"Actually, I would," Gina said, enjoying the notion of sending this barbarian on an errand. "I should like a glass of champagne, please. The pink kind."

He looked about and poked one of the footmen standing next to the door. "You! Fetch me two glasses of pink champagne, if you please."

The footman looked around, startled, but leaped to obey.

"You're not supposed to do that," Gina said, laughing despite herself. "The butler has positioned those two men at the doors in case they are needed."

"For what?"

"What if someone faints?"

He looked her over from head to foot. "You look hearty. Are you feeling like fainting?"

"No, of course not." Something about his leisurely gaze sent hot blood to her cheeks and made her a bit dizzy.

To her relief Sebastian appeared. He bowed punctiliously. She could tell he wasn't pleased to find her with her husband. He had said earlier that he thought the duke should return to London so as to avoid complicating the annulment proceedings.

Cam thought of bowing and decided to skip it. He was getting tired of looking at the floor. Just then the footman reappeared, holding two glasses. "Thank you very much," he said, taking them and handing one to Gina. "Sorry we don't have a glass for you, Bonnington."

Gina sighed. Sebastian's mouth closed like a steel trap. Clearly he thought she'd had more than enough to drink and, to be honest, she had. There was nothing she disliked more than feeling sluggish in the morning. "I don't wish for any champagne. Would you mind terribly fetching me some lemonade, Sebastian?"

He gave her an approving nod and plucked the champagne out of her hand. Then he bowed again and began making his way out of the room.

"How the devil did he manage to bow without spilling the champagne?" Cam asked. "Damn! Now you'll have to share mine, and I was looking forward to swilling the lot." He held the glass out to Gina with such a merry, wicked look in his eyes that she took it without thinking and drank some.

He comfortably leaned against the wall next to her. "Shouldn't some man be pestering you for this dance?"

"I had promised it to Sebastian." She took another sip of champagne, wondering why her pulse was racing.

"But you can't dance twice with the same man," he said. "Remember those letters you wrote me when you just came out?"

"I can't believe you remember that! Why, that was years ago."

"I have a good memory," he said lazily. "So are you risking scandal by loping around the dance floor with your betrothed twice?"

"Oh no," Gina said. "Those rules only apply to girls just out of the schoolroom. Although Sebastian does restrict himself to three."

He turned his head and looked at her. "If I was betrothed to you, rather than just being your husband, I wouldn't let you dance a single dance with anyone else."

Gina felt a lick of fire in her stomach. "Oh," she said lamely. Her conscience prompted her to defend her betrothed. "Sebastian feels we are in a very precarious position. Here I am, married, after all." She took out her fan and waved it gently before her face. There was nothing worse than a flushed face with red hair, as her mother had repeatedly told her.

"Yes," he said meditatively. "Here you are, married, after all." He reached over, plucked the champagne glass from her hand, and took a drink.

Gina licked her lips. There was something incredibly intimate about sharing a glass. Perhaps the bubbles were going to her head again.

"Shall we sit down?" he asked.

"All right," Gina said.

He walked straight across the room and ducked into one of the little alcoves off the ballroom. Heavy ocher silk swung closed behind them.

Gina sat down on the little velvet sofa, flustered. "I never enter these alcoves."

Cam looked around and then sat next to her. "Why on earth not? It's a little airless, to be sure. And I don't think much for Lady Troubridge's artistic sense." He peered at a picture of a lackadaisical Cupid sitting on a buttercup.

"Curtained alcoves aren't considered proper."

He looked at her with frank amusement in his eyes. "I'd just as soon spend all my time in an alcove and none of it skipping around. Have some more champagne." He handed her the glass. "I think we should finish it before Bonnington returns, don't you think?"

She pushed it back into his hand. "I don't care for any, thank you very much."

"How are you, Gina?"

"Absolutely fine," she answered, startled.

He leaned toward her. Gina smelled his soap. Her heart beat a rapid tattoo against her rib cage.

"No, I mean how are you truly?" he said. "After all, we are intimately related, though I haven't seen you for twelve years. We were first cousins for years. Then when it was suddenly revealed that you were not my blood relative, you became my wife."

"I'm just fine," she said, getting more flustered. She tapped her fan closed and looked at it rather than meet his eyes.

Marissa's face was a perfect oval. When Gina's eyes were hidden by those sooty eyelashes—she must color them, he thought absentmindedly—her face looked almost as perfectly oval as Marissa's. Odd he hadn't noticed that earlier. It must be her eyes. They led him astray. She was smoothing each stick of her fan with a delicate finger.

He was jolted by a stab of lust. Did she touch the lofty Bonnington with those long fingers of hers? With that smooth a stroke? If she hadn't, she would. He pulled his thoughts back from that image.

"Gina," he said.

She looked up. Her eyes were a bewitching green, the color of a deep pool of Mediterranean water.

"Aren't you going to welcome me home?" he said, rather huskily. And then, before he thought twice, his lips drifted down on hers. He tasted surprise on her lips. He was surprised too. What the devil was he doing? Still . . . a woman's lips, a curtained alcove, a waltz playing dimly in the background. England at its best, he thought dimly. He cupped the back of her head in his large hand and relaxed into the kiss.

Except that one moment he was feathering his lips over hers in a sweet, welcome-home kind of way, and the next his wife gave a startled little squeak and so, of course, he took the invitation and—her open mouth.

At which point waltz, curtains, and champagne fell away. His groin tightened; he tilted her face so that he could crush her mouth under his. He cupped that delicate oval of a face in his callused hands and drank from her as if she were nectar. The mating game. Not nostalgia anymore, nor greeting. In the flick of an eyelash, their kiss had transformed into a bewildering, lusty meeting of mouths. He had a sweep of her hair in his right hand and her hand was curved around his neck. His mouth was hard on hers, sweet kisses, hot kisses that burned the air between them.

Except she stopped kissing him back and shoved at his shoulder, hard.

He pulled back. For a moment they just stared at each other. Then she reached out a hand and pulled open the curtains. Sure enough, her fiancé was making his way across the ballroom floor.

"You must excuse me," Gina said. "I believe I momentarily forgot who you were."

Cam felt a bolt of anger. No one forgot who he was when he held her in his arms—no one. Especially not his own wife.

"It appears that Bonnington is about to save us from a spot of marital embarrassment," he drawled.

"Are you embarrassed by something?" she asked, raising a delicate eyebrow.

He had to admit it. She was as cool about it as he was. Damned if he believed that she'd never been in an alcove before. He answered without pause for thought. "I've always thought it must be unpleasantly embarrassing to feel desire for one's wife. Rather like a disreputable longing for the bread pudding served in the nursery."

She turned a little pink at that. "Bread pudding?"

"Yes," he said. "Bread pudding. Because one can go without bread pudding for long periods of time, can't one? In fact, it is hardly seen on a civilized table. But then sometimes one has an alarming"—he paused—"*lust* for just that homey concoction."

There was a moment's pause as Gina untangled his metaphor and discovered she was being compared to a soggy concoction that she hadn't willingly eaten in years. Fury polished her tone to a smooth honey. "I understand your embarrassment," she cooed. "Because it is embarrassing, some would even say humiliating, to experience an unreturned lust, is it not?"

He smiled at her, one eyebrow raised. "Then why on earth are you engaged to that man?" He nodded toward Sebastian.

Gina gasped.

It was much more comfortable to have her in a state rather than himself. "Do you know, a flush really isn't very attractive on a red-haired person," he said with an air of discovery.

Bonnington approached, holding a glass of sickly yellow liquid. Gina walked into the ballroom, giving him a melting smile.

Cam was amused to see that the slightly hunted look in Bonnington's eyes only increased. If she wasn't careful, she'd flush that partridge too early.

"I have been longing for some refreshment. Unfortunately, I am beginning to find this assembly has become quite tedious." She paused. "Perhaps it is the sedating effect of reacquainting oneself with childhood playmates. I'm sure you won't take offense at that, sir. I'm afraid that I've quite lost my taste for the nursery." She favored Cam with a cool smile. "Shall we stroll into the garden?" She slid her hand into Bonnington's elbow with a jolt that brought her body up against his jacket.

Cam watched with hooded eyes as Bonnington automatically edged back so as to achieve a proper distance between their bodies. "I trust you will excuse us," he said.

Deep in his eyes Cam saw a glimmer of manly panic that made him feel much kinder toward the fellow. After all, why judge a man based on his finicking deportment in public? Some of the most polite fellows he knew were outrageous in private.

If anything, he should feel sympathy for the poor blighter. Caught, he was. He watched as they strolled away. Unfortunately, Bonnington had gotten himself into the mess by proposing. He would soon find himself walking down the aisle of St. James and, in the natural course of marriage, would be driven around the bend by his wife.

A jaundiced, beery voice sounded at his ear. "Hello there, duke," it said.

Cam looked about.

"Richard Blackton, second cousin on your mother's side," the man said, swaying and catching his balance with the ease of a habitual drinker. "Recognized you at once. You look just the same as your father, you know. What're you here for, then? Annulling the one marriage, are you? Going to take on younger game? Why don't you try one of Deventosh's daughters? They've got red hair too. Not so many women with red hair in the *ton,* you know. If you have a penchant for the color, well, beggars can't be choosers."

Cam's head had begun to pound in an unpleasant fashion. "I am honored to meet you," he said.

The drunk looked confused and said, "What? What'd you say, son?"

"I am ravished with pleasure to meet you."

That silenced him. "Foreign manners," he said, looking suspiciously at Cam. "Foreign manners and red hair. I need a brandy." And he turned and tottered back to the decanters lining the sideboard without another word.

Cam retreated to the chambers allotted him by Lady Troubridge, trying to dismiss a nasty suspicion that was creeping into his mind. Marissa had black hair. Midnight black. So black it was . . . black.

Gina had hair the color of a ripened orange.

Perhaps he *did* have a penchant for red hair. It was a bewildering thought and didn't fit his vision of himself as an Englishman who lived in a cheerfully godforsaken country and fashioned plump naked women out of marble, a man who spent most of the day covered with gray marble dust.

There was no room in his life—in that life—for an irritating duchess.

For a wife.

Chapter Seven

The Afflictions of Memory Following Lady Troubridge's Ridotto

The following morning Gina could not bring herself to visit the breakfast room. She huddled in bed, reliving every exchange with her husband. He was so very different than she remembered. How *male* he had become, she thought with a shiver. The way his shoulders—but no. It was more his eyes. There was something about the way he looked at her, as if she were a delicious private joke. She curled deeper under her covers, ignoring the way her stomach tingled at the memory of their kiss.

If the truth were told, many of Lady Troubridge's houseguests were similarly afflicted by an attack of memory. Sir Rushwood was also abed, brooding over an unpleasant remark made by his wife after he danced a waltz with the beauteous Mrs. Boylen. Tuppy Perwinkle had glimpsed his wife, Carola, dancing at least three times with a foppishly elegant man. Now he was in the breakfast room gloomily chewing toast and wondering if a new wardrobe might win back his wife's affections.

Gina was startled out of her reverie by the sound of her mother's voice followed by a swish of silk.

"Darling!" her mother announced. "Open your eyes. I am here. I arrived late last night."

"I gathered that," Gina mumbled, pushing herself up on the pillows. "May we have this discussion at a later hour, Mother?"

"I'm afraid not," Lady Cranborne said, "given that I have made this trip merely to speak to you. I must return to London immediately for a meeting of the Ladies' Charity Organization. I have received another one!" she announced. The edge of hysteria in her voice finally caught her daughter's attention.

"Another what?" But she guessed, even before her mother answered.

"Another letter of course!" Lady Cranborne half screamed. "And what am I to do about it? My brother is dead!"

"Well, that's true," Gina answered, startled. "But what does his death have to do with the arrival of this letter?"

"Everything!" said Lady Cranborne in anguished tones that might have come from an overwrought Ophelia.

Gina waited.

"Last time, I summoned my brother and he took care of it all. Everything! I didn't have to worry about the letter again. I believe he even hired a Bow Street Runner, although since he said nothing about it, I suppose the man was unsuccessful. And now we are alone. Even Cranborne has been dead these five years, although he was utterly useless when we received the first letter, *utterly useless*! All he could say was, 'Thought the woman knew how to keep her mouth!'"

Gina had heard this summary of her father's abilities many a time, and reiteration was tedious.

"Thank God, Girton was a different kind of man from my husband," Lady Cranborne continued without pause. "Thank God he saw immediately that you had to marry his son, because if it was up to your father, you would have been branded a bastard the length and breadth of England before he even understood the consequences. He was *that* beef-witted."

"Yes, but Mother—"

"My brother simply took charge. He grasped the situation in two seconds and summoned Camden back from Oxford that very afternoon. And there you were, married the next day. If there's anything I admire, my dear, it's a man of *action*. Which your father was *not*!"

"Did you receive another blackmail letter?"

But her mother was striding back and forth so furiously that she didn't hear. "I begged your father, when you were brought to us, as a baby," she cried. "I said, Cranborne, *if* you have an intelligent bone in your body, you'll pay That Woman off!"

Gina sighed. It was clearly going to be a lengthy conversation. She climbed out of bed, pulled on her robe, and sat down next to the fire.

"Did he obey me? Did he even *listen* to me? No! All Cranborne did was mumble about how distinguished That Woman was, and how she would never betray her own child. And what happened?"

"Nothing so terrible," Gina put in. "I became a duchess, remember?"

"Due to my brother, never to Cranborne!" she said triumphantly. "The first letter arrived—and who would write an anonymous letter? A French person. *Obviously* it was That Woman who wrote the letter. And this one as well, no doubt."

"Mother," Gina repeated.

Lady Cranborne paced.

"Mother!"

"What? What is it?" She stopped her frantic walk in mid-step and automatically put her hands to her hair. "Did you say something, dearest?"

"Countess Ligny cannot have written you a letter. She died last year."

Lady Cranborne gaped. *"What?"*

Gina nodded.

"Your—your—the woman who gave birth to you is *dead*? Impossible!"

"Mr. Rounton wrote me a letter, and he enclosed a notice from the Paris *Express*."

"Why didn't you tell me?"

Gina saw the warning signs of an attack of temper. "I didn't want to upset you by even bringing up her name."

"And what did you *do* about it?" Lady Cranborne asked.

"Do?"

"I know you, Gina!" she snapped. "I may not have given birth to you, but I did raise you! What did you *do* after receiving Rounton's letter?"

"I wrote a letter to her estate," Gina admitted. "I was wondering whether she left a message or a note . . ."

Lady Cranborne rustled across the room and patted her daughter on the head. "I am sorry, dearest," she said, dropping a kiss on pale red hair that precisely matched that of the infamous Countess Ligny. "I *am* truly sorry. The countess was an ingrate and a fool, even though her loss was my blessing."

Gina took a deep breath. "It's all right. She paid no attention to me during her life, but I thought perhaps . . ." She shrugged. "The puzzling thing is, though—"

"Lud!" Lady Cranborne broke in, hand to her mouth. "If That Woman—if Countess Ligny didn't write this letter, then who did?"

"What does the letter say?"

Her mother fished in her reticule. "Here it is." It was written on heavy stock, in a precise secretary hand.

For a moment Gina's eyes danced over the ornate loops and twists of the script without being able to decipher its meaning. Then suddenly the text jumped at her.

Might the Marquess be miffed?
The Duchess has a Brother.

"I have a brother," she whispered. "I have a brother!"

"Must be a half brother," Lady Cranborne corrected. "I never allowed your father anywhere near the continent after that trip to France had such ghastly consequences." She caught herself. "I didn't mean that, darling. You are a blessing to me. Thank *God* That Woman didn't want to raise her own children. Lord knows where this brother of yours might be. Likely she threw him back at his father, same as she did with you."

"But who on earth could have written this letter?"

"Obviously, the countess was careless. She assured your father that no one even knew that you existed. As soon as she realized she was *enceinte,* she retired to her country estate. And you appeared at our doorstep as a babe of only six weeks." She gave her daughter an impulsive kiss. "It was the happiest day of my life."

Gina smiled. "The happiest and the angriest, Mama."

"True. But by then I had Cranborne's measure, my dear. If there was another such fool in the world, I never met him. If I hadn't kept him on a short leash, he'd have sprouted children like brussels sprouts in a cabbage patch, I swear to God."

Gina was staring at the anonymous letter again. "Perhaps they'll write again and tell me where to find my brother."

"More likely they will write and ask for money," her mother pointed out. "The letter is clearly a threat. How do you think Bonnington will feel about you having an illegitimate brother?"

"Oh, he'll be—" but the words caught in her throat before she said that Sebastian would be happy for her. The fact was that from the moment she confessed the truth of her birth—that she was, in fact, her father's illegitimate child with a French countess—Sebastian had never mentioned the disreputable fact again. In fact, she suspected that he was pretending he never heard it. The story believed by most of England, that Gina was the orphaned child of one of Lady Cranborne's distant cousins, was far more palatable.

"He won't take it well," Lady Cranborne pointed out. Then, with a faint giggle, "He'll be *miffed*."

Gina had to admit the truth of that. "He won't like it. Particularly if there is a chance that the letter writer will actually spill the news to the public."

"Thank goodness your father was never allowed to meddle with the estate. We're certainly rich enough to pay for this horrid person's silence."

Gina sat down on the end of the bed. "I'm not so sure that is wise," she said slowly. "The blackmailer has been waiting, hasn't he? Uncle Girton thwarted the initial threat of exposure by marrying me to Cam. But then Cam fled to Greece. So the letter writer has waited and waited. He must know that Cam is about to annul the marriage. And he thinks I will pay a fortune to ensure that Sebastian's offer of marriage holds."

Lady Cranborne nodded. "As the Duchess of Girton, you could brazen your way through a scandal about your birth. But as an ex-duchess and a bastard, you make a poor prospect for a marchioness. Perhaps you should throw over the marquess now, before he has the chance to throw you over," her mother suggested.

Gina looked at her suspiciously. "You simply don't like Sebastian."

"True," Lady Cranborne said, preening before the dressing table mirror. "I think he's a stick, my dear. But then I'm not marrying him."

The words "Thank God" echoed silently in the room.

"Cam arrived last night."

"Did he? How lovely! I can't wait to see the boy. I'll have to try to catch him at luncheon. Did I tell you that there is a meeting of the Ladies' Charity Organization tonight? I can tell you, in the darkest secrecy, of course, that there is a *small* chance that I shall be elected president. I shall refuse, of course." Lady Cranborne looked affectionately at her aristo-cratic countenance. A thoroughly modern matron, she spent most of her time rushing from philanthropy to philanthropy.

"Congratulations, Mother!" Gina said, summoning up all the enthusiasm she could. "That would mean you are the head of four organizations, wouldn't it?"

"Three," Lady Cranborne said. "I discarded the Golspie Cripples' Committee last week. Just a group of muddleheaded old ducks who didn't understand leadership. If there was one thing my brother taught me, it was how to lead. Although I must say that he handled young Camden very badly. *Very* badly. One of the few areas in which I'd seen him act in a bacon-brained manner, and so I told him."

"Yes," Gina said, remembering the battles that enlivened the house after Cam had fled to Italy, leaving his bride *virgo intacta* in their marital bedchamber.

"It wasn't your fault, dearest. My brother had a heavy hand."

"He could be cruel, Mother."

"I wouldn't go so far. His harshness was due to his great intelligence." Lady Cranborne patted her hair before the mirror.

Gina bit her tongue. The Girtons had made a practice of worshipping at the altar of intelligence over humanity; who was she to try to change her mother's mind? "I suppose we must simply wait for another communication," she said.

73

"Do you plan to inform Bonnington?" her mother asked.

"No."

Lady Cranborne glanced over her shoulder with a glimmer of amusement in her eyes. "Careful, darling," she said. "Keeping secrets from one's husband often signals the beginning of trouble in a marriage."

"He is *not* my husband," Gina said sharply. "Cam is my husband."

"Well, then, tell Camden," Lady Cranborne said, tucking an errant ringlet back under her cap. "He was shaping up to be almost as intelligent as his father, from what I remember."

"More so, I think."

"I wouldn't be surprised. Girton always complained that the boy was afraid of the dark and afraid of guns and who knows what else. All because he disliked hunting. Girton thought Camden was a milksop simply because he spent his time carving wooden boats rather than shooting animals. But I thought he showed signs of early acuity."

"He's not a milksop. Not at all."

"I never thought so," her mother said. "Could tell he'd inherited the family brains. As did you, darling," she added loyally.

Gina forbore to point out that she was no blood relation to the Girtons. Yet even in her brief reacquaintance with her husband, it was clear that conventions wouldn't bother him. "I wouldn't mind discussing the letter with Cam," she said slowly.

Her mother nodded. "We could use some help. We'll need a man to deliver the money once it is demanded, for one thing."

"I don't like the idea of paying for silence."

"I don't like the idea of you being foisted out of society either. Small minds must be appeased, and so we will pay through the nose to ensure you marry Bonnington, if that's what you wish. And then we will never pay another red cent! Because I don't care what the letter writer thinks; the *ton* will never ostracize the wife of a very wealthy marquess. Perhaps we'd better consider having the wedding directly after your annulment is obtained, however."

"Sebastian has already obtained a special license."

"Excellent. I shall leave you the note so that you can show it to your husband, darling. Do talk to him as soon as possible, won't you?" She hesitated. "I need hardly ask—but you have gotten rid of that dreadful little tutor of yours, haven't you?"

"No," Gina replied.

"No?" Lady Cranborne's voice rose. "In my note, written the very minute that scandalous piece appeared in the newspaper, I instructed you to let him go *immediately*!"

It was times like this that reminded Gina that Lady Cranborne and Cam's father were siblings. "I can hardly do that, Mother. He is my husband's employee—"

"I shall never understand why you brought him to a house party in the first place," her mother declared. "Such a dreadful little—"

"He's not dreadful," Gina put in. "He's just rather awkward."

"There's something very peculiar about him. I can't fathom why you didn't simply leave him at the estate, if you couldn't bring yourself to let him go."

"He wanted to come."

"He wanted to come! *He* wanted to come!" Lady Cranborne's voice had risen to a shriek now. "You took into account the wishes of a servant. What else did he want, a visit to Buckingham Palace? No wonder *The Tatler* caught hold of this!"

"Mother!"

75

"Girtons do not behave like common rabble!" her mother said. "We do *not* abandon our dignity, ever, nor do we do odd things which allow the hoi polloi to mar your virtue. What on earth were you thinking of, Ambrogina?"

"It was foolish," Gina admitted. "I merely said that I was sorry to suspend our tutoring, and he expressed such a wish to accompany me that I couldn't very well leave him behind. He's not a nuisance, Mother. I do enjoy learning Italian history."

"He must go," Lady Cranborne said ominously. "I shall speak to your husband immediately. Now I must leave. If I don't see you at luncheon, au revoir, dearest." And she swept off with an expression that made it clear that she would be mollified only when one history tutor had walked out of the house with his bags in hand.

Chapter Eight

In Which Beautiful Men
Frolic by the River

Gina didn't see Cam until late afternoon. Lady Troubridge had organized a picnic al fresco at the banks of the River Saddler, which ran at the bottom of the gardens. Gina strolled down the hill with Esme.

"My goodness," Esme said, as they neared the river. "Who is that *exquisite* young man?"

Gina looked. "An actor. His name is something absurdly theatrical. Reginald Gerard, I think."

Tables had been set out in the shade of some old willow trees that spread themselves like gossiping matrons on the riverbank. The actor was crossing the river by leaping from one protruding rock to the next, grabbing apples from a low-hanging apple tree, and returning them to the young ladies waiting on the bank.

Every once in a while he tottered and seemed sure to fall into the river, eliciting little shrieks from the flock of debutantes clustered on the bank.

"What a nauseating spectacle," came a drawling voice at Gina's ear.

She turned to smile at her husband, quite as if she hadn't spent the whole morning watching the parlor door for his arrival. "Hello, Cam."

"Will you introduce me?" he said, looking appreciatively at Esme.

Esme curtsied, a little smile lurking at the corner of her mouth.

"This is Lady Rawlings," Gina said. "Esme, my husband."

"A true delight," Cam said, kissing her hand.

Gina felt a stab of annoyance. Cam *was* married, after all. As was Esme.

"Oh look, Esme," she said coolly. "There's Burdett."

Her friend managed to tear her eyes away from Cam and waved to Bernie, who came loping over with the eager pace of a well-trained retriever. "How do, then?" he said cheerfully. "How do? I'm Bernie Burdett."

Cam bowed. "I am the Duke of Girton."

"Oh," Bernie said, clearly nonplussed. But then his face cleared. "Your Grace? Your Grace!" Confident now of the proper salutation, he managed to reiterate his own name without prompting.

"Well done, Bernie," Esme said, tucking her hand into his arm. "Shall we sit down, everyone?"

Cam fell in beside Gina. To her annoyance his eyes were fixed on Esme's slender back. "What on earth is she doing with him?" he asked quietly.

"Bernie is a very, very—"

"—very picture of a fool?" Cam supplied.

Esme and Bernie had reached the edge of the river. As they watched, Bernie took off his jacket and threw it on the riverbank. Then he leaped gracefully from rock to rock without a moment's hesitation, putting the young actor and his overdramatic stunts to shame.

"Aha," Cam said, with amusement roughening his voice. "I see the light."

Gina followed his gaze. Bernie's gray morning trousers were molded to legs as muscular and shapely as it was possible for a man's legs to be. In truth, with the sun shining on his golden hair, Bernie Burdett probably looked as well as he had ever looked in his life. He had reached the other side of the river now and reached up to pluck an apple. White linen stretched across beautifully defined shoulders. A second later he was back at Esme's side.

"Yes," Gina murmured.

"Well, don't go into a trance," Cam snapped. "Physical beauty is not everything."

She looked at him curiously. "I would think that a sculptor would value beauty above all other attributes."

Cam shrugged. "I could sculpt Burdett, but I couldn't do much about his brains. He would still look like a Jack Pudding." Bernie had handed over his apple and was kissing Esme's hand as a reward. "How can she bear to be around him?"

Gina didn't ignore the innuendo, because there was no scorn in Cam's tone, only genuine curiosity. "Esme has a great love of beauty," she explained. "At the same time, she seems to choose friends who have—who are—"

"Half witted?"

"Well—" Gina said reluctantly.

Cam shrugged. "It's a common decision in the male case. The ideal mistress is beautiful, cheerful, and indolent. Bernie seems to fit the bill."

"Do you—" Gina caught herself. There was something about Cam's beguiling curiosity that lured her into saying whatever came to mind.

"I don't have a mistress, at the moment," he said obligingly. "But when I did, she fit precisely into the parameters I just outlined."

"And wives," Gina said, feeling dispirited, "should wives be the same?"

"Less beautiful is acceptable, but they must be even more obedient," Cam said. "Do you think you could live up to the bill, had we been married in earnest?"

"I never gave it a thought," she said, sweeping him a glance under her eyelashes. He had the most suggestive grin she'd ever seen on a man, this husband of hers. "But I doubt it. Obedience is not one of my virtues." She turned to walk toward Sebastian, but Cam stepped directly in her path.

"One doesn't wish a wife to be obedient at all times, you know."

He looked as if he were laughing at her, but she wasn't sure why. "What are you saying?" she asked.

"Obedience is such a complicated issue," he said dreamily. "For example, with regard to the bedchamber, one must choose a wife—"

Gina cut him off. "That is of no concern to me. I am quite aware that you did not choose me as your wife."

"True enough," Cam said. "I remember my father telling me that you would ripen into a beauty, though, and you certainly have fulfilled his prophecy."

Gina gaped. "Your father said *that*?"

Cam nodded. "Is it so surprising?"

"When I made my debut, he remarked that I should be thankful I already had a wedding ring, so that I needn't try to parade my wares on the market. I always took that to be an insult."

"Quite right too," Cam remarked. "My father was a master of the insulting remark. In fact, he said very little that one could not take offense at."

"Besides, I am not beautiful in the way Esme is beautiful," Gina remarked, wondering why on earth she was saying something so pitiful.

Cam looked over at Esme. "Yes, Lady Rawlings is certainly one of the most classically beautiful women I've ever seen, in England at least."

"I can't imagine why we're discussing such a foolish topic," Gina said airily.

"Come along!" Esme called, waving at them.

Cam turned toward the classical beauty, but Gina walked toward Sebastian instead. It was best that she not spend time with her husband. She certainly didn't want to weaken her chances for an annulment.

Sebastian was sitting alone at a small table. He had an expression that she secretly thought of as his puritanical look. She slipped into a seat with her back to Esme and Cam.

"How *is* Lady Rawlings this morning?" Sebastian asked disagreeably. "She certainly seems to be enjoying herself."

"I'm sure that she is," Gina said, glancing back. Esme was ensconced between Bernie and Cam, and shining with pleasure. Cam was leaning toward her as if she were speaking pearls of wisdom.

"I suppose if she keeps your husband occupied, it will be all the better for the annulment," Sebastian remarked.

"I expect so," Gina murmured.

It was unfortunate that Sebastian was facing Esme's table, because he didn't seem to be able to keep his eyes off her. All the way through lamb à la béchamel he kept up a hissing commentary on Esme's bold seduction of Gina's husband. "At this rate, your annulment proceedings will be twinned with a bill for divorce from Rawlings," he said disagreeably.

Gina was beginning to feel slightly sick. "Sebastian!" she finally said, "don't you think that I am the one who should be upset, if anyone? And I'm not. Who does it hurt if Cam and Esme grow acquainted? No one." She took a bite of chicken. It tasted like a wrung-out piece of dishcloth.

"I suppose you're right. I just don't like to see a good man drawn in—"

"You are forming a veritable obsession!" Gina said, exasperated. "To be honest, you are quite impolite to even air this subject in my presence."

Sebastian look startled, and then appalled. "You must forgive me, Gina. I completely forgot that you have no more experience of the world than a mere green girl."

"I'm not quite that uninformed."

"No, I insist on apologizing." Sebastian's blue eyes smiled at her so warmly that Gina felt more friendly despite her annoyance. "I allowed your innocence to slip my mind. And yet that is one of the qualities I most love about you, Gina: your air of being untouched by the seamier side of life."

"And what will happen when we are married and I am no longer so innocent?" she asked baldly.

Sebastian smiled. "You will always have an innocent beauty. There is something untouched and untouchable about you—the mark of good breeding bred in the bone."

"But, Sebastian—" Gina began, entertaining for one reckless moment the idea of discussing her newly discovered illegitimate brother.

Lady Troubridge was clapping her hands for attention and Sebastian instantly turned toward their hostess.

"Hear ye! Hear ye!" Lady Troubridge cried gaily. "Mr. Gerard has agreed to organize a small performance for the weekend—just a few scenes from Shakespeare. Anyone who would like to take part in a reading, will you make yourselves known?"

To Gina's dismay, Sebastian's brow darkened again. "Performing with a professional actor? Grossly *improper*!"

"Oh, Sebastian," she said, "sometimes I think that is your favorite word."

He opened his mouth and then paused. To her inexpressible relief she saw a glimpse of the old Sebastian, before he became so intent on his rank and title. "I'm getting to be stiff-rumped, is that what you're saying?"

She smiled gratefully into his eyes. "Only a little bit."

"My father was an old stick. I was thinking about it last night. I reckon you're right, Gina. I'm getting prudish." He looked horrified at the thought.

Gina patted his hand, wishing she could be more demonstrative, but that would shock not only Sebastian, but the rest of the assembly as well.

"I have you," he said, looking into her eyes.

"Yes, you have me," she repeated, rather heartily.

"Well, isn't that endearing? We should all be so lucky as to possess Gina," Cam continued silkily at Gina's shoulder. "In fact, I do believe that we both have the *same* good luck! Isn't that extraordinary?"

"I am a lucky man," Sebastian said, too loudly.

"And so am I, so am I."

"Gina and I were about to volunteer to take parts in the Shakespeare reading," Sebastian said, standing up so quickly he almost knocked over his chair. "If you'll excuse us—"

"Don't let me hinder you. I was thinking of joining the performance myself, and I know that Lady Rawlings will feel the same," Cam remarked. He turned and waved at Esme, and to Gina's disgust, her best friend smiled at him so warmly that she felt a curl of embarrassment. Esme had no right to openly seduce *her* husband.

"Come along, Sebastian!" she snapped, walking toward Lady Troubridge without waiting for Esme.

The young actor, Reginald Gerard, was surrounded by a fluttering group of debutantes who all seemed to be giggling and begging to play the heroine. But their hopes were quickly dashed by Lady Troubridge.

"I'm sorry, girls," she said briskly, shooing them away with a brightly colored handkerchief. "But your mothers and I have decided that performing a play is a little too daring for girls who are unmarried. I'm not having any scandal attached to my party!" She sanguinely ignored the fact that her house parties invariably provided the prime gossip for the first two months of the season. "No, Mr. Gerard will have to make do with married women, that's all. You four will be perfect!" she exclaimed.

Gina watched as Reginald Gerard's face fell. It was clear that he didn't wish to spend his afternoons with married couples. Likely he hoped to elope with an heiress.

"I agree with you, my lady," Sebastian was saying to Lady Troubridge. "Dramatic prose is entirely too exciting for young ladies."

"What play are you considering?" Cam asked.

"A few scenes from *Much Ado About Nothing*," the young actor replied. He might have been disappointed, but he rallied and bowed politely enough. "May I introduce myself? I am Reginald Gerard."

"I believe I saw you at Covent Garden this past season," Sebastian said, bowing. "I am Marquess Bonnington. This is the Duchess of Girton, and Lady Rawlings. And the Duke of Girton," he added.

Reginald smiled at the little circle. "I think we shall be able to come up with an enchanting little performance here. Perhaps the duchess could play Hero and—"

"I think not," Cam interrupted. "The duchess and I had better play Beatrice and Benedick. After all, we *are* married, and it would be quite harrowing for me to see another man at my wife's bedchamber window."

"Oh, of course," Reginald agreed.

Sebastian frowned. "What's this about a bedchamber window?"

"In the play, Claudio—that would be you, my lord—believes that his betrothed, Hero, has been unfaithful to him when he thinks he sees another man at her window."

"That sounds most unsuitable to me," Sebastian said, frowning. "Is the play appropriate for mixed company?"

"It was performed with great success only last season," Reginald said politely. "Besides, we will only do a few scenes. If there is anything that you and Lady Rawlings do not feel quite comfortable with, we will avoid that section. I suggest that we meet in the library before supper, and decide on the scenes."

Gina felt a warm hand at her waist for a split second. "Do you suppose that we will survive a foursome for an hour or more?"

"Why, what do you mean?"

"Surely you've noticed your fiancé's preoccupation with the beauteous Lady Rawlings?" He nodded toward them. Sure enough, Sebastian appeared to be lecturing Esme as she absentmindedly ate an apple.

"You seem to suffer from the same affliction," Gina remarked.

Cam laughed. "What's not to love? She's beautiful, curvaceous, and apparently quite friendly."

Gina's lips tightened. "She's not *that* friendly!"

"I'd give a groat that Bonnington is lecturing her on her friendliness."

Gina looked again. True enough, Esme was starting to champ her apple, and a flush was rising up her cheeks.

"She would make a superb Diana," Cam said.

"Diana, the goddess of virginity?" Gina asked, with a touch of skepticism.

"Odd, isn't it? But she has a touch-me-not air, for all her friendliness. Perhaps I'll see if she will pose for me."

Gina glanced up at her husband. He was looking at Esme with the critical eye of a master jeweler assessing a perfect diamond. "I thought you were already working on a Diana. Won't it be tedious to do another figure of the same goddess?"

"No. Each woman is different. Giving them the names of goddesses—that's just putting a name to what you see in their faces. In the case of Lady Rawlings, she is provocative, beautiful, even erotic. But at the same time, she is distinctly reserved. I would guess that she is not sharing a bed with Burdett, for all she acts as if she is."

Gina looked at him with new respect.

Sometime later she and Esme walked up the hill in silence, returning to the house. Gina was longing to know whether Cam watched them leave, or whether he turned blithely away. She almost turned, but Esme caught her elbow.

"Don't look!" she whispered, eyes dancing. "I'm sure he's watching, but you don't want him to suspect, do you?"

"Sebastian?"

"Of course I don't mean Sebastian, you half wit!" Esme exclaimed. "I mean your oh-so-gorgeous husband, of course!"

"Well, I'm glad you think so," Gina said tartly.

"Of course I think so." Then her eyes widened. "Gina, you didn't think that I—"

"No, of course not!"

"Yes, you did!" Esme had delightful dimples, Gina had to admit. No wonder every man she met fell in love with her, including Gina's own husband. "Don't be silly. You know I have no use for intelligent men." She tucked her hand into Gina's elbow. "May I say one thing though?"

Gina nodded.

"I think you should keep him."

Chapter Nine

A Slab of Pink Marble and a Contemplative Duke

Cam stared at the piece of marble three footmen had gingerly deposited on the Axminster carpet. There was no doubt that Esme Rawlings, with her generous curves and glossy hair, was as close to Marissa—and therefore to goddesslike beauty—as he was like to find in England. It even seemed possible that Esme would lend herself to such a risqué project as being sculpted in pink marble as a seated, half-naked deity.

But somehow the idea of creating a shapely goddess of the hunt had little interest at the moment, not to mention Stephen's insistence that he sculpt something other than a female torso. He kept turning back to the copy of *Much Ado* Lady Troubridge had sent to his room. In the throes of loneliness when he first left England, he had read Shakespeare's plays over and over. Lonely for English hearth and home, for English phrases and English ale.

But he never thought to play Benedick to his wife's Beatrice. Well, he never thought of himself as having a wife at all, so why should he? But there Gina had been all the time he was reading Shakespeare, trotting around England with that slim body and silky red hair, that indomitable curiosity and keen intelligence. Wearing his ring all the time, even though he hadn't given it a second's thought.

He eyed the marble again. Gina would make a terrible Diana. She had a far too eager look in her eyes. The misanthropic goddess never regarded a man with Gina's frank and appreciative gaze. Would never greet him with pleasure, as if she had genuinely missed him. Certainly the goddess would never write that delinquent husband hundreds of letters.

It hadn't occurred to him that once they were no longer married, Gina wouldn't write to him. Her letters had followed him from country to country. He frowned down at the book in his hand. Hell, if the truth be told, he'd hounded those letters from country to country. He always wrote her before he moved, because he didn't want to miss a letter. And there was that time when he sent Phillipos on a three-day trip back to an inn they had long since left to retrieve one of her letters they had missed.

The thought made him uncomfortable. She was his link to England, nothing more. In fact, the *letters,* not Gina, were his link to home. It was nothing to do with his wife. It was the letters that mattered to him.

Of course.

He tossed the slim volume of plays on the ground where it slid across the carpet and rested next to the obscenely pink marble. Damn it, but Stephen had done him a disservice. Now he looked at the stone and saw fleshy thighs and vulgar hips, whereas always before he had seen the potential to shape a nubile and beautiful woman. Pink, plump, and naked. He curled his lip. Stephen made him sound like a purveyor of pornographic etchings.

His wife wouldn't want to pose as a member of the pantheon of Roman goddesses. Although the idea of Gina wearing nothing more than a transparent piece of veil was enough to fire any man's loins.

He wouldn't make her into Diana, of course. Not Venus either . . . too bland. Besides, he wasn't even certain that he *could* sculpt Gina. Her sliding mass of hair—how did one turn that into marble? And the way she was always in motion, always turning, always moving. It was impossible to imagine Gina pausing long enough to catch her on paper, let alone in stone. And yet his fingers itched to try.

But sculpting Gina was a moot question, because after this visit he wouldn't return to England for years. No point in that. No point in coming back to see his former wife presenting the turgid marquess with babe after babe, enthusiastically produced in a marital bed.

No, he'd stay in the village, thank you very much. At least there he was the unquestioned master of his fate. No wives around to send hot blood pounding to his loins with their innocently seductive remarks . . .

It's just lust, he thought. After all, he and Marissa had stopped what lackadaisical sexual activity they used to perform a few years ago. And although he'd enjoyed a woman's company now and then, it had been months. That's why he was annoyingly, humiliatingly watching his wife's slender hips and the creamy skin on the inside corner of her elbow. That's why—that's why he insisted on playing Benedick. Because Benedick kisses Beatrice, unless he was much mistaken.

Suddenly impatient to confirm his memory, Cam scooped up the play again and leafed through its pages.

It wasn't that he really wanted to seduce his own wife, he reasoned. Or even to kiss her, in the way a man kisses a woman. It was just that his sexual appetite had grown out of control, due to abstinence. Wasn't good for a man, abstinence. Led to madness and uncontrolled lust. And the woman *was* his wife. If he felt like kissing a woman, well, he might as well kiss one who already belonged to him.

He tossed the book again. Was there a point to lying to himself? He wanted more of Gina. More of her surprised kiss, soft lip, sweet curve, silky hair. The way she melted into his arms just before she remembered who he was and pushed him away. Next time . . . Next time she'd remember who he was *and* stay exactly where she belonged.

In his arms.

He didn't bother to follow the logic of that thought. After all, men are known for thinking with their loins rather than their brains, and Camden Serrard, Duke of Girton, had just succumbed to a common male complaint.

Edmund Rounton was having no trouble arranging the Duke of Girton's annulment. In fact, he was a little appalled at how easy the business was. Everyone he consulted seemed to nod and instantly agree that annulment was by far the best solution and should be effected as rapidly as possible.

"Used to be difficult," Howard Colvin, Esq., commented. Colvin was England's leading authority on annulment.

"Dear me, yes, I remember when we desperately needed to put through an annulment—that would be the Duchess of Hinton from her husband. Man was absolutely incapable. Couldn't even piss in the proper direction, if you catch my meaning. Took us months, and she finally had to undergo a virginity trial!" He looked outraged. "Of course, that was back in '89."

"I trust that particular ordeal is no longer in use?"

"Of course not. We're much more humane these days. The Regent is partial to annulments. Thinks it saves on the scandal of a divorce, and of course it does. I got one for the Meade-Featherstonehaughs last year. Did you hear of it?"

Rounton shook his head.

"We kept it quiet, and for good reason," Colvin said. "Meade-Featherstonehaugh had taken three wives! Mad as a hatter, he is. Most men wish they didn't have the one, and the featherbrain brought two more into the house."

Rounton blinked. "How'd he do that?"

"Took 'em to Scotland. One at a time, of course. The second and third had no idea until they returned to the house. Of course, it was the first, the only legal one, who annulled." He hoisted himself out of the low leather chair. "Shouldn't think there'll be any trouble with the Girton marriage. Although I have heard that the duchess is a bit of a wild one, isn't she?"

Rounton looked him steadily in the eye. "Her reputation is much exaggerated by jealousy, sir. She is a beautiful young woman."

"She'll have to be, to get married again. Must be getting long in the tooth by now."

"I believe that she has many suitors," Rounton said stiffly.

"No offense! You'd think she was a relative of yours," the old man chortled. "Just send the papers over to my office, boy, and I'll have it all sewed up tight as a jug of malmsey. Talk to the Regent myself. I expect under the circumstances we can waive the parliamentary approval business."

Rounton bowed. "Thank you very much."

"Not at all, not at all." And England's leading authority on annulment tottered out of the club to his waiting carriage.

Rounton walked back to his legal chambers in a dark mood. Annulment shouldn't just be another case of divorce, to his mind. If a man takes three wives, then he should be jailed, and that's the end of it.

He pushed open the door and called for his junior, Finkbottle, without noticing that Finkbottle was sitting just before him. The man jumped several inches in the air. His hair stood on end as if it were caught in a brushfire. Rum thing, having that color hair, Rounton thought.

"Now," he said briskly, "I'm sending you down to Kent today. I have the first bunch of annulment papers here for the Girtons, and the rest should be along in a few days. But your job, Finkbottle, is to delay. *Delay.* Do you understand?"

A familiar look of panicked confusion spread across Phineas Finkbottle's face.

"Pretend you don't have the papers. Pretend a rainstorm sent the messenger off the road. Use finesse." Rounton lowered his voice.

"I have a particular task for you during your stay in Kent."

Chapter Ten

The Fruits of Regret

Carola Perwinkle, sometime wife to Tuppy Perwinkle, was near to tears. She sat at her dressing table, her hair tied back with a ribbon. It was the same room she had slept in for a week; the same rather weary face looked back at her from the glass; the same empty bed loomed behind her in the faint shadows.

She had, in essence, spent the previous evening dancing with Neville. They danced the ridotto, they danced the quadrille, they danced the waltz three times. No need for her to have worried about encountering Tuppy. He was there: she glimpsed him at the far end of the room. But he hadn't even bothered to greet her. She bit her lip, and tears gathered in her eyes, not for the first time that afternoon.

She bit her lip, hard, until the sting made the burning pressure behind her eyes recede. She was going to be twenty-five next week. And every year she realized with a keener and keener sense just what a fool she had been. Soon she'd be a thirty-year-old fool and, in a matter of minutes, a forty-year-old fool. Fifty—she might as well be dead by then. Fifty-year-old women don't gallivant around the ballroom dancing the waltz. They sit at tables and watch their daughters, or sit at the edges of rooms and whisper tales of their sons' extravagance—except she wouldn't have any children to talk about.

There was a soft scratch at the door, and her maid appeared. "My lady, the Duchess of Girton's maid would like to know whether Her Grace might visit for a moment."

"Of course," Carola said tonelessly. She pulled the ribbon from her hair and began brushing. Her maid automatically moved toward her, but she waved her from the room.

It wasn't the best of cures, she thought, seeing her oh-so-perfect friend the duchess. Gina had a husband *and* a fiancé, and unless she was much mistaken, they both wanted Gina. Lucky woman. No one wanted Carola. Tears mounted with her self-pity, and she swallowed hard.

Gina entered the room looking quite as delectable as someone so lucky ought to be. She also had an air of slight hesitation that Carola thought was very nice of her. Gina was probably the most beautifully behaved woman in the *ton*.

"Are you feeling terribly ill? Is there anything I can do?"

"Actually, no. I simply couldn't face leaving the room," Carola said flatly.

Gina sat down in a chair to the left of the dressing table. "I felt that way as well, but since then I have been to a picnic and had yet another quarrel with my betrothed, and now I am almost myself."

Carola smiled at that, just a lift of her lips. "What did you fight with Lord Bonnington about?"

"Whether he is a stick in the mud," Gina said gaily. "And— wonder of wonders!—he agreed. And so we are to act in a less than absolutely proper Shakespeare play, as recompense."

"He must truly love you," Carola said, startled. "Because it is very difficult to imagine Lord Bonnington engaged in something as dashing as a theatrical."

"Yes, of course," Gina said, wishing she could affirm Sebastian's love more enthusiastically. It wasn't his *love* that she worried about.

"Don't mind me," Carola said with an apologetic smile, mopping up tears. "It's been happening all day."

"Are you crying because of your husband's arrival?"

There was a moment's silence while Gina wondered if she should have phrased the question more tactfully.

"Yes," Carola said, finally. "Yes and no."

Gina waited.

"Every year it grows worse. Every year I regret more and more. And every year the possibility of reconciliation is further in the past."

"Well, why don't you speak—"

"Impossible. You don't understand, Gina. There you are with a betrothed who looks at you as if you were a goddess, and now your husband arrives in the country and looks at you the same way."

"That isn't true!"

"Of course it is." Her voice was sharp. "I'm a grown woman, who was a wife, *once*." She sniffed disconsolately. "I recognize the look in a man's eyes. Tup—Tup—Tuppy used to look at me that way!" And now she broke out into true sobs.

Gina sat next to her on the padded bench and wound an arm around her shoulder. "Darling, if you still love your husband, then you must make amends with him. Court him, if you have to. That's all there is to it."

Carola was struggling with tears and reaching blindly for her handkerchief, so Gina put it in her hand. "You don't understand anything," she said in a rather wavery, ungracious voice. "What you suggest is impossible."

"Why?"

"It just is."

"Why?"

"You can't understand!"

95

Gina was starting to feel annoyed. "Why not? You'll have to make yourself clear. It seems obvious to me that given that you left your husband rather than the other way around, it is your responsibility to approach him. In fact, to woo him back."

Carola took a deep breath and wiped her eyes. "It's not so easy. I made a mistake, a horrible, horrible mistake, and now I simply have to live with it, that's all." She kept talking, sensing that Gina was about to query her again. "I'm not crying because of Tuppy—well, not really. I'm crying because I can't have back what I lost." There was savage belief in every word she spoke. "You wouldn't know about that, Gina, because you haven't made any mistakes. Two men look at you—that way. You can choose either one. It doesn't matter which; either way, you'll be living with a man who loves you and desires you."

"How can you say that my husband loves me? I hardly know the man."

"Well, it's clear to me that he *wants* you and Bonnington *loves* you. My husband doesn't want me *or* love me." She started to cry again.

"I had no idea you felt this way about your husband," Gina said, rocking her friend against her shoulder. "That you were still so much in love with him, I mean."

"I'm not!"

"It certainly sounds as if you are."

Carola gulped and straightened again. "I'm not *so* in love. But I saw him last night, twice. He didn't even bother to greet me. Usually, he . . . he takes my hand, and he asks me how I have been. And—and—this is so humiliating!"

"Not humiliating," Gina said. "Interesting. What on earth have you been doing, pretending that you enjoy living apart from your husband?"

"I don't pretend," Carola said wretchedly. "I just go on, day after day. And honestly, in the beginning I didn't care much. It was only when he didn't come fetch me, and then I started watching for him on the street, and wishing I would meet him—so he would know how happy I was, you understand. And then somehow I never saw him enough, and I would end up thinking about him at home."

Gina handed her a fresh handkerchief. She had discovered a little pile of them.

"When we were first married, I wasn't in love with him *at all*. My mother made me marry him. He was the best offer I got. She didn't want to fund another season, and there was my younger sister coming up. And then, just at the end of the season, Tuppy appeared," Carola continued. "I'd hardly met him four times before he asked for my hand. In under a month, we were married."

"Was being married so objectionable?"

"It wasn't. But I never admitted it to myself, because that would mean that my mother was right. She said"—another sob fought its way up her chest—"she said that if I just lost some of my vanity, I would settle down nicely in the stable with Tuppy."

"Oh," Gina said, rather nonplussed by the description.

"I was so angry," Carola said. "I had come to her after . . . after the first night." She stopped. "Do you know what I mean, Gina?"

"Of course."

"And all she said was a mingle-mangle of metaphors about horses and stables and settling down to my feed. She said he was an awkward rider, and I should try to be a docile mare. So I went home and fought again with Tuppy, and then before I hardly knew it, I had run back home to my mother's and he never—he never came after me."

97

"Just like a man," Gina said with exasperation. "Nary a one in ten has a sense of responsibility. Tuppy is just like Esme's husband. If he had come after you, and demonstrated his constancy and faithfulness, you might have had a family by now."

Carola shrugged. "I don't see where responsibility enters the picture." She'd stopped crying and was just staring at her shadowed face in the mirror. "He doesn't give a fig about me, Gina, and why should he? I was barely in his house and his bed before I fled screaming to my mother. All I did while I was with him was whine and yelp about how much it hurt. It *did* hurt, too," she said suddenly. "But no one bothered to tell me that it would stop hurting eventually."

"How do you—" Gina broke off.

"Oh, I haven't broken my wedding vows," Carola said. "Somehow I never really wanted to. I've heard other people talking, of course. Look at Esme. She wouldn't risk her reputation if it wasn't pleasurable, would she? And now . . . and now I only want to live with my husband, and he doesn't even greet me."

"I'm sure he meant to. He probably couldn't find you amid all your admirers."

"I saw him, last night, talking to that young red-haired snip who is suddenly so fashionable. The sullen-looking one."

"Penelope Deventosh?"

Carola nodded. "He could divorce me on grounds of desertion, you know."

"He could have done that years ago, if he wished to."

"But perhaps Miss Deventosh will win his heart."

"Not if you do so first. You're going to have to court him."

"Court him!"

"Yes. It sounds to me as if you probably wounded his pride. Did you tell him that you had consulted your mother?"

"You mean the bit about the awkward rider?"

Gina nodded.

"I'm afraid I embellished on my mother's comment. You see, I really *did* find the whole business painful and messy. And marriage too."

"Even worse, then. Of course he didn't go after you."

"I don't know how to court someone." She sniffed disconsolately.

"It's that or let him marry Miss Deventosh."

Carola was silent for a moment. "I'll kill her first," she said tensely. "I want him—even if he is too tall for dancing and cares only about fish."

"Did you tell him that as well?"

Carola nodded. "And more."

"Goodness. I think we had better ask Esme for advice."

"Do you think that she knows how to court someone?"

Gina thought about how her husband's eyes brightened when Esme smiled at him. "I have no doubt about it." Her tone was rather grim.

"But I don't want to be seductive," Carola whispered. "I'd rather die than let my husband think I wanted to bed him. It would be such a victory for him. I'd rather *die*."

Gina felt her way cautiously into an answer. "I think you're going to have to let him know. Why would a man want to live with a woman who—" But then she remembered Sebastian's insistence on her innocence. It was more than a belief; Sebastian was convinced that she had no desire whatsoever, all evidence to the contrary.

"You're right," Carola said dispiritedly. "Why would he want me back if he thinks that I'm just going to shriek like a peacock every time he tries to bed me?"

Gina's eyebrows went up as she met her friend's eyes in the mirror. "That bad?"

"I was young and stupid."

"Some men dislike the idea of marrying a desirous woman," Gina offered. "Do you think Tuppy is one of those?"

"I've noticed that," Carola replied. "But I think the men who feel that way invariably don't love the woman in question. I've seen it over and over. They marry a woman for her purity. Then they fall in love with a woman who certainly isn't innocent."

Gina swallowed. Surely it wouldn't be that way with Sebastian.

"I've heard women complaining about it," Carola continued. "Make the smallest advance to a man of that stamp and they scold you because you've walked off your pedestal and stained your innocence. I don't *think* Tuppy is that sort."

"I hope not," Gina murmured. There was no avoiding the fact that Sebastian *was* that sort. It gave her a queer stifled feeling in her chest to think about it. "Here's what we'll do," she said with sudden vigor. "How long do you think Tuppy will stay at the house party?"

"He generally stays for at least three weeks. He has to, or Lady Troubridge threatens to disinherit him."

"Has she ever urged you to reconcile?"

"She's never said anything about it."

"First thing, we'll speak to Lady Troubridge," Gina said. "Because she is in charge of seating during meals."

"Oh yes," Carola exclaimed. "I could sit next to Tuppy!"

"And she assigns bedchambers," Gina said, a wicked twinkle in her eye.

Her friend gasped. "Bedchambers!"

"Only as a matter of last resort."

Carola's eyes were round. "That would be bolder than I feel capable. I couldn't do it!"

"Likely you won't have to," Gina said reassuringly. "After all, men court women all the time. How difficult can it be? And we have Esme for advice."

Carola blinked and whispered: "Bedchambers, Gina?"

"Only if the man holds out beyond the point of reasonableness," Gina promised.

Had Lady Cranborne seen her daughter at that moment, she would have been quite proud: in Gina's eyes shone the unmistakable stamp of a Girton.

Chapter Eleven

Improper Shakespeare, in the Library

Gina dressed very carefully for the evening. She had decided to put Sebastian to the test. Common knowledge had it that men's sexual appetites are barely held in check: she meant to find out whether Sebastian's urges were in perfect working order. Because the more she thought about it, the less she wanted to find herself on a pedestal her entire married life, while her husband gallivanted about with a lively and lascivious mistress. She was starting to worry that she might have overrated constancy as a husbandly trait.

She drove her maid to distraction by changing her gown three times, but finally she was ready to descend the stairs in an inky blue evening frock of heavy silk. It laced behind and was made to display the whole of her neck and shoulders. But the pièce de résistance, from Gina's point of view, was that the hem was looped up at the sides, showing her satin slippers. Her ankles were among her best features, and it couldn't hurt to display them. She wore her hair high, with silky ringlets falling over bare shoulders.

In sum, the gown was her most daring, what with the lacing behind and caught-up hem below. *If this doesn't fire Sebastian's heart,* Gina thought as she left the chamber, *nothing will.*

Since Lady Troubridge did not care for reading, and rarely ventured into the library, the chamber hadn't changed since the early 1600s. It was dark and tranquil, with its barrel roof arched high above, and brass-fronted bookshelves set between narrow windows. During the day it received southern light, but in the evening the windows were nothing more than smudges of darker gray between the bookshelves. The only lamps burning were at the far end of the room, where a wide pool of light edged toward her and then fell into darkness.

Gina walked toward the light, her slippers making no sound on the thick carpet. The rest of the cast had already assembled. The young actor, Reginald, was holding forth on something; Cam was listening courteously, but she could see a glint of amusement in his black eyes. Sebastian was frowning down at his book, his hair shining in the light of the fire behind him like a new-minted penny.

Esme was seated on a low stool next to Cam, ideally positioned so that the neckline of her evening dress revealed all to anyone who cared to glance.

Gina walked into the circle of light. The men rose, of course, and Esme smiled from the stool. "Do listen to this, dearest. Mr. Gerard has cast me as a poor maiden who faints and almost *dies* when she is accused of loose behavior!"

Gina couldn't help smiling back. Whatever one could say about Esme, one could not say that she deluded herself. She was the first to see the pleasure of that incongruity.

"Perhaps we should switch characters," Esme continued. "Your claims to an unspotted character are far greater than mine."

Sebastian answered. "I do not care for that suggestion," he said, frowning. "Beatrice seems to be a lively but not unladylike young woman. Far more suitable for Her Grace."

"Ladylike?" Cam murmured as Gina walked over and sat at a chair by his side. Part of her plan involved using her husband to demonstrate to Sebastian just how pedestal-unworthy she was. The more she thought about the way her husband had kissed her, the more she realized that it was likely representative of his daily behavior. The man probably lusted after any woman he had close at hand. She sat down gracefully and watched with satisfaction as her dress fell open over her ankle.

Cam looked down at her slender leg and then quickly up at her face. His eyebrow rose and he surveyed her slowly, from the tip of her head to the tip of her slippers. "I presume this display is not solely for my benefit?" he whispered. His eyes were alight with laughter and something—something Gina wasn't certain she could identify.

"Be still, you wretch!" she whispered back, turning a little pink. Of course he saw straight through her—he always had, even when they were children. But that made him the perfect man to inspire Sebastian's jealousy. He would never take a flirtation seriously: not Cam.

Sebastian had sat down again after greeting her, and was turning the pages of his book. "Yes," he said weightily, "I think the part of Beatrice is quite appropriate for Her Grace. *I had rather hear my dog bark at a crow than a man swear he loves me.* Quite appropriate."

"What? Do I say that?" Gina opened her book. "Where?"

"I gather you don't agree with the sentiment?" Cam asked.

"Of course I do," she replied. "I'm simply trying to find the text."

"Let me help you," he said, leaning over and taking her book in his large hands. "Bonnington is reading from Act One."

He had an indefinable scent, Cam did. Clean and autumny, like wild leaves in the outdoors. Unlike most men, he wore no perfume. Her cheeks were burning by the time he drew away, pointing to an open page.

She looked down at the text rather dubiously. Her character, Beatrice, seemed to be a bit of a shrew.

Cam leaned over her shoulder again, confusing her. A hand came across her book. "We're a quarrelsome pair," he said. "Look at this." He pointed to a line. "You're threatening to scratch my face."

"You seem to be a boastful sort." She recited, mockingly: *"But it is certain I am loved of all ladies, only you excepted.* What a braggart! *All ladies* indeed!"

His face was so close to hers that she could feel his breath on her cheek. "You may have a point," he said, so softly that she could hardly hear him. "We shall have to read on to see whether you bring me to my knees or not."

Gina caught her breath. For a moment her eyes met his, dark with promise and wicked with intent. A restless cough jerked her back into the room. She turned her head, suppressing a satisfied grin. He *did* notice. "How is your part, Sebastian?" She refused to address him formally. They were among friends, after all.

Sebastian's mouth tightened, indicating that he noticed her disobedience.

For that's how it felt, Gina noticed with surprise. As if she were disobeying him.

"My role seems to be unexceptionable. Apparently I believe that I see my betrothed at her bedroom window, embracing another man, and so naturally I repudiate her. It's in Act Four:

> *Would you not swear*
> *All you that see her, that she were a maid,*
> *By these exterior shows? But she is none:*
> *She knows the heat of a luxurious bed.*

Of course I don't marry her, under those circumstances," he said with some satisfaction.

But Gina was confused. "I never read this play. Is Esme playing the woman whom you refuse to marry?"

"Yes," Sebastian agreed.

"So I'm the one who looks like a virgin but isn't, and knows the—what did you call it?" Esme asked.

"The heat of a luxurious bed," Sebastian repeated with emphasis.

"How typical of a man to jump to such an absurd conclusion," she said.

"What's absurd?" Sebastian said with a shrug. "Where there's smoke, there's fire. Wouldn't you concur, Lady Rawlings?"

Gina glanced between them. For some reason Sebastian and Esme's customary level of tension seemed particularly high tonight. "But your fiancée is not truly betraying you?"

Reginald Gerard took over. "She is not. A villain has convinced another woman to act the part, standing in her bedchamber window."

"I make some excellent points," Sebastian said, looking back down at his book. *"But, as a brother to his sister, show'd bashful sincerity and comely love."*

"What are you talking about?" Gina asked.

"My attitude toward my future bride, played by Lady Rawlings," he explained. "Naturally, I never stepped outside the bounds of virtuous behavior, but behaved as a brother to a sister."

Was there a hint of meaning in his voice? Gina cast him a look through narrowed eyes. Sebastian seemed to have a rather smug look about him. How *dare* he lecture her. She closed her book with a snap.

"I would appreciate the opportunity to call my wife a parrot," Cam said. "Why don't Gina and I perform this bit from Act One?"

"Fine!" Reginald said. Obviously he had caught on to some worrisome undercurrents among his cast. "And shall we have the scene that you so admire, Lord Bonnington? And then perhaps one other scene—"

"I suggest we do the entire fourth act," Cam interrupted.

"Of course," Reginald agreed.

Gina narrowed her eyes. For some reason Cam looked mighty pleased with himself. "What is it?" she demanded.

He met her eyes with such a flare of amusement that she felt a jolt in her stomach. "It's a good piece, Gina. You'll enjoy it."

"I doubt it," she said, swinging her foot a little. Sure enough, his eyes turned for a second to her slender leg. She giggled, feeling dizzily triumphant. She might not be able to entice her fiancé, but she certainly had an effect on her husband.

"You have some interesting lines," that husband said.

"Oh?"

"Indeed. For example, you swear to love me forever."

Gina put her hand to her heart. "Oh, how will I say such an untruth!" she said dramatically.

He leaned closer. "I'm sure it will come easily."

"I doubt that!" she said tartly. "Not to a swinish boaster like you!"

"That's Shakespeare's character, Benedick, not me," Cam corrected her. He lowered his voice. "But after all, you are accomplished at this sort of thing, aren't you?"

She blinked and looked at his eyes. They were lined with such a thick row of eyelashes that she almost lost track of her point. "In fact, this is my first theatrical performance."

"Ah, but you presumably told that poor sod over there that you loved and adored him," Cam said gently.

Gina took a deep breath as outrage poured through her.

"Am I to understand, my lord, that you have experienced a change of heart?"

It was his turn to blink.

"I can only think," she continued, "that you are afraid to find yourself unmarried, given that you are decrying my future husband." She patted his hand. "Please don't worry so much. I'm sure we can find *someone* who will marry you." There was just a touch of doubt in her tone.

"Vixen," he growled.

Gerard was speaking. Gina's heart was beating so fast that she could hardly hear what he was saying.

Given that her plan involved driving her betrothed into a display of jealousy, it was unfortunate that Sebastian seemed oblivious. She could hardly inspire jealousy if he didn't notice that she was flirting with another man. Instead he was quarrelling with Esme again. In his anger, he had scooted his chair closer to her stool, and their heads were bent over their books as they argued over their lines.

Reginald clapped his hands again, pleading for attention. "Ladies and gentlemen," he said, "I suggest that you take your books back to your chambers and spend the remainder of the week memorizing your lines. Lady Troubridge has suggested that we perform on the weekend."

"Memorize our lines?" Cam sounded shocked.

"Too much of a strain for an elderly brain?" Gina cooed.

"At least I managed to read the play before this evening," he retorted.

"Very good, Your Grace!" Reginald said. "We shall meet in three days, and I would be most grateful if you knew your lines from Act One and Act Four."

Gina stood up and shook out her skirts. Then she deliberately drew off the cashmere scarf she had been wearing around her shoulders. With a quick glance under her lashes, she saw

Cam glance at the swell of her breasts. He looked away immediately but took a deep breath that gave her untold satisfaction. Her fiancé, however, was helping Esme to her feet as he hurled a last comment, and paid no attention.

Esme moved away without a word, leaving Sebastian in mid-sentence. Her eyes met Gina's with a hint of desperation. "Shall we join the rest of the party?"

"Of course," she said. They walked out before the men.

"I'm so sorry that you and Sebastian are not more at ease together," Gina said.

"Yes," Esme said. But she shut her lips tight.

"Do you think it would help if I spoke to him?"

Esme turned and clasped her arm. "Please don't mention it. I believe he can't help being so censorious. Lord Bonnington is quite honorable and distressed by lesser behavior in others."

"Of course," Gina murmured. "I just wish he didn't behave like such a prig around you."

"He's not a prig. He simply has the . . . the courage of his convictions."

"Yes," she replied, her mood turning to depression. "Of course."

They walked through the doors of the Long Salon. Lady Troubridge had arranged for card games that evening. In front of them was a small table graced by Esme's husband, Miles. As they watched, he brushed his hand gently over Lady Childe's cheek.

"Better a prig than a reprobate," Esme said bitterly. "Bonnington will never humiliate you in public. That sounds like paradise to me."

Miles Rawlings looked up and waved, beckoning them over to his table.

"He's very friendly," Gina pointed out. "At least you and your husband don't live in a state of armed warfare."

"No, not at all. We are the very epitome of a civilized couple. Well, shall we greet him? I managed to avoid him last night."

Esme's husband was a blocky, solidly built man. When one glanced at him across the room, he gave an impression of bullish masculinity, but at close range he had an oddly feminizing dimple in the middle of his chin.

To Gina, it seemed that his eyes were shining with genuine delight to see his wife. He kissed her on each hand with a good deal of flair. Lady Childe too had risen and was murmuring a welcome that held the note of apology missing from Rawlings's tone.

"How have you been, my dear?" Rawlings asked, beaming at his wife.

"Quite well, thank you," Esme replied, disengaging her hands and curtsying. "How pleasant to see you again, Lady Childe. Are you enjoying the country?"

Lady Childe was about fifteen years older than Esme, and looked it. She was a horse-loving matron who had given her husband two boys and after her second lying-in never, it was widely rumored, shared his bed again. Or any man's bed, until she met Esme's husband.

They chatted pleasantly for a moment until Esme's fingers tightened on Gina's arm. "Please forgive me," Gina said, smiling at the couple. "But I must return to my husband. Esme, will you accompany me into the supper room?"

"I think it could be much worse—" Gina began, as they walked away.

But Esme interrupted. "May we drop the subject? Please?"

"Of course," she agreed. "Are you all right?"

"Certainly. Marriage is—difficult, that's all."

Gina nodded. "You're four times as beautiful as she is," she said reassuringly.

"That should matter, shouldn't it?" Esme was walking faster and faster, her stride lengthening. "But it doesn't. And I don't mean that I want him. I don't. I certainly don't want him in my bed, so I should be grateful to Lady Childe."

Gina kept silent.

"The only reason I'm not grateful is that I'm a jealous, horrible person," Esme said vehemently.

"No, you're not!"

"I am. He's in love, you know."

"Not for the first time," Gina pointed out.

"Ah, but for the last time, I think. I truly think it. He's been lucky enough to find someone whom he loves. And if society were any different, they would live together for the rest of their lives. In fact, I'm not sure but that they will anyway."

"I doubt that," Gina said after thinking about it. "Lady Childe's sons would suffer from her lack of reputation."

"I suppose so," Esme agreed in a dreary sort of way.

"Darling, what *is* the matter?"

"She has sons."

Gina could think of nothing to say to that, so she twined her arm around her friend's waist and they walked into the supper room together. Carola was ensconced at a table and surrounded by her usual lively circle of young men.

"Carola needs your advice."

"My advice?" But Esme let herself be drawn over to the table.

As soon as Carola saw them, she stood up and shooed off her admirers. "Go along, do! I must speak to these ladies." Grumbling, three of them left. Only Neville remained. "Neville!" Carola said. "I'll dance with you later."

"I shan't go," he said, bowing to Esme and Gina. "Your

Grace, Lady Rawlings." He deftly handed them into chairs and then sat down again. "I know the look of a witch's coven as well as the next man. And you know, darlings, I *always* fancied myself in a coven."

Carola rolled her eyes. But Neville smiled so beguilingly that she gave in. "All right, you may stay. But this is a secret conference, do you understand?" She fixed him with a fierce gaze.

He bowed his head. "May all the starch in England be turned to butter before I breathe a word," he said devoutly.

Gina eyed his elaborate, starched neck cloth with some interest. "Would that be so terrible?"

"There is no reason to live without a perfectly starched neck cloth in the morning," Neville replied.

Carola tapped him sharply on the hand with her fan. "This is a council of war, and if you can't be serious, you must take yourself off."

Neville straightened up immediately. "War! I always wanted a pair of colors!" he cried. "I would look so dashing in uniform."

"No starch on the battlefield," Gina pointed out.

"Please, let's be serious," Carola said. "Esme, I need to ask your help. Your aid in—in—" She didn't seem to be able to formulate her request.

"May I?" Gina interjected.

Carola nodded.

But Neville's eyes were bright with affection as he looked at Carola. "Let me guess. My own Lady Perwinkle wants to win back the hand of her lamentably dressed husband, and so she is employing the help of the ravishingly seductive Lady Rawlings."

Carola swallowed hard. "Am I that obvious?"

"Am I your closest friend?" Neville asked.

112

Carola nodded.

"Besides, you never showed any interest in *me*," he went on, "so I knew within moments that you must be still attached to your husband."

"Oh, Neville." She laughed.

"The point is," Gina broke in, "that Carola needs to court her husband. He's only likely to stay at the house party two to three weeks, Esme, so we haven't much time."

"I don't foresee any particular problems courting your husband," Esme said.

"Can you—could you seduce anyone you pleased?" Carola asked, rather awed.

"Men are like children. You can't take their claims to independence seriously."

Neville laughed. "I knew I would find out some home truths if I remained."

Carola ignored him. "I have to tell you that Tuppy pays me no attention whatsoever. In fact, he didn't even greet me when he arrived last night. I'm not certain he remembers that I exist."

"If he doesn't know you exist now, he will soon," Esme said reassuringly. "Now, Lord Perwinkle appears to me to be the sort of man who will respond to—well, to put it bluntly—to a woman desiring *him*."

Gina nodded. "That's what Carola and I thought as well."

"I can't do it," Carola whispered. "It would just be too humiliating!"

"There's nothing obvious about it. The man won't even realize what's happening," Esme explained. "Now—here's what we're going to do." She paused and cast a glance at Neville. "Off with you! You've heard enough."

He acceded to a greater authority and rose. "You may be

right," he said with mock gravity. "This is a conversation that would strike fear in any man's heart." He bowed and kissed Carola's fingertips. "The first minuet?" She nodded and he strolled off.

Chapter Twelve

In Which the Marquess of Bonnington Suffers an Insult

Cam entered the Long Salon after eating supper with Tuppy, Stephen having fled back to London in the afternoon. He spotted Gina immediately, standing with the poker-faced man she wanted to marry.

She was fingering the sticks of her fan in a dissatisfied sort of way while the marquess lectured her about something or other. Cam felt a low simmer in his belly that he had no trouble identifying. He wanted the chit. Unfortunately, she was his wife and un-haveable. But perversely he meant to torment her for being so desirable.

Gina's face lighted up as he approached. "Cam!" she exclaimed.

Bonnington had screwed his mouth into a line again. "I think it inadvisable that Your Graces should overly associate."

"I am quite certain it is of no concern," Cam remarked. "Rounton writes me that annulments are alarmingly easy to achieve. In fact, he intimated that they are growing as common as divorce."

"Divorce is not common in England," Bonnington pointed out. "I am certain that you would not wish any unpleasant rumors to sully your wife's reputation."

Cam frowned. "That reminds me," he said. "What the devil is going on with your tutor, Gina? Rounton told me some nonsensical tale that people believed you were dallying with the poor man."

Gina laughed, but Bonnington interrupted, scowling. "Such matters are inappropriate for Her Grace's ears," he said heavily. "While I share your concern, naturally, perhaps we should discuss it at a later time."

Cam met the marquess's eyes with a raised eyebrow. "Damned if you aren't the most poker-faced type I've met since my dear departed father," he said. Then he turned toward his wife. "Gina, what the devil did you do to poor Wapping? The man couldn't throw his leg over a lady if you paid him, and here you are, ruining his reputation."

She giggled. "I told everyone that. He is quite the shyest man I've ever met."

"Damned if I'd send some Lothario to hang about my wife," Cam said.

"It was all a mistake. A horrid gossip column printed something about us, and then we were surveying a meteor shower in the conservatory, and we were seen by Mr. Broke and his wife."

"A meteor shower?" Cam looked skeptical. "What the devil did you want to see one of those for?"

"There was a meteor shower the night that Florence fell to the Medicis," Gina explained. "Mr. Wapping thought it would be salutary for me to experience it, since the meteors had a marked effect on public opinion. But the almanac was mistaken and it was a dark night."

The corner of Cam's mouth quirked up. "Thought you'd like Wapping," he said. "I had the idea from your letters that life was beginning to pale a little."

Gina met his eyes and found complete understanding. "Are you ever bored?"

Cam spread his large hands and looked at them briefly. He wore no gloves, unlike the rest of the men in the room. "I would be if all I did was dance and change my clothing," he said, dropping his hands.

The Marquess of Bonnington was not having a pleasant evening. First he had been tempted into rash words by that witch of a woman, Esme Rawlings. Then, when he tried to explain his entirely justified attitude, his future wife disagreed. Finally, Gina was discussing her tutor with her husband as if *he* didn't exist. And as if *his* feelings about her tutor were of no account. He forgot that he didn't give a hang about Gina's tutor.

"I am happy to say," he said, staring down his patrician nose, "that Her Grace and I do not engage in menial labor as a pastime."

The duke looked back at him from heavy-lidded eyes. "Quite so," he said with a drawl. "I declare I almost forgot that Gina neither weaves, nor does she spin. One of the lilies of the valley, aren't you, my dear?"

Gina glanced at her husband-to-be, who was sporting a dangerous flush high on his cheeks. "Sebastian," she said placatingly, "may I speak to you for a moment?"

But fury was growing inside Cam. "It's admirable that you are such a modern fellow, Bonnington," he remarked. "To look at you, I'd never think that you were the type to marry an illegitimate woman. By-blow of a French countess, aren't you, Gina?"

Bonnington's eyes narrowed. "And you, sir, are no gentleman even to mention such a thing in a public setting!"

"I see," Cam said. "Trying to pretend it's all hum, are you? Well, it isn't, Bonnington. I've been meaning to tell you," he said, turning to Gina who was standing frozen at her fiancé's side. "I have something for you from your mother. Your real mother, that is."

She gasped. "You have?"

117

He nodded. "No idea why it was delivered to me; I expect her estate made some sort of mistake. Remind me to give it to you tomorrow." He turned away.

"Wait!" Gina said, catching his sleeve. "What is it? A letter?"

He met her eyes and suffered a shock. "I'm sorry, Gina," he said. "I didn't think you would care much about the gift, and so I forgot to mention it."

"Is it a letter?" she repeated.

"There might be a letter inside," Cam said. "It's a box, about yea high." He sketched a smallish box with his hands.

"I'm a selfish ingrate. I should have known that the gift would be meaningful to you. I'll go get it now, shall I?"

"No!" Sebastian said sharply. "You will *not* give my future wife the object sent by that disreputable woman. Act responsibly for once, and discard it as the trash it is."

Gina looked at him incredulously. "You're making fun, aren't you, Sebastian? You would never keep my mother's present away from me?"

"Your mother," he said between clenched teeth, "is Lady Margaret Cranborne. And naturally I would never limit any correspondence between you and your *mother*. But as for this disgraceful woman, yes! No husband would allow his wife to receive letters—gifts—from an infamous highflier, countess or not!"

Gina swallowed hard. "The question is not whether my mother was a countess, Sebastian. She was . . . she was my mother, and she left me something."

"In my opinion, she gave up the title of mother when she discarded you on your father's doorstep," he said icily. "And I cannot emphasize how utterly inappropriate I think it is to have this conversation in an open room!"

Cam shot Gina a swift glance under his lashes. Two tears were standing on her cheeks. A swell of rage almost led to the self-righteous bastard stretching his length on the floor. But he caught Gina's eyes just as another tear snaked its way down her cheek.

He bowed instead. "Bonnington, your servant. Gina." He held out his hand.

But she didn't take it.

In that moment, it was absolutely clear to Gina that if she walked off with Cam, her engagement was over. She looked up into her betrothed's furious blue eyes, and knew that he recognized it as well.

"Sebastian," she said shakily, "I find I am not as composed as I might wish. Will you accompany me on a brief walk in the gardens?"

Not even a flash of triumph appeared on his face. He held out his arm. "It would be my greatest pleasure," he said.

Cam stepped backward and bowed again. Then he watched until Gina's slender, naked back disappeared into a crowd of overdressed aristocrats. He uncurled his hand and looked at it. His fingers were shaking slightly with the strain of not hitting the pretentious, stiff-rumped snob whom his Gina wanted to marry.

He caught himself. *His* Gina? Only in the legal sense, he told himself.

And it wasn't as if she gave a damn about him anyway. She had walked off with her marquess without a backward glance.

Cam's jaw tightened. His fingers instinctively curled into a large and dangerous fist once again.

Chapter Thirteen

Tasting Rain

A summer rain shower began just as Gina and Sebastian walked out the wide doors of the Long Salon. They watched for a moment as water splattered the terrace into dark gray and made fat red roses tremble with tiny blows. Gina took a deep, unsteady breath and tried to calm herself. Logic was what was needed here.

Sebastian shifted his weight from leg to leg. "It's come to rain," he said.

He's not sure of me, Gina thought. He knows I almost left him. "I still want to marry you," she said, diving straight to the point. Although to be honest, she wasn't quite certain of the truth of that statement.

She felt a tiny jerk in the arm she held, a small instinctive reaction. "That is," she added, "if you want me to."

"Of course I do," he answered rather roughly, and without his usual sangfroid.

Chattering voices approached from behind. They moved to allow a cluster of damsels in diaphanous gowns to peer at the plump drops falling to the ground.

"Isn't that a *shame*?" one of the girls cried. "It's all wet!" They all laughed and retreated quickly back into the warmth of the room, with just a curious glance or two at the Duchess of Girton and her companion.

Gina heard one clear voice, louder than her owner meant

it to be. "She's not *so* old, Augusta. I don't believe she's yet twenty-five . . ."

"Would you like to go for a walk?" she asked, looking up at Sebastian.

He frowned. "You would take a chill, dressed as you are."

"Oh no, the air is warm. I promise you, I never take a chill. Why, I believe I haven't been sick a day since I was a child."

He was looking at her with a speculative concern that made her bristle inside. "It's *raining,* Your Grace," and then, catching her eyes, he corrected himself. "Gina."

She opened her mouth but he wasn't done yet. "We do not go outdoors in the rain." He said it slowly, with attention to each word.

Gina felt such a fillip of rage in her chest that she almost slapped the man. He stood there in the glow of torches lighting up the wet terrace, so rigid, so—*poker-faced,* came an unwelcome memory of Cam's remark.

He saw something of her thoughts in her face because he held out a hand to the sky. There on his hand were two, or perhaps even three, silvery raindrops. "It will destroy your gown," he said. "Water stains silk."

She sighed and gave up the idea. "I should retire for the night. Would you accompany me to the library, Sebastian? I left *Much Ado About Nothing* there."

He turned readily enough and offered his arm. They walked to the library without saying another word. Gina was trying her best to think logically, a difficult task when one felt like bellowing one's anger to the skies.

She wanted to marry Sebastian. She *did*. He was calm and steady. He had stood at her side, offering welcome advice in the difficult years when she was a young married woman without a husband. He would be a responsible, loving

121

husband and father. And he was handsome too, a pleasure to look at. Of course she wanted to marry him.

It was simply that he was so rigid in his morality. So absurd in his insistence that she reject her mother's gift. Perhaps it's a good thing that Countess Ligny died before I married Sebastian, she thought, remembering the letters she had hopefully written and sent to France. None of them were ever answered. But she had kept writing, up until the day Rounton informed her of the countess's death.

"Do you truly wish me to reject the gift from Countess Ligny?" she asked.

They were in the library now. The fire had burned down. He picked up a poker and struck at the blackened logs. "Disgraceful. Lady Troubridge's servants are taking advantage of her, most certainly due to her widowed status."

"Sebastian?"

He leaned the poker back against the fireplace brick and turned about. "I think it would be best." But his eyes were troubled. "Yet she *was* your mother, Gina. And she is dead. Perhaps there is no harm in accepting her final gift."

She breathed a silent sigh of relief. "Thank you," she said, the two words tripping over each other.

"I am disappointed by your husband's readiness to discuss such a subject in public." Sebastian's face had a look of disdain, almost of contempt. "He seemed to have no concern for the extreme delicacy of the situation."

"Cam has always been at loggerheads with propriety," Gina explained. "His father was rigidly observant."

He nodded. "From everything I know, the duke acted precisely as he ought in every situation."

Gina drifted over to him and lifted her hands to rest lightly on the front of his black evening coat. "And you, Sebastian? Do you always act precisely as you ought?"

He stared down at her as if she'd asked him an obscenity. The half-born, half-acknowledged hope that she had kept with her all evening flickered and died. She let her hands slide from his chest.

"Gina, are you feeling all right?" he asked, finally. There was nothing but kindness and affection in his eyes.

"I believe so."

"Ever since your husband has returned, you have not been yourself."

"Cam only arrived yesterday."

He nodded. "And you've not been yourself: the Gina I know." *And love* hung in the air between them.

"You mean that I have tried to make you kiss me," she said in a high, clear voice that masked the tears crowding the back of her throat. "But I also tried to tempt you into unsightly behavior at the picnic, before Cam arrived, if you remember. That's what you called it—unsightly behavior."

He hesitated and looked quickly over her shoulder.

"We're quite alone," she said with a touch of scorn in her voice. "There's no reason to worry about your reputation."

"I worry about *your* reputation, Gina." What she saw in his eyes was disarming, and made her rage drain away.

"Your reputation is fragile, being a married woman. I would hate to see you punished by society for your husband's childish lack of consideration."

"Is that what you think of Cam?" she asked, startled.

"As does every right-thinking gentleman. The man's an irresponsible cad, leaving you here for years at the mercy of every rakehell who strayed across you. If you weren't such an inherently virtuous woman, there's no telling what might have happened to you, living without a husband's guidance."

"I had no need of male guidance!" she flashed back.

123

"I agree," he said, blue eyes meeting hers steadily. "You are a most unusual woman. Truly. Many of the young women of the *ton* never had the untouched, innocent air you have, even when they debuted. They would have fallen into some man's bed long before now. Just look at Lady Rawlings."

The last thing Gina wanted was to get into another argument on that subject. "Esme's situation is entirely—"

But Sebastian jumped in. "I blame Rawlings. If rumors are true, he deserted her bed within a month. He stands responsible for leaving a beautiful young woman to the mercies of fribbles like Bernie Burdett."

"I'm not certain this is an appropriate subject," Gina said. Sebastian's eyes were flashing and he was showing a good deal more passion than she'd ever seen from him.

"Rawlings should be *hanged*," he snarled. Then he seemed to remember where he was and turned back to Gina.

"Only a woman with your extraordinary chastity could have preserved her virtue intact."

Gina sighed. At least she had a clearer understanding of why Sebastian repudiated her every effort to further their intimacy.

"That's why it doesn't overly concern me," and he lowered his voice, "that your mother was unmarried. And why I pay no mind to foolish rumors about your tutor. As a true gentlewoman, you are untouched by the low and dissolute emotions that rule so many women these days. I shall be proud to make you my marchioness."

"I have no extraordinary virtue," Gina said. "I simply never wished to be akin to my mother."

"I should think not," Sebastian huffed.

She touched his sleeve. "But do you love *me,* Sebastian? Do you love me, or just the idea of me?"

He stared down at her. "Of course I love you. Haven't I always said so?" Then his eyes brightened. "Is that the problem? You've been worrying that I don't love you? Well, I *do*." He beamed at her as if he'd handed her the moon and the stars.

Then he took her arm. "There!" he said. "Now we can be comfortable again."

Gina walked up the stairs without another word. Lord Bonnington clearly felt all the relief of a soldier released from battle; he talked merrily of plans for the next day. They stopped at her chamber door. He bowed and kissed her gloved hand.

She tried to smile and failed, but he didn't seem to notice.

"I feel the better for this little discussion," he said. "You must forgive me for my lack of comprehension. I had forgotten how emotional and high-strung ladies are. I will be careful to ensure that my feelings for you are absolutely clear, so that you need not embarrass yourself in the future."

And Gina, handed neatly in the door of her bedchamber, had no doubt but that he would do just that. Likely he would dutifully inform his wife that he loved her, each and every morning before breakfast, so as to preserve marital harmony. Because being married to such an *emotional* and *high-strung* woman was certain to be difficult.

She unbuttoned her glove and threw it on the bed. When the second glove stuck, she ripped it off and tossed it next to its brother. A pearl button skipped and hopped across the floor, creating a counterpoint to the splatters of rain hitting the windows.

For a moment she thought about ringing for Annie. Yet she felt so *high-strung* at the moment that she might shriek at the poor girl simply from vexed nerves.

There was a push of emotion in her breast that made the thought of bed intolerable. She was engaged to a poker-faced marquess who did precisely as he ought, in every situation. And he would continue to act precisely the same when they were married.

What had she been thinking? She walked to the windows and pushed back the heavy velvet drapes. That Sebastian would become affectionate once his ring was on her finger? She undid the latch. He *was* affectionate, she thought unwillingly. It was just that he wasn't . . . he wasn't passionate. Passion was the look she saw in Esme's eyes when she talked of Bernie's muscled arm. Passion was the way Esme's husband touched Lady Childe's cheek.

Yet she herself was to receive affection rather than passion, that was clear. Sebastian was responsible, level-headed—and he didn't desire her. They stood at her shoulders like a good and a bad angel: Desire and Responsibility, Cam and Sebastian.

I could court him, she thought suddenly. Carola is wooing Perwinkle; I could do the same. A pulse of excitement danced down her spine: to woo Cam of the dark eyes and strong hands. Woo him—to what? To bed her: certainly. To love her: doubtful. To live with her and raise children, and be duke to her duchess: *never*. Better to stay with Sebastian, and try to woo him into desire.

The garden breathed a dark and dreamy scent of rain-washed roses and black soil. The rain was splattering down in such a lazy, halfhearted way that the air had hardly cooled. She threw off her cashmere shawl as she stood in the window.

I believe I'd like to have my mother's present now, she thought after a moment. Of course she always meant to have it, no matter what her future husband said about it. The question was, how to find Cam?

Annie darted into the room before she had time to change her mind. "Good evening, my lady!" she said. "Are you wishing to retire for the night?"

126

"Not yet," Gina replied. "I would like to visit my husband. Could you find out where his chamber is located?"

The maid's eyes widened slightly.

"We have some legal matters to discuss," she told Annie.

"Of course, my lady. Would you like me to see whether His Grace is still downstairs? I think that most of the ladies and gentlemen have retired by now." She trotted to the door. "If he's not downstairs, I'll ask Phillipos where he is."

Gina looked an inquiry.

"Phillipos is his man," she explained, an impish smile on her face. "He's Greek, and such a character! Quite the charmer, *he* thinks."

Gina sat down in a chair and waited with ill-concealed patience for Annie's return. It had been hurtful to think that her mother had cared nothing for her, and didn't even leave her a note at her deathbed. But surely the present meant that Countess Ligny did care for her daughter. Perhaps she *had* read her letters. Perhaps she loved her . . . if only a little amount.

What I would most like is a letter, Gina thought. Or a portrait. A letter would be marvelous, she thought again. A personal letter, from my mother.

Annie reappeared. "His Grace retired for the night just a few minutes ago, madam. He's four doors down, on the left. Phillipos was already downstairs. Apparently His Grace never requires assistance preparing for bed."

Gina raised an eyebrow, looking at her maid's pink cheeks. "I hope Phillipos did not charge a toll for this information?"

The young girl giggled. "A toll is a good way of putting it, madam."

"I should be back in a matter of five minutes or so, Annie. You need not wait. I shall go directly to bed on my return." She took a deep breath and left the room.

127

The long corridor was shadowy and lit only by wall sconces at the far ends. Gina felt her heartbeat speed as she counted the doors. What if Annie had made a mistake and Cam's door was the third, rather than the fourth, from her own? Could there be any greater humiliation than knocking on the wrong door? Her reputation would be in shreds and tatters.

She reached the fourth door and knocked softly. There was a sound inside of someone walking to the door. Her breath caught in her throat; the door swung open.

There he was.

It was just as it had been when she first caught a glimpse of him in the ballroom. Gina's trepidation fell away and she smiled with genuine pleasure. "Hello, Cam!"

"Jesus!" he said roughly, and looked up and down the hall. Then he grabbed her arm and yanked her into the room.

"What the devil are you doing here?"

She smiled again. "I thought I would visit." To her relief he was still dressed. It would have been quite embarrassing to see him in night clothing. She shook off his grasp and walked into the chamber.

His room was a flowery, silk-hung boudoir that looked exactly like hers. Obviously, Lady Troubridge had decorated the guest rooms to one standard. There was a signal difference, however. Resting in the corner of Cam's room was a hunk of rock. It looked absurd, a dusty, coarse lump plopped on the flowered carpet.

"What on earth is that?" she said, walking over to it. "Will you make a sculpture right in your bedchamber?"

She turned to find him leaning against the wall. It felt dangerously intimate to be alone with a man wearing only a white linen shirt and pantaloons.

"Well?" she asked impishly.

"No, I do not chisel rock in my bedchamber. Gina, why are you here?"

She stooped and touched a jagged corner of the rock with one pink-tipped finger. "Then why is *it* here?"

"Stephen gave it to me. I will probably have to knock it down, as marble that size can't be fashioned quickly. I'll be back in Greece long before it could be finished."

"Is it pleasant living outside England?" She poked the rock again, afraid he would read envy in her eyes.

Cam strolled across the room. "No gloves, Gina? Since entering this house, I had forgotten what a woman's hands look like."

He picked up one of her hands and looked at it speculatively. Her fingers were long and very thin. "Perhaps I'll sculpt one of your hands," he said.

Gina tried to ignore the tingle in her hands.

"What are you doing here?" he repeated.

But she had been looking at the heavy, sensual line of his lips and she lost track of the question.

His eyes narrowed. "You didn't mistake my chamber for Bonnington's, did you?"

Nonplussed, she just stared, her mouth forming a small O.

He dropped her hand and dragged a hand through his thick black hair. "Forgive me. Of course, Bonnington would never get up to shenanigans with another man's wife."

"No," Gina said, recovering herself. "Besides, according to Sebastian, I have rare and extraordinary virtue for a woman." She said it airily.

The look in his eyes made her skin heat as if by the sun's glare. "Doesn't know you very well, does he?"

"Of course he knows me. He's been a close friend for years!"

He tipped up her chin. "Was it so difficult after we married? I feel like a damned reprobate to hear Bonnington talk. The truth is, I thought your mother was taking care of you. Or rather," he said ruefully, "I didn't give it much thought one way or the other."

Gina gave a tiny shrug. A smile tugged at the corner of her mouth. "For a lady of such extraordinary virtue as I, your average rakehell presents no temptation."

"Vixen." His hand slid from her chin to her neck, large callused fingers oddly gentle. Gina shivered but didn't look away. "I'll ask you again, wife. Why are you visiting me in my bedchamber in the middle of the night? I'm fairly certain that Bonnington wouldn't approve."

"No, he wouldn't." For a moment she couldn't think why she was there. "I came to fetch my mother's present."

"Oh." He stared at her a moment and turned to his wardrobe. "Here it is."

It was a wooden box, sturdy and nicely made but not elegant. A wooden box with an ordinary latch.

She took the box from him. "It's heavy."

"I haven't opened it."

"I know that." Cam would never open a gift meant for another person.

Gina took a deep breath and swung the little metal latch up. All she could see was a mass of poppy-red satin, a florid ripple of shining cloth.

Cam peered over. "Rather gaudy," he said. She seemed to have temporarily frozen, staring at the bright cloth, so he said, "May I?" and at her nod, pulled back the top layer of satin.

Inside was a statue.

Gina picked it up. It was a woman, standing about two hands high. Her fingers automatically curled around its naked waist to protect it from Cam's sight.

"That's a very fine quality alabaster." He reached out but her fingers tightened. He couldn't see more than the statue's head and legs. "It might be Aphrodite," he said curiously. "The face resembles a painting by Titian, of Aphrodite rising from the waves. Is she wearing clothing?"

"No," Gina whispered. "She is quite, quite naked. My mother gave me a *naked* statue."

To Cam's dismay, her face crumpled. "It's not just a naked statue," he said quickly. "Pink alabaster is very valuable."

She bit her lip and stuck the figure back into its crimson bed, facedown. "It seems that Sebastian was right," she said in a hard voice. "My mother apparently believed that I would be grateful to have a naked figure of a woman—for my bedchamber, perhaps?" She snapped the top down on the box and placed it to the side.

Cam had seen women in a fury before, and the one before him looked delirious with rage.

"I'm going for a walk," she said.

He cleared his throat. "It is raining."

"No matter." She walked to the door and paused. "Are you coming?" Her voice was impatient.

"Of course."

Cam waited as Gina took the statue into her own room. She was gone for only a second. Probably threw it in the fireplace, he thought regretfully. It was a pity: he would have liked to examine the figure more closely.

They walked from the darkened and empty salon into the dripping garden without saying another word. A gentle breeze was indolently throwing a few drops of rain here and there.

Gina wished a blizzard were raging: anything to match the agitation in her chest. Her mother was just as Sebastian had pictured, a loose woman, a degenerate. The kind of woman

131

who sent her child over to a foreign country without a second's thought for whether the father would accept her. No wonder her idea of an appropriate gift was a lascivious statue. Gina swiped at an overhanging apple bough.

There was a muffled curse from Cam, walking behind her.

"What happened?" she said, savage disinterest in her voice.

"You shook water down my neck."

Her gown was sprinkled with dark splotches, only barely visible in the moonlight.

"Listen," came a male voice behind her.

She stopped for a moment and heard the liquid trill of a bird.

"A nightingale," he said.

The bird sang on. It sounded sorrowful to Gina. As if the nightingale sang of lost love and an impure life. Tears fell down her cheeks.

"Are you crying?" Cam said in the suspicious voice of a man who hated female tears.

"No," Gina said shakily. "It's just rain on my cheeks."

"Warm rain." He stepped in front of her and touched her cheek with one finger. "Why are you so upset?" He sounded genuinely mystified.

"My mother sent me a naked statue," she said, swallowing the hysterical note in her voice.

His whole body resonated with puzzlement.

"She was a lightskirt," Gina said shrilly. "A woman of pleasure." She almost spat the words. "And she obviously thought I was one as well!"

"A woman of pleasure? The Countess Ligny?"

"A strumpet. A *prostitute,* for all I know!"

"Nonsense," Cam said. "She may have given birth to a child out of wedlock but that doesn't make her a strumpet."

Gina started walking back down the dark path, wet silk dragging against her legs. "What's nonsensical about it? She didn't have only one illegitimate child. She had two."

"Two?" Cam caught up with her.

"I gather my mother didn't tell you that she received another blackmailing letter."

He grabbed her arm and stopped her. "What does it say?"

"That I have a brother," she snapped.

Cam stood in the pathway, blocking her way to the house. "Did the letter request money? Did you show it to Rounton?"

"No money was mentioned. The letter was delivered to my mother's home and Rounton hasn't seen it yet."

"I'll speak to him," Cam said. "We'll have to hire the Bow Street Runners. Damn. I'm sorry this happened again."

"I think your father tried Runners."

"Was there anything that might serve as a clue? Was the letter in French?"

"No, English."

"Curious," he said. "The first letter was in French."

Gina frowned. "It was oddly phrased, but the note clearly said I had a brother."

Cam's eyebrows rose. He had curled his hands around her upper arms, just below where her little sleeves ended. He started rubbing his thumbs in gentle circles over her chilly flesh. "Perhaps it was oddly phrased because it was written by a Frenchman."

"I don't think so. But how could anyone but a Frenchman find out about the countess? I mean, enough to know whether she had other children?"

He was still caressing her arms, and it was causing a little quake in her stomach. He stood in the path, just under a pear tree. The moon was full and shining through the leaves, light falling on his shoulders in a dancing pattern.

133

Suddenly she was very aware of his large body, standing just a hair's breadth from her own.

"I always wanted a brother," he said.

"That's not the point!" she said irritably. "Who could want an illegitimate brother?"

"*You* are illegitimate, Gina," he pointed out.

She tried not to think of herself in those terms and was generally successful. "Yes," she said in a subdued tone. "Of course."

"I didn't mean to be unkind," Cam said. "But I've never seen much point in worrying over one's parents' mistakes. God knows, if I indulged myself, my father left a good deal for me to worry over."

"The duke was very proper. I'm sure you don't have illegitimate siblings."

"Perhaps. But he considered himself above the law," Cam remarked. "I was around fifteen when I discovered just how many illegal schemes he was involved in. It's a miracle he managed to die without being found out."

Gina was looking very surprised.

"Oh yes," he said. "Did you ever wonder where all his money came from, given that the estate has little land attached?"

She shook her head.

"Gambling. Not gambling in a gaming hell. On the market, the mercantile exchange. And only when he knew that he could make a small fortune, generally because he had previously arranged for that to happen."

"Oh."

"Money gained by using his title to attract investors to fraudulent schemes, cashing in before the companies went bust." He dropped his hands from her arms. "So a few illegitimate children wouldn't have bothered me."

"I'm sorry," Gina said, looking up at him.

He shrugged. "We are not our parents' keepers."

A fat drop of water landed on her back, and she shivered. A large hand replaced the cold trail of water with an intoxicating touch. Back up the curve of a creamy white shoulder, shining in the moonshine like the highest quality alabaster.

When he bent his head, she held her breath.

But he didn't stop. His hands tightened on her shoulders and his lips met hers.

There was no reverence. There was no sweet touch of lips, pleasant, pleasurable and altogether agreeable.

Instead his lips brushed against hers, once, twice, hard and demanding. Gina opened her mouth to protest and he brazenly took what was offered: she tasted him and smelled him at once.

His mouth was wild and wet and hungry. She was shocked into silence, and only blindly aware when his hands stroked down her naked back and slid to her waist. She didn't even notice the moment when her own arms reached around his neck to hold him in case he tried to escape.

But then, she was not kissing Sebastian. There was no feeling of elusiveness about her husband, no sense that the moments were being counted for suitability or lack thereof. No unspoken sense that the kiss was dipping into unsuitability.

She could feel his hard body against hers. Silk, the midnight-blue silk of her gown, was no barrier to feeling.

Their tongues and hearts fell into a rhythm that beat through blood and bone and blinded her senses to anything except the intoxication of his arms and lips and mouth.

He responded to her grasp with a satisfied kind of growl and pulled her even more tightly against his body. She clung and squirmed closer, lusting for the heat, the need and hunger

135

that pulsed between them. Her tongue met his timidly. He made a hoarse sound in his throat, and the blood beat through her bones.

He broke away.

Her heart was beating heavily in her chest. Finally she had to open her eyes.

"God," he said huskily. Then he seemed to lose track of his thought. "Were your eyes this green when I married you?"

She opened her mouth to answer, but he surrendered to instinct again. Her lips were crimson, wanton, *his*. He plundered his own possession.

His hands molded her slim curves to his body, pressed every curve and hollow against the answering swerve in his own body.

She broke away.

Her lips were stained crimson from kisses. He watched, spellbound, as her tongue touched her bottom lip.

"I tasted you." She swayed toward him, put her arms around his neck. "You taste marvelous," she whispered into his mouth.

He took her lips with the ruthlessness of a man tasting rain in the desert. And still, when she drew back her head, he let her go.

"I don't *like* wet kisses," Gina said wonderingly. Her arms were still around his neck.

Cam looked down into her green eyes. They looked darker now, the color of fir trees.

"No?" he asked. Then he brazenly licked her lips. They were tempting beyond all measure. He pulled her even more tightly against him. "I think you do," he said, voice dark with need and amusement, mixed.

She tried to speak and her voice came out a hoarse gasp.

"Did you say something, wife?" came a voice.

"Are you licking my ear?" Gina asked, shocked into coherence.

"Mmm," Cam said. "You see, I love wet kisses. Wet," he said, licking the curl of her delicate ear. "Wet," he said, licking the sweet swan curve of her neck. "Wet," he said, licking his way across her rain-drenched cheek to her open mouth.

Not a word came from that mouth indicating a dislike of his wet kisses. Pleasure burned in his loins as a tongue innocently—but oh so ardently—met his. Burned down his legs as Gina's hands clasped his face, drawing him closer. Raged in his chest as she trembled against his body, as she answered the hard arrogance of his hips with a tiny undulation that said everything of innocence and even more of desire.

But something was nagging at Cam's mind. An annoying, pestilent, pestering voice was saying over and over, in the inner recesses of his head, *She's your wife. She's your wife.*

"You're my wife," he repeated, kissing her eyes.

Gina wasn't listening. She was discovering precisely why Esme's eyes flared at the sight of Bernie's arm. Running her hands over Cam's chest, she could feel muscles under the thin linen: heat, life, intoxicating strength under her fingertips.

But Cam, by saying it aloud, had woken to the truth. "Oh God," he said, pulling his hands away as if he had touched molten iron. "You're my *wife.*"

He stepped back and ran his hands through his hair, leaving it standing straight up. "This is not a felicitous way to conduct our annulment," he said dryly.

She smiled at him. "I found it very pleasurable. And there is nothing wrong with kissing, after all. Kissing is not, is not—"

"Intercourse," Cam said.

In the moonlight, Gina's cheeks flushed a color that could never be caught by oil paints, a translucent, rose-stained tint he'd seen only on the inside of a large shell. But she maintained her composure. "Kissing is only kissing. And I enjoyed it." She looked at him, head held high. "I have kissed other men. I have kissed Sebastian, many times. I am a married woman after all."

"Married to *me*!" Cam barked. The idea of Bonnington kissing Gina made him hot with irritation.

"All the more suitable," Gina said. She turned back to the house. Her heart was thudding in her breast and making it difficult to speak coherently.

She looked back to find he hadn't moved from the path. He stood there, spangled by moonlight, black eyes inscrutable.

"I am rather cold," she stated.

He ran his hand through his hair one more time and then started walking.

"No more kissing." His voice was dangerously quiet.

Gina pushed a damp lock of hair behind her ear. Her fingers were trembling but she managed to steady her voice. She would *not* show a reaction. "It was just a kiss," she said, with just the right touch of impatience in her voice. "The fact that we are married doesn't make it more or less than just a kiss."

He looked at her sideways, from underneath long lashes. There was a sardonic gleam in his eyes and he brought her to a halt with just a touch. "A *wet* kiss, Gina," he said softly.

She said nothing and lost her air of sophistication in an instant.

He bent his head and deliberately swept his tongue across her beautiful, cherry dark lips. They opened, just an inch, but he took the invitation. When he finally raised his head, blood was pounding through his body in a demanding rhythm. "No more kisses," he said. His voice was ragged.

This time she didn't look so disinterested. She looked up at him and nodded.

They walked into the salon together, Cam mentally castigating himself for telling implausible lies. No more kisses: it was as if his father promised not to cheat anyone.

He would stop kissing his wife . . . the moment she wasn't his wife anymore. After all, a kiss is nothing more than a kiss, to quote that same wife.

But somehow he managed to stop himself from pinning that wife to the corridor wall and covering her mouth. "Good night," he said nonchalantly.

He fancied he saw a flash of disappointment on her face.

She curtsied. "Your Grace."

He bowed. Bowing brought his head past the flimsy silk of her darkened bodice. Brought him eye to eye with nipples grown cold and tautly visible through thin silk. His hand stirred at his side as if it had a will of its own. "You'd better go to your chamber," he said, voice harsh.

A glint of amusement lit her face. "I won't forget," she said sweetly, tapping his chin with one slender finger. "No more kisses—from my husband at least."

She was very pleased to see his mouth tighten. "Good night, Cam," she repeated. And closed the door to her chamber in his face.

Chapter Fourteen

The Truth Is Sometimes Displeasing

"I'm not saying that it was humiliating, precisely. But it was unnerving."

Esme regarded her closest friend with a smile that was almost—not quite—a smirk. "Then what happened?"

"Nothing, of course. I went into my room and presumably he went into his."

"A pity," Esme said.

"I thought so too," Gina remarked.

Esme laughed. "That kiss did you some good, my girl. You don't want to become a stick in the mud like your fiancé."

"Sebastian isn't a stick in the mud." But her voice didn't have much conviction and Esme ignored her.

"I forgot to tell you," Gina said. "I received a bequest from Countess Ligny."

"Bequest? From your mother?"

Gina nodded. "Cam gave it to me last night. Her solicitor must have mistakenly thought that I live with my husband, so he sent it to Greece."

"What is it?"

"A statue," she said. "A statue of a naked woman." A night's sleep had blunted her rage and embarrassment, and she said it without inflection.

True to form, Esme grinned. "Salacious, is it?"

She nodded. "Pink, and all polished. The woman doesn't have a stitch of clothing on."

A peal of laughter rang out. "You have to say this for your mama: she died as she lived, didn't she?"

"You could put it that way," Gina said, feeling peevish again.

"Do you dislike the statue?"

"No. It's precisely what one would expect from a woman who gave her child away."

"That's harsh," Esme said. "It is remarkably difficult for an unmarried woman to raise a child. Look at you. You're a duchess. You're happy. What would your life have been like if she had kept you?"

"I would have had a mother."

"You *do* have a mother. Lady Cranborne loves you dearly, so don't weave me any Banbury tales about a sad childhood."

"You're probably right," Gina admitted.

"Where is the scandalous nude?" Esme looked around the room.

"I've put it in the cupboard, of course."

"Why *of course*? Unless you're afraid of the competition, which you shouldn't be. I'd put it next to my bed, if I were you."

Gina colored. "I'm *not* you!"

Esme rose and gave her a quick kiss on the cheek. "I don't mean to tease, sweetheart. It was a wise move. What if Bonnington caught sight of it? Disaster!"

"He doesn't enter my bedchamber."

"Just as well. If he knew you were concealing scandalous statues in cupboards—especially bequests from your inconveniently unmarried mother—there'd be no controlling his righteous indignation. Why, he'd probably turn as orange as a pumpkin and blow smoke from his ears."

Gina sighed. "Couldn't you two simply ignore each other?"

Esme regarded herself in the cheval mirror. "Is this gown dowdy?"

"No. You look exquisite." And it was true.

"Lady Childe looks very well these days."

"She's old. And not nearly as beautiful as you are."

Esme sighed. "I'm a competitive beast. I can't bear it that everyone knows whose bed my husband is frequenting."

"Everyone knows whose bed you are frequenting as well," Gina pointed out, unable to stop herself.

"You know I rarely frequent beds," she answered, unruffled. "I enjoy, I sample, but I don't partake."

"Miles's mistresses never bothered you before. You sound like Carola, hoping to win back her husband. Do you wish to court him, then?"

A look of pure revulsion passed over Esme's face. "Absolutely not. I am only vexed—and this is horrible of me—because he is in love. Isn't that dreadful?"

Gina rose and slung an arm around her neck. "Dreadful," she agreed. "Natural, though."

Esme stared at their reflection in the glass. "She has children, Gina." Her voice was tight. "That's what really bothers me."

"I know." Gina tightened her arm. "I know." Their eyes met in the mirror. "Now, what do you say if we two childless crones make our way out for luncheon?"

Esme smiled, with only a tiny waver. "Is Holy Willy going to be there?"

"Sebastian may be a little stiff in his manners, but he is *not* a Holy Willy!"

"Hoity-toity," Esme retorted. "Why don't you bring *Much Ado* along? We could practice our lines after the meal, if you don't have other plans."

"All right," Gina agreed, picking up the little leather-bound volume. "I can't practice too long, though; Mr. Wapping and I are still working on the Medicis."

"I don't understand how you can spend so much time with Wapping, Gina. One would think you missed the school-room! What on earth do you get out of it? What do you gain? I would almost think you *were* having an affair with him except—"

"Except?"

"Except Mr. Wapping is . . . Mr. Wapping!"

"*The Tatler* described him as an extremely handsome young man," Gina said loftily. "I should be fortunate to attract such a beau."

Esme chuckled. "If you like them short and rather furry."

"Rather like a squirrel, isn't he?" Gina said. "Someday he'll marry a small—"

"—*very* small," Esme put in.

"—a very small woman and they'll have little furry babies."

"Who will all speak Greek. In fact, if you keep him around long enough, he could teach your children to speak Greek."

"As soon as he finishes his book I'm sure he'll be invited to teach at Oxford or Cambridge. He has innovative ideas about the political situation in the Italian Renaissance," Gina said.

Esme rolled her eyes. "What *are* you doing with him?"

"I think Cam found him in a Greek temple somewhere. At any rate, he sent Wapping over to me so that I could keep him fed. I agreed to be tutored because that was the reason Cam sent him to England. And then the subject grew interesting."

"For goodness' sake, why couldn't your husband feed the man himself?"

Gina thought about it. "I suppose he just thought it was easier to send Wapping to England. That would be like Cam. And I do enjoy the tutoring."

"Ah well." Esme sighed, giving her gown one last twitch. "I flirt and you learn history: it's clear who will get into heaven, isn't it?"

The moment Gina walked into the Long Salon, Carola dashed up and whispered in an anguished undertone: "Tuppy is here, and I'm supposed to begin courting him. But I can't gather my courage to do it! In fact, I think I'd rather faint than speak to him. At least I wouldn't feel so distressed."

"All you need to do is speak to him. Remember Esme's lessons. Show interest in whatever he says."

"I don't even have the courage to approach him. Not that it matters, because I always seem to fall silent whenever he's around."

"I don't believe you," Gina said. "I've never seen you act in a shy manner."

"It's different with Tuppy. I can't explain it. I go clammy and fall utterly silent."

"I'll go with you." Gina patted her arm. "I'll start a conversation and you join in when you wish."

Carola nodded and began to tow Gina through the room so quickly that an elderly gentleman almost spilled his wine as they rushed by.

"Slow down!" Gina hissed. "You don't want to be obvious!"

She stopped, panic-stricken. "I know that," she said. "Do I look all right?"

Gina nodded. "You look charming. Did Esme choose that gown?"

"Yes. I wanted to wear a yellow one that is more cheerful. It has ruffles all along the hem, and a sweet little parasol. But Esme said that this one is more elegant. It certainly has a low neckline. Do you think I ought to change?"

"Absolutely not. You look charming and cheerful."

"Not desperate?" Carola asked desperately.

"No. Now let's make our way gracefully over to where Tuppy is standing. Yes, I see him. *Drift,* Carola, *drift.*"

Carola looked agonized. "Drift," she muttered to herself, making an odd crablike motion to the side.

Gina swallowed a giggle. A moment later they gracefully placed themselves in front of Lord Perwinkle. Gina was glad to see that Carola didn't faint. Even more interesting was the fact that her husband went silent as a rock. Very interesting.

Of course, while Carola didn't faint, she didn't say anything either. So Gina automatically became a duchess. The duchess effect worked wonders with people who were uncomfortable: she told stories, she told a mild joke or two, she laughed at her own jokes. She smiled encouragingly and asked Tuppy question after question until the man gathered himself together and began to speak civilly enough.

In fact, after about a half hour, she and Lord Perwinkle had had an interesting conversation about the life cycle of trout, although Carola had still to utter one word. And Gina had had enough of marine life.

"My lord," she said, giving him her very widest smile. "This has been a tremendous, tremendous pleasure. I trust that we can speak of your fascinating experiments again in the very near future."

He bowed. "I would be happy to, Your Grace." He looked rather more cheerful. In fact, in a rangy, unpolished kind of way she could see why Carola hankered after him. When he grew excited about baby trout, his hair fell over his eyes in an engaging fashion.

"I must say hello to my husband," Gina said. "He just entered the room." And she drifted away at top speed, leaving Carola and Tuppy staring at each other.

When she reached Cam she grabbed his arm and swung him around so that she could appear to be talking to him but really watch the Perwinkles over his shoulder.

"What the devil are you up to?" he asked.

"Hush!"

Cam started to turn so she jerked him back around. "No, you look at me and pretend we're having a riveting conversation."

"Well, this is interesting," Cam said, starting to enjoy himself. He'd been awake half the night, and when he finally went to sleep, his dreams had been full of one overseductive wife who had transformed mid-sentence into a naked statue. And then he spent the morning staring at the marble lump in the corner of his bedroom. Should he sculpt Gina as a pink, naked Aphrodite? A pleasant thought.

Even more pleasant when the duchess herself stood before him. She would make a lovely Aphrodite. Unusual for an Aphrodite, of course. She was slimmer than the normal model, and her face was far more intelligent. The Aphrodites he could bring to mind had sensual, indolent faces, like that of Gina's statue. Whereas her face was thin with a look of curiosity. But why should Aphrodite, as the goddess of eros, of desire, be indolent? Why shouldn't she have precisely that innocent look combined with a gleam of erotic curiosity—the look in his wife's eyes?

"Who *are* you watching?" he asked, casting a look over his shoulder. "That woman who's rouged to the eyeballs?"

"No," Gina said absently.

"Everyone is looking at us. They think I'm about to lunge down your bodice."

At that, her head swung up. Sure enough, a good portion of the room did seem to be entranced by the intimacy being displayed by the Duke and Duchess of Girton. A little group

146

of dowagers turned back among themselves with a general titter.

"I'll go flirt madly with that gorgeous friend of yours," Cam offered. "It will mitigate the burning anxiety the ladies clearly feel about our annulment."

"Quite a sacrifice," Gina remarked, a drop of acid in her voice.

"Are you staring at Tuppy Perwinkle?" Cam had finally managed to locate the site of interest.

"Yes," she admitted.

"Why on earth?"

"That's his wife he's speaking to."

"I thought he lost his wife three years ago."

Her eyes grew wide. "He told you that his wife had *died*?"

"Oh no, just that he had misplaced her."

Gina nodded with some satisfaction. "I don't think he's overlooking her now." In fact, Tuppy and Carola seemed to be having an animated conversation.

"You know," Cam said, "I'm not certain that Tuppy wanted to rediscover his wife."

"Too late," she said. The couple were standing very close together and Carola was talking with great emphasis.

"Look! They must have found something to talk about besides trout. Isn't that sweet?"

"Does she know anything about trout?"

Gina gasped.

The sound of Carola's slap could be heard throughout the room.

"That's what comes of rediscovering a lost wife," Cam said cheerfully. "I told you he didn't want her."

"I think one could say more precisely that she doesn't want him," Gina retorted.

★　　★　　★

147

At luncheon, his wife was seated next to her fiancé. Just to amuse himself, Cam had started a list of epithets for the man. "Poker-faced" he'd already used. He needed something more vulgar to truly make an impression on Gina. "Uppish" sounded almost complimentary. "Wiggy" was a good one. Had a pedantic yet tedious air. Wiggy Bonnington. He liked it. He ambled over to the table where they were seated and, as luck would have it, the seat next to Gina's luscious friend was unoccupied.

"Hello there, Lady Rawlings," he said with just a touch more pleasure than was called for by common politeness. "Bonnington, your servant," he remarked. "I'm afraid I didn't register your presence immediately." And he smiled, an indolent type of smile.

The wiggy one stiffened but confined himself to a cool nod in response.

"How's your hysterical friend? The one who belted Perwinkle?" Cam asked, looking at his wife across the table.

"She didn't *belt* him," Gina snapped. "Carola is absolutely fine."

Cam grinned at her and then turned back to Lady Rawlings. He felt more cheerful just sitting next to a bosom as lovely as hers. Somewhat to his surprise, he encountered a ferocious glare from the wiggy marquess. Interesting, Cam thought. Bonnington doesn't like it when someone throws the lovely Esme a lusty look.

He decided to try a little experiment. He leaned forward across the small table and gave his wife the smile he generally reserved for his rare encounters with an exotic dancer named Bella who lived in the next village. It was a slow, heated smile that started at Gina's sensual lips and didn't go anywhere but down.

To his utter shock, Cam found that certain parts of his body sprang instantly into ardent attention, a level of

148

attention that lusty Bella never received. He hastily looked back up into the startled eyes of his wife.

A tiny blush, a sweet cherry flush crept into her cheeks. For a moment those wild almond-shaped eyes caught his and turned a smoky, darker green.

Cam sat back, feeling poleaxed. Then he remembered to look at Gina's fiancé. Old Wiggy was looking utterly relaxed and didn't seem to have even noticed.

What he should do now was stare at Lady Rawlings's bosom, but for some obscure reason he needed to take a breather. His wife didn't have half the cleavage of the bountiful lady next to him and yet . . . and yet.

He leaned closer to Esme. She had a spicy perfume that suited her sensuous, available air. He took a manful breath and leaned even closer, giving her the Bella smile. It was rather less of a success. For one thing, in comparison to Gina's, her bosom was wildly overfleshy and he had a sense of vertigo, as when one dives from a high cliff. And when he met her eyes, there was no surprised welcome mixed with a hint of erotic pleasure, as Gina's had had. Instead, they were flatly amused.

She leaned forward and asked huskily, "Are you enjoying yourself, Your Grace?"

He blinked and remembered to look at Bonnington. Sure enough, the man appeared to be on the verge of exploding from rage. He had turned dark red and was visibly clenching his teeth.

If Sebastian had ever seen death in another man's eyes, it was in those of the marquess. In the oh-so-civilized Wiggy's eyes was the promise of murder: swift and unrepentant murder.

"I believe so," Cam said, pulling back from Lady Rawlings. He had no intention of going to grass for the sake of a well-endowed Englishwoman. But he did have a question or two that she might be able to answer.

She jumped in before he could formulate a question. "How is your memorization of *Much Ado* coming?" There was a warning in her tone. Obviously she knew exactly what he was thinking, but she was not going to admit it. A good girl, Cam thought suddenly. Loyal to Gina. And damn beautiful as well.

"Would you do me the honor of allowing me to make a sculpture of you?" he asked impulsively.

She looked surprised. "Do you sculpt real people then? I have heard of your work, as it is very well known in London. But I didn't know that you sculpted actual people rather than mythological figures."

"I don't. I would probably sculpt you as Diana." He had decided on the moment.

"Diana? Isn't she the goddess who hated men?"

He considered. "I think of her as the goddess who tempted men by bathing outdoors, and turned them into animal life if they succumbed to the lure of bare flesh."

There was more than a gleam of laughter in her eyes. "You're not as blind as the average man, are you?" she said, lowering her voice so she could not be overheard.

Cam smiled. He liked Gina's lusty, not-so-lusty friend. "Would you like to be shaped in pink marble?" he offered. "I guarantee a scandalous response from the *ton*."

Esme cocked an eyebrow. "And why would I be interested in creating yet another scandal in the *ton*? I assure you that I do scandals quite well on my own."

Cam bent closer. "The wiggy marquess will particularly dislike the idea."

Esme gave him a guarded look. "Hush."

Cam glanced up to find his wife and her betrothed looking

at them with matched frowns. "Lady Rawlings has just agreed to be a model for my next work," he said.

Something flashed across Gina's eyes and disappeared. "Esme will make a beautiful goddess."

Cam nodded. What was that look in her eyes? She wasn't hurt, was she? Damn it, he probably should have thought about it before making such a rash offer. An hour ago he had decided to shape Gina into Aphrodite, and here he was with a Diana instead.

Bonnington was looking more starched than he'd ever seen him. He was obviously longing to scold Lady Rawlings, but he turned to Cam instead. "I thought you specialized in less-than-respectable statues. Are you broadening your focus?" His tone indicated that it wasn't possible.

"In fact," Cam said, "Lady Rawlings and I have just agreed that she would make an admirable Diana."

Bonnington's nostrils flared.

"I am so looking forward to it," Esme cooed, leaning forward so that her bosom brushed Cam's arm. "The duke suggested Diana in the bath . . . but I think that would be a *wee* bit too scandalous, don't you, Lord Bonnington?"

Cam privately thought that if looks could kill, his half of the table would be stretching their length against the ground.

"Not at all," the marquess bit out. "It sounds remarkably appropriate. I saw a piece of yours in Sladdington's entryway, Your Grace." He turned his scathing eyes to Esme. "I'm certain that you will enjoy being depicted in marble. Sladdington uses the statue as a hat stand. Perhaps Lady Rawlings could become something so . . . *useful.*"

Cam felt Esme's body go rigid next to his arm. He gave her an encouraging nudge. "Touché!" he whispered. "Your turn."

But before she could speak there was a sharp squeal of a chair pushing backward. Cam looked up to see his wife looking icily detached. "Please excuse me," she said. "I must have eaten something amiss. I'm feeling a touch of nausea." She turned and walked off. Bonnington stalked after his betrothed.

Esme snorted. "Touché! *Your* turn."

Cam surveyed his remaining luncheon companion with a raised eyebrow. "You're playing with fire, you know that?"

She picked up her fork and stirred her mushroom fricassee. "Not in truth," she said. "I am—" But she caught herself and snapped at Cam: "This is a *most* improper conversation."

"True enough. Do you have a husband, then?" he asked, with some curiosity.

"Oh yes," Esme said, just the faintest shade of bitterness to her voice.

"Is he here?"

"Naturally." She nodded toward a table to the left.

"Which one?"

"Miles has brown hair," she said dispiritedly.

"Don't you mean that he used to have brown hair?"

"Well, he still has some," she said, looking over. "He's the one snuffling Lady Childe's shoulder."

"Snuffling is a nice word for it," Cam said thoughtfully. "It has a gently porcine ring that pleases, in the context. Would you like me to get his attention and then snuffle your shoulder?"

"No, thank you," Esme said, eating a mouthful of fricassee.

Cam felt she didn't have to sound so completely uninterested. But he suspected that the audience for most of Esme Rawlings's scandalous behavior had just stalked out of the room.

"In that case, would you like to help me memorize my lines?" he asked, putting on a pathetic tone. There wasn't any point in letting the woman lapse into a melancholy.

Esme sighed and agreed.

And that was how Gina found them, thirty minutes or so later when she came looking for Esme. Her husband and her best friend were snuggled before the fire in the library, heads bent over a copy of Shakespeare. Esme's black curls looked like glossy silk next to Cam's unruly locks.

She was giggling.

"Stop laughing, wench," Cam said. "I'll try that line again: *What, my dear Lady Disdain: are you yet living?*"

Gina turned and walked out of the library without disturbing them. Mr. Wapping would be expecting her. And the fact that she had a headache beating in both temples had nothing to do with what she just saw.

Esme deserves some happiness, she told herself.

Cam doesn't deserve any, she told herself just as fiercely.

By the time she reached the third floor and prepared herself to learn about the escalating difficulties of city-states in the thirteenth century, she was fairly certain that she'd never suffered such a terrible headache in her life.

She was also absolutely clear about whose fault it was.

Her degenerate husband had decided to seduce her best friend. Never mind the fact that Esme was married and had already gotten herself into enough scandals. Never mind the fact that she was only hanging on to her place in the *ton* because, to Gina's private knowledge, Esme's men rarely managed to get her into bed, try as they would, and therefore she had never actually been caught in a compromising situation.

Cam would have no such problem. There was no point in thinking about how quickly any woman would succumb to

153

his large, relaxed body and laughing, seductive eyes. He looked at one and made the world spin crazily, if only for a moment. Wait until he started sculpting Esme in marble. Looking at her. Naked?

Mr. Wapping tidied his mustache and his beard and set a stack of books on the table. "I have some very exciting information to share today, Your Grace," he said with a good deal of self-importance. "I believe that my research will shed an entirely new light on Machiavelli's place within the Florentine government. You do remember what we talked about last week, don't you?" Sometimes Mr. Wapping tended to forget that he wasn't instructing a class of undergraduates.

"Yes, of course," Gina said obediently. "The Medicis took over Venice and Machiavelli was exiled."

"*Not* Venice—Florence," Mr. Wapping said, with a faint air of disapproval.

He snapped open his books. "Now I'm sure that you'll find this discrepancy between Sandlefoot's and Simon's hypotheses regarding Machiavelli's attempt to gain a place on the Medici council as interesting as I did, Your Grace."

Gina nodded. She was having trouble breathing—due to pure rage, she assured herself. It was because she didn't wish her best friend to fall into the trap of the first lazy and degenerate duke to come along.

That was the only reason.

"Your Grace? Your Grace? Are you feeling well?"

"Of course," Gina snapped.

Mr. Wapping blinked. "I only mentioned it because you are uncharacteristically inattentive." Then he clearly recollected to whom he was speaking. "Shall we return to the subject? Machiavelli, of course, was a profound strategist, especially when it came to war. He favored an indirect approach, what he called a 'silken and indirect appeal.' Of

154

course, he also noted that some situations warrant a blunt and forceful attack."

Gina smiled weakly and thought dark thoughts about her husband.

"Would you care to recapitulate Sandlefoot's hypothesis regarding Machiavelli?"

"Not at the moment," she admitted.

So Wapping did so himself, which was by far his favorite mode of instruction.

She needed a strategy. Nothing came to mind but attack. I'll go to his room and brain him with the piece of marble, she thought. Blunt, forceful, and effective. The thought made her feel better and she nursed it for the next hour, finally refining her strategy into a plan to brain her husband with the pink Aphrodite. That attack had a silken and indirect resonance that she found immensely soothing.

"Mr. Wapping," she said, breaking into a learned demolition of Sandlefoot's conclusions, "what do you know about Aphrodite?"

He broke off with an oddly strangled sound.

"I'm so sorry," Gina cried. "I did not mean to interrupt you, Mr. Wapping. I am simply concerned about something—"

"Not at all," he said. "Aphrodite." He paused, stroked his mustache, and rolled back on his heels. "What would you like to know?"

"She is a married goddess?"

"Exactly. Aphrodite was married to Lord Hephaestus."

"And was she unfaithful?"

"Homer has it that Aphrodite slept with Ares, god of war, in her husband's bed. But she had several other lovers, including two mortals, Adonis and Anchises. Is there any particular reason that you wish to know about Aphrodite?"

Gina shook her head. "So Aphrodite is not a very respectable goddess?"

Wapping smiled. He had a rather secret and irritating smile; Gina had noticed it before. "There I would have to agree with you, Your Grace. Aphrodite is the goddess of eros, or physical love, often confused by careless scholars with the Roman goddess Venus. She is not respectable by any means."

Later Gina sent her apologies downstairs and ate supper in her room. Carola wasn't eating either. She had declared that she would rather die than sit next to her husband, although she wouldn't tell Gina what Tuppy had said that drove her to the point of violence. And Gina had no wish to watch Cam smiling at Esme.

She took a leisurely bath and sat in a chair by the fire to tackle a pile of estate papers that had been delivered that afternoon. After an hour or so she took the Aphrodite from its box. The statue certainly was beautiful, in a luscious, depraved type of way.

She was starting—just starting—to relinquish her dream of braining her husband. He's not worth it, she told herself. Let him go back to his squalid little island and shape squalid naked statues for the rest of his life.

She was going to be a marchioness and raise hundreds of children who would all have blond hair, gold as the sun, and godlike beauty. Certainly none of them would have unruly hair and snapping black eyes.

When the knock sounded on the door, she hastily stuck the Aphrodite under the ruffled edge of her chair. It was unusual for Annie to return once dismissed, but perhaps she had forgotten something. Gina stood up and turned around, calling out, "Enter."

The moment she saw who it was her entire body was swept by a wave of sensation that was as hot as flame and as embarrassing as it was hot. She reached up to draw her robe closed over her thin nightrail and realized she'd left it on the bed.

He cleared his throat. For some reason, he sounded almost hoarse. "May I come in?"

There was silence while she contemplated her plan to brain him with the Aphrodite. He looked entirely too endearing and delectable to live. It would be unfair to married women everywhere. She took another swallow of brandy.

"Gina?" he said. "I'm in the hallway. May I come in?"

She stepped back. "If you must," she said ungraciously. After all, she could hardly inflict bodily harm if her husband and the Aphrodite weren't in the same room.

It was the kind of tangled reasoning that Il Segretario Machiavelli would have deplored. Chapter Ten of his treatise *The Prince* spelled it out. One should only consort with the enemy under conditions of extreme caution, given that the danger of secret attack was so great.

Alas, with the tumult of the last few days, the Duchess of Girton hadn't read past Chapter Five, "The Virtues of the Blunt and Forceful Attack."

Chapter Fifteen

A Duchess in Dishabille

Cam told himself that the tentlike effect in the front of his knitted pantaloons was not a concern. Gina was obviously a virgin, given Bonnington's sense of propriety, and so she likely wouldn't even know what caused it. If she noticed. Everyone knew that virgins had no practical knowledge of the male physique.

"I came to look at your blackmailing note," he said, strolling over to the small table on which stood a decanter of brandy. "May I congratulate you on your taste in beverages? What the devil did they give you a single glass for?"

He turned around and surveyed the room. Then he gave a satisfied nod and snatched a water glass from beside her bed.

"They gave me a single glass because I sleep alone."

He poured the brandy and thought about the faint hint of a sultry complaint in her voice. Did he hear it only because he wished it was there?

A moment later, he sharply revised his assumption about virginal innocence. As he turned around, her eye ranged over his body and then caught. She was apparently fascinated by his pantaloons. Cam resisted the urge to rearrange his equipment.

"See something you like?" he asked.

She turned her head away without a glimmer of embarrassment. "Certainly," she said in an offhand, polite way. The way you assure a woman that she has not gained weight when the lady is either *enceinte* or has recently eaten a side of beef.

"Good," Cam said, unable to come up with a witty remark. What happened to the days when virgins screamed with fear at their first sight of a man's rod? He hadn't lived outside England that long.

Gina was gazing into the fire without even a blush. Looked as if she hadn't a care in the world. In fact, she was brazen in her attention and, rather more galling, in her dismissal. Blood throbbed through Cam's body. That sort of insult might drive an unprincipled man to toss the wench on her own bed.

But of course he had no interest in that, except the usual arousal a man feels for a half-dressed woman in his presence. "Couldn't you put on a robe?" he asked.

She lifted one eyebrow and took another sip of brandy. "It's quite warm in here and you *are* my husband."

He stared at her until she rose with a graceful shrug of one shoulder. "If you insist." She walked past him to reach the bed. The scrap of cloth she was wearing was made of the thinnest, pale yellow silk that Cam had ever seen. It draped and clung to the long line of her thigh in a way that made a mockery of his unclothed statues.

Of course she didn't put on a sturdy cotton garment. The robe matched her gown, except most of it was lace. It hid nothing. Granted, Cam was already in a state of arousal. But even so, the faint swish as she walked past his chair was one of the most seductive sounds he'd ever encountered. It spoke of sweet skin and soft belly curves.

She jumped up again. "I forgot the letter." She walked over to the cupboard and opened it up; Cam cursed his wayward body and stared hard at the flames, trying to force the pounding in his loins to dissipate.

His wife was playing games with him. She was the antithesis of a virgin. Probably slept with Bonnington, Wapping, and a hundred other men. Her languid way of walking wasn't a virgin's gait. Everyone knew that virgins clamped their knees, crossed their legs at the ankles, and turned pink at the very idea of a man in their bedchamber.

But here was his wife, having summoned him from Greece so he could inform the entire Parliament that she was still a virgin, drinking brandy and wearing a garment a Cyprian would be proud to call her own. She walked back holding a folded paper.

"Do you do this every night?" he asked in a fury of resentment.

"Do what?" There was a look of mild inquiry on her face. Didn't she realize that the hazy light from the fireplace outlined every curve of her legs? He could even see a round and tender curve on the top of her inner thighs. Cam crossed his legs again. This was getting ridiculous.

"Do you always sit around like a bird of paradise, drinking brandy and entertaining men while half clothed?" His tone was brutal.

She chuckled. "Is that the life of a courtesan? I must say, I would have assumed a less peaceful and far more . . . rigorous evening. But I bow to your greater knowledge, naturally."

It was all Cam could do to stay silent. Some virgin his wife was turning out to be.

"Goodness me," she said with an air of discovery. "You're turning quite plum-colored, Your Grace. I warned you that my chamber was overheated. But to answer your question. I prefer to bathe in the evening, and my hair is slow to dry. I have fallen into the habit of drinking a brandy while working. I find brandy so restful, don't you?" She almost cooed it. "After drinking a small amount, I am utterly relaxed and ready for a sound night's sleep."

160

The vixen, Cam thought. She's deliberately trying to drive me to distraction, God only knows why. But two can play at this game.

He gave her a brazen look that was a kiss in itself. "What sort of work do you find so exhausting, my dear? As your husband, I would be happy to take some of the burden from your shoulders." He took a meditative sip of brandy. "I find a shared burden at bedtime even more relaxing than liquor."

Gina choked on a sip of brandy.

"For example," he continued, "should I ever have the good fortune to be married—and here I refer, of course, to a consummated marriage—I shall insist that my wife calm herself each evening. Or rather, that I help her in that worthwhile endeavor."

She gave him a limpid smile. "What a lucky woman she will be. Will you manage the estate business yourself, or will she be doubly burdened?"

He met her eyes with a gleam of pure enjoyment. Then he frowned. "What estate business?"

She pointed to a large heap of papers, stacked untidily on a stool next to her chair. "Your estate, which I currently manage. Once our marriage is annulled I will, naturally, cease to do so."

Cam blinked. "I thought Rounton and Bicksfiddle handled all that. Why on earth are they bothering you?"

"Bicksfiddle cannot make important decisions himself, Cam. You must know that I handle most of the estate business. I've written you about various things."

"But I didn't think you were *working* on those problems. I thought that Bicksfiddle consulted with you once or twice a year."

She snorted. "Once or twice a year?" She pointed to the heap on the stool. "Bicksfiddle's inquiries for this quarter. All of them need immediate attention."

"Damnation!" Cam exclaimed. He snatched up a sheet. It was a note from Bicksfiddle requesting hardship funds.

"Who are these people? Henry Polderoy and Albert Thomas from Upper Girton. Eric Horne and Bessie Mittins from Lower Girton."

"Oh dear," Gina said. "Bessie must be in the family way again."

"Is she a servant at the house?"

"No, those are people living in the village. You *do* remember that the estate includes two villages, don't you? Henry Polderoy used to be the blacksmith, but he suffered an injury to his right arm last winter, and he hasn't been able to keep up with his work. He has three little sons, all born on the same day. It was the funniest afternoon, Cam!"

He met her green eyes, dancing over the rim of her glass. "Mrs. Polderoy had very kindly asked me to be the godmother. And as luck would have it, I was in the village when the first babe, Henry, was born. So I paid a visit to see my new godson. Well, Mrs. Polderoy was still feeling distressed, and out came a second son! We named him James. He was the sweetest little poppet, and was just bathed and wrapped up, when Camden arrived."

"Camden?"

Gina nodded. "He's yours. Let's see, I think there are two or three Camdens in the village, counting Camden Webster in the next parish."

"What the devil are they doing, naming their children after *me*?"

"They name their children after you because you are the owner of the estate. You own the land they live on; they depend on you for their support and their livelihood. If you withdrew herding rights, they would starve. If you ceased hardship funds, they would find themselves in the poorhouse."

162

Cam didn't know what to say. He looked back at the sheet in his hand. "What's the matter with Bessie Mittins?"

"Nothing's the matter with Bessie besides the fact that she keeps having babies."

"What does her husband do for a living?"

"Oh, she doesn't have a husband," Gina replied cheerfully. "I'm afraid she's the proverbial loose woman. She says that she can't resist a good pair of legs—and I gather the men of Lower Girton are well endowed." She giggled.

"In *that* respect."

But Cam only smiled. He was thinking. "Do you mean to tell me that you were present at the birth of Henry Polderoy's children?"

"Not for the first one. But yes, I was there for James and Camden."

"Have things changed since I left England?" he demanded. "I could have sworn that young virgins would not be allowed to attend a lying-in."

"An unmarried woman is unlikely to," Gina agreed.

"But you are not married, at least not in the important respect!"

Gina looked at him. "I am the duchess," she stated. "For Bessie Mittins or Mrs. Polderoy, it doesn't matter whether you fled from my bedroom the night of our marriage or the next night. They need a duchess, and I'm the one." She finished her brandy.

Cam looked back at the sheet in his hand. "Why are we paying hardship for the neighboring parish? Isn't that Stafford's land?"

"He's an absentee landlord," she explained. "Doesn't give a rat's tail for his people. They'd starve, unless we helped. And luckily the estate is quite solvent."

"I thought *we* were absentee landlords," Cam said, stunned. "I thought you lived in London."

163

"I used to." She shrugged, with an easy, elegant rise of her shoulders. "But for the past five years I've spent at least half the year at Girton. I find it too difficult to keep the estate running smoothly without close attention."

"Damned if I don't fire Bicksfiddle," Cam snapped. "My instructions were clear enough. After father was bedridden, I instructed him to handle everything himself."

"I am the Duchess of Girton," she repeated simply. "I have been the duchess for twelve years, and I've run the estate for eight, since your father became incapacitated."

"I know how long we've been married!" He snatched a second sheet from the stool. "What's all this about tweed?"

"I'm trying to revive the homespun tweed industry in the village. We've had droughts repeatedly in the past few years, and sheep farming is not sustainable without better harvests."

Cam was growing aware of an unpleasant ball of guilt swelling in his belly. He tossed the letters he held toward the stool, but they drifted to the ground.

"You're turning the estate into a charity concern," he said. "My father would have loathed that."

"If your father hadn't extracted every cent he could without returning any to the land, we wouldn't have so many impoverished tenants."

Cam felt another twinge of guilt. Luckily, he was a past master of ignoring uncomfortable feelings, and he deliberately put them out of mind now, letting his eyes drift from Gina's scarlet lips down her long, slender neck.

When he looked back up, startled by his own fierce reaction to what was, after all, just a neck, she handed him another piece of paper. "My blackmailing letter," she said, rising from her chair. "May I give you a touch more brandy, Your Grace?"

"Why are you suddenly 'your gracing' me?" he asked irritably. "You called me Cam a moment ago."

She poured a little golden liquid, just a drop or so, into her own glass. Then she turned around and reached for his glass. He waited, eyebrow cocked.

"I am annoyed with you," she said composedly. "I daresay it is a feeling that your near acquaintances suffer from daily, and so I shall not make more of it than that."

Cam almost apologized but caught himself. He *never* apologized. The most useful thing his father ever taught him was never to admit guilt.

"You're likely right about my annoying my acquaintances," he said. "I'm afraid that Marissa complains quite loudly sometimes."

"I'm certain that she does," Gina said, just a trace of sympathy in her tone.

He waited, but that was all she said.

"Don't you wish to know who Marissa is?" he demanded, finally.

"I expect she is the buxom young lady who has served as a model for your goddesses," she replied, handing him a hearty dose of brandy and sitting down. She stretched her pale yellow slippers toward the fire and wiggled her toes comfortably. "She must be a close friend of yours."

He felt a shock of disbelief that stretched to his fingertips. "Don't you give a damn whether Marissa is my mistress or not?" he growled.

Gina considered. "No. As your wife, I should greatly dislike it if you fashioned my naked body into a hat rack. But if Marissa does not mind being shaped into a useful occupant of the cloakroom, who am I to object?"

"Damn it! Not all my sculptures are used to display hats!" Cam roared. "Only one of my statues does that duty."

A small smile curled at the edges of Gina's mouth. "I fear that your hat stand has achieved a level of notoriety in London

165

that none of your previous works—at least those to reach this shore—has done."

"I never should have sold the piece to Sladdington. Proserpina wasn't meant to be a hat rack, you know. If you look under all the hats, she is holding flowers. I should never have let a bumbler like Sladdington buy her. But it never occurred to me that he would transform her into a hat rack."

Gina looked at him sympathetically. "It—she—looks quite comfortable in his front hall."

"You've seen her? Damn it, she's *naked,* Gina! What were you doing in Sladdington's house anyway?"

"I wished to see my husband's triumphant piece of art. I must have heard about it from a hundred people. I believe Sladdington traveled to Greece solely to obtain one of your statues, and it certainly has raised his consequence."

"Bastard," Cam said. "What's he doing exposing young women to naked statues, anyway?"

"Oh, you don't have to worry about that. She's not naked," Gina corrected him.

"She's *not?*"

Gina shook her head. "He's wrapped something about her waist."

Cam was silent, appalled. "He's given Proserpina a nappy?"

"Not a nappy. More a—a—" She stopped, clearly at a loss for words.

"That's perfect," Cam said gloomily. "I'm known in London as the sculptor of Proserpina in a diaper."

Gina barely stifled a yawn. "I'm sorry," she apologized.

"Might the Marquess be miffed?" Cam read aloud. *"The Duchess has a Brother.* What the devil is this?"

"The blackmailing letter. It was sent to my mother, at her house in London."

"Very odd," Cam said, frowning. "This letter is nothing like the first."

"I never saw that one."

"When I wouldn't believe the letter existed, Father had to show it to me. I can't remember exactly, but I think the handwriting was different. And it was in French."

"But it must be from the same person," Gina objected. "How many blackmailers are there who know this particular piece of information?"

Cam shrugged. "Could be many, by this time. Who have you told about your real mother?"

"Only my closest friends."

"Well, that was damn stupid if you wanted to keep your birth a secret!"

"I prefer not to be called stupid," Gina remarked. She tossed off the few drops remaining in her glass and stood up. "This has been an absolutely charming interlude, but I am growing weary."

Cam looked up at her from under heavy-lidded eyes. "No need to take a snit."

"Your comment is preposterous. No matter how many people I told about Countess Ligny, none of them had any idea that I have a sibling."

"If you do have a brother. The phrasing is extremely odd. Don't you think so?"

"I thought it was rather amusing."

"That's what I mean. *Might the Marquess be miffed?* The first letter was awkwardly phrased. I remember that my father came to the conclusion that a servant in the countess's household was responsible. No person who writes uncomfortably in his native tongue could turn out a pertly alliterative question in English."

Gina leaned against the fireplace. Cam pretended to study the letter while he watched the line of her thighs. She had the

167

prettiest legs he'd ever seen. She was fine-boned and slender, from the tips of her elegant fingers to the tips of her slim feet.

He didn't want to leave. So he kept pretending to look at the paper in his hand and, at the same time, reflecting on how much he would like to have those legs wrapped around his waist.

After a while she cleared her throat.

He looked up.

Their eyes met: green, mocking female eyes and darkly lustful male ones.

"See anything you like?" she asked, gently.

He stood up and took one step forward.

Chapter Sixteen

The Bedchamber of a Spurned Woman

Carola Perwinkle was not resting peacefully. She was reclining on her bed, to be sure. But she was clenching her teeth and quivering with rage. Her husband—her despicable, dislikable devil of a husband—had not only ignored her, he had not only forgotten to say hello or goodbye to her, he had committed the cardinal sin.

"Fiend!" she whispered to herself, under her breath in case her maid heard from the other side of the room. "Satan! Devil!"

She lapsed into silence, staring at the gathered silk canopy that topped her bed. There was a light knock on the door. Her maid bustled over to answer it, standing in such a way as to shield her mistress from the open door. But Carola recognized the voice and sat upright. "Please, do come in," she called.

"Good evening," Esme said, strolling into the room. "I saw a light under your door, so I thought I would check on our little project before going to sleep."

"It's no use." Carola looked at her in anguish. "Tuppy has fallen in love."

"Really? With whom?" She looked interested but unworried.

"Gina!"

Esme snorted. "He'll find no success there."

"Of course he won't!" Carola snapped. "No one but me would want him, that disgusting, depraved reprobate." Then her face crumpled again. "It's because I'm so stupid. He's not even interested in me because I don't know anything about trout."

"About trout," Esme repeated, rather stunned.

"I read a book about newts because he used to talk about them." She pointed to it on the table. "*Cooke's Guide to Newts, Frogs and Lizards*. He didn't even mention newts. Instead, Gina started discussing the life cycle of the trout—did you know that she had spent the last few years restocking the trout streams at Girton?"

"The subject has never come up."

"Well, she has. Apparently the fish died because of mining runoff or something. If I was dramatic-looking, *and* I knew about trout, I might have a chance," Carola wailed. "I was ready to talk about newts. But he didn't even mention lizards!"

"You're not being fair to yourself. You have beautiful, creamy skin. And lovely curls." Esme wound a soft lock of hair around her finger. "Look at this! You're a hairdresser's dream. Gina would love to have short hair. You look like a cherub."

"It doesn't matter," she said morosely. "He doesn't even notice me. After Gina left all he could talk about was how intelligent she was. I'm boring! I'm wallpaper."

Tears started to well in her eyes. "I walked all the way across that room just to speak to him. Just so that I could listen to his tiresome stories about newts! And what does he do? Lust after my friend! *Fiend!*" she repeated furiously.

"They're all fiends."

Tears snaked down Carola's face. "But I love him! He's a boring, fiendish—"

"—newt-discussing," Esme interjected.

170

"—newt-discussing man, but he's mine. And I want him back!"

"Then you must attend meals. Lady Troubridge shuffled the seating, and I sat across from the poor man. An empty seat next to him will not increase his affection."

"I tried to have a conversation in the salon. But all he could talk about was how interesting Gina was because she knows about trout ponds, and I ended up slapping him!"

"I've been wondering . . . so why did you slap him?"

Her jaw set. "He insulted me."

"What did he say?"

"First he talked about Gina. And then, as if that wasn't insult enough, he made a horrible remark."

"What was it?"

"He asked me if I had cut my hair. I said yes, and he said that Gina's hair was one of the most beautiful things about her."

Esme frowned. "That was certainly inconsiderate."

"Then he asked me whether I had gained weight."

"You haven't gained any weight, have you?"

"I don't think so. But he was looking at my bosom. Now I think about it, it's your fault. Because you told me to wear the crimson gown, and obviously it exposed too much of my f-f-fat!" Tears poured down her face.

"He looked at your chest, did he? And then asked whether you'd gained weight?"

"Yes," Carola choked. "I said no, I hadn't gained any weight. And he said that it must be that I was changing my shape as I grew older!"

Esme took a deep breath. "You behaved correctly, Carola. The man deserved to be slapped."

"I should have kicked him. I should have slapped him and then kicked him!"

"I wonder what he was thinking." Esme's eyes narrowed into thoughtful chips. "It's out of character for Tuppy to be so rude."

"He probably just blurted out the truth. I am getting old. And dried up like a prune. And fat too."

"That's enough! Those things he said are nonsense. You're no prune. You're like a luscious plum, all sweet and curly." Esme pulled out one of Carola's curls and let it go again. "I wish I had your lovely hair."

"I would rather look like you. You stand a good head taller than I do, and it makes you look so elegant. I look like a dumpling. I think I'd better give up hope. He obviously doesn't give a rat's ass for me."

"Carola Perwinkle!" Esme said, grinning.

"A rat's ass," she repeated firmly.

"In fact, I think we're making progress. Tomorrow I want you to flirt with another man while wearing an even lower bodice, if you have one. And be sure to stand directly in front of Tuppy."

"I don't want to," Carola said. "I'm not very good at flirting."

"Of course you are good at flirting. It's an innate female trait. Who would you like to flirt with?"

"No one." Then she brightened up. "Perhaps Gina's husband. He's rather handsome, don't you think?"

"I suppose. He has a nice laugh."

"Oh, Esme," Carola said with disgust. "I don't know how you got that reputation! You don't seem to notice a thing about a man except the width of his arms."

"I have found a man's arms to be prophetic of the rest of him," Esme said with a wicked twinkle. "Would you like me to lend you Bernie? He responds to flirtation about as well as a piece of firewood, but he is a sweetheart, and you can depend on him not to take you too seriously."

172

"Isn't he yours?"

"At the moment, Bernie thinks quite correctly that he is far too foolish for me to consider as a sexual partner." Esme paused. "That is, if he thinks at all. Bernie is definitely limited in his mental abilities."

"I'll flirt with Neville. After all, he already knows about the plot. I'll send him a note directly, and we can begin at breakfast." Carola looked marginally more cheerful.

Esme kissed her cheek. "Mmm, you smell like peaches." She walked to the door.

"Thank you!"

"My pleasure," she called back, and stepped into the hall.

She bumped directly into a large male body.

"Excuse me," came a steely voice just over her head.

Esme steadied herself against the wall. Then she pushed herself upright and dropped a slight curtsy. "There's no need to apologize, my lord. I should have paid attention to where I was going." Finally she couldn't put it off any longer and looked up.

Why did he have to have such beautiful eyes? They were cobalt blue. Too beautiful for a man.

"Whose room is that?" he snarled. "Was it a *great* pleasure?"

Esme had an icy stare that had held her in good stead over the years. "A *great, great* pleasure." She let a little kindness leak into her tone. "I only wish that you might experience such happiness some day." She started to edge around his large body.

But he put an arm out to stop her passage.

"Lord Bonnington?" She had perfected the art of the withering glance and she gave him the full treatment.

But Sebastian had never shown the slightest sign of being cowed by her, and he didn't now.

"You should stop visiting men's rooms. What if someone other than myself had caught you emerging from a man's bedchamber? Your reputation is already hanging by a thread."

Fury was building in the back of her throat. But it was against her code of ethics to betray anger—or any other genuine feeling—to a man. So she fluttered her eyelashes instead. "A man or a woman?" she cooed.

"What?"

"Am I discovered by a man or a woman?"

He visibly ground his teeth. "A man!"

She looked at him for a moment, counting silently to forty. Then she rearranged her low bodice with an easy, lazy movement of her shoulders so that it slid even lower, just barely covering the tips of her breasts.

"You needn't bother to answer," Sebastian said, his voice grating. "I gather you would buy your way out of trouble. A lucky gentleman indeed."

She gave him a seductive smile. "I always pay my debts." Her stomach was seething but not a flicker of anger crossed her face. She gave him a slow smile and was trying to think of another provocative comment when he reached his hand out and touched her face, just for a moment.

"Don't."

There was a stark moment of silence in the corridor.

"Don't what?"

"Don't *do* that. It's not necessary."

The sexy air fell away from her like a heavy cloak. "You've made your feelings perfectly clear, my lord. You need not fear that I will try to seduce you."

Damn those blue eyes. They were pleading with her now, trying to take away her anger.

And then he reached out, grabbed her shoulders, and slowly, slowly drew her toward him. He looked in her eyes

174

the whole time. And she went. Heaven help her, she drifted toward him like a rabbit in the glare of a snake.

His mouth was gentle but her mouth opened, and then their tongues met, and then his mouth wasn't so gentle anymore. And it wasn't until some time later that Esme felt his hands on her breasts, and realized that she had just moaned into his mouth and that she was shaking—

Finally her common sense reasserted itself. She pulled back so sharply that her head rapped against the wall. "If you will excuse me."

Something faded from his eyes and they were just blue again. "I should apologize."

She paused.

"For detaining you," he finished.

A fillip of rage replaced the pounding in her heart. "May I take it that you consider my debt canceled, my lord?"

She made a deep curtsy, making certain that her breasts were entirely visible as she swept down. Only she knew how much her knees were trembling. She could only hope she was smiling. It seemed to be hard to control her mouth.

"Please, *don't*." His voice was unsteady and low, and their eyes met.

There was that strange feeling again, as if all the sound in the world had been swallowed up.

"I must go," Esme said, not at all seductively. And she pushed past him without another glance and ran down the corridor.

Chapter Seventeen

In Which Desire Comes to the Forefront

Her throat was dry. She curled her fingers around the belled shape of her empty brandy glass.

"As it happens," said her husband, "I do see something that I like. Very much."

The fire crackled behind them, and he stepped closer, so he was standing just before her.

"May I take it?"

For a moment she didn't understand his question. He wore no scent, just a smell of himself, an open-air, woodsy smell with a touch of chalk.

"Why do you smell like chalk?" she asked, stalling for time.

"Before I start a sculpture, I work on paper."

"So you've been sketching goddesses," Gina said, desperately trying not to think about his question. "Does Esme—"

But he took the words from her mouth and kissed her, his mouth sweet against her lips. Large hands gently uncurled her fingers from the brandy glass. She relaxed into his arms thinking: *Yes, take what you want.* But she didn't say it out loud. It would be too easy to add: *Please, please, please.*

He seemed to have forgotten the question altogether. He was running his fingers through the long strands of her hair, brushing his lips gently across hers. "You have lovely hair," he whispered. "It shines in the firelight like fire itself."

"Very poetic," she said, trying to lean closer against his body.

He kissed her again, his lips soft and coaxing.

"I didn't sketch a goddess. I found myself sketching you," he remarked, with just a shade of surprise in his voice.

"Well, I'm no goddess," Gina admitted. That truth took a bit of the enjoyment out of her.

"You're better," he said, rather thickly. Enjoyment flowed right back into the pit of her stomach. He was kissing her neck as worshipfully as if she were a goddess.

But it wasn't what she wanted. It wasn't—*wasn't* the same. So she took her arms from where they were docilely slung around his neck and let them slide down his back.

He was delicately kissing the side of her cheek. He started kissing her ear.

She trembled, spreading her fingers against the lean muscles of his back. Then she pulled, sharply, snapping his body against hers.

He was muscled, Cam was. She could feel muscles all over his back, through the thin linen of his shirt. The feeling made her heart pound in her chest, and made her press closer and closer to his body.

"If you won't take it," she said huskily, *"I will."* She twisted her head to capture his mouth and licked his lips so that he had to open them and kiss her, kiss her the way he had yesterday. He tasted dark and delicious and like Cam.

Finally his mouth lunged against hers. He licked her lips, great stroking, predatory kisses that made heat surge through her legs. It was a kiss that let time pass, a lazy, impassioned, heartbreaking kiss.

His hands slid over her breasts. She cried out, soundlessly, against his mouth and arched into his hands. But he couldn't get any closer.

"Cam!" she choked. She opened her eyes and saw him looking down at her, laughing eyes looking as depraved as ever.

"Were you wishing to experiment, lady wife?" he whispered.

His hair was standing on end, dark eyes, dark lashes that made her feel dizzy with desire. She nodded, hearing the ocean pound in her ears.

But he waited, eyebrow raised. His hand kept up a lazy sweep over her breast until she pulled him to her again. She held him as tightly as she could. It couldn't be called a caress since she had the grasp of a drowning woman.

"Damn you," she whispered, "kiss me."

"The duchess is swearing," laughed the duke. His eyes searched hers. "Kisses only?" Why did his voice sound so calm when hers was raw with desire?

She nodded.

He swept an arm under her legs and cradled her against his chest. Then he took her to the bed and yanked at her bodice. It came down, and his mouth closed on her breast. Gina cried out loud.

She couldn't seem to stop herself. Every time, every single time he suckled at her breast, she cried out again and arched up against the weight of his knee as it parted her legs.

He wrenched at her gown and it ripped neatly down the seam between lace and silk.

Then he bent his head again, and she sank her fingers into that wild black hair and writhed under him, clutching at his shoulders.

Suddenly he moved and lay on top of her, with only the cloth of his pantaloons and the frail silk of her ruined gown between them, and rocked downward hard. Without conscious thought she pushed back, rubbing against his hips.

He made a hoarse sound and opened his mouth over hers, great throbbing, tormenting kisses. She closed her eyes and begged silently. Begged that he would know what she wanted without her having to say something so humiliating.

He stopped. Took his hands away.

"No," she gasped.

She closed her eyes tight against what she saw on his face.

"Gina."

She pretended not to hear.

"Gina. We have to stop now." His voice was far too controlled.

"No!" she said sharply.

He laughed, and she opened her eyes.

"How can you laugh?" she demanded.

"Not for want of desire, if that's what you're asking." Even a novice could hear the rasp in his voice. He pulled away and sat on the edge of the bed.

Every inch of her body was quivering with pleasure and frustration and desire, all mixed together. She glanced down at the rip in her nightrail. Yellow silk was pushed to the side and a round, plump breast with a pale pink nipple lay open to the air, rising and falling with her breath. It was beautiful; it looked different, felt different, than an hour ago.

She looked up to meet her husband's eyes. A moment later a dark hand curved around the firm weight of her breast.

She sighed and arched her back, just a little, so she plumped into his hand.

"Damn it, Gina," he said, his voice strangled in his throat. "You're driving me insane—" And he bent his head.

It seemed to be some kind of involuntary reaction, she thought shakily, hearing her own cry echo a second later. He kissed her and she . . . again. And again.

179

He had both breasts now, and she twisted up against his hands, his mouth; soft hair brushed her skin and he suckled hard, harder. Cries flew from her lips until a large hand covered her mouth. She bit it.

He rolled away, breathing hard. Gina followed him, enjoying the way her ravished nightrail fell in shreds over her creamy skin.

She came up on her knees before him. "Men have nipples too, don't they?"

He seemed to be trying to catch his breath, so she pulled up his shirt. He did have nipples, beautiful and flat, like ha'penny pieces on his muscled chest. She ran a finger experimentally around one and he shivered, as if she'd touched the surface of a lake.

"If I kiss you there, will *you* moan?"

"Absolutely not," Cam said, staring at the ceiling. She guessed he was trying to ignore her until he got control of his breathing.

So she dipped her head and continued on her experimental way.

Somewhat to her disappointment, he didn't make a sound. But his body quivered and one hand came up to her shoulder, slipped under the ruined lace and ran a delicate caress over her naked skin. She could hear the air shudder in his chest. It was sound enough.

She came up for air and he pushed her away. His breathing was wild and his eyes were wilder.

"Damn it, Gina!"

"The duke is swearing!" she mocked. "Call out the army! Summon the militia!"

He rolled his eyes at her. "Be still."

She bent over, green eyes alight with mischief, cradled his face in her hands, and pursed her lips into an exaggerated kiss. "Mayn't a wife kiss her husband?"

180

Her lips were full, cherry red, swollen, luscious.

Cam could feel a headache coming on.

"We have to stop this nonsense," he said woodenly. "Enough. Another few moments and your marquess will find himself cheated."

"He would be cheated if I lost my virginity," Gina said. "But we're nowhere near that point."

"So you think!" he snapped.

White arms entwined his neck. The thought made him shudder. If he didn't get himself out of his chamber, he'd make Gina his. No question about that. Except that she had her pompous marquess.

A sweet, warm voice breathed into his neck. "Thank you, Cam. I . . . found it very enjoyable."

He grabbed her arms and pulled them off his neck. "I agree. Very enjoyable." He stood up and moved away. But when he met her eyes he couldn't keep up his bad humor.

She was laughing. "I can't tell you what pleasure it gives me to realize that I, plain old Ambrogina, have driven a man to the edge of despair."

"I wouldn't call it the edge of despair," he replied rather stuffily.

She grinned. "That's how Esme describes it."

"Well, she might not be so far off," Cam admitted. Just watching Gina sit on the bed was enough to drive him to despair.

Even as he watched she swung her long, slender legs from the bed and pulled on her robe. He could still see one beautiful breast peeking out. Then she pranced over to him like some sort of exuberant femme fatale.

"You're not supposed to be so triumphant about it," he muttered.

"I didn't think I had the ability to drive a man—"

"—to the edge of despair," Cam filled in.

A smile trembled at the corner of her mouth, but her eyes were serious. "Sometimes I feel as if I grew old without ever being young."

"Old! You're what? Twenty-two?"

"Twenty-three. That's old to be getting married for the first time, Cam."

"Not in the real world. In Greece, most women marry in their twenties."

"I don't know the real world. I only know this world, and I've heard many young women called dried-up old maids, who were my age or only slightly older. I thought perhaps . . ." Her voice trailed off.

"Are you trying to tell me that you feel *dried up*?" His voice was ripe with disbelief.

"Not—it's just—" She fidgeted with the tie to her robe, and finally looked back at him. "Because I'm married, I have heard many conversations about bedroom matters."

"I can guess. Women talking about what they enjoy in bed."

She looked faintly surprised. "Actually, they mostly talk about what men enjoy. But I didn't have—" She started again. "It's obvious that men like very young women. You see it everywhere. Wives and their husbands rarely sleep together, and husbands have young mistresses. Not my age: younger."

"Those men aren't married to you." He let his hands slide through the silk of her hair, down the curves of her shoulders, brush her breasts, curl over the sweet curve of her bottom. "If a man was married to you, he would never want anyone else. Not younger, or older."

"You don't think I'm too old?" Her eyes met his, and he was startled by the anxiety in them.

182

"Too old for *sex*? Are you addled, Gina? Your husband will probably be dragging you over to the bed when you're both eighty-five and barely moving." He risked looking down at her body, only to find that her robe had opened again, thanks to her fumbling with the tie.

He slid a rough thumb over one rose-colored nipple and a little sound escaped her, a little puffing moan. He did it again. She squeaked again.

"Gina, if I touch you there"—he did it—"what does it feel like?"

She gasped.

"What does it feel like?" he persisted.

"Quite lovely," she whispered, so quietly he barely heard it.

He curved one arm around her back. She had turned a little pink and looked confused. Then, without warning, he sucked one of those luscious nipples into his mouth. After all, they were just sitting there, begging to be kissed.

She screamed, her knees buckled, and he barely managed to catch her weight in his arm.

"You're a shrieker," he said with satisfaction. "In fact, I would say without hesitation that you are one of the most sensual women I've ever had the pleasure to kiss." *If not the most,* he silently acknowledged.

She looked at him, green eyes lustful and embarrassed all at once. He smiled and decided to embarrass her some more. He tightened his left arm around her waist. "Dried up?" he said softly, into her ear. He let his right hand slip down the silky front of her gown. Suddenly his hand curved over the sweetest mound he'd ever felt. Even through silk he could feel heat. She quivered all over. "If you were any more responsive," Cam said hoarsely, "a man would never let you leave your bedchamber."

He couldn't stop himself and pulled her against him, hard. His tongue slipped inside her mouth, and his body strained against hers. He pushed her back on the bed, and she went willingly, clinging to him. He spread the rip on her gown open wide so her whole delectable body lay there. He bent to kiss her and his hand drifted down . . . down.

She leaped against him when he touched her. Oh God, she was soft. Sweet. His mind went black with desire and he turned and took her mouth, plunging with his tongue while he longed to do the same with his body. Her eyes were shut and she was clutching his shoulders, gasping things he couldn't understand. But he didn't care.

He moved from her mouth to her breast and she twisted up against his body and screamed, a gasping little scream. And now he had her luscious body where he wanted it, his hand in her softness, sleek now, wet now, plump, throbbing around his fingers. When he lifted his mouth from her nipple she began to pull away, gasping "No," and other foolish things. So he simply put his lips back and suckled. Small cries flew from her mouth, and there was no resistance, just that gorgeous body laid out for him, all sweet cream and silky skin, a tuft of hair between her legs like pale port wine.

To kiss her there . . . He raised his head. Instantly she clutched his arm and said, hoarsely, "Cam! You must stop—"

"Hush," he said. "Hush." His lips roved over her breast, shaped her, created that breast into something far more beautiful than mere marble.

She was panting, her eyes blurred, a smoky green. He let his hand take on a rhythmical cadence he knew as well as he knew his name.

"Oh, Cam," she panted. Her body moved up against his fingers.

He longed to roll over on her, to do the thing as it ought to be done. My wife, he thought dimly. She's *mine*. Take her, pounded his loins. Take her, urged his heart. It was only a growling voice in his head or wherever conscience was located that said: She doesn't want you. She wants the petulant marquess.

He pushed the voice away and slung a leg over her slight form. She was innocent, he could tell that. Unknowing and yet . . . knowing. She bucked against his leg, arched up against his urging fingers. Sobbed into his shoulder, clutched him, begged, "Please, Cam . . . please . . . *please.*"

It would be forcing her to marry you, growled the voice in his head. It was a voice distilled from hatred of his father, hatred of his own forced marriage. It chilled him just slightly, gave him control enough to shift away from tempting proximity.

He dipped his mouth and kissed her, ravished her sweetness while his fingers took a practiced turn that she had no power to resist. He kissed her once, kissed her twice. His fingers urged her on, a cadence beating through his loins and only barely held in check.

Then he rubbed a thumb over her nipple and . . . like that, as easily as that, his sometime wife, his own Gina, arched up against him in a great shaking surge.

She was a shrieker, all right.

She shook like a new-fallen leaf against his hand. He gritted his teeth together against the urge to enter, to feel the last clench of her body, to replace emptiness with himself, warm, throbbing—

He pulled away.

Gina opened her eyes but she didn't really feel like waking up, so she let them drift shut again. Her whole body was glowing, pleasure heavy in her legs.

But Cam was muttering. "I must go, Gina. This is not a good idea." His voice was thick. She opened her eyes again. He ran a hand through his hair. It looked as if it had been raked in four or five different directions.

185

Of course it wasn't a good idea. She was engaged to someone else, and he was Cam, her childhood friend. She tried to pull herself together but she was caught by a wave of limp satisfaction.

"I won't visit your room again," Cam was saying. "So there'll be no repeat of this . . . this incident. I—"

"Don't apologize," she murmured.

He looked surprised. "I hadn't thought of it. Ought I to?"

At that, Gina smiled. "Men have apologized after a single kiss. Whereas you—"

He grinned. "Ah, but we're married."

"For the moment."

"The moment is all that's necessary. And we didn't do much more than kiss anyway."

Much more than kiss? Her legs were throbbing, and her breath was still racing, and he called that *kissing*?

He started to stuff his shirt back into his trousers. "I'd better get out of here," he remarked. "Be damned awkward for our annulment if someone caught me in your room."

Gina was definitely coming back to herself now. She pulled her robe closed. It took a moment for the truth to sink in: she was still annullable, to his mind. Staying married wasn't in his consideration.

A moment later he looked just as neat as he had when entering her chamber. She felt a spurt of pure rage. How could he look so untouched?

"But I should thank you," she said, reaching out and catching his arm as he started for the door. "You were very reassuring."

He instantly took on a cocky, smug air.

"I'm so pleased that I was able to explore this problem with you rather than with Sebastian," she cooed. "Now I shall go to his bed with a newfound sense of confidence."

He stilled and looked at her for a moment. Then he bowed. "I am, of course, glad to be of use," he said. And left.

Gina spent the rest of the night thinking of far more clever exit lines. By the time dawn crept through the windows, she knew exactly what she should have said, if she had any brains at all.

Actually there were two options.

Option number one would have been delivered with scalding effectiveness: *I am particularly grateful to know that I will go to my beloved Sebastian's bed with an enthusiasm to match his.*

Option number one sounded as if Sebastian lusted for her. Never mind the truth of that.

Then there was option number two. It varied throughout the night, and was punctuated by the riveting memories. It ran something like this: *I'd like you to come back to bed now.*

Sometimes she added *please*.

And sometimes she let her ruined gown fall off her body as she said it.

Chapter Eighteen

Houseguests Need Not Rise Before Noon

Gina woke very late, with a calm sense of returning to herself. Gone was the flushed, exultant woman of the previous evening. Which was just as well, she told herself, because it was important to keep these experiences in their place. It had been deliciously enjoyable. She should thank her husband for it. Really. Because now she didn't have to feel nervous about her wedding night—her real wedding night, with Sebastian. She had experience, finally. Some experience.

In the morning's crueler light she looked unkempt rather than seductive in her ruined nightdress. She bundled it away and pulled on a chemise. Still . . . A secret, luxurious smile curved her lips. It wasn't the memory of her pleasure that pleased.

It was the memory of Cam's wild eyes and the way the breath pounded in his chest. It had done miracles to dispel her secret fear that her fiancé didn't respond to her because she was too old. Too stiff, too duchesslike, too thin. Cam didn't seem to think she was too thin. True, he still wanted an annulment. But that was due to his basic nature, she decided. He would always avoid the kinds of responsibility that go with having a wife. The important point was that he had wanted her last night, and now she knew how to make Sebastian want her too.

Annie popped into the room. "There's plans for the afternoon," she said, sometime later, her fingers briskly weaving

Gina's hair into a long braid. "The ladies are invited to practice archery on the west lawn. The Chaplins are going to give
a fencing exhibition at three o'clock. Oh! And Lady
Troubridge asked whether you would like to join her. She is
going to visit the village in the pony cart, because there's a
new baby."

"I'd love to go see the baby," Gina said. But the mass of
papers, still untidily stacked on the footstool, caught her eye.
"I have too much work to do."

"You work too hard, you do," Annie said. "All this work
isn't good for a soul."

"Ah, but those letters must be answered."

"Would you like to wear the morning dress with half
sleeves today, madam?" Annie knew a losing argument when
she started one.

When Gina slipped into the drawing room, she barely had
time to greet Sebastian before Lady Troubridge clapped her
hands and they all filed into luncheon. Soup was already
served by the time Cam strolled in. His hair looked almost
composed. But there was a streak of white chalk on his shoulder. She looked away. It was nothing to her that Cam headed
toward Esme like a bee toward a rose.

"Sebastian!" she said, inspired. "I must find a quiet corner
in the library and write some letters for a few hours. But will
you join me in the latter half of the afternoon?"

He bowed his head. "I would be most honored." He
escorted her back to her chamber and was just bowing goodbye when Gina pushed open the door and gasped.

The room was a mess. There were clothes all over the floor
and books heaped higgledy-piggledy, wherever she looked.
The doors to her wardrobe swung open, and the drawer to
her dressing table hung from one corner, the bright ribbons
that Annie used in her hair spilling to the ground.

A look of acute annoyance crossed Sebastian's face. "It would seem that someone has robbed your chamber. Was your jewelry accessible?"

"No. Lady Troubridge insisted that all jewelry be kept in her safe. Annie has been taking it back every night."

"A wise precaution," he observed. "I doubt they got much then." He strode through the room, the breeze of his passing making piles of soft chiffon on the ground stir and billow, and looked down at her dressing table with disgust. "They rifled your table, hoping you'd left something. Bold devils coming during the day. They might easily have been caught by a maid." He picked up a tipped glass and set it back on the dressing table with a small rap. Water dripped slowly over the side of the table onto a pile of frills and ribbons.

Gina moved slowly into the room. Her mirror had been taken down and was leaning against the wall. Her bed was stripped, the covers thrown on the floor. "I've never been robbed before," she said, with just the smallest shake in her voice.

"You have not been robbed now," Sebastian replied. "Since there was nothing to steal, you've merely been inconvenienced. You're not feeling hysterical, are you?" She shook her head. "Your maid will straighten your room. I wonder if they tossed more than one room? There's no particular reason they should target yours, after all." He turned. "I had better leave. I wouldn't like to be seen in your chamber."

"I hardly think that anyone would believe that you ripped the covers off the bed in a moment of passion, Sebastian."

His eyes narrowed.

"It was a jest!" she protested. Then she aimlessly bent down and picked up two corsets. "This is rather unpleasant. Have you been robbed before?"

190

"Several times. In fact, robbery during house parties has become endemic. My room was searched only last year at Foakes Manor, and a pair of cufflinks was taken."

"Did they turn out your undergarments . . . everything?"

Sebastian looked at the delicate twist of cotton and ribbon in her hand and quickly looked away again. "They were looking for your jewels. It's quite common to hide precious objects among one's intimate clothing. I shall inform Lady Troubridge of this incident. She will likely wish to question the servants." And he disappeared.

Gina looked around. Bicksfiddle's stack of paper had been tossed this way and that. She picked up a silk stocking from the ground but couldn't see its mate. Finally she sat down on the naked mattress to wait for Annie, looking at the ground rather than looking around the room at her crumpled belongings. No matter what Sebastian said about inconvenience, it felt a great deal worse to her.

"Hell and damnation!"

He was standing in the doorway looking huge and male and utterly outraged. She sniffed. Tears welled up in her eyes. "I've been inconvenienced."

Cam took one quick look at her, swore again, and strode over. Then he picked her up in one swift, economical movement, sat down, and plopped her onto his lap.

Too surprised to protest, Gina leaned her head against his chest and listened to him swear a blue streak.

Finally he wound down. "Did they take anything?"

She shook her head, but elevated the little pile of corsets she held. "Look!"

"Despicable bastards," he snarled.

Her chin started to wobble. "I don't think I ever want to wear them again."

"Bastards!" he growled. "I should shoot them just for that."

Gina let a few tears soak into his black coat.

He stroked her up and down her arm in a comforting kind of way and handed her a large white handkerchief.

Lady Troubridge herself rushed in the door. "Oh dear, oh dear!" she shrieked. "I simply loathe thieves, loathe them! Are you quite all right, my dear?"

Gina knew that she should leap from her husband's knee. But his arms were large and tight around her, and she didn't move.

"Her Grace is, of course, distressed," Cam said. He stood up. "I shall escort her to the library while the room is put to rights."

"An excellent idea," Lady Troubridge said, with a speculative gleam in her eyes.

He walked from the room without another word. Out in the corridor she began to struggle. "Put me down, Cam. I don't wish to fall!"

"You won't fall."

"I am too large to be carried all the way downstairs. You must put me down—I mean, please, put me down."

"I shall not. I enjoy carrying you." And he gave her a little squeeze.

"Cam!"

"Mmm," he said. "There's something to be said for carrying women about. It gives one such good access." He looked at her with an amused twinkle and his hands—

"Cam!" She almost jumped out of her skin.

"That's better. You don't look quite so much like a scared rabbit."

"I don't!"

"Red eyes and all," he nodded. He kept walking.

"Please may I walk downstairs?" Gina pleaded. "This is embarrassing."

"Who's embarrassed?" He inched his right hand forward and let out his breath in a big whoosh. They had reached the landing when he said, "you may be right," and set her down. Gina looked up at him. It wasn't that she *wanted* to be carried, of course.

"I might become embarrassed," he said, looking her straight in the eye.

But Gina saw a suggestive glint in his eye and looked down. It was a split-second glance, but enough. "Dear me," she said. "That's quite a problem."

He took a quick look around. They were at the turn of the landing, and there was no one in sight. He put his arms around her, running his hands down her back and the delicious curve of her bottom. "It was an act of charity," he said soulfully. "I had to take your mind off your loss."

Her eyes narrowed. "What loss?"

"How soon you forgot! Remember those corsets? I was just anticipating how you were going to look with nothing under your gown but your own sweet skin."

"Why—"

He took the words from her mouth with his lips. "Why, without a corset, you will be—" but he lost track of what he was saying because her lips were warm on his, and his hands had jerked her against his embarrassing body.

And then he did exactly what he spent the entire night planning: he put a hand on her breast, and even through three or four layers of cloth, she arched her back into his hand and opened her lips—he barely caught her squeal.

"I thought I imagined that," he said with satisfaction, looking down at his wife. She was looking at him, lips open and eyes dazed. "But I didn't." His hand tightened and he caught her cry in a kiss again.

"You will never be able to make love outdoors," he whispered into her ear. He was getting a little worried that someone would come up the stairs, so he pushed her back and tugged at her dress. "There! You look just the same."

"What are you talking about?"

But before he could answer, she answered herself. "Heathen! I'll have you know that Englishmen don't ever do—*that*!"

He laughed. "I'm willing to believe that some of them never do that, or did you mean that they never do it outdoors?"

Gina turned to look at him as she descended the stairs. He was struck with an irresistible urge to dishevel her hair. She was such a duchess, with her proud gait and calm way of talking.

"If I were married to you—" he said.

"You *are*," she put in.

"You know what I mean. Someday when I am truly married and living at Girton, I will take my wife out to the bluebell wood. Being the heathen that I am."

They had reached the hallway. Cam self-consciously adjusted his jacket. He needed to stop this conversation or risk social humiliation. He glanced over at Gina and made a quick decision to go for a walk outdoors. She had her brows knit, and she looked as if she were musing over a particularly difficult problem.

"Don't you remember the bluebell wood?" he said into her ear.

"Of course I remember the wood!" she snapped. "You left me there in the middle of the night. How could I forget?"

"I'd forgotten that," Cam chuckled. "Stephen and I ran away, didn't we?"

"You told me there were ghouls in the woods first," Gina said indignantly.

"You were too good at fishing. We had to bring you to a sense of your place in the world. Besides, we rescued you after five minutes, didn't we?"

194

"Humph," Gina said and pushed open the drawing room door. She was met by a level of talk that rose like a storm of bees. Clearly the party had been informed of the indignity suffered by the duchess. Cam bowed and backed away. The all-male companionship of the stables sounded comforting at the moment.

Something about his wife was driving him insane. He gave a bark of rueful laughter. He'd been without a woman for too long, that was it. And since she was the only woman in the world he couldn't sleep with, given that the act would terminate their annulment proceedings, naturally he was being driven to distraction by temptation.

That explained it all.

He strode out to the stables. In the middle of the night it had occurred to him forcefully that the key point of an annulment was virginity.

There were many, many pauses on the way from virginity to the lack thereof. If his wife wanted to experiment with him before she hopped into bed with her stuffy marquess, who was he to complain?

He wandered to the stable door musing over a few questions he had for Lady Troubridge.

For example, was there a bluebell wood tucked away on the estate?

Chapter Nineteen

A Piscatory Discussion on the Riverbank

Neville was so critical that Carola wished she had chosen Esme's Bernie to flirt with instead. They hadn't yet made it down to the river, because he kept adjusting this or that about her apparel, and giving her more and more instructions about how to be flirtatious.

"Neville!" she finally cried in exasperation. "I assure you that Tuppy won't notice anything about my garments, not even if I appeared in sackcloth!"

"Don't underestimate yourself," he said, giving her a last critical glance. "No. That cloth must go." And with one swift lunge he plucked away the kerchief that had taken her maid at least a half hour to arrange.

Carola futilely grabbed at it. "This gown is far too low without that handkerchief! I can't be seen like this!"

"Of course you can. Now you look much more the thing," he said with satisfaction.

She looked down at her plump breasts with horror. "He already thinks I'm *fat,* Neville! Can't you understand that I have to cover up all this flesh? At this rate, he'll think that I've grown at least two sizes!"

"When did you marry the poor man?"

"Four years ago. Why do you ask?"

"I believe that your chest has grown in the interim. It certainly has since I first met you, darling green girl that you were."

Carola narrowed her eyes. "My clothing size is private information."

"Even if I promise not to hanker after your large and luscious bosom? I never allow myself to desire impossibilities. But I think it's quite likely that your poor besotted husband *is*."

"Besotted? Not likely!"

"Besotted," he returned. "I saw him looking at you, after you walloped him in the drawing room. He looked blue as one of those fish he loves so much. If I had any hope of catching you for myself, I gave it up that moment."

Carola slipped her arm through his and smiled. "Oh, Neville, you are the best friend a woman could have!"

"Don't smile at me that way or I'll change my mind about letting Tuppy have you," he said.

She squeezed his arm.

They were almost down to the river when he paused. She dragged him forward. "There he is. I recognize his back!"

"Just a moment, Carola."

She looked up at him.

"You need to think about *me*."

She nodded. "I am."

"No, really think about me." He tipped up her chin with a strong hand. She stood, brown eyes blinking innocently at him. "Damned if I don't envy Tuppy, fishmonger that he is," Neville muttered.

Then he lunged at her rosy mouth, ignoring the ineffectual way she batted at his chest.

"There!" he said a moment later. Her cheeks were pink and she looked thoroughly aroused. Which she was—by anger if not by lust.

"You! You!" she spluttered. "You must not behave in that outrageous fashion, Neville Charlton!"

197

"Next time someone grabs you, kick him in the ankle," he advised, turning her back to the river. "Now remember to look at *me,* Carola. Not the fishmonger."

"He's not a fishmonger!" Carola said, turning even pinker.

"Good afternoon!" Neville called. Two elderly gentlemen were sitting beside Tuppy and taking bait from a bored footman. The men stood up as they approached.

Carola was careful not to look at her husband, but she did notice that the only free chair was next to him. She started to move toward it when Neville preempted her.

He sat down and smiled provocatively at her. "I'll take you on my knee, my lady," he said with an unmistakable leer.

Carola's eyes widened. She'd never done such a fast thing in her life as to sit on a gentleman's knees. But here was Neville, stretching out his hands. The two old men had already gone back to talking about trout lures and were paying no attention. She walked over and delicately perched on the very end of his knee.

He made a production out of putting his arms around her and showing her how to handle the rod the footman handed him.

"Relax, you little idiot!" he breathed into her ear.

"I am!" she said indignantly. He put his hand over hers, and demonstrated the proper grip on a fishing rod.

"I've sent a servant to fetch a chair," came a stern voice at her right.

Carola finally looked at Tuppy. What she saw in his eyes stiffened her backbone. He looked scornful. In fact, she realized with horror that he probably thought that she was too plump to sit on a man's knees. He probably ordered the chair so as to save Neville from her weight.

Without further thought, she giggled softly and looked up at Neville. "I'm quite comfortable here, sir. Unless you foresee a problem?"

Neville had that leering glance down to a science, she thought. It was truly amazing the way his good-natured face turned so suggestive. He put his hand over hers again. "I would never dream of anything more delicious than you on my knees," he said soulfully.

It wasn't until he poked her in the side that she remembered her part. She cast Tuppy a glance under her eyelashes. He was looking rather grimly at the rod he held in his hand. Surely he had heard Neville's comment. "I could never deny you anything that you desire," she said in a clear voice, remembering at the last moment to smile intimately at her fishing partner.

"Pretty good," Neville breathed in her left ear.

He glanced at Carola's husband. Tuppy was glaring at the two of them. So Neville took a long and deliberate look straight down Carola's gown. She did have luscious breasts, damn it. He moved uncomfortably. It was all in the name of friendship, of course.

"Lean back against me," he whispered to Carola.

Of course that brought her breasts right under his nose. He risked another look at Tuppy. Unless he was much mistaken, the man was planning a massacre. And he, Neville, would be the first to go. Just then the two elderly gentlemen rose and began to stroll back to the house.

Neville jerked his fishing line just slightly, just enough so that the hook and line flew out of the water, splashing as they fell back into the river.

"Botheration!" he cried. "There's river water on my trousers. I shall have to change immediately! *Nothing* stains as badly as river water."

"River water?" Carola said with surprise. "I don't see any." She leaned forward to look at his lemon-yellow pantaloons, inadvertently giving Tuppy a fine glance down her bodice.

Neville grinned to himself. After he took care of Carola's little problem, he might hire himself out as a marriage broker. "I assure you that I felt the chill of river water. And naturally I cannot be seen in soiled clothing." He stood up, gently pushing her back into the seat and handing her the fishing rod.

"I shall return in the flash of an eye," he announced. He gave her his finest leer. "And then I shall accompany you to the house. I am certain that this excursion has been most exhausting. Perhaps you will need to rest, Lady Perwinkle."

Without waiting for an answer, he strode briskly toward the house. He was feeling remarkably hungry. Probably all that leering at a heaving bosom that would never be his. A warm crumpet would be just the thing. Perhaps three or four. Let the two lovebirds gawk at each other for an hour or so.

Carola leaned gingerly back in the chair and picked up her rod. She kept her eyes on the river and didn't look at Tuppy. Instead she practiced breathing shallowly so that her chest wouldn't rise and fall too much and look even larger than it was.

There was a noise beside her. It almost sounded like a growl. She turned to look at Tuppy. "Did you say something?" she asked.

He stared back at her, eyes narrowed. "You are still my wife, even if you seem to have forgotten that fact."

"I am aware of my marital status," she said, trying to push all the air into her stomach so that her chest wouldn't catch his attention.

"Then why are you acting like such a trollop?" he asked grimly.

Carola forgot about her chest. "I am not a trollop!"

"You certainly act like one. *I could never deny you anything that you desire!*" He made a scoffing noise.

Unless she was much mistaken, Esme's plan was working. "Oh, but I couldn't deny Neville," she said, looking up at Tuppy from under her lashes. "He's been a dear, dear friend to me in the past year."

His jaw set. "I can see that for myself." He looked back at his fishing rod.

It was time for a change of topic. "Are you using a lure?" she asked, jiggling her line so that perhaps a fish would bite. It would be splendid if she could catch a fish in front of Tuppy.

"A warbling minnow," he said.

She nodded. "Made with bucktail?"

"Wood," he said, casting her an unfathomable glance.

Carola almost quailed at the look of indifference in his eye, but she barreled ahead. "I prefer a bucktail lure myself. Finkler says that they are by far the most useful in country streams."

He narrowed his eyes. "Finkler is an idiot."

There was a moment's pause, broken only by the weedy song of a kingfisher on the opposite bank.

"What the hell do you know about Finkler?" he demanded.

"I happened to hear him speak," she said airily. Actually she had gone to the lecture in hopes that Tuppy would attend, but he wasn't there. "And then I read his book. I thought it was quite interesting, except when he starting talking about eviscerating the poor fish." She shuddered. "*That* was disgusting."

"Just when did you become interested in fishing?"

Carola was starting to lose courage. Was it worse to lose her husband forever, or to humiliate herself by letting him know that she had sneaked down the Lady Troubridge's library the previous night and escaped back to her room with not one but two books on trout fishing? She swallowed and prevaricated.

"Neville taught me. Why, fishing has become my favorite sport in the world, thanks to him. He is a highly skilled fisherman," she announced. "You can judge that for yourself by his excellent handling of the rod."

"Ah yes," Tuppy said frostily. "We fishermen are always so careful about the stains caused by river water. I can't tell you the number of yellow pantaloons that I have damaged with water."

Carola sat up a little higher. "Neville is a fine fisherman," she said with her nose in the air. "He carves his own lures."

"So do I!" snapped Tuppy. "So does any competent fisherman!"

"He's not merely a competent fisherman," she flashed back. "He handles his rod with flair!" That was something that Finkler had talked about in his lecture—handling one's rod with flair. But Tuppy didn't seem to think much of that as evidence. If anything, his face grew even more stern.

"I trust you know what you're saying, madam," he said in a steely tone.

"Of course I do!" How dare he question her knowledge of fishing after she read all those books? "Neville is a better rod handler than you any day, Lord Perwinkle!"

"I didn't know we were being compared." He stood up, throwing his rod on the ground. His face had gone dead white.

Carola stood up as well, clutching her fishing pole. "Why, Tuppy—"

"So now it's *Tuppy*, is it? What happened to Lord Perwinkle?" He strode over to her, eyes blazing. "And why didn't you let me know that I was involved in a fishing contest?"

Carola blinked. "It's not a contest."

"Fishing for trout in a particular pond!" Tuppy snapped. "And you, madam, appear to be the pond in question!" His eyes dropped to her chest.

Carola looked down. She'd forgotten all about taking shallow breaths, and her breasts looked monstrously plump from this angle.

His eyes were burning. "I believe these are still *mine,*" he said with so much rage in his voice that she shivered. Then he reached forward and jerked her into his arms. Carola felt a moment of humiliation as her bosom pressed against his chest. But then his mouth was on hers, and it was so sweet . . . she melted against him. And wound her arms around his neck. And generally acted as if kissing, rather than fishing, was her favorite sport in the world. She felt dizzy with it, with the smell and the taste of Tuppy.

Until he put her away from him and looked down at her with inscrutable eyes. Carola's chest heaved as she tried to get her breath, and his eyes lingered there for a moment. She felt desperately ashamed that she no longer had her kerchief. It was absolutely clear that he was thinking about her new plumpness. His mouth had grown so tight that it had a little white line around it.

But he spoke courteously enough. "I see that I have not yet lost the contest."

She paused, bewildered, and tried to think what to say. He waited. "No," she said uncertainly.

His eyes changed. "I must admit, my lady, that I thought it lost long ago."

"Not necessarily," she whispered, lowering her eyelashes.

A finger touched her cheek, whisper-soft.

"Then I shall endeavor to handle my rod with flair," he said. "As Finkler admonishes one to do."

Carola took all her courage and raised her head. She could tell that crimson patches were burning in her cheeks. But she refused to flop into his arms like a dying trout. "He also says that fish must be courted."

There was a tiny curl at the corner of his mouth. "It must have been too long since I read his book. I confess I don't remember that part."

"It's a whole chapter," Carola said. "Another fisherman is always waiting to steal your fish."

"Ah," Tuppy said. "I stand corrected, madam. I shall definitely have to consider my science more closely."

Carola was feeling much better. She took a deep breath and didn't even look to see whether her breasts had popped free of her bodice. "I have found this fishing excursion quite exhausting," she said. "I shall take a rest. No, you needn't accompany me."

She turned with a swish of petticoats. She could feel his eyes on her back, so she turned around after a few steps. He was standing there, brown curls all messed, looking so dear, and ungentlemanly, and beautiful, that it was all she could do not to run back down the slope and leap into his arms.

He raised his hand, so she waved as well.

"I will see you tonight," he called.

She turned faintly pink.

"At dinner," he finished.

"Yes," she said. "Isn't it providential? Lady Troubridge told me this morning that she has moved dear Neville to sit at my left. My two favorite"—she paused—"fishermen, on either side of me. What a lovely meal!"

He looked as if he was grinding his teeth. She *hoped* he was grinding his teeth. She waved again and walked back to the house.

Chapter Twenty

In Which the Question of Marital Beds and Bedchambers Comes to the Fore

Gina didn't see Cam again until early afternoon. Lady Troubridge had arranged a piano recital to be given by some of the young ladies attending the house party. Miss Margaret Deventosh was pounding out Handel with far more flair than talent when Cam slipped into the seat beside her.

"Have you seen the Aphrodite?" he asked.

She frowned at him. "Hush!" She turned back to watch Miss Margaret beat the keyboard into submission.

"The girl has even more spots than she had three days ago," Cam whispered.

At that, she glared at him. "Be still!" On her other side, Sebastian stiffened.

"Have you seen the Aphrodite since your room was robbed?" he asked, quieter this time.

This time Gina took in what he said. She shook her head. "But I'm quite certain it's there," she whispered back. "Who would want it?"

"I would, for one. For all you know, madam, that Aphrodite was sculpted by Cellini himself."

"I have no idea who Cellini is. But my statue is rather slap-dash. I was looking at it carefully just last night. You can see lines where it was put together."

"Put together?"

Sebastian tapped her arm with a finger. Gina gave her husband another frown and turned back to the music. Miss Margaret was just winding to a tumultuous conclusion with a great slamming of her feet on the pedals.

"God in heaven, who taught her to play?" Cam groaned into Gina's ear. He was clearly unmoved by the fact that people all over the room were sending them disapproving little glances.

Margaret wound up her song with a heavy emphasis on the pedal.

"Thank God!" Cam dragged Gina to her feet. "We must check on the Aphrodite."

"What?"

Sebastian was looking at Cam with a darkening frown, but he ignored it. "We have to make certain that your Aphrodite was not stolen."

Gina helplessly waved goodbye to Sebastian.

"Your chamber was the only one ransacked by thieves, although it would have made a good deal more sense for a thief to toss a room occupied by an elderly lady. Everyone knows they leave their jewels about and sleep with money under their mattress. Just from the look of you, anyone could tell that your jewels are safely locked up."

"And what do you mean by *the look of me*?" Gina demanded.

He snorted. "Have you ever left a string of emeralds hanging about while you slept?"

"Well, perhaps not, but—"

"Have you ever hopped into bed before washing and creaming your face and applying Lord knows what other cosmetics?"

"I don't wear cosmetics to bed," she snapped.

"Have you ever slipped into your sheets naked? Rushed outdoors in the morning before brushing your teeth? Danced on the lawn in your bare feet?"

"A good many of your fantasies seem to involve being both unclean and unclothed," she replied with dignity.

He laughed and started up the stairs. "Come along then, duchess."

"I often rise early in the morning. Just last week I went into the conservatory at three in the morning."

"That would be the meteor shower that led to you and poor Mr. Wapping being suspected of extramarital pleasures?"

"Yes," she said. "No stars fell, even though the almanac announced they would."

When he turned into the corridor she stopped and leaned against the wall to catch her breath. "For goodness' sake, Cam! I can't imagine why we have to rush up the stairs in this helter-skelter manner. I'm certain that Lady Troubridge and her guests are wondering what on earth came over you."

"Oh, I'm certain that they know precisely what came over me."

"No one knows about the Aphrodite except you and Esme," she pointed out. "You haven't told anyone, have you?"

"That wasn't what I meant."

"Oh," she said, feeling foolish.

"Come along, then." He held out his hand to her.

"Do you ever wear gloves?"

"Never. I dislike cloth between me and the world. You women seem to wear them constantly. Don't they bother you?"

She looked down at her pearl-gray gloves. "No, although I do grow annoyed if I am wearing a pair with too many buttons. I'm particularly butterfingered and I can't undo the right hand without a maid. Eating while wearing gloves is quite tedious."

They were at her door. The room was neat as a pin, and looked as if nothing had occurred, thanks to the ministrations of Lady Troubridge's maids.

"Where is it?" Cam demanded.

"The Aphrodite? In its box."

Cam strode across the room and flipped open the box. The froth of red satin no longer cradled a naked woman.

"Oh my," Gina breathed. "It *was* stolen." But something was nagging at her mind. "No, I stuck it under here last night." She bent down and plucked out the figure from under the ruffled skirt of her fireside chair.

"You left a priceless statue under a chair?" Cam bellowed.

"No one says it's priceless except for you. And she was quite safe." Her fingers instinctively curled around the poor woman's waist to hide her naked state.

"May I hold her for a moment?"

"I'm not interested in her value," Gina said, her jaw setting mulishly. "You can see for yourself that she hasn't been stolen."

"This statue has to be the reason your room was torn apart. As I said, yours was the only room searched, which is unusual. In general, thieves strike three to four rooms when they rob a house party. The thief had to be looking for the Aphrodite. Except it never occurred to the poor sod that you, who would never leave a paltry string of emeralds on your bedside table, had flung the statue under a chair."

"I didn't *fling* her. And I think your scenario is extremely unlikely. How would a thief know that I owned the statue in the first place?"

"Perhaps the statue and your blackmailing letter are linked."

"Even more unlikely. Why would my mother give me a priceless statue? She never bothered to answer a single letter I wrote her. Why would she leave me anything of value?" She

208

looked down at the Aphrodite. "This is a salacious little object to decorate my bed table. An afterthought on her part."

Cam looked at her but she turned away. "The countess was a fool not to answer your letters," he said bluntly.

Her eyes prickled but Gina bit her lip hard. She refused to become a watering pot before her husband.

"She may not have written back, but I expect she read them," he said. "She may have left you the statue in gratitude."

"Absurd! If she were the least bit grateful, she would have bothered to dip pen in ink and say so herself."

"Perhaps . . . May I see the statue?"

At first Cam said nothing. He looked at the Aphrodite's face for a long time, and then turned her over and over, his large fingers soothing every curve. He held the figure up to the sunlight. He even pried at the crack that ran down her sides.

Finally Gina joined him at the window. "Is she priceless?"

"I don't think so," Cam admitted. "I don't recognize the artist's initials: FF." He showed her where they were scratched in the base. "She's beautifully made though. See the upturned arm, almost hiding her eyes? And the way her hair splashes down her back? It's very difficult to fashion alabaster in such fine detail."

"I knew she wasn't valuable," Gina said, feeling cross.

"She's oddly made, as you noticed. It looks as if she was fashioned from two pieces of stone. I've never seen such a clever fit, as a matter of fact. There is absolutely no give in the join."

Gina took her back. "I like her face."

"I like her body, myself."

"She looks embarrassed. I don't think this Aphrodite likes being naked."

"I would guess that she is fleeing from Vulcan's bed. She has just been caught by her husband, and she's taking one last look back at her lover. Aphrodite is generally depicted either rising from the waves or fleeing from Vulcan's bedchamber. Here the artist was thinking of the latter situation because she is looking back, over her shoulder."

"That's *wonderful.*" Bitterness sharpened her voice. "My mother sent me a statue of a naked woman caught in the moment of adultery."

Cam's large hand came under hers and pushed the statue into the sunlight coming in the window. "Your mother gave you an object of great beauty."

They stared at her together for a moment. Sun beams played over marble, making the pink alabaster glow as if rosy blood danced just under the surface of Aphrodite's skin.

"You think she is looking back because she misses her lover. But I think she's sad because she betrayed her husband."

A wry smile lit his face. "There's my moralistic little duchess. For goodness' sake, woman, uncurl your fingers!" With an exasperated noise, he unwrapped her fingers. "She has lovely hips. It's a sin to cover them up."

"Have you made Aphrodites like this one?" Gina asked.

Cam shook his head. "Marissa has a much lusher figure here"—he pointed to her breasts—"and here"—he touched the statue's thighs.

Gina's mouth tightened. "Perhaps you could make me an Aphrodite," she remarked. "Then I'll have a statue from each of the people who—" She caught herself.

"Who what?" he asked.

"Who are related to me," she said lightly.

"That's not what you meant," Cam observed.

She shrugged. "I have a nonmother and a nonhusband. It just seems odd that both of you chose to send me naked statues. Do you remember the naked Cupid you sent for my twenty-first birthday? If you fashion me an Aphrodite rising from the waves, I'll have a matched pair."

"Your future husband will love that," Cam drawled. "Your bedchamber will look better than a brothel."

Gina put the statue down with a little click. "Our bedchamber," she corrected him. Then she colored. "I didn't mean ours as in yours and mine, but Sebastian's and my bedchamber." She turned around briskly, pretending her cheeks weren't on fire. "Don't you think we should return to the musicale now?"

"You mean that you and the stuffy marquess are planning to share a room?"

"Certainly. And I would prefer that you did not add insulting epithets to my fiancé's name. Are you coming?"

"We can't leave the Aphrodite. The thief might return. By rights, it should be in Lady Troubridge's safe, tucked snugly next to your emeralds."

"I would prefer that she not know of its existence. At any rate, if the thief was looking for the statue, he has surely given up."

He frowned.

"You can put it back under the chair, if you like."

There was nowhere else to hide the piece so Cam bent and tucked the statue back under the chair ruffle.

He walked silently down the corridor. When he spoke, it was in a tone of casual curiosity. "When did you and Bonnington discuss your future bedding arrangements?"

She consciously emptied all the irritation out of her tone. "I'm afraid that is none of your business."

"It will be an unusual arrangement. You do know that, don't you?"

Her shoulders grew a little stiffer. "Of course I am aware of that fact."

"Most couples sleep in separate rooms, if not in separate houses." There was something in his tone that made her skin prickle. "And then, once a month or so, the husband knocks politely on his wife's door and requests fulfillment of marital duties. After all, one must produce an heir, no matter how unpleasant the task."

"Sebastian and I will have a different sort of marriage," Gina snapped, starting down the stairs. "This is a most improper conversation."

He caught her wrist. "It's just me, after all. What makes you think that your marriage will be different?"

"Because Sebastian and I are in love, you idiot!" she hissed at him. "Now, will you have done with your questioning?"

"No. I'm agog to hear how you managed to talk the stuffy marquess into sharing a bedchamber. I would have written him off without a second's thought as the once-a-month type. With a mistress on the side, of course," he added.

"He will *not* have a mistress on the side!"

"No? Well, you know best, of course." He began walking down the stairs before her.

She rapped him sharply on the shoulder. "You should not say those things! Sebastian will not have a mistress. And we will sleep together more than once a month!"

He grinned at her over his shoulder. "Given your behavior last night, perhaps I should warn the poor marquess to throw over his mistress and get into fighting shape before the annulment takes place."

Gina blinked. Before she could untangle the metaphor—fighting shape?—they were back in the entranceway. She wandered back into the long drawing room.

Sebastian was still seated in the middle of the parlor, but her seat had been taken by Esme. As she watched, Sebastian bent his head and whispered in her ear. She was obviously

212

laughing, from the way her shoulders were shaking. Gina sighed.

This always happened. Just when she would start to think that the two of them hated each other so much that they would never speak again, they would about-face and talk as if they were the best of friends. Until the next spat.

At any rate, it would be best if she returned to working on the estate papers. She had promised to practice the play with Sebastian, and she still hadn't read the Machiavelli chapters that Mr. Wapping had assigned. Silently she backed out of the room, found a footman, and sent him to fetch her papers.

Then she retired into the library with a tea tray. It was very pleasant, alone in the hushed room. She spread her papers out on the long oak table and wrote letters for almost an hour. Dusty sunlight spread over her shoulders from the high mullioned windows behind her. Mites danced in the rays, pranced over the papers, swirled in the air when she lifted her quill or put it down again. The light was just starting to fade when Sebastian strode into the library.

She smiled up at him. "Can you give me one moment? I am just answering the estate manager's questions about sheep breeding."

"Why on earth haven't you given these questions to your husband?"

"I could have," Gina said, finishing the letter. "But I actually enjoy managing the estate. I'm afraid I'm a managing sort of woman. Will you be able to bear it?"

He bowed gallantly. "I should warn you that I am lucky enough to have two excellent estate managers."

"Shall we practice our lines, then?" She walked over to a sofa.

Sebastian joined her, opening his Shakespeare.

"I believe I have finally memorized the opening scene," Gina said. "This is my favorite line: *I thank God and my cold blood, I am of your humour for that: I had rather hear my dog bark at a crow than a man swear he loves me.*"

"I can see why," Sebastian said. "It suits you."

"Suits me?" Gina repeated, startled.

"Your wonderful air of independence," Sebastian explained.

"Oh."

"I too have my part memorized," he said, leafing through the later scenes. "However, Lady Rawlings informed me during the musicale that she has not even begun to work on her part. Perhaps since you seem to know your lines, I should seek her out. She's so flighty that I wouldn't be surprised if she never learned her lines without explicit guidance." He smiled down at her. "Not a bit like my duchess."

Gina sighed. "In that case, I will write a few more letters."

"Your sense of responsibility is admirable. But you need more light," Sebastian said, jumping from the sofa and ringing the bell. He bowed and strode over to the door. "I'll instruct the footmen to bring you plenty of candles."

Gina stared at the closed door with a sense of mild shock. Sebastian couldn't have made it clearer that he had better things to do than sit about with his future wife. Slowly she walked back to the library table and sat down, pulling another sheet toward her. Bicksfiddle wrote that the bridge spanning Charlcote Stream appeared on the verge of collapse. Would she like to repair the existing span, or tear it down?

Gina was gazing blindly at the estimated cost of the project when Cam walked in. "A man from Rounton's office is asking if he might speak to us," he said without greeting, walking over to where Gina was sitting. "Since his business is likely to address the annulment, I told him to join us here."

He read over her shoulder. "Bicksfiddle wants to pull down the bridge over the Charlcote?"

She nodded. "Apparently the timbers are rotting."

"Pity. It had the lovely high span you see in Elizabethan bridges. Is this the estimation for a new one?"

"Yes."

"He doesn't say whether the bridge will achieve the same height."

"Probably not," Gina said. "Bicksfiddle is rather wanting in imagination. I expect that he simply instructed an architect to build a flat bridge."

Cam drew up a chair. "We can't have that," he said. He pulled over a piece of paper. "I'll send him a picture myself. Now I think about it, I'd like to have the arch rise well above the surface." He started to sketch quickly.

Gina watched, rather fascinated, as the bridge grew under his hands. It arched up with a lovely span.

"Are those supposed to be stones?" she asked, watching him crosshatch the span.

He nodded. "If the old timber bridge has to go, I'd prefer to replace it with a stone arch. This is a reproduction of a bridge in Florence. We'll have to scale it down, of course, but—"

"Cam," Gina interrupted. "We can't possibly spare the funds for a stone bridge. Do you know how much masons cost? We spent over a thousand pounds just repairing the courtyard last year!"

He looked at her sharply. "I hope you didn't replace the star in the middle with gravel or some such abomination."

"Of course I didn't! But that's how I know the expense of masons. It took four of them months to repair all the brick in the central pavement. We simply can't afford to build a stone bridge this year."

Cam was finishing his drawing. "I don't see why not. I remember glancing over the figures Bicksfiddle sent me. Didn't the estate make around eleven thousand pounds last year? Where's it all gone?"

"That was two years ago," she said. "Last year was an even better year. We made fourteen thousand pounds on rents and properties alone." Pride leaked into her voice.

He smiled at her, and his eyes crinkled at the corner in such a way that her stomach curled. "Good work, Gina!" He looked back at his drawing. "Let's put some of those pounds into a new bridge."

"We can't. I've already earmarked all the money not needed for the London house and my allowance for building drains in the village."

"Fourteen thousand pounds worth of drains? Impossible."

"It's not at all impossible. I'm afraid that your father neglected the village shamefully during his lifetime. All the cottages were in terrible repair when he died."

"Dear Father," Cam remarked. He picked up the quill and began fussing with his drawing.

"In the years that I've been running the estate, I've managed to rebuild most of the cottages, or at least repair them to a livable state. But every extra penny is needed to build some sort of a sewer system."

She poked him. "Do you know that the villagers were simply emptying their slop into the river? That river flows directly past Girton House *and* close to our well! Last year we discovered that all the trout were dying."

"Because of the nasty habits of the villagers?" Cam asked rather absentmindedly. The bridge was growing more ornate by the moment.

"In fact, it turned out that the mining projects upstream were leaking into the river and killing the fish," she explained.

216

"Mr. Rounton had to serve papers before the miners stopped shoveling ore into our stream. Then when the stream was clear again, I restocked it with trout. Unfortunately, they all died. But Bicksfiddle reports here that there are still living fish in Charlcote Lake, so perhaps it was a matter of—"

He gave her a swift hard kiss.

She stopped in mid-breath and blinked.

"Did anyone ever tell you how beautiful you are when you talk about trout?"

"Never."

"You are," he said. "What do you think?" He pushed the paper around so that she could see.

"Oh," Gina said, rather lamely. "It's lovely, of course. But—"

"You see, there's a statue of Neptune here." He tapped with his quill. "And these two are water nymphs. Two more water nymphs over there."

"Are they clothed?" she asked, narrowing her eyes at the drawing.

"Absolutely," he said. "You know water nymphs. Never seen abroad without a corset and gloves." He grinned at her.

Gina bit her lip. "You want to turn the old wooden bridge over the river into a stone bridge guarded by *naked water nymphs*? I suppose that Neptune is naked as well?"

Cam looked forward and peered at his own drawing. "Here." His quill scratched the parchment for a second. "Now he has an artistic bit of seaweed around his middle."

"Absolutely not!" Gina cried.

He was wicked, *wicked,* to laugh at her like that.

"You don't understand," she said. "Girton is a beautiful property, built in—"

"Built just in time for one of Queen Elizabeth's progresses in the 1570s," he filled in. "I know all that, Gina. A few naked

217

statues will enliven the grounds. They were deadly boring, from what I remember. Is that ghastly formal garden still in place?"

"Yes, it is!" Gina snapped. "And I don't want a thing changed about it. Your mother designed it before she died, and it stays as a monument to her."

"As if she'd give a damn," Cam drawled.

"She would!"

"How do you know?"

"Because she didn't have anything else to do. Your father barely let her leave the house, you know."

"I was too young to realize." He had pulled forward a new piece of foolscap and was sketching with great concentration.

"I'm certain *she* would never have allowed the cottages to fall to pieces."

Cam frowned at her. "You never met my mother. Hell, I barely met my mother. Why all the passion over her garden?"

Gina stopped. "After you left, I didn't—I was rather lonely, so I . . ."

He put his quill down. "What do you mean, you were lonely? Where was *your* mother?"

"She returned home and left me there," Gina said. "The duke said I had to begin my duties immediately, and you know how he and Mother used to quarrel. I begged him to let her visit more often, but he refused."

"Damn it to hell," Cam said. "But you had a governess, didn't you? Pegwell or Pegworthy, wasn't it?"

Gina nodded. "Mrs. Pegwell was a very good woman. She lasted quite a long time as your father's employee, four years, I think. By then I was fifteen years old, and old enough to do without a governess."

"I feel like a blackguard."

"Your father was difficult."

"Not difficult: an utter bastard. I should have taken you out that window with me. I never thought your mother would leave you to Girton's tender mercies."

"I was fine. What are these blocks?" She pointed at the bridge.

"They're called abutments," Cam explained. "We can put figures here and here, on the abutments."

"You cannot ornament Girton with naked people," Gina said. "I won't allow it, Cam."

"But that's what I'm planning. Naked Venuses in the front hall. Naked hat racks in every room. Naked Cupids in the dining room."

She wrinkled her nose at him. "Impossible. The villagers would be horrified."

"Not by Neptune and his nymphs," Cam said, leaning over so he was touching her shoulder. "How would you feel if I changed—"

But Gina wasn't listening. What was it about her husband that made her quake, deep in her stomach, every time he touched her? He was scribbling all over the bridge, his head bent just in front of her. Her whole body tingled with a desire to sink her fingers into his hair. Turn his face toward her.

He straightened. "If we change these arches, Gina . . ." His voice trailed away.

She swallowed.

His eyes were lit with a deep, sinful amusement. He leaned toward her. "It was the picture of Neptune, right?" He almost whispered it against her lips. "Before I added the seaweed, of course."

"I don't know what you're talking about," she managed.

They were so close that he didn't have to pull her far. Those big hands simply lifted her up and transferred her to his lap.

"I'm talking about you," he said, tracing the shape of her lower lip with a finger. "You and the way you look at me."

"I don't look at you!" she snapped, mortified. She pushed his hands away.

"The same way I look at you. Want to know how that is?"

She shook her head firmly. She really ought to get off his knees. Except she didn't want to. "Of course I don't," she added, for good measure.

"When I look at you I pretend that you threw out those corsets you were clutching this morning. That would mean that under this cotton dress you're wearing there's nothing but rosy, creamy curves, smooth skin"—he was embellishing his words with kisses—"mmm, lovely breasts, damned if you don't have the most beautiful breasts in England, Gina"—and his hands were following his words.

Except that he stopped talking because his wife had grabbed his hair and muttered something that sounded suspiciously like "Shut up"—except that very proper duchesses never say something so impolite. At any rate, it was a good thing he did stop talking because, as Cam had lately discovered, he couldn't put a finger on Gina's breasts without her making little squealing noises that made him crazed with lust.

And when he discovered that she had held to her word, and discarded her corsets, his hands wandered in such a way that the gathered bodice of her gown soon lost its claim to decorum. But he couldn't let his mouth follow his hands because of the inarticulate noises his wife was making, the ones that made him long to do nothing more than sweep up her dress and satisfy both of them.

Of course, if he hadn't been busy stifling all those little squeals with his mouth and causing new ones with his hands, he might have heard the library door open.

It was really a circular argument. Because if he had heard the library door open, he and his wife wouldn't have been caught kissing by one of the solicitors working on their annulment.

Or, to put it another way, they wouldn't have been caught looking about as close to consummation as was possible while clothed.

Chapter Twenty-One

A Scandalized Solicitor

"Ignore it," Cam advised the solicitor standing in the open library doorway. Lady Troubridge's butler had taken one quick glance and fled the scene.

The young man's face was as fiery as his hair. "I will return at a . . . a more convenient time."

Gina wanted to sink through the floor in mortification or, at the very least, drop into a dead faint. But her disobedient heart kept beating in a steady rhythm.

Cam came around the end of the library table, casually rearranging his neck cloth. "I heartily apologize, sir," he said, bowing. "But I have clean forgotten your name. It must be the excitement of the moment."

"My name is Finkbottle," he said. "Mr. Rounton's junior solicitor. We had the pleasure of meeting last week in the *Queen's Smile*."

"Well, Mr. Finkbottle," Cam said. "May I have the pleasure of introducing you to my wife, the very one whom I'm annulling?"

Gina dropped into an awkward curtsy. Her knees were still trembling. "I apologize for my disarray. I was unprepared for your arrival." But that sounded as if she were casting blame on him—something no proper duchess ever did. "It was entirely our fault," she added. "Please forgive us."

"May I return at a later moment?"

"No, no. I imagine you've come to speak about—" she stumbled over the words—"about our annulment. Please, do be seated."

"Mr. Rounton desired me to inform His Grace that your plan to remain in England only a week appears to be inadvisable," Mr. Finkbottle reported.

"What on earth is taking him so long? The duchess wants to remarry immediately. And I need to return to Greece," Cam said.

"Mr. Rounton is, of course, aware of your wish to fulfill your commitments in Greece in a timely fashion," Phineas Finkbottle mumbled. He'd never been much good at fabrications. The duke and duchess's annulment papers were burning a hole in his chest pocket as he spoke. But Rounton's command was clear: *delay*. "I am expecting a communication from Mr. Rounton within a day or two. I am staying in the nearest village and I will—"

"Oh no," Gina said. "Lady Troubridge will surely be pleased to have you remain here. We wouldn't wish you to be housed in a dreary inn on our account. I insist," she said, jumping to her feet. "I shall speak to Lady Troubridge at once. Your Grace, Mr. Finkbottle." She curtsied without meeting either man's eyes and left the room at what she hoped was a dignified pace, rather than an indecorous trot.

"Where did you train?" Cam inquired. "Lincoln's Inn?"

"Unfortunately, no," Mr. Finkbottle replied. But he seemed reluctant to continue.

"Sergeant's Inn?"

"I trained on the continent."

"Ah," Cam replied. He eyed Finkbottle's red hair speculatively.

"Are you French, by any chance?"

"There are Frenchmen among my ancestors."

"And have you worked for Rounton long?"

"Not very long," Finkbottle replied, courteously enough.

Cam watched him go with a slight frown. Something about the man didn't fit his prim solicitor's garb. Something awkward in the way he moved, as if he was about to trip over his own feet.

Esme was not particularly happy to find herself seated next to her husband at supper. Lady Troubridge apologetically explained that she was having remarkable difficulty working out an appropriate seating plan.

"The pleasant thing about you and Lord Rawlings," she confided to Esme, "is that you are so remarkably civil. I'm afraid that does tempt one to seat you together."

"Miles and I do not hesitate to dine together. He is my husband after all."

"That's very kind of you." Lady Troubridge patted her arm. "Yet one hates to force propinquity where none exists on its own."

"Please do not be concerned," Esme assured her.

Thus she found herself elbow-to-elbow with her spouse. "Good evening," she said, accepting a helping of bombarded veal from a footman. "How are you?"

He beamed at her. One could never say that Miles was handsome or particularly gifted, but he had a genuinely kindly disposition. There wasn't a bit of hesitation in his face on seeing with whom he was seated. More the opposite.

"I am quite well," he answered. "The better for seeing you, my dear. In truth, I've been meaning to ask you this age what you think we should do about the local church. The vicar writes me that the steeple is tumbling down."

"Oh dear," Esme said. "I believe he had some eight hundred pounds last year to rebuild the cemetery wall."

"Was that the amount? I knew there was a substantial sum, but I couldn't remember precisely. Shall we mend the steeple, then? The estate seems quite solvent, goodness knows why."

"It would be a shame if the steeple fell," Esme pointed out. It was an example of Miles's innate goodness that he bothered to ask her opinion. In fact, that he kept her as his wife at all. Many a man would have cast her off years ago.

"Are you quite all right, Esme?" he asked. "You don't seem to be as jovial as I am accustomed to finding you."

"Oh yes," she said, rather bleakly. "I am quite myself."

Really, Miles had the kindest eyes she'd ever seen outside the calves' pasture. Unbidden, tears rose to her eyes.

He took her hand under the table. "I may not have been the best of husbands. But I am very fond of you. Is there anything I can do to make you more cheerful?"

"I do have one question," she said. Yet now that she'd broached the topic, she hardly knew how to continue. To ask such a delicate question here—in company! But a quick glance told her that no one was paying attention. After all, there is nothing more uninteresting than a married couple having a civil conversation.

"I am at your service," he assured her, patting her hand.

She lowered her voice to a whisper. "Do you still wish for an heir, Miles?"

His eyes widened and he spluttered into speech. "But you—you—you were—"

"I know, I said many things. But I was very young when we married, Miles. I am ten years older now and more aware of my responsibilities."

"My nephew," he began and stopped himself. "Are you quite certain, my dear?"

When she looked at his plump face and plumper body, she wasn't at all certain. But how many times could it take? Surely there would be only a few uncomfortable encounters, and then she would have a child.

She clasped his hand under the table. "I would like to make amends for my foolishness years ago, Miles. I had no right to deny you an heir."

His cheeks turned a little pink. "In truth, my dear, it has been my fondest wish. These past few years I have felt the lack of a son keenly. Except"—he chewed his lip—"I will have to discuss the matter with Lady Childe."

She flinched. "Is that absolutely necessary?"

"A child will change a great deal in our lives. You and I will have to live together, for instance, once the child is born. I'll release the lease on my house in Porter Square."

"Could we not continue living as we are?"

"Oh no," Miles said, with a firmer tone than she'd ever heard from him. "I would have to live in the house and set a good example." He hesitated. "We will both have to be a good bit more discreet. It wouldn't be right for the child."

Esme had never been one to overlook the absurd, and she could certainly see it in this conversation. "Perhaps if we maintain the lease in Porter Square, you could, ah, visit Lady Childe there. At the same time that you were setting a good example at home."

"It would be a delicate situation. She's a wonderful woman, Lady Childe. In truth, she's changed my life. I'm never late—never late anywhere. Why, I actually gave a speech in Parliament last year! She wrote it, of course. So I'll have to bring up the subject gently." He unthinkingly clutched Gina's hand so hard that it began to ache.

"I am certain that Lady Childe will be understanding," she said. "She has children of her own, and she must know how important this is to you."

226

"Even if she throws me over, it would be nothing compared to the happiness of starting a family," Miles said.

"My goodness." Esme looked more closely at her spouse. "I had no idea that you were so attached to the idea of reproducing yourself."

"When we first married, I didn't give a hang," he admitted. "But I'm not getting any younger, my dear, and the idea has grown on me. There was nothing I could do about it." He swooped and suddenly kissed her cheek. "This means the world to me."

Smiling into his beaming eyes, Esme could see her future changing. No longer a scandalous married woman, she was about to become domesticated, even matronly. She would live with her husband and set a good example, whatever that entailed. Unfortunately, she was not greatly enamored of principled activities.

"Shall we say, in two days?" Miles was asking.

For a moment, Esme had no idea what he was talking about.

"That will give me ample time to discuss the situation with Lady Childe."

She finally caught his meaning. Apparently domestic life would begin directly after Lady Childe had (presumably) given her approval.

"You're a good person, Miles," she said. "It is honorable of you to be so forthright with Lady Childe."

Miles turned the ripe color of an embarrassed Englishman, and mumbled something. Esme let her eyes drift down the long table.

Sebastian was seated next to his betrothed, of course. Gina was laughing delightedly.

And Sebastian . . . just for a moment, she gave herself the luxury of looking at him. He was bending his head to listen

227

to something Gina was saying. His hair gleamed in the light of the candelabra.

Her heart thumped unhappily.

She sighed and looked up to find Miles watching her with a look of distress.

"I'm very sorry, my dear," he said quietly.

She hated it that Miles was not only extraordinarily nice but also perceptive. Far too perceptive for a man.

She managed a weak smile.

"You're a good woman," he said. "And don't think I don't know it."

She chuckled at that. "I doubt anyone at this table would agree with you."

"They would be wrong," he said. He smiled once again, and turned to his neglected dinner companion to the right.

Esme turned to Bernie. But even Bernie's shoulders held no appeal. Moreover, he was beginning to take on a beaten, petulant air that indicated that she would have to give him his walking papers.

"How was the hunting today?" she said, shaping her lips into a smile.

As she listened to the demise of three grouse, a game hen, and two rabbits, Esme tried to imagine herself in bed with Miles. Impossible. It was literally impossible to imagine. Even ten years ago, they had hardly slept together after the first few weeks of marriage. What had her impulsiveness led to?

But the truth was nestled in her heart. She wanted a baby more than she wished to continue being the scandalous Esme Rawlings. She wanted a baby to nuzzle and hold and cuddle and kiss. She was tired of muscular arms and seductive glances.

The truth was that she would exchange them all for a sweetly fuzzy head. Thinking about it, she smiled at Bernie in such a way that he forgot his newfound belief that Lady Rawlings was merely toying with him.

"I say!" he said, pressing her hand.

Esme winced. That hand had just been crushed by her husband.

"May I have the first dance this evening?"

A fleeting image shot through her head of the last time she and Miles had danced together. He had floundered about the dance floor like a dying fish. She turned her mind away from the obvious parallel.

"I would be pleased to dance with you. The second dance as well, if you wish."

Bernie glowed. He'd had the idea lately that Lady Rawlings was too much of a high-stepper for him. Obviously he had been wrong.

Chapter Twenty-Two

Lady Helene, Countess Godwin, Escapes an Unpleasant Experience in the City

Carola Perwinkle was beside herself with a combination of nervousness and joy. "I think the plan is working. I believe—he kissed me." She stopped for a moment. "Isn't that *wonderful,* Esme? Isn't that simply wonderful?"

Esme pretended that she was too busy adjusting a pincurl to turn around. They had retreated to the ladies' dressing room. She had her hair up à la grecque again, and her toque had a lamentable way of lurching to the side. "It *is,* darling," she said, injecting warmth into her voice. "I'm so happy that Tuppy is seeing the light."

"Perhaps he'll kiss me again during the evening." Carola smoothed the front of her straw-colored crepe ball gown. "I wasn't going to wear this because it's so low around the bosom, but then I remembered—" She was interrupted by the door opening.

Esme turned around and a genuine smile broke out on her face. "Helene, love, what a pleasure to see you! I had no idea that you were planning on making us a visit."

The Countess Godwin had sleek blond hair caught up in a complicated arrangement on her head. She was tall and slender, with cheekbones so prominent that she gave the impression of being too thin for perfect health. "Good evening, Esme. And what a pleasure to see you, Carola!"

Carola rushed over like a kitten, words tumbling over each other.

Helene relaxed into a chair, laughing at Carola's exuberance. "Let me get this straight," she said. "You have decided that you want your husband back, for goodness knows what reason, and our own Esme has given you such excellent advice that the poor man is beside himself with lust after one fishing excursion. I hope that rain is not forecast for tomorrow. It would put such a damper on this budding affection."

"Rain calls fish to the surface," Carola said, grinning. "I'm quite the expert."

"What a lovely image," Helene replied. "You and Tuppy shivering on the riverbank while you exchange heated glances in the rain. Even the thought makes me glad not to be a fisherman."

Carola broke into a peal of laughter. "Oh, Helene, one cannot imagine you on a riverbank at all. You are far too elegant!"

"Thank goodness," she replied, turning to Esme. "Well, how is our local heartbreaker? Is Dudley as luscious as you said in your letter?"

"Not Dudley, *Bernie*. And yes, he is luscious. But as a matter of fact, to use a piscine reference, I am about to throw him back into the sea."

Carola had bent over the dressing table to tuck in an errant curl, but she turned around at that. "You *are*? But I thought"— she smiled mischievously—"that you hadn't quite reeled him in yet."

Esme wrinkled her nose. "Enough, pipsqueak." She shrugged. "I'm borrowing a leaf from your book, Carola. I'm taking my husband back."

Carola gasped. "Miles! You're taking back *Miles!*"

"He's my only husband to date."

Helene didn't say anything, but her eyes narrowed.

"I want a child. And Miles is the obvious man to fulfill that desire." There was no point in dressing up the truth, at least not in front of her friends.

Carola sank into a chair, dismay written on her face.

Esme almost laughed. "You both look as if I had announced a funeral."

"Won't you miss Bernie?" Carola asked.

Esme shook her head. "Absolutely not."

"That is quite a sacrifice," Helene said, watching her.

"I want a baby rather terribly," Esme replied. "It's grown so that I don't care very much about Bernie, or his muscles, or indeed any man's muscles. I just want a baby."

Helene nodded. "I know what you mean."

"I don't!" Carola said. "I don't think that Esme should reconcile with Miles—I mean, *Miles!* He's run to fat. And he's slaveringly attached to Lady Childe."

"Not anymore," Esme said, with a gleam of amusement in her eyes.

"He threw her over for you?" Carola exclaimed.

"There's no need to sound so surprised," Helene said with a gurgle of laughter. "Miles would be lucky to come within ten feet of his wife, and I'm certain he knows it."

"Miles is a nice man," Esme said. "A very kind man. He genuinely loves Lady Childe. But he wants an heir."

"Well, it's true that I've never known you not to win any man you desired, Esme," Carola said. "It's just such a shock to think of you with Miles. Goodness' sakes! He doesn't compare to Bernie, does he?"

Esme picked up her fan from the dressing table and waved it before her face. "I haven't the faintest idea what can be found in Bernie's head: whatever it is, there aren't many brains to challenge it."

"Still, what a change this will be. Here I am, reconciling

with Tuppy—or I hope to, at least. And Gina is about to marry her marquess—"

"Perhaps," Esme interjected.

Helene raised an eyebrow, but Carola kept going. "And you are going to have a child with Miles. Are you planning to live with him?"

"Yes. He thinks it would be best for the child. And I believe I agree with him," Esme said with an air of surprise.

"How odd," Carola exclaimed. "There will be three of us actually living with our husbands. No longer the most scandalous set in the *ton,* by any means."

"I shall have to hold up the torch for the rest of you," Helene put in.

Carola grinned. "Oh, Helene! You are the antithesis of scandalous."

"I am not," she said with faint indignation. "After all, I don't live with *my* husband, and since I couldn't contemplate lying next to him unless we were both in a tomb, I won't be joining the three of you on your merry, married adventures."

Esme gave a wry smile. "You think I'm making a devil's bargain, do you?"

"No, I don't," Helene said. "I would love to have a child. And if my husband were even half as respectable and kindly as yours, I would break down his door demanding my marital rights. But as it is—"

"Why did you join us here?" Esme asked, carefully not looking at her friend, but instead watching the lazy sway of her fan. "I thought you were determined to stay in London for the month."

There was a moment's pause.

"He attended the opera last night," Helene said. "With his young woman in tow."

Carola gave a squeak of disapproval. "That dissipated, degenerate—"

"—debaucher," Esme chimed in.

"I was going to say bounder," Carola said with dignity.

"You could say dog," Esme added.

"Or dastard," Helene put in.

"Lord Godwin is a pig! I can't believe he brought that trollop to the opera. Don't tell me they entered the box!" Carola's eyes grew round at the thought.

Helene sat with her back perfectly straight, a posture normal to her. But her chin rose just a fraction of an inch in the air. "They did."

"Oh my goodness!" Carola cried.

Esme snapped her fan shut. "*Dastard* is too good for him."

"I was seated with Major Kersting," Helene said. "It was a difficult moment."

"It must have been horrible," Carola said. She pressed Helene's hand.

"I wouldn't describe it as horrible. But it was difficult."

Esme grimaced at her. "Cut rope, Helene! Difficult? It sounds hellish to me!"

A smile curled the edge of Helene's lips. "Major Kersting was a support to me."

Esme snorted. "About all he could be, the old stick. I can't understand why you like going about with him."

"He knows his music," she replied. "And he has no interest in making advances."

"I should say not!" Esme said. "Why everyone knows that—" She broke off.

"Knows what?" Carola asked. "I never heard it rumored that Major Kersting was enamored of any particular woman."

"He isn't," Esme replied. "That's the point, Carola. He prefers male companionship."

"Oh!" When Carola was shocked, her eyes grew as round as a baby's, and she looked even more cherubic than ever.

"He's a dear man," Helene said, with a hint of sharpness in her tone.

"I didn't mean to disparage one of your entourage," Esme remarked. "I like Kersting, for all his primness."

"At any rate," Helene continued, "Major Kersting was very helpful. He talked . . . talked to *her* until the theater was darkened, and then we left, of course."

Esme opened her fan again. "I don't see why your husband takes such great delight in tormenting you. Isn't it enough that he moved the woman into your house?"

"I expect he didn't consider whether I would be there. He simply wanted to introduce the girl to *Cosi Fan Tutte*. He says she has a voice."

"Oh, I'm sure!" Esme said in a tone of pure disgust. "A voice that she—"

"I have come to the conclusion that she is not to blame for her situation. I had the sense that she was only fourteen or fifteen. She spoke in an extremely youthful fashion."

"Fourteen! Your husband is *disgusting*!" Carola squealed.

Esme threw her a quelling look. "That has been an accepted fact since Godwin invited his youthful trollop into the house. There's no need to reiterate it."

"I would antedate general acceptance to the point when he invited three female members of a Russian singing group to live with him," Helene said thoughtfully. "It was a low moment for the ancestral mansion, or so the servants said. They left in droves and informed most of London of their reasons. That was before you debuted, Carola."

Esme nodded. "I remember. The girls were dancing naked on the dining room table when the butler walked in. It was just after you left the house, wasn't it?"

"Oh yes. Perhaps he was lonely," she said with a touch of irony.

"Not for long!" Esme pointed out.

"I can't believe you two are funning over this!" Carola said. "Helene's husband is a disgusting, degenerate—"

"You're repeating yourself," Esme put in.

"It's not a laughing matter! Here's poor Helene, living in her mother's house while her husband turns her own house into a bordello."

"You also live in your mother's house," Helene pointed out. "And, happily enough, I like my mother."

"But Tuppy isn't running a bordello out of my former bedchamber."

"Tell me more about Tuppy," Helene remarked. "I am agog to hear when you decided that you wished to take him back."

Carola erupted into a tangled speech about dancing and fish, with a few references to brown curls thrown in.

"Perhaps we should repair to the ballroom," Helene suggested, smiling. "It sounds as if your Tuppy might be pining in your absence."

Esme fixed Carola with an admonishing look. "You must not make your feelings obvious. It's all right to crow over it among us, but you must not—must not!—by any gesture or even a blink of the eye, let Tuppy know that you prefer him over Neville."

"Well," Carola said, "surely I could just—"

"No," Esme said. "You may not. Let me put it this way: you must make certain the fish is well up on the bank before you remove the hook."

"I know," Carola said, sighing.

Chapter Twenty-Three

A Brazen Challenge and an Injured Jawbone

The ballroom was sparsely populated, since only the house party was in attendance. A small orchestra played a waltz at one end. Neville and Carola were soon circling the room, Neville swinging her in great arching circles with his usual flair.

"Lud!" Esme said, looking around. "There are no men tonight. Not that it signifies, given my new marital status."

Helene was not a demonstrative person, but she gave her friend a fleeting kiss on the cheek. "I would give anything to trade places with you."

"You would? I never knew you wanted a child!"

"There was no point in airing the subject. My husband and I will never reconcile."

"And you are not the type of woman to have an illegitimate child."

"I have considered it."

"Helene!" This was truly a night for surprises.

"But quickly rejected the idea," she continued with a fleeting smile. "For one thing, I have no interest in muscled bodies like that of your Bernie. So who would play the role of father?"

"Why don't you ask Rees for a divorce? The two of you have so much wealth that surely it would be possible."

"I have thought of that as well," Helene replied. "But who would I marry? I am not like you, Esme, with hundreds of beaux wilting at your feet. I am a dull person, who only likes music. No man has made me an indecent proposition for years, let alone suggest that I divorce my husband and marry him."

"Nonsense! You are a beautiful woman, and when you find the right person, he will fall at your feet. You would never wish to marry one of the fools I play with."

"I wouldn't mind marrying your Miles," Helene admitted.

"That's absurd!"

"No, it's not. I have come to value kindness above all."

"He's plump."

Helene shrugged. "I am too thin."

"He's going bald."

"I have enough hair for both of us."

"He's in love with his mistress."

"That's the best part about resuming your marriage. Miles will never pester you for displays of affection that you are unwilling to give."

Esme looked at her friend curiously. "Poor darling," she said, taking her arm. "You must be properly blue to consider such a horrid fate. Leave the plump balding men to me. We will find you a willowy man with a passion for music, and kindness dripping from his fingers."

Helene laughed.

"Meanwhile, I'll introduce you to Bernie," Esme said, seeing him plowing toward her. "Unfortunately, he has none of the qualities you respect. Given his extraordinary bloodthirstiness on the hunting field, I'm afraid he can't even qualify for kindness."

Sometime later, Esme found herself dancing with her husband. Miles was not a good dancer: he tended to bounce on the tips of his toes, and wipe his face repeatedly with a large handkerchief, but he smiled so gaily and was so complimentary that it was a pleasant experience. He was considerate, Miles was. He never glowered. In fact, she couldn't remember him ever being in a bad mood.

"Why did we separate, Miles?" she asked impulsively.

He looked surprised. "You asked me to move out, my dear."

Esme sighed. "I was a horrid little beast, and I'm truly sorry."

"No, you weren't," he replied. "I was tedious. I wanted too much from you."

"Nothing more than a wife ought to give her husband," Esme said.

"But those are wives who actually knew their husbands," he pointed out. "Your father did you a disservice. He should have waited until we knew each other."

Esme shrugged her shoulders. "It's a common state of affairs."

"It shouldn't be." There was an edge to his voice that made Esme look at him in surprise. "I don't feel right about it," he confessed. "I feel as if I bought you. I saw you dancing, and I had to have you. Presented myself to your father the very next morning."

"Yes," Esme said, feeling very tired. "I remember." She remembered the summons to come down to the library, to answer a plump, yellow-haired baron who had just asked for her hand in marriage. Given her father's approval, there was no answer other than yes expected, and she had said yes.

"It wasn't right." The dance was over and they walked toward the chairs at the side of the room. "I should have introduced myself to you, courted you, but I was overcome by your beauty. All I could think of was asking for your hand before someone else took you. They were calling you the Aphrodite, that season."

"I'd forgotten that," Esme said, thinking of Gina's statue.

"So I bought you," he repeated. "I shouldn't have done it. I've felt it was a wrongful action ever since I saw you crying before the wedding."

"You saw me crying?"

He nodded. "I came around the church and you were crying and holding on to your mama. I felt shabby. And I've felt shabby ever since." He pressed her hand. "I want to apologize before we try a new life together. Will you forgive me, Esme?"

"Of course."

He looked rather pink. "If it is quite all right with you, I might visit your room day after tomorrow, if you . . . you—"

"That would be lovely."

"Are you quite certain?"

"Quite, quite certain. You see," Esme said, grinning at him, "I am choosing you, rather than my father doing so. And that makes all the difference, Miles."

He smiled too, rather uncertainly.

"Have you spoken to Lady Childe, then?" she asked.

"Yes," he said, turning even redder. "She is most understanding, most kind, most understanding . . ." His voice trailed away.

Esme took his hand. He had a beautiful, fine-grained hand, quite unlike his ungainly body. "If you ever change your mind and wish Lady Childe in your life," she said in a low, clear voice, "I would understand."

He shook his head. "That would be shabby as well. I've grown too old to behave like a child. My opinion of myself matters a good deal to me these days."

Esme leaned forward and dropped a kiss on his lips. His eyes were blue and utterly round. "There are a good deal of

240

people, myself among them, who act like children every day. I am proud to think that the father of my babes is not one of them."

A flush jumped up his cheeks. "No need to say that. Ah, here is your next partner, unless I miss my guess." He stood up and beamed at Bernie Burdett.

Esme choked back a giggle. Only Miles would smile at the man half the *ton* believed to be his wife's lover.

Carola was still dancing with Neville when Tuppy entered the ballroom. She gave her partner a huge, glimmering smile.

"Let me guess. Perwinkle has arrived," Neville said.

"How did you know?"

He rolled his eyes. "Remind me never to partner you in whist."

"Do you think Tuppy will ask me to dance?"

"Has he *ever* danced with you?"

"I think so. We must have danced when we first met. But he absolutely refused to dance in the year during which we were married. I mean," Carola said rather confusedly, "during the first year of our marriage."

Neville expertly swung her in a circle. "I expect he hates dancing, in that case. The fact that it is your favorite activity might give one pause."

Carola nodded, keeping her eyes fixed on his face so as not to look at Tuppy.

"Are you quite certain that you want to reclaim your boring husband? Because I love dancing."

"Thank you, Neville, but no."

"I am ten times more handsome."

"How very ungracious of you to point it out!"

"You don't seem to have noticed my manifold virtues," he complained. "So I am forced to bring them to your attention.

Shall I end this dance next to your beloved, then, and hand you over?"

"I don't think so," Carola said, succumbing to an attack of shyness. "You have to act naturally. I shall die of humiliation if he suspects my intentions."

"Of course he suspects. Didn't he kiss you?"

"Anyone could have kissed me."

"Men rarely kiss women without provocation. For example, I've never kissed you," he pointed out.

"Perhaps you should," she said with a speculative gleam in her eye. "Is Tuppy watching?"

"Carola, kissing on the dance floor is paramount to declaring that we are engaged in an extramarital relationship," Neville objected. "Not only would it damage your reputation, perhaps irredeemably, but it isn't the case, more's the pity."

Her mouth set in a stubborn little line. "Will it damage *your* reputation?"

"To the contrary."

"Then kiss me. Now, please."

Neville slowed his dance step to a near standstill and leaned forward so his face was a fraction of an inch from hers. "When I kiss you, I'd like you to think only of me."

"I'll try," she said with a little giggle.

He looked over her shoulder. "I think we have achieved the desired resolution without endangering your reputation overmuch. Your husband is coming this way looking like a thundercloud."

She gave him a smile so brilliant it looked as if it had been painted on. "Don't leave me!" she whispered.

"Only if violence is imminent." Then he bowed urbanely.

"Lord Perwinkle, what a pleasure to see you again. How was the—"

But whatever kindly remark Neville was about to offer was cut off by a solid *thwunk* of fist meeting chin.

He flew backward, unconsciously trying to regain his balance by tightening his grip on the nearest support—Carola. And Carola, being a little pint of a person, flew through the air even faster than Neville, and landed even harder.

He grunted; she shrieked. The orchestra stopped playing instantly and craned their necks. Tuppy Perwinkle, maker of his own fishing lures and a man resigned to the bachelor state, stood over his two victims trying to figure out what the hell had happened.

"Carola," he growled, "get off the floor."

But she had landed hard on her bottom. Worse, her dignity had taken an even harder beating. She ignored him and came to her knees next to Neville. "Dearest!" she cried, "are you all right?"

Standing to her right, Mr. Reginald Gerard rolled his eyes. Amateur actresses invariably overacted, and Lady Perwinkle was no exception. Neville Charlton, on the other hand, was maintaining an enviable calm, and seemed a good candidate for the stage.

Neville opened one eye and peered at Carola. Then the other eye opened and he regarded the concerned and excited faces that ringed his vision.

"Ow!" he said, rubbing his chin.

Carola ignored her husband's outstretched hand and scrambled to her feet.

"You must be cracked!" she said, fists clenched. The circle of faces around her nodded. They agreed. The provocation (while notable) was not equal to the punishment.

Then everyone looked back at Neville, still on the floor. He came to his feet in a leisurely kind of way and began to repair his neck cloth.

243

Tuppy was beginning to feel like an almighty fool. "You look all right."

Neville fingered his jawbone. "I believe I shall survive," he said, as if discussing a fall from an apple tree. "Do you intend to air your reasons for this assault?" He said it in the nicest possible tone.

"No," Tuppy replied. "I do not plan to do so." Despite himself, his hands curled into fists again when he saw how Carola was fluttering around Neville, brushing his coat.

Neville pushed her away. "Let's not provoke the maddened bull, shall we?"

But Carola was beside herself with rage and humiliation. She flew back to Neville's side and clutched his arm. "How dare you assault my future husband!" she shouted at Tuppy, her voice high. "The man I love more than anyone in the world!"

Tuppy turned even paler. "I foresee a small problem—" he began.

"As do I," Neville put in.

But Carola was almost panting with rage. "You had the temerity to assault the man I love! You must *apologize at once!*"

There was a dreadful moment of silence.

"All right, I apologize," Tuppy said, turning to his victim.

Neville was still rubbing his chin and trying to pretend that he was elsewhere. He dropped his hand and raised an eyebrow inquiringly. Surely Perwinkle was saner than his wife? But alas, not so.

"You can have her," Tuppy snapped. "Take her. I don't want her. I can't imagine why I tried to protect her reputation." With that he turned on his heel and walked from the room. Bystanders fell back in utter silence as he walked by.

Helene stepped forward and took Carola's arm. She smilingly looked around at the fascinated eyes of the women surrounding them. "Lady Perwinkle must refresh herself," she announced. "Men are exhausting, are they not? So much passion. Only a woman as beautiful and chaste as she could provoke so much passion!"

Lady Troubridge nodded, and everyone else followed their hostess's lead. Helene drew Carola from the room.

Gina felt her husband's presence at her elbow before he made a sound. "Good evening," she said. "Did you see your friend Perwinkle's remarkable performance?"

"Make sport of the throes of passion at your peril," he said with mock gruffness.

"What do you know about the throes of passion?" she laughed.

"Too much," he said, his voice taking on a husky undertone. His wife was wearing an absurd evening dress. It was extremely tight in the upper body and trimmed with a little frill around the neck. With her red hair and white skin, she looked like a seductive Queen Elizabeth.

"And when was the last time you defended a lady's virtue?" she asked.

She had eyes the color of a piece of glass fished from the Greek ocean. And hair like an early sunset.

"Do you want to go back to the library and pick up where we left off?" he said. "It would be a shame not to answer Bicksfiddle's letters promptly. Perhaps there are emergencies we should be discussing."

Her smile transformed into something altogether more mysterious and seductive. Damn! He had better watch his step. Unless he wanted to sign up for a life supervising bridges over Charlcote Stream, he couldn't go much further than—

"No, thank you," she said.

He couldn't remember what she was talking about.

"I would rather not continue working on estate papers in the library," she clarified, a thread of laughter in her voice.

Cam grimaced. The orchestra had started up again. "Let's dance," he said, taking her by the hand.

"We can't," Gina protested. "This is a roulade, and Lady Troubridge has not yet arranged sets."

"It's a waltz." He flipped a coin to the conductor that shone gold as it turned over and over. The roulade turned abruptly into a waltz.

"I'm not sure this is a good idea," Gina said, looking up at her husband. "We're supposed to be awaiting our annulment, not dancing together. People will talk."

He considered that idea for a moment. "If you don't dance with me, I shall kiss you, right here on the dance floor."

"*What?*"

"On the other hand, if you dance with me, I won't kiss you . . . at the moment." His eyes glinted with promise. "You had better dance, because I don't think that Bonnington will appreciate the kiss. Given Tuppy's example, he might feel honor-bound to protect your reputation by trying to floor me. And"—he grinned—"I'm not sure he's up to it."

He danced the way he spoke, the way he lived: in bold impetuous dashes and wild seductive turns. Gina could tell that people were staring at them. She felt a prickling in her shoulders. She wrapped composure around her like chilly velvet and dared onlookers to make a comment.

Cam felt the change in her body and looked down to find that he was holding a Duchess in his arms. A Duchess with a capital D. Gina's beautiful lithe body was as rigid as a board. No one could possibly interpret their dance in a suggestive light: in fact, her chilly indifference was positively marital. He felt a ripple of extreme annoyance. He preferred his wife with a blush and a giggle.

"I believe your brother might be a member of the house party," he said.

"Why on earth do you think that?"

"Just because."

"Remarkably poor reasoning. If my brother were here at the party, he would have identified himself."

"What would he say?" There was more than a trace of scorn in Cam's voice. "How do you do, Your Grace? I'm your illegitimate brother?"

"Why not?"

"What if your brother sent the blackmailing letter? Pardon me," he said over his shoulder as they bounced off another couple.

"I don't think we should speak about this in public," she hissed. She had lost her composure. One curl had fallen from the complicated arrangement on her head and was bobbing against her neck.

Cam thought about kissing that neck, and white-hot lust shot through his limbs. "Let's retire to the library and discuss it at liberty," he said silkily.

"I don't know what you think you're doing," Gina hissed, having discovered that her husband's crooked smile had the disconcerting ability to make her blood race. "We're getting an annulment. We are annulling our marriage. Our marriage is ending. Our marriage is—"

"I agree," he interrupted.

"Then why are you courting me?"

When Gina was uncertain, she turned into a duchess extraordinaire. Her question sounded like a royal proclamation. Her eyes had never looked more commanding, her tone more utterly self-possessed.

He wanted nothing more than to shake that composure from her and return her to the impulsive, shrieking girl he had once deserted in a bluebell wood.

"I'm not courting you," he said, condescension intentionally underscoring his tone. "I'm seducing you, Gina. There *is* a difference."

There was a fractional pause. The music came to an end.

"Seduction would be remarkably foolish, given your wish to be rid of me." Her tone was thoughtful. "In fact, I think it could fairly be said to be the opposite of what you desire."

He raised his eyebrows. "I do not wish to be rid of you. And if you are not certain about what I *desire,* I would be happy to illustrate it at great length."

The corner of her mouth curled up unwillingly.

But she caught Lady Troubridge's interested eyes and remembered the more important subject. "What do you mean, you don't wish to get rid of me? We are not even in a real marriage, for goodness' sake."

"You asked *me* for the annulment. I like having you around—well, I like reading your letters."

"You don't want me as a wife," she pointed out. "Merely as a correspondent." She colored slightly, but continued. "Seducing me will not encourage me to write you letters. You don't want me to be your wife, Cam."

"Only because I'm not the wiving sort," he replied. "I think the more pertinent fact is that *you* don't want me as a husband. I'd be perfectly happy to continue as we are. In fact, with a few modifications in our arrangements—"

"What are you talking about?"

"Our marriage," he explained. Then he wondered what on earth he was saying. So, in the way of all men, he retreated. "I hadn't found our arrangement too onerous."

"That is not what you said. You said something about making modifications—in fact, it sounded to me as if you suggested that we halt the annulment."

248

Cam felt the blood drain from his head. Had he really said that? Surely not. His eyes drifted to his wife's creamy, delicate shoulders and long neck. He had said that.

"Well?" she demanded, voice as sharp as any Shakespearean heroine.

"There's no need to be triumphant about it," he said, trying for an easy tone. "If you lost your nerve and decided not to marry your icebound marquess, I'd be happy to keep you on. No one could complain about the work you've done at Girton."

Her cheeks were flagged with crimson patches. "Oh really? Isn't that nice? I can move from being the invisible wife who causes no trouble to being an invisible wife who causes no trouble, while continuing to do a great deal of work. How splendid for me. I shall give up a man who loves me and wants me to have his children, for a man who admires my letters and my management abilities."

"It was only a suggestion," Cam said, feeling a wash of relief. It must have showed on his face.

"I should like to know what you meant by modifications." Her eyes were narrowed. When he didn't answer, she gave him a sharp poke in the ribs. "Cam!"

He had that amused, sleepy look about him that made her stomach tighten. "I was talking about bedding," he replied, without even looking about to see whether anyone was listening. "If we stayed married, I think we should share a bed—at least when I'm in England, don't you think?"

"Even better!" she said shrilly, trying to ignore the little voice in her head that seemed to be—traitor!—welcoming the idea of sharing Cam's bed. "I gather that I become an estate-managing wife who raises a family alone while her husband frolics in a foreign country."

249

"Ah, but we could have a good deal of pleasure before I left. And I would visit." His whole face was wicked now. He wasn't even touching her, and she felt as if he was caressing her. A glowing weakness lay low in the pit of her stomach.

She opened her mouth to say something. But what?

A cough sounded at her elbow. Marquess Bonnington gave Cam a scant bow. "The evening has deteriorated into an unpleasant display," he said with glacial emphasis. "I propose that we adjourn to the library and practice our roles in *Much Ado About Nothing*. Lady Troubridge has just informed me that she has invited a large party to see the performance day after tomorrow."

Gina's eyes widened. "She promised it would be a simple skit for the house party alone!"

"Apparently she changed her mind."

Cam chuckled. "I hope she is not expecting us to match the thespian abilities of Lord and Lady Perwinkle."

"The less said about that disgraceful scene the better," Sebastian commented.

"Quite," he replied.

Gina had the horrible suspicion that Cam was laughing silently at her betrothed. "Come along, then. If we are to make fools of ourselves, we might as well practice our humiliation beforehand."

"There's the spirit," Cam said. He turned and scanned the room. "Where, oh where, is the beauteous Ophelia?"

Sebastian frowned.

"That's from *Hamlet*," Cam noted, adding painstakingly, "another Shakespeare play. I was referring to the more-than-beauteous Esme."

"The line reads *Where is the beauteous majesty of Denmark?*" Sebastian snapped, walking toward the library. He paused when they all reached the room. "Shall we begin with the first act?" A less dignified man might have been described as barking.

"That would be us," Cam said in a sunny tone. He caught Gina's hand, but Sebastian was holding her arm. "If you would allow Beatrice and Benedick to sit down?"

He drew Gina to the couch. Esme sat down opposite them, looking amused.

"You had better take your gloves off," Cam said, handing Gina a book. He frowned when he saw the myriad of tiny buttons extending to her elbows.

She watched as his dark head bent over her wrist and he began nimbly pulling apart the small pearl buttons on the inside of her wrist. "I'm perfectly capable of reading with my gloves on."

Sebastian made an irritable gesture and sat down next to Esme. "When you are *quite* ready," he said, with a biting edge to his voice.

Cam drew off both gloves and tossed them aside without giving Sebastian a second glance. "There we are," he said, in such an intimate tone that Gina felt as if she were transferred to the bedchamber.

"Begin, then!" her betrothed snarled from the opposite couch.

"What, my dear Lady Disdain! are you yet living?" Cam said, with so much amusement in his voice that Gina's mouth curled upward, despite the fact that she was still annoyed with him.

His eyes met hers, black and laughing, and her heart hiccupped.

"We can't sit like sticks," Cam remarked. "We'll have to act this thing out, now that we are to have a proper audience." He picked up her hand and kissed the palm. Sebastian made a growling noise.

"Is it possible disdain should die while she hath such meet food to feed it as Signior Benedick?" Gina said, trying to ignore the tingling in her hand.

Miracle of miracles, Esme had managed to engage her irate future husband in conversation. "Why are you deliberately antagonizing Sebastian?" Gina hissed.

"Forgot the rest of your speech?" Cam replied with an irreverent smirk. "Prompters at the theater charge a penalty when actors haven't learned their lines properly." His eyes drifted in such a way that his idea of a penalty was readily obvious.

"Thankfully, my memory is excellent," Gina snapped. *"Courtesy itself must convert to disdain, if you come in her presence!"*

"Then is courtesy a turncoat," Cam responded. "And by the way, I think I've done you a signal favor by drawing off that boarhound you call your future husband."

"Nonsense," Gina said. "You are playing with his feelings the way you play with everything. Aren't you ever serious, Cam?"

"It is certain I am loved of all ladies, only you excepted."

Annoyance boiled in her chest. She snatched away her hand. Somehow he'd kept hold of it and was smoothing each finger in a way that made nerves tingle all the way up her arm. "I don't believe you care about anything. You're nothing more than a care-for-naught, as my old nurse would say."

Cam's face lost a bit of its impudent seductive quality. *"Truly, I love none,"* he remarked.

Gina's jaw set. "That is just like you," she hissed. "I insult you and your reply is a joke."

"It's the line from the play," he protested. "Benedick says that he doesn't love anyone."

Gina scowled at her script. *"A dear happiness to women: they would else have been troubled with a pernicious suitor."*

"You needn't sound so fervent."

"Why not? It's true enough. You *are* Benedick, in the flesh. You love no one, except perhaps your Greek Venus."

"I do care for Marissa. She's a passionate, loving woman." Cam decided that he didn't have to mention that Marissa's passion was reserved for her husband.

"How lovely," Gina cooed. "I shall marry Sebastian"—she threw a reckless smile toward the other couch—"and you can return to your cozy domestic goddess."

Cam was happy to see that Bonnington was absorbed in a heated quarrel with Lady Rawlings. "I wouldn't call her merely cozy," he said, dismissing the memory of his echoing house in Greece. "Marissa is such a *warm* person that she seems to fill the house with laughter. So why don't you continue with that line about your cold blood?"

"I thank God and my cold blood," Gina said between clenched teeth, *"I had rather hear my dog bark at a crow than a man swear he loves me."*

Cam gave a mock little bow of his head. "Said with true flair. Beatrice to the life. Hopefully that cold blood will sustain you during your marriage with yonder icy marquess."

"How dare you!" Gina gasped. They both involuntarily looked at the opposite couch, but Esme and Sebastian were paying no attention.

"God keep your ladyship still in that mind," Cam said. *"So some gentleman or other shall 'scape a predestinate scratched face."*

"Scratching could not make it worse, an 'twere such a face as yours were," she taunted.

"Oh really?" Cam snapped back.

"That's not in the play." Her green eyes were glowing with the pleasure of battle. He felt an unwilling surge of lust that rocked him from head to toe.

Esme interrupted. "Lord Bonnington and I are going to take a brief turn in the garden. We will return in five minutes."

Cam gave them a tight nod.

"Forgot your line?" Gina said, the moment the door closed.

"I believe so." His hands bit into her shoulders and he jerked her toward him.

"Then I own the forfeit," she said. Her tone was just a little uncertain as she watched his mouth descend on hers.

Now he had her where he wanted her: on his lap, with her lips under his. She wiggled for a moment and then her body melted against him, slender perfection and creamy, delicate curves.

"I determined the forfeit before we began." His voice was a husky rumble.

"Um-hmm," she said.

He deepened the kiss. His hands roamed greedily, molding sweet curves, tracing breasts hampered and constrained by tight silk and a corset.

"What's this?" he whispered, tracing a whalebone curve. "I thought you forswore all corsets."

"I changed my mind."

He stood, pulling her to her feet.

Gina's knees were weak. Before she knew what was happening, he was towing her out of the room.

"Where are we going?" she cried.

He didn't even pause. "Your bedchamber."

"What?" She put all her weight in her heels.

He turned around. "We're going to your bedchamber, Gina." He tipped up her chin, and what he saw there made him shudder. *"Now."*

Still she held back. "We can't, unless—" Her cheeks were wild rose and her voice faltered. "I must bring virginity to my marriage bed, Cam."

He felt as if she had dashed him with cold water. His voice

254

was flat. "You really do think I'm an irresponsible lout. A—what did you call it?—a care-for-naught."

She felt the way his body stiffened as if his skin were her own. "No! That isn't the case. I trust you. I know you wouldn't do—*that*."

He waited, mouth grim.

"I don't trust myself."

The words faltered from her lips, and she turned a deeper shade of rose. He thought about it. Her hair was swept high on her head, and diamonds shone on her ears. She looked precisely like a young, regal Queen Elizabeth. Except that Cam knew he could turn this queen into *his* with a touch of his lip.

As he said nothing, her shoulders grew perceptibly stiffer. She turned with a swish of skirts. "Shall we return to the play, sir? Your next line is, *Well, you are a rare parrot-teacher.*" She sat down and picked up her book as if it were the most fascinating document she'd ever seen.

Camden Serrard, the Duke of Girton, never acted out of pure instinct. Since hopping out the window of his father's house with literally tuppence in his pocket, he had survived by using his wits, acting not by instinct but by logic, combined with a strong wish for self-preservation.

Until that moment. He found himself, Lord *knows* why, on his knees before a young and imperious queen.

He reached out, cupped her face in his hands, and crushed her mouth under his. Large hands cradled her face as if she were the most delicate piece of statuary ever made.

She sighed into his mouth, an erotic little squeak, and strained against him. He let his hand run across her bodice, feather light over smooth cloth, cupped the curve of her breast, and ran his thumb over silk.

"Oh, Cam," she gasped.

His eyes glinted with satisfaction. His other hand danced enticement, teased and caressed.

She cried out, unable to keep the sound inside. He kissed her again so that he could taste her gasps in his mouth. His hands went their sinful way until she was boneless, gasping against his mouth, squirming for satisfaction she couldn't have, given the restraints of silk, taffeta and one corset.

Until a noise outside the door reminded an erring duke and duchess that they were not, in fact, in the duchess's bedchamber.

Gina pulled back and stared at her husband. When he touched her, her breath turned to silken fire in her breast. When he kissed her, she became shameless. Everything about him, from his black eyes to his callused hands, made her pulse with desire. I will never feel this for anyone else, she thought. The knowledge was very clear in her heart.

Cam smiled at her easily, and tucked the frill about her neck into order. He looked unmoved, as if they'd spent their time reading Shakespeare.

I mustn't do this again, Gina thought, out of the new knowledge in her heart. I must not touch this man again: he is not mine, and will never be mine. That way lies only heartbreak.

The remainder of the evening passed in a blur. They ran through the play three times, with her betrothed acting as a taskmaster. By the second time they were reasonably proficient, and she was drooping with fatigue.

In the last run-through, Beatrice snapped at her Benedick with passionate emphasis. Benedick, conscious of growing frustration every time he looked at his delectable wife, snapped back with such intensity that even Marquess Bonnington watched and wondered.

Chapter Twenty-Four

The Second Council of War

"I don't think you've destroyed *everything,*" Esme said, judiciously choosing a grape before she popped it in her mouth. "But you certainly have made your life difficult."

Carola shuddered. "I don't see how you can eat at a time like this." Her voice had an edge of hysteria. "You must come up with a plan to save my marriage!"

Esme raised an eyebrow. "The number of grapes I consume has no effect on my sympathy, I assure you."

"The fact remains that Carola is right. We need a plan of action," Gina pointed out.

"I am very sorry to say this," Helene added, "but Lady Troubridge informed me that Lord Perwinkle is leaving at first light tomorrow."

There was a wail from Carola's side of the table, and Gina automatically handed her a handkerchief.

The four women were sharing a meal in Carola's chamber, since she had once again refused to descend for luncheon.

"I believe the time has come for strong measures," Esme said, eating a grape.

Carola lowered the handkerchief just enough to blink despairingly at her. "I truly don't wish to marry Neville."

"More to the point, he shares your feelings," Gina noted.

Carola scowled. "He'll marry me if I tell him to. And I may have to, if . . . if Tuppy decides to divorce me!" She burst into tears again.

Gina looked at the handkerchief Carola held to her face and decided it had two or three more bouts of tears left to it.

"I believe that a bed trick is necessary," Esme said. "Very appropriate, given that we're performing Shakespeare tomorrow. His plays are full of bed tricks."

Helene looked pained. "What on earth is a bed trick?"

"A bed trick is the substitution of one person for another," Gina explained. "The obvious problem would seem that, to the best of my knowledge, Tuppy has not invited anyone to share his bed. For whom will Carola substitute?"

"That's the tricky bit," Esme admitted.

"Impossible," Carola sniffed damply. "He doesn't want to sleep with me."

"One of us will have to seduce him, making an assignation for a later hour. Then Carola will be waiting—"

"And Tuppy will leave in disgust," Carola interjected.

"No, he won't," Esme said. "Because it will be *dark*. Don't you know anything about bed tricks?"

Carola shook her head. "It sounds like just the sort of activity my mama deplores."

"I believe it's the only solution. Tuppy has reason to believe that you dislike his performance in bed, and you have made it clear that you wish to end the marriage. You must convince Tuppy that you wish to be in his bed—nay, that you are willing to embarrass yourself to be there."

"The question is, who is going to make the assignation?" Esme looked brightly at her two best friends. "Gina? Helene?"

"You," they answered in chorus.

She grinned. "As it happens, I've made an appointment

258

with my husband for tomorrow night. Tonight is my last night in the solitary comfort of my bed, given that Miles's girth is likely to have me sleeping on the floor."

"I cannot believe we are engaged in this disreputable conversation," Helene said, very pink in the face. "However, I assure you that I cannot make an assignation. I haven't the faintest idea how to go about it."

"I disagree," Esme remarked. "You simply haven't had the impulse yet."

Six eyes turned to Gina, who was eating a tart and clearly considered herself merely a spectator.

"Oh no!" she said, startled, putting down her tart. "I couldn't possibly!"

"Why not?" Esme said. "Apparently Tuppy likes you already, given your knowledge of trout."

"I can't! I'm already—"

"Already what?"

"I won't allow it," Carola broke in. "Tuppy likes Gina far too much. In fact, I don't like this plan *at all,* Esme. I don't want to watch someone flirting with my husband. You are all more beautiful than I am, and tall in the bargain. I won't have it!"

Three tall women looked at her affectionately. Her halo of golden curls was gleaming in the sunlight, and she looked as adorable as a new-hatched chick. "You're a fool," Esme said affectionately. "But if you don't want Tuppy seduced, so be it."

"Why not just put Carola into Tuppy's bed late at night?" Gina asked. "He won't expect her, and it will be a lovely surprise. That is, if you really think Carola has to take such a drastic measure."

"I do," Esme replied. "Tuppy has been humiliated before a large part of the *ton*. He's a man, with a man's dislike for

259

embarrassment. If I were Tuppy, I wouldn't go within a yard of my wife, no matter how besotted I was. Because he is besotted with you, darling," she said, turning to Carola.

"He can't be that besotted, given that you think he would invite any one of you to join his bed."

"We are not mere girls," Esme announced. "I have complete faith that any of us could usher a defenseless male into our bed without undue exertion. And that includes you," she said, giving Helene a stern look.

"What will I say when he enters the room? Oh, I couldn't!" Carola cried. "I forgot about his valet."

"We'll bribe his valet," Esme stated. "With no valet, he'll have to undress himself. All of Lady Troubridge's guest chambers look precisely the same." She nodded toward Carola's heavily curtained bed. "He won't even know you're there until he's unclothed and in bed."

"But then what will I say to him?"

"Nothing," Gina put in.

"Nothing?" Carola's eyes were big.

Gina's smile was full of mischief. "Nothing at all."

Esme looked at her with admiration. "You are changing before my very eyes, Ambrogina Serrard. Whatever happened to your duchesslike facade?"

"Duchesses grow accustomed to saying nothing when the occasion calls for it."

"So I gather," Esme replied, twinkling.

"All right," Carola said, bowing to the weight of necessity. "I'll do it."

"Good. I shall instruct my maid to bribe his valet. And then we"—Esme cast a glance at Gina and Helene—"shall detain Lord Perwinkle in the ballroom until the right moment."

"What moment?" Carola asked.

"Eleven o'clock. We won't allow him to leave before that, Carola. So you must be snugly in his bed by then."

"I have to ask you all to excuse me," Gina said, casting a hasty look at the mantel clock and rising.

"Why so?" Helene said. "I was hoping you would take a ride with me."

"I said I would meet Cam in the library this afternoon," Gina said, with just a trace of self-consciousness in her voice.

"Oh," Esme chortled. "The handsome husband!"

"He's not my husband," Gina retorted. "Well, he is, but not for long. I have promised to explain Bicksfiddle's letters to him. Cam is going to take over management of the estate."

"Well, that's an improvement!" Esme said. "Perhaps he's finally leaving the ranks of childhood."

"That's not fair," Gina protested. "Living in Greece, Cam had no idea how much work the estate can be."

Helene touched her on the wrist and said in her light, clear voice, "but how splendid of him to take over the work the moment he realized."

"Humph," Esme snorted. "If I were you, I'd keep that husband of yours on a tight leash. He'll give all that work back if you give him the smallest encouragement."

"I shall miss it," Gina admitted. "You know I enjoy it. How am I going to fill my day? Sebastian tells me that he has two excellent estate managers."

"Trust the marquess to have two when one would do," Esme snapped. "I suspect you won't have time for doing estate work. It will take you all day just to live up to Bonnington's expectations of fair ladyhood."

Gina took up her gloves. "I shall leave, Esme, before we exchange words. I will see you all for supper, I hope."

After she was gone, Helene looked at Esme with some concern. "Why so sharp, dearest?"

Esme bit her lip. "I'm a pig, aren't I?"

"Not quite that dreadful."

"I'm consumed with jealousy these days," Esme burst out. "I feel like a five-year-old visiting someone else's nursery. I desperately want everyone else's beaux, and I don't want my own."

"I don't remember Gina's husband," Helene said. "I believe I met him before he left, but I was a mere child. Is he so handsome?"

"It's not the duke," Esme replied.

Helene reached over and touched Esme's cheek. "Poor duck," she said.

"I'd give you Tuppy if you wanted him," Carola said damply.

Esme giggled. "Then we'd be a proper mess, wouldn't we? Tuppy chasing after Gina's trout, and you and I both chasing after Tuppy!"

Helene stood up. "Shall we go for a ride? My mare arrived this morning, and I'm eager to take her out. Carola?"

She looked up from woeful contemplation of her handkerchief. "I couldn't."

"You could," Helene said firmly. "You will be unfit for the evening if you mope around your chamber all day."

Carola swallowed. "Every time I think about this evening, I feel ill," she whispered.

"Let's go for a ride. I shall work off my evil temper, and Carola will lose the doldrums, and Helene will stay her calm self . . ." Esme grinned impishly. "Someday you will behave as nitwitted as the rest of us, Helene, and I shall be there to crow over you."

She smiled. "Not I."

Gina entered the library with the firm conviction that there would be no more dalliance with her husband. Enough was enough. The mortifying truth was that she found Cam's kisses nearly irresistible. But she hadn't spent the majority of her life waiting to be a real wife, to be part of a real family, only to fall prey to a few kisses. The idea of going back to Girton House by herself while her husband sailed away chilled her blood. She couldn't do it. She couldn't live that lonely, duchess-life without a husband or children even a day longer. She wanted the things Sebastian offered: a family, stability, faithfulness, and love.

After all, she'd seen many a marriage begin with passion and end with nothing. Helene and her husband were a good example. When they were both young girls, she'd been green with envy after Helene ran away to Gretna Green with a handsome nobleman. Gina nourished that envy for at least a year, until the countess moved out of her husband's house and he promptly replaced her with a bevy of Russian singers.

Cam was waiting for her at the long table. There was a streak of chalk on his temple.

"Have you been drawing again?" she asked.

He nodded. "It was a fine morning. I have an idea or two for Stephen's marble." But he didn't say anything more, and Gina felt hesitant about asking. After all, he was sculpting Esme. She wasn't sure that she wanted to know.

Cam took the stack of papers she had brought. "Inquiries from Bicksfiddle?"

She nodded. "Some of them he simply forwards. Others he writes himself. I've sorted them into piles." She lifted off a good third of the stack. "These are questions to do with land improvement and farming, these have to do with the house itself, and the last are a motley assortment."

"Let's do the motley ones first," Cam said. He held out a chair for her, sat down, and picked up a letter. "Why does he want to trim the hedges? Why not simply let them grow?"

"The fields are separated by hedges," Gina explained, "and if they are to be negotiated by fox hunters, they must be jumpable."

Cam scowled. "Who hunts our land?"

Gina raised her eyebrow. "You?"

"I do not hunt!"

"Oh. Your father was—"

"I know," he said, a tired note to his voice. "My father was a great hunter. Enjoyed it even more if he could trample someone's kitchen garden while pursuing a small wild creature. Have the hedges been kept at a jumpable height?"

Gina hesitated for a second and then said, very collectedly, "I allowed the hedges to grow after your father was bedridden in 1802. Bicksfiddle greatly disapproves, and therefore he issues an annual plea that we trim the hedges."

His smile made her blink and she quickly pulled forward the next sheet. "These are the plans for the harvest dinner in the village."

"I don't remember a harvest dinner," Cam said.

"Well, 1803 was a terrible harvest year," Gina said. "So I instituted the dinner. And," she added firmly, "I opened the forest for gaming as well. I'm afraid that Bicksfiddle will complain about that rather bitterly when you see him next."

"Why would he bother one way or the other?"

"Bicksfiddle has firm ideas of the ducal role," Gina explained. "He particularly disliked it when I let the gamekeepers go. But really, there was no point to retaining them, given that I had no intention of allowing hunting parties on our land."

Cam's lopsided smile made her feel warm to her toes. "Let me guess," he said, putting a finger on her nose for an instant. "The gamekeepers left in 1802, which just happens to be the year my father was bedridden."

The intimacy of the situation was unnerving Gina. She could feel a little flush rise up her cheeks. "Let's begin with the house," she said.

Cam looked at her for a moment, and then nodded. "Of course."

And so they sat side by side, the duke and duchess, and worked their way through a large stack of papers. At some point, a footman brought them tea; they kept working. Finally Cam stood up and stretched. "Lord Almighty, Gina, my back is breaking. We'll have to return to it tomorrow."

She looked up, surprised to find that the thin ribbons of sunlight coming through the library's mullioned windows had long since faded.

"I still cannot believe that the household consumes so much oil," Cam remarked. "Six hundred gallons seems excessive."

"There are a great many oil lamps," Gina pointed out. "We could consider putting in gas lamps in the town house, I suppose. The banqueting rooms at Brighton Pavilion are being fitted for gas, but what if it explodes? Someone told me that gas is terribly dangerous."

"I know nothing about it," he said.

"What do you use for light in Greece?"

"Candles . . . the sun . . . the skin of a beautiful woman." He bent down and kissed her cheek, so swiftly that she hardly felt the imprint of his lips.

Gina looked down at her hands for a moment. She'd managed to get an inkstain on her wrist. "Cam," she said quietly, "we must stop this—behavior."

He turned around from where he was standing, surveying Lady Troubridge's books. "What behavior?"

"Kissing."

"Ah, but I like to kiss you," said her reprobate husband.

Gina shivered. That would result in a lonely bed, tending to all of Bicksfiddle's letters while her husband bathed in the Greek ocean. She looked away, tightening her lips against the sight of him.

But he was moving, pulling her to her feet. "Gina," he said, and his voice was deep and full of passion. He kissed her just at the corner of her mouth, and her whole body trembled. "Gina," he said. "May I accompany you to your chamber?"

She trembled in his hands like a bird caught on its first flight. He trailed kisses down her high cheekbones. "I want you," he said, in a voice burnished and dark, a voice that spoke of laughter, irresponsibility, naked statues, and the Greek sun.

It was all wound up in Gina's mind: the statues, the naked women, his Marissa waiting for him—

She pushed his hands away. Her cheeks were flushed, her lips trembling, but her voice was firm. "That is not a good idea."

His face became instantly guarded and casual. "Why not? We could both find pleasure without anyone being the wiser."

Her eyes were scornful. "You would like to take pleasure, and leave without injury. That's just like you, Cam."

"I don't see anything wrong with it." He fought to keep his temper.

"Perhaps there isn't anything wrong," she said, "from your point of view."

"That's quite a little moralistic statement." His voice was cruelly polite. "May I remind you, lady wife, that I have had every opportunity, and legal right, to take your body wherever I please? But I have chosen to ignore the signs of your oh-so-willing character, although I have had the distinct impression—"

She interrupted. Duchesses never interrupt, but this one was losing all claims to dignity. She was rosy with pure embarrassment. "I enjoy kissing you." Her voice shook. "I enjoy the way you, the way you . . ."

He stared at her, silenced by her truthfulness.

"But you're just talking about pleasure, not anything else," she continued, meeting his eyes.

"What more do you want?" he asked, genuinely bewildered.

"I am twenty-three years old. I want to live with my husband and have children together, which is not an unreasonable request. What you offer is pleasure alone. You are too good at ignoring unpleasant truths, such as the fact that you've had a wife sitting at home for twelve years while you dallied with your Greek mistress."

Cam frowned. "You never said that you cared about where I was. You never asked me to come home until you requested an annulment."

"And would you have returned, had I asked?" She waited but there was no answer.

"Would you have given up Marissa, had I asked?"

He just looked at her, jaw set.

"I believe that marrying is not in your nature."

Cam had always said he wasn't the marrying kind. He had made a joke of being the earliest-married among the never-meant-to-be-married. But he didn't like the prickling feeling it gave him when Gina pointed out his unsuitability.

He rallied quickly, the veteran of a thousand unpleasant family battles. "None of this started with a question of marriage," he remarked, deliberately pulling down his sleeves and readjusting his jacket. "It is merely a question of desire. Since you are honest, I shall be as well. I want you, Gina."

He walked a step closer and stared down at her. "I want to plunge inside you."

She looked away to escape the intensity in his black eyes. He forced her chin back up. "And you want the same from me." She didn't answer, unable to balance the scorching glow in her belly and the shrinking humiliation of hearing such a thing said out loud.

"Desire is a normal, human emotion," he said. "I can certainly understand if you would rather experience it with your future husband than with me."

It didn't take a genius to realize that she and Sebastian would never share anything of the sort.

"But there is no need to insult me. As an eighteen-year-old, I did not indicate a wish to marry you, Gina. If I ever have a real wife, a wife I myself chose, I will not leave her for twelve years, nor take a mistress, for that matter. It is not fair to criticize me for breaking vows dictated by my father."

He let his hand drop.

She felt a wave of shame so profound it was as if she'd been dipped in hot water. "I'm sorry," she whispered.

"There's nothing to be sorry for. We're both victims of my father, two of the many."

Gina looked at him and knew, in that instant, that she loved him. He stood in the last rays of dying sunlight and there was chalk in his hair. He stood smiling that lopsided smile of his, and she wanted nothing more than to hold out her arms and say: *Come. Come kiss me. Come love me. Take me to your chamber.*

The words wavered on her lips but she couldn't say them.

He met her eyes. "Marissa is married to a nice fisherman," he said. "She was my mistress, but I danced at her wedding some three years ago. We had an enjoyable time but our friendship was of no great consequence to either of us."

"Oh," she breathed. And she knew that what mattered was love, her love for him. Not the future: the present.

He had her hands again. "I have no right to ask. But may I . . . may we . . ." He didn't seem to know what he meant, or how to phrase it. He cleared his throat and put out his elbow. "I will be a sometime husband, Gina. But I would like to be yours. May I escort you to your chamber?"

Gina took a deep breath.

"I believe you may," she said. Her voice was faint but clear.

He looked at her for a moment and then bent his head and kissed her. Gina's whole body sang at his touch. He turned and wrapped an arm around her waist, and they walked toward the library doors.

Chapter Twenty-Five

In Which Mr. Finkbottle Proves Himself a Worthy Employee

Phineas Finkbottle was not having a pleasant evening. It was very kind of Lady Troubridge to invite him to the house party, and goodness *knows* he needed ready access to the duke and duchess if he were to carry out Mr. Rounton's instructions. But how the devil was he supposed to ensure that the duke and duchess remain married? He had spent the morning shut in his room, miserably aware that he ought to be talking the duchess out of an annulment. Except the duchess was so very *duchess-like*. He couldn't imagine bringing up the subject of whom she should or should not marry. At any rate, after yesterday, when he walked into the library and saw the duke kissing his wife, he was hopeful that the man would take care of the matter himself.

Still, it was better to sit glumly in his room than sit silently at the supper before dancing. The three elderly ladies to whose table a footman had escorted him responded to his introduction with the briefest of nods and turned back among themselves with a little titter. He ate wafers of ham and thought loathful thoughts about Mr. Rounton. If the man wanted his clients to fall in bed together, why the devil couldn't he arrange it himself? Phineas's ears grew a little pink even thinking about it. The duke was at least ten years older than he, and far more sophisticated and experienced. He could hardly urge the man to visit his wife's bedroom. His skin crawled at the very thought.

The ladies' conversation drifted into his thoughts.

"Indeed, my dears," said an elderly woman named Lady Wantlish, "I can tell you quite honestly that her tears were soon dissipated. Why, I believe she mourned the man for all of a fortnight, if that!"

Phineas sighed. He was discomfited by the fact that the ladies ignored him, and mortified by the realization that they were right to do so. He wasn't dressed in the first stare of fashion. He was only a solicitor, even if his father was a gentleman. Worse, he didn't know a soul at the party except for his clients and his hostess.

"They were in the conservatory together for at least two hours!" shrilled the plump woman named Mrs. Flockhart, to his right. "*Two hours,* my dears. I had it on the best authority. There are those who say that her mother locked the door until enough time had passed. Her father demanded satisfaction, of course."

"How disgraceful!" chimed in the lady in yellow, whose name Phineas couldn't remember. "Although I don't believe it of her mother. Why would she bother to lock her daughter in the room with a second son? No, no, the girl is fast. I always thought so, since the moment she debuted. You know, she tripped over her train when she bowed to the Queen. Careless chit."

"I think it's likely her mother was instrumental in locking them in the room," Mrs. Flockhart insisted. "She always was a wily one. When we were just girls, she used to swear that she was going to catch a duke. Never did, of course. The boy may be a second son, but he's got a nice income of his own."

Phineas narrowed his eyes. If the duke and duchess were locked in a room together, would they be forced to remain married? Surely the marquess would discard his engagement if the duchess was compromised.

271

"What room was it?" he asked.

Three pairs of sharp eyes looked at him. "What the devil are you talking about, boy?" screeched Mrs. Flockhart.

Phineas felt his ears turning crimson. "The room," he said. "Where were they for two hours?"

There was a cackle of laughter. "Not the bedchamber, if that's what you're thinking!"

"It is not a good way to win yourself an heiress," said Lady Wantlish. At least she had a twinkle in her eye. "Too risky."

"I am not hoping to win an heiress," Phineas said with dignity.

"Good," Mrs. Flockhart said acidly. "I don't think there are any here who are uncompromised."

"Now, now," said Lady Wantlish. "Miss Deventosh is quite a catch. She was the recipient of her late aunt's estate. And I assure you that she is uncompromised."

"That red-headed little snip?" The old woman was scathing. "If she's an heiress, why is she wearing those dreadful clothes? She looks like a ruffled turnip."

Phineas felt a stab of sympathy for the unknown Miss Deventosh. He felt like a turnip and apparently she looked like one.

"They were locked in a conservatory," Lady Wantlish commented, turning back to him. She had a friendly look in her eye. Or perhaps she just wanted him to create a scandal.

"Ah," he said, trying to sound uninterested. He felt a sharp dig in his ribs.

"Who are your parents, boy?"

"My father's name is Phineas Finkbottle," Phineas said, starting to blush.

"Finkbottle? You're Phineas Finkbottle's son?" To his amazement, Lady Wantlish softened all over and looked as sweet as butter. "He was one of my very first beaux. That was before he lost all his money, of course."

"Good thing you didn't take him," Mrs. Flockhart observed.

"My father wouldn't allow it," Lady Wantlish admitted. "How is he now?"

"He's lame, madam," Phineas stammered. "He suffered a carriage accident a few years ago."

"Are you good to your parents, boy?"

He started to turn purple with embarrassment. "Yes," he mumbled. "At least I think so. My mother died in the accident."

The old woman nodded. "Thought I heard something about that. A few years after Finkbottle lost his money on the 'Change, wasn't it? You have a nice look about you. Doesn't he, gels?"

They all stared at him with beady eyes.

"I expect you're right," said the plump one to his right. "He *does* have a nice look." She sounded quite surprised.

"I'll introduce him to the Deventosh chit," Lady Wantlish announced. "She's my goddaughter, after all. As you said, Mrs. Flockhart, she dresses like a turnip and she's unhappy as a turnip too. Told me she doesn't want to marry a useless aristocrat. I'll hand her a nice young solicitor. Mind you"— she gave Phineas a sharp look—"no locking yourself into a conservatory with my goddaughter. She's a good girl, for all she has advanced ideas."

Phineas turned quite purple with shame. Thankfully the ladies were gathering their scarves and reticules and preparing to leave. He bowed, and bowed again as they left, swallowing a lump in his throat that made him positively long to jump into a coach and flee to London. Except then he would lose his position, and . . . the thought of his father at home stilled his nerves. He had to keep this job. He simply had to.

I'll lock the duke and duchess in a garden building, he decided. If that doesn't work, at least Mr. Rounton couldn't say that he hadn't tried. That very night he would do it. It would be easy enough. All he had to do was send the duke and duchess out individually, follow, and lock them in. As for the key . . . the key. What key? For that matter, what building? He set off with renewed vigor. He'd have to walk the grounds until he found a structure that locked.

By a half hour later Phineas was quite discouraged. Wandering around in the dark, he had found two little garden buildings, but they were so dirty that he couldn't imagine the elegant duchess entering either of them. Then he found an outdoor earth closet that looked like a little house from a distance. But inside it was quite malodorous, and what would the duke and duchess do for several hours? It was extremely difficult to imagine them sitting peacefully on stools.

The problem was that none of the little grottos or conservatories scattered about the grounds locked. And when he discreetly asked a gardener about keys to the Roman temple, he got nothing more than a suspicious look and a muttered response that there weren't no need for it.

Finally he was driven back into the house. He'd have to lock the duke and duchess into a room. Which sounded better, in truth, because they were bound to create a greater scandal by being locked in right under the house party's noses.

But he encountered the same problem. The library locked, but only from the inside. In the end, he found only two possibilities: the billiard room and the cupboard water closet off the ballroom. On the whole, Phineas thought the billiard room sounded the better proposition. He walked out of the water closet, contemplating ways by which to maneuver the couple into the billiard room. To his horror, a gentleman was standing just outside. Phineas turned scarlet with confusion.

"Interested in the facilities, are you?" the man asked jovially. "As am I, as am I! I'm thinking of putting a Stowe water closet into my own house. My wife wants one in her dressing room. Have you seen the plunge-bath?"

Phineas shook his head.

"Come along, let's find it, shall we?" The man blew out his walrus-type mustache. "My name's Wimpler."

"I am Phineas Finkbottle," Phineas replied, bowing.

"Good!" Mr. Wimpler exclaimed. "Good, good, good. Now, the butler told me that the steps down to the plunge-bath come from the east portico. Must be this way." And he set off vigorously, Phineas trailing behind.

They walked down a set of narrow, winding steps and peered into the plunge-bath. It was lined in brick.

"What do you think?" Wimpler shouted. "Think I ought to have one of those?"

"It looks chilly," Phineas pointed out.

"Now there you're wrong," Wimpler said. "Lady Troubridge told me that it's heated. Somehow . . . ah! Steam heat, I would guess. Look at that!"

Phineas looked.

Wimpler smirked. "Lovely place for a ron-dee-vous, wouldn't you say?" He elbowed Phineas cheerfully. "A little splash and tumble? Don't suppose that's what Lady Troubridge had in mind when she installed it, though!" He laughed at his own cleverness and set off back up the stairs. "Come along, then," he called back. "We shouldn't like to be late for the dancing."

Phineas followed more slowly. What really struck him about the plunge-bath was the key on the door. The key, and the silent, oiled way in which it turned. If he could lure the duke and duchess into visiting the bath, he could lock them in. Moreover, since the entrance was on the east portico, the couple was unlikely to be discovered before sufficient time had lapsed to ruin their reputations.

The next question was how to lure them to the plunge-bath.

But that turned out to be quite easy. As he was walking back along the corridor, Mr. Wimpler having dashed away to find his wife, he saw the duke and duchess just leaving the library.

"Your Graces!" he called, rushing toward them.

The duchess had just begun to climb the stairs and didn't turn her head immediately. The duke stopped, however, and greeted him rather curtly.

"Lady Troubridge requests your presence," Phineas said, catching his breath.

The duke had a hand on the duchess's waist. For a moment Phineas had a qualm: what if the duke was, indeed, going to take care of the problem himself? But then the sight of Mr. Rounton's apoplectic face shot across his memory. No: he couldn't trust the duke. It was for his own good, after all.

"Her Ladyship would like to see you *immediately*," he said, injecting urgency into his voice.

The duchess turned around, finally, and smiled. She put a hand on the duke's sleeve. "Why don't you greet Lady Troubridge for me? I shall take a small rest."

Perhaps he *was* making a mistake.

The duke was grinning back at his wife. "No indeed. I couldn't let you do that. Not without exerting yourself first."

Phineas was fairly sure that there was a double meaning to the conversation.

But the duke and duchess began walking quickly down the hallway. He actually had to run after them to direct them to the plunge-bath. Luckily, they didn't seem to notice where they were going, and accepted his hasty explanation that Lady

Troubridge was down the stairs off the portico without even glancing at him. The duke was whispering in the duchess's ear; Phineas could see that she was faintly pink in the cheeks.

He hesitated, swung the door shut behind them, and turned the key. Instantly he felt enormous relief. He'd done what needed to be done.

He would return with witnesses in three hours. At the end of the evening. Surely people would notice the duchess's absence during the dancing. He smiled with newborn confidence. He, Phineas Finkbottle, was a man of action. A man who came up with a plan and satisfied his employer. He strolled in the door of the ballroom full of well-being.

Chapter Twenty-Six

Cabined, Cribbed, and Confined, as Hamlet Put It

It took a good two minutes before Cam and Gina realized that not only was Lady Troubridge not in the plunge-bath, but Phineas Finkbottle, for reasons known only to himself, had locked them in.

"What the devil?" Cam banged on the door. It was made of such solid oak that his fist only made a dull thunk.

"What could that man have been thinking?" Gina asked.

"He won't be thinking long once I get out of this dungeon!" Cam snarled.

"It's not a dungeon." She retreated back down the stairs. "He can't be planning to murder us, because Lady Troubridge told me herself that she takes a plunge-bath every morning. In the worst case, we shan't be discovered until morning."

"Perhaps Finkbottle doesn't know that Lady Troubridge is addicted to the bath," Cam pointed out.

"He doesn't seem a murderous type of person."

He tramped down the stairs after her and then stopped. "He's stealing the Aphrodite!"

His wife looked up at him and smiled. "I gave it to Esme for safekeeping this morning. I decided that you may be correct in insisting that the thief would return."

"Damn him. It crossed my mind that he was your no-good brother, and I ignored it. More fool I." Cam was filled with the rage of a man unable to rescue his lady, even though she was only debatably in danger.

"You think Mr. Finkbottle is my brother?" Gina gasped.

"He has red hair. He trained on the continent. And he's off stealing the Aphrodite. Only your brother could possibly know about the statue."

She froze for a moment, thinking it through. "Mr. Finkbottle is my *brother*?"

"It's the only explanation that makes sense." He stomped down the rest of the stairs. "I expect he's turning over your mattress at this very moment, looking for the statue."

"Why didn't he simply ask me for it?"

"Because he's a criminal," he snapped, still smarting over their enforced imprisonment.

"Still, if he'd asked me, I would have given him the statue." Her eyes were so sad that Cam felt some of his annoyance melt away.

"Fools, both of them," he said, a bit more gently. "Your mother didn't answer your letters and your brother didn't introduce himself properly."

Her chin wobbled.

"Oh for goodness' sake," he said with exasperation, and tucked her into his arms. "Why would you want your by-blow of a sibling to introduce himself anyway?"

Gina bit her lip hard and didn't say anything because she might cry. Duchesses *never* cried in the presence of others.

"Well?" Her husband sounded cross but he was holding her so sweetly that it almost—almost—made up for the fact that neither her mother nor her brother cared to meet her. Cared to speak to her, or write to her, or know her at all. She deliberately pushed the thought away and thought: *Duchess is as duchess does. Duchess is as duchess does. Duchess is as duchess does.*

279

"What is a plunge-bath anyway?" Cam asked, looking around at the vaulted brick ceilings.

"They're quite the newest thing," she said. "That's the bath." She pulled herself from his arms and pointed down at the tiled bath. "One enters by those stairs. It's really quite clever. The water is piped across the kitchen hot wall, so it's already warm by the time it arrives in the bath. And one could make it hotter by turning this switch."

"I gather Finkbottle doesn't mean us to freeze to death then," Cam said, walking over to inspect the pipes. "This is ingenious. Perhaps we should put in a bath at Girton."

"I thought about it," she said. "It would be quite easy to pipe the water through the kitchen, since it is set so far to the east."

"That's an optimistic way of looking at the kitchen's location. Father always cursed the fact it was so far away from the dining room, but I suppose a warm plunge-bath is better than a cold meal."

"We have the cold meals anyway," Gina pointed out. "We might as well have a warm bath."

Cam climbed the steps down into the bath and was fiddling about when suddenly a huge gush of water erupted from the pipe.

"Damn it to hell!" he howled, jumping back on the stairs. But it was too late: he was completely soaked from his knees to his boots.

Gina giggled. "More fool you. What did you think would come out? Air?"

Cam ignored her. "Lady Troubridge is right: the water is quite warm." He walked back up the steps, sloshing as he went. "Perhaps I had better remove these wet clothes." He grinned at her. "I wouldn't want Finkbottle to succeed in murdering me due to a chill."

Gina blinked. "You may not undress in front of me!"

"Have a heart," he said pathetically. "I shall freeze if I stay in wet clothing. Besides"—he pointed to the water splashing into the bath—"I believe when all's said and done we might as well experiment with Lady Troubridge's invention."

"Take a plunge-bath with—with *you*? One takes baths alone."

His smile was secret and inviting and passionate, all at once. "Not always." He sat down on the top of the stairs to the bath and pulled off his boots.

"You are really going to undress? What if someone arrives to let us out?"

"They won't. I would guess that we're here for the duration, duchess. Finkbottle is searching your room at leisure; it should take him at least an hour. And then I expect that he'll make good his escape. You might as well make yourself comfortable."

"I am quite comfortable, thank you." His wife put her nose in the air and tapped her foot with annoyance. He thought she was quite the most delectable woman he'd ever seen in his life. The more he thought about it—he pulled off his second boot—the more he had a mind to give Phineas Finkbottle a handful of bank notes when they got out of the bath. After a trouncing, of course.

He stood up and put his hands at his trousers. Gina was watching him with fascination.

"You mustn't do this." Her voice sounded weak, to his mind.

He grinned and undid his trousers, pulled them down, and threw them to the side.

She didn't shriek and run up the stairs. Of course, his shirt did hang rather low. He started to unbutton it.

"Cam!"

She said his name in a sort of gasping way.

He stopped unbuttoning and walked over to her. Then he kissed her. He couldn't stop himself, not with her lips so plump and rosy. She sighed and he put his hands on her shoulders to steady her.

"Gina, what did you think we were going to do in your bedchamber?"

She looked at him with those lovely green eyes, secretive and inviting and passionate, all at once. The edge of her mouth curled up. "Take a bath?"

"No. But undress . . . I would have undressed you, duchess," he whispered against her ear and the soft skin of her neck. He pulled her into his arms, holding her tightly against him. Without trousers, he was fairly certain that she would know exactly what was on his mind. "Gina, my love, I would have undressed you."

She looked at him: at his wild smile and high cheekbones, at the mischievous twinkle in his eyes.

She was no idiot. He would take what he took, and leave for Greece. But before he left . . . And he called her "my love." Her heart melted. Her conscience scolded, but some other part of her melted when he said that. He called her "love."

The plunge-bath was housed in a small room, and it was quickly growing toasty warm from the water pouring into the bath.

Cam kneeled before her. "May I remove Your Grace's slippers?"

Gina's heart was singing. She was quivering all over. She delicately raised her skirts in both hands and pointed her narrow shoe at Cam.

His smile had no hint of complacency, just a pure joy that sent a burning heat to Gina's middle. His hand slipped around her slender ankle and pulled off her shoe. He set it precisely to the side, and she offered her other ankle.

"Beautiful," he said, and she thought he was talking of her legs. He drew off her other slipper and put it to the side.

Then he ran his hands slowly, slowly up one leg, sliding up the graceful curve to her knee. He stopped at the garter, untied the knot, and flung it to the side. A stocking fell in a silky rush to her ankle. He looked up at her briefly and then curled his fingers around her other ankle. Obediently she let him take the garter and the stocking. She was bare-toed and bare-legged under her gown.

He didn't move immediately. His hands returned to her ankles, and slid up the smooth flesh, sweet, peachy smooth. She quivered.

"What are you doing?" she asked.

"Caressing you." His hands were inching up, up into the curve of her thigh. She was on fire. But some primitive female spirit of defense aroused itself.

"No!" She reached down and pushed at his shoulders. But he was like a mountain, fixed in a position of worship. He threw his head back, tossed hair out of his eyes, and grinned at her.

"It's naught but a gentle touch."

She trembled under that gentle touch and her mouth formed a small circle.

"It's nothing more than a caress one might give a child, or a baby lamb."

She could feel her knees shake. She broke away and pulled back. He stood up and pulled his shirt over his head. And there he was: strong of thigh in the flickering gas light, wearing only white smalls. His chest was broad and muscular, his arms even larger.

She didn't know what to say or where to look. But she couldn't look away. He was too beautiful, too *male,* too unlike herself. There was nothing sleek about him. He was all hard muscle with a dusting of black hair.

"Why are you so muscular?" she asked. She had a fair idea that most men in the *ton* had no muscles at all.

Cam shrugged. "Sculpting is hard work. I quarry my own marble."

He looked at her. "Duchess." His voice was a command. "Here." He pointed to a point just before him.

And she obeyed. Ambrogina Serrard, Duchess of Girton, dutiful daughter, dutiful wife, dutiful duchess, walked to her husband in her bare feet. But she didn't look at him with the prim and proper air of a virgin faced with her first ungarbed male body. No: Gina looked at him with the frank and thirsty gaze that was hers alone. Cam felt his blood race. Go slow, he cautioned himself. Keep her virginity in mind. The thought cooled him down a bit.

She looked at him. "Well?"

He cleared his throat. "May I remove your garments?"

"I can manage," she said quickly.

Cam grinned. Did his duchess even realize that he had tricked her into undressing? He had discovered that Gina never, ever asked for help. She seemed to think that she could go through life unaided, except when it came to her right glove.

But she wasn't doing so well at the moment. "Perhaps we should extinguish the oil lamps," she said, just a bit desperately.

"Absolutely not. I want to see you."

Her cheeks were flaming. "I don't wish to do this on the floor."

"There is a chaise longue," Cam said, and only the laughter in his eyes betrayed his grave tone. "But a duke and a duchess would never make love other than in the ducal bed."

284

Gina chose to overlook the little edge of mockery in his voice. "Exactly."

Cam looked down. There was nothing he could do about the state of his body. In fact, he had a fair idea that this would be his normal state for the next forty years or so. Whenever he was around his wife, anyway. "In that case, shall we sample the bath, duchess? May I suggest that you remove your gown and"—he forestalled her objection with a swift kiss—"bathe in your chemise?"

Gina bit her lip. Really, she could have no objection to bathing in her chemise. It wasn't as if she was naked.

Her gown had two buttons at the neck. She drew it over her head and then, in one beat of her heart, the cool yellow fabric rushed past her eyes and was gone. There was no difference between a chemise and a nightgown, after all. Cam had seen her nightgown—nay, he had ripped open her nightgown. Gina's cheeks pinked at the memory.

Cam took a deep breath. Gina was wearing a chemise of the thinnest cotton. It was white, simply fashioned, and the essence of modesty. Yet it was more sensual than the richest silk.

"Shall we to the bath, Your Grace?" She gave him a slow smile, a smile like liquid molasses. The Duchess of Girton was discovering the manifold pleasures of seduction.

He said something, had to clear his throat, finally said, "Yes."

She held out her hand. But he wouldn't let her draw him toward the stairs into the plunge-bath. Instead he turned her palm against his mouth. Did she know what would happen to her delicate cotton chemise when drenched? Did she care? His prim duchess was gone, replaced by a sultry sprite—the woman who greeted him in yellow silk with a brandy in her hand.

He kept his eyes on hers and tasted her wrist, sweet skin, white even in the twilight of the bath. Finally he let her draw him to the steps.

At the bottom, Cam plunged into the water. Gina paused at the last step above the water and poked in a toe. "It *is* warm," she said with delight.

"I turned on the warming switch," Cam said. He was up to his waist in water. She walked slowly, step by step into the bath, until she stood before him, the water just lapping at her breasts. As she watched, he ducked under the water and came up a gleaming water animal, sleek and dark, drops sliding from his chest back into the bath.

Not to be outdone, Gina did the same. She splashed back up, laughing. "This is the first time I've been in something larger than a tin bath. Isn't this glorious, Cam!"

"Glorious," he said.

Her eyes followed his. "Hmm," she said. "It appears that my chemise has lost its—"

He stopped her amusement with his mouth.

Gina had never been a coward. It was with dismay that the old duke, Cam's father, had discovered that his son's young wife had too much backbone for her age. He had succeeded in molding her into a proper duchess, but only at the expense of his nerves. Mr. Bicksfiddle, the estate manager, would have echoed the old duke's statements. Once the Duchess of Girton decided to do something, not hell nor high water could stop her.

She stepped back and pulled her sopping chemise over her head and tossed it to the side. It billowed when it hit the water, and sank.

The look on Cam's face was everything a woman could hope to see, under the circumstances. She ignored the burning heat in her belly and the unsteadiness of her limbs and splashed a little water in his direction.

"You will love bathing in the Mediterranean," he said hoarsely. He walked one step toward her. His large hands touched her as if she were marble sculpted by Michelangelo himself. "Ah, God, you're so beautiful," he said. And in the wonder of his voice, she felt truly beautiful for the first time.

There were strands of wet hair caught on her cheeks; he carefully pushed them away. "There's paint on your cheeks," he said, and rubbed with his thumb.

She looked puzzled and then laughed. "I darken my lashes."

"I thought you did," he said with satisfaction. Then he brought his great, wet hands to her face and rubbed. "They're beautiful without paint. Like strands of sunlight." She caught his hands in hers, and he bent his head to her lips.

She came to him with a little sigh that set his pulse racing. He lingered on her body, molding its sweet curves to his fingers, memorizing the delectable curve at the inside of her hip. She turned out to be a laughing mermaid, his wife, liable to fall backward into the water. He had to punish her with kisses until she clung to him trembling, her breath caught in her throat. Begging . . .

He climbed from the bath, holding his wife in his arms. Carried her to Lady Troubridge's chaise longue and laid her down.

She was a wanton woman, his duchess. She didn't lie under his hand, as had most women of his experience. Let alone a woman with no experience. She twisted and turned, begged and cried. Turned to him. That was the truly unexpected thing, from his point of view. She not only took, but she gave. Where he kissed her, she kissed him. Where he touched her, she touched him. She was a born coquette, a ravishing combination of innocence and innate knowledge.

And she laughed. She giggled when he kissed his way down the curve of her breasts, the delicate curve of her rib cage. Stopped giggling and they had a brief argument as he continued. He won when he distracted her by letting one hand stray to her breast. His Gina could no more contain herself when he touched her breast than a young boy can resist being tickled. There was no laughing then. He made his sweet way where he wished, and kissed as he wished, and she twisted and gasped and cried in his arms.

The shocking part—not to put it too bluntly—was that she pushed him away and demanded her own rights. "Ladies don't do this sort of thing," he warned her. His body went rigid as a board as she kissed a little path, a winding, smiling path down his stomach. "Gina—" he said, but she paid him no mind. She probably never would, he thought dimly. They'd be—but he lost the thought. His fingers caught in her sleek, wet hair, and a low groan burst from his chest.

When he pulled her up, covered those red lips with his own, he closed his eyes in the face of her delight.

"He can't have you." His voice was rough and his hands were shaking. He rolled her on her back and ran a hand down her sleek legs. They fell open and she arched against him. He was afraid to diminish her pleasure, afraid of the pain. "It won't hurt long," he said into her ear.

"I know. Please, Cam. I want you . . . I want you!" Her hands clutched his shoulders.

He thrust. And waited to cause pain. Dimly, he was aware that his body was shot with ecstasy, demanding more, demanding—but he waited. She had her eyes closed. He kissed her eyes, her cheeks, her lips.

"Gina!" he whispered. "Are you all right?"

She opened those eyes, the exact color of the Mediterranean at sunset. "Do you think that you could do that again?" she said. He wasn't mistaken. She was going to laugh all the way through making love. There was laughter gleaming in her eyes and in the tremble of her mouth.

He withdrew, slowly, and plunged deep. The laughter disappeared and she gasped. It seemed to him not an unhappy gasp. So he did it again. And this time she met him halfway. He could feel his vision slipping.

"It doesn't hurt, does it?"

"A little bit," she replied. "You're—you're—bigger than I am."

He could feel that for himself. Every inch of his body was telling him the same thing.

"But it doesn't hurt, it feels—ah—I don't know. It makes me feel *hungry*."

A slow smile curled Cam's lips. "I can help you with that," he said against her mouth. He plunged again, again, again.

She was a screamer, his duchess. He knew it, and he was right.

What he hadn't known was that she would make him into one.

Cam rolled onto his back, carrying his wife with him. He put her on top of him as if she were a blanket. She slumped boneless, her head tucked into the curve of his neck. He stroked the long line of her backbone and thought pleasurably about nothing. Thought about staying in the plunge-bath forever. She was sleeping, so he dragged Lady Troubridge's blanket over her sleek skin and kissed the top of her head.

Perhaps they should get dressed . . . rescue might come at any moment. He wrapped his arms around his precious bundle of a wife. He'd made one decision: he wasn't going to let her go until they did that again, oh, perhaps a thousand times. Two thousand. His eyes drifted shut.

Chapter Twenty-Seven

Lady Troubridge's Plunge-Bath, a Dark but Not Unpleasant Habitat

Gina woke to darkness so profound, so thick and silent, that she literally couldn't see anything. For a moment she was mortally frightened.

But then she realized that while she couldn't see, she could feel. And hear. It wasn't utterly silent. She could hear Cam breathing. Moreover, when her heart stopped beating frantically in her ears, she could hear his steady heartbeat, not so far from her ear. And she could feel her own boneless, satisfied body. A grin curled her mouth.

There had been no excruciating pain, as she'd heard it described. She had heard all about the marital act. She knew it was pleasurable, in the right circumstances. And that some women didn't enjoy it, while men always did. She turned her lips against the warm skin beneath her. She had an idea that those women weren't as lucky as she.

He woke up like a cat, straight from sleep to awake. His body went rigid. "What the *devil* happened to the light?"

"I think the oil lamp burned out." She kissed his throat, tasted salt.

He said nothing and his body didn't relax.

"Cam?" She found his lips. An involuntary shudder went through her body. Perhaps, she thought, her body would never be the same. Blood danced under her skin, speaking of the hair-roughed skin beneath hers, the hard angles and

290

muscles she lay on, the luxurious weight of her own breasts against his hard chest.

He kissed her, but it was no more than a pucker of the lips.

"I'll have Finkbottle's skin for this," he said, and he sounded a good deal more furious than he had when they were first shut in the bath.

"The lamp was bound to burn down," she pointed out. "Do you have any idea how long we slept? Perhaps it's already near morning."

"It's between ten and eleven o'clock in the evening. We've been here approximately three hours."

"How on earth can you tell?" she asked, nuzzling his neck with her lips.

"Excuse me," he said, lifting her off his body and putting her to the side. A moment later the blanket tucked around her shoulders.

"How can you see what you're doing?" she asked. "And how do you know what time it is?"

"I have had similar experiences," he said. His voice didn't echo even a trace of the pleasure they had shared. Gina huddled in her blanket.

Cam had walked away. She strained her eyes but couldn't see anything at all. "Don't fall in the water!" she cried, suddenly afraid.

"I won't." His voice came from the right. "Would you like to wear your gown?" His voice came back toward her and the gown fell into her lap. Gina clutched it gratefully. She dropped the blanket and pulled on her gown. It took a moment to make certain that she had it on correctly.

"I've found your stockings," said the voice, dimly. "But I can't seem to locate one of your slippers."

"You threw it to the right."

A moment later she was drawing on her stockings—a far more difficult task in the dark than in the light. Then she was as dressed as possible. She shuddered to think what her hair looked like. All she could do was comb it with her fingers.

"Cam?" she asked.

"Yes?"

"Why am I bothering to get dressed? Aren't we likely to spend the night here? It seems to me that Finkbottle would have returned if he was likely to."

"I doubt he ever meant to return," he said in a brutally angry voice. "I plan to kick that damn door until someone hears me."

Gina thought for a moment. "Cam," she called. "Will you come here, please?"

She heard his footsteps, but it was still a shock when he touched her. "Will you sit with me?"

He hesitated. "Of course," he said, sitting beside her.

"What is the matter?" she said, in a tone carefully empty of blame or reproach.

"Nothing," he replied, just as calmly. "Other than the fact that I dislike being imprisoned in a dungeon by a solicitor who has likely stolen a priceless artwork."

She held on to his arm so he couldn't slip away. Perhaps men grew irritated after—a more dreadful thought struck her. Perhaps he was in a rage because, having taken her virginity, they would no longer be able to procure an annulment. A pang of distress sounded all the way from her heart to her stomach.

"Are you angry because the annulment won't go through?" she asked, before she could rethink the question.

"No," Cam said shortly, sounding uninterested. "You're mine now." Gina felt a thrilling dip in her stomach. She'd never been anyone's before. Even her mother had not really been her mother, and her husband had not really been her husband. There was something oddly reassuring about the briskness with which he announced it.

"Then what is the matter?" she repeated.

"For God's sake, I just said that nothing was the matter," Cam roared, starting to his feet. Gina came with him. She loathed the idea of stumbling after him in the dark.

But he tore away her hand and walked off. "It's only dark, Gina," he said roughly. "There's no reason to go into a tizzy."

"But I'm not—" Gina said, and stopped. It was he who was scared—how odd that she hadn't seen it immediately.

He hadn't gone far, so she simply walked in the direction of his voice until she bumped into a warm body. He was leaning against the wall. His body was rigid. She cupped his face in her hands and kissed him. At first he didn't respond at all, and then his lips softened.

She almost thought she had done it, when he pushed her away and said, in a strained sort of way, "Lord save me from an insatiable woman."

Gina bit her lip and counted to ten.

"It was supposed to be a joke," said a voice just in front of her.

She counted to ten again. As she had told Carola, silence was sometimes extremely useful.

Sure enough, his arms reached out. He put his lips in her hair, and at first she couldn't understand what he was saying. So he repeated himself.

"Did you hear the jest about the preacher, the Puritan and the vintner's daughter?"

"No," Gina said.

"I can tell you a riddle, if you like," he offered.

"I would prefer not. I've never been any good at riddles."

"I would not wish you to be afraid of the dark." There was a driven rage to his voice. "I shall have Finkbottle's head for putting you in this intolerable situation."

"I'm not afraid," Gina said flatly. She reached up and pulled down his head so that she could kiss him. "Would it make it easier if I told *you* some riddles? I cannot always remember the correct answer, more's the pity."

There was a moment of silence broken up by a drop or two of water falling from the pipe into the bath.

"Am I twittering?" he said, finally.

"You're distressed. I myself am thrown into paroxysms by snakes. So be warned."

A kiss landed on her nose. "I suspect if I were capable of paroxysms, this is the situation that would bring them on."

"Shall we sleep with a lamp burning?"

"No. I am only disturbed by rooms with no light and no window." He hesitated. "My father used to close me in closets and cupboards for punishment."

"He tried that with me! That is, he did it once. He shut me in the wine cellar. But I described the punishment in a letter to my mother. The duke never recovered his hearing in his right ear after her visit. At least, that's what he blamed his deafness on."

Cam's arms tightened around her. "I'm sorry he did that to you. It never crossed my mind he would do it to someone other than his own child. More and more, I think I should have taken you with me out that window."

She laughed. "You couldn't have! Imagine how annoying it would have been to be burdened with an eleven-year-old wife."

"Well, if I had known he was going to lock you up in the cellar, I would have pulled you after me," he said.

"To be honest, the cellar didn't bother me very much. I am such a practical kind of person, and even at eleven, I wasn't very imaginative. But if he did it when you were a child, it must have been dreadful."

"The first time I remember it was the day of my mother's funeral. He thought that I hadn't shown proper respect because I fidgeted during morning prayers. So he closed the doors to the chapel and locked me in with her body."

"That's horrid!" she gasped. "Dreadful old man that he was. You were only seven or eight, weren't you?"

"Five," Cam said. "After that, he locked me up fairly frequently. I like to tell myself that I wouldn't have become a coward except for the things he said."

"You are not a coward!" They had ended up back on the chaise longue, and Gina had her arms slung around his neck. "What things did he say?" She thought that his body was slightly less rigid than it had been.

"That my mother was going to haunt me. I believed him of course. He could be quite graphic about decaying flesh and worms."

"Cruel old man," Gina snapped.

"Yes," he agreed. "It took me some years to realize it. And coward or not, I am not comfortable in the dark, even now, years later."

"That was a despicable thing to say about your mother," Gina said. "She loved you so much."

"How on earth do you know?" There was an amused note to his voice.

"Because I know," she retorted.

He shrugged. "I have no memory of her at all. I expect she was a conventional woman of the *ton* who greeted her son and heir with a pat once or twice a week."

"No," Gina said. "She wasn't that type of woman at all. I was given her bedchamber after our wedding, you know."

"Her room? It was locked up during my entire childhood."

"When he discovered that you had fled, your father locked your room instead and pushed me inside your mother's."

Cam's lips were warm on her ear. "Tried to terrorize us both, didn't he? It's lucky that you have such a strong backbone."

"It was odd at first," Gina admitted. "All her clothes were in the wardrobe, and her hairbrushes were on the table, just as they were when she died. But my governess didn't make anything of the fact that your mother's things hadn't been touched in over a decade. Instead, we started folding all the gowns and putting them away. And in the pocket of one of them was a little book. Your mother's diary."

He had started caressing her neck in an idly interested sort of way, but his hands stilled when she said that.

Gina leaned back into his arm in case he wanted to lower his hand just a trifle. "She writes about you as a baby," she said. "I gather you were the sweetest baby ever born in England, Scotland or Wales. She used to sing you to sleep every night. Even when they had guests, she would slip away to the nursery so she could sing you to sleep."

His hand had started its caress again, but she could tell he was listening.

"You had huge black eyes, and a plump lower lip. You had a special smile just for her, and your first tooth was just *here*." She put her finger on his lips. He licked her finger, and she put it in her mouth. "Mmm," she said dreamily. "You taste very sweet, even grown up."

He made a low sound in his throat and his hand danced over her gown. "Why'd you put this rag back on?" he demanded.

She ignored him. "I daren't tell you what she called you," she said with exaggerated timidity. "I'm afraid you would be too humiliated."

He was tracing a lazy path up her thigh. "Try me," he said, kissing her eyelids.

"Buttercup," she said, somewhere between a gasp and a cry. His thumb was doing . . . something. "She called you her little buttercup because you—oh, Cam, that feels *so* good."

He pushed her back onto the chaise longue, and yanked up her gown. "You mother loved you more than anyone in the world," she said, in the moment before she forgot what she was thinking. She reached out blindly and managed to catch his face in both hands and draw it to hers. Unfortunately, that brought his hard body down on hers, which destroyed the little thinking capacity she had left. So she spoke quickly. "Your mother was likely with you in those dark rooms, Cam. She was sitting next to you and crying because she wasn't able to rescue her own little Buttercup." Tears stung her eyes at the thought.

"I hope she's given up her guardianship by now," an amused voice said from the darkness above her. "I'd rather we were alone at this particular moment."

"Oh *you*," Gina said crossly. Without warning his head descended to her breast.

She melted, raising her body to his hand, writhing, crying out. He slipped in as if he was born to answer the throbbing sensation that had engulfed her thighs. She clutched him, hard, and tried to regain the sense of rhythm they had last time. It came quicker this time. She was learning, she thought. Then he did something different, lifted her legs, and half understanding, she wrapped them around his waist and—

This time he didn't roll over and pull her on top of him. He was too tired. She took too much out of him, his delicious wife.

He slipped to the side, took his weight off her but stayed where he could keep his hand on the silken skin just under her breast. "So what color was my hair when I was born?" he said, when his heart had slowed to a reasonable rate.

"Huh?" She sounded dazed. Cam grinned to himself. He'd pleasured a few women in his day. But he had never seen a woman as passionate as his own prim and proper duchess.

He let his lips slide across her cheeks. She had beautiful high cheekbones. All this darkness was excellent for the sculptor in him. He was feeling her bones rather than seeing them; it made him itch to hold clay in his hands, to pick up a chisel. "Did my mother say whether I had hair as a baby?"

"Of course you did," she said. "You had adorable little black ringlets."

He smiled into her neck. "I hope you're not one of those people who goes to sleep every time you have a little pleasure."

"Mumph," said his wife with a huge yawn. And she seemed to think that her response was sufficient.

But Cam felt as if his body was one huge grin. He scooped her up and strode toward the bath. Then he paused because he didn't want to break a leg. He was pleased to find that he had walked unerringly to the top of the bath steps.

"Cam, what are you doing?" She nuzzled her face against his neck.

By now he was up to the knees in water. "Dropping you," he said cheerfully.

She shrieked lustily when she hit the water. No reason for that, Cam thought. Lady Troubridge's heating pipe was working just fine. Wait till he dropped her in the Mediterranean in December. Now that was chilly water!

She came up with a squeak and before he knew it she'd launched a counteroffensive that employed all kinds of body parts generally ignored in polite circles.

"I can't believe you did that," he said a few moments later, panting and laughing at the same time. He had the advantage because of his uncanny night vision, but she was so slender and slippery that she seemed to disappear from his hand. And she attacked without warning—

"No, you don't!" he said with a shout of laughter, heading off an attack that might have had serious consequences. He caught her against his body and kissed her, a slow molasses kiss. "You wouldn't want to jeopardize our future little butter-cups, would you?"

It took her a moment to remember. To think about butter-cups, and him and her, in the same breath. But he was crush-ing his mouth against hers, and if her foolish heart melted even more . . . well, what could she do about it?

It was the second time that Phineas Finkbottle had observed the duke and duchess crushed in a passionate embrace. In the moment before he turned away he saw the duchess's slender, milky back and the duke's hand on the curve of her bottom. Phineas put down his lantern and turned to go without a sound. He couldn't let his witnesses see the duchess unclothed. But his heart was filled with glee. He, Phineas Finkbottle, had stopped that annulment in its tracks.

"I'm sorry," he said, pulling the door shut behind him and looking at the little circle of dowagers whom he had prom-ised to escort into the plunge-bath. "I'm afraid that this is not a suitable time to visit the facilities."

"Why on earth not?" screeched Mrs. Flockhart. "What on earth is stopping us?"

He almost quailed but then he straightened his shoulders. He was a man of resource, a man who got things done. "I saw a rat," he said crisply. "Not an appropriate place for delicate ladies such as yourself."

Mrs. Flockhart voiced what several were thinking. "Well! I do expect that Lady Troubridge, *poor dear,* will be rather horrified to know that she has been sharing her bath with rats! She is so insistent on the health benefits of a plunge-bath!" she tittered.

Chapter Twenty-Eight

Mr. Rounton Defends His Heritage

"Do you know what I love about your eyes?" Gina said dreamily. "The way your lashes are so black. And they're all spiky from being wet. I would love to have black lashes, truly that color, I mean."

"I like yours as they are. They're—" Cam broke off. "I can see your eyelashes."

She turned her head and stared at the stairs up to the house.

"Look at that," Cam said. "Someone's come in and left us a lantern. Thoughtful of them. Nice not to interrupt us."

Gina looked down and felt as if her blush must cover her entire body. "I must dress," she said.

"Yes. I suppose the door is no longer locked."

He picked her up and strode back through the water and splashed his way up the stairs. Then he let her slide down his body, onto her own feet.

She looked at him, and smiled, a cat-in-the-cream smile. "You didn't seem to mind the dark very much."

"Think you've cured me, have you?"

"You didn't need curing," Gina said, standing on her tiptoes so she could look straight into his eyes. "All those kisses your mother gave you were in your memory. You just needed reminding that she loved you—*Buttercup*."

His smile was reluctant, but none the less sweet for that. "Perhaps you're right," he drawled. She turned away to pick her gown off the floor. He pulled her back against him, holding her naked bottom against him.

Feeling rushed through her legs and her knees almost buckled.

"I'll be joining my lady in her bed tonight," he said.

She couldn't even answer. The blood was pounding so hard in her ears that she wasn't even certain that she heard him correctly.

He let her go and strode over to his trousers. She stood for a moment, letting the fact that she was utterly, absolutely, in love with her fool of a husband sink into her head.

"And I'll be sculpting you with that piece of marble," he tossed over his shoulder. "I've been working on the sketches for the last two days."

Wonderful. Now she was to become the naked resident of cloakrooms. She didn't even care. She put a foot on the chaise longue and slowly pulled on a stocking. Her body twinged and protested. She was going to live among naked sculptures, become one herself. Her heart sang.

He was already dressed and had turned off the warming switch. "Cam," she said, "do you see a garter anywhere?"

He plucked it from the floor and walked over to her. She took it and tied it just over her knee, shaking her gown down to the ground.

"I'm going to do your head and shoulders," he said, tracing a line that ended just above her collarbone. "I'm not certain that I can do your eyes justice, especially the way they tilt at the corners. But this beauty here"—his thumb rubbed the back of her neck—"this is lovely and I know I can do it."

Her relief must have showed.

"Thought I'd turn you into a naked Diana, did you?"

She nodded.

"I'll be damned if I ever let another man see your body," he said. "In stone or in the flesh. You're my wife, Gina. Really my wife now. Not that I won't sculpt other naked bodies," he added.

Her eyes narrowed. "Marissa?"

"Who else? I'm not putting you out in the marketplace. You'll be naked in my bedroom, and no other place."

There was something about his eyes that made her trust him. Fool that she was, she couldn't even bring herself to question what he meant. Did he mean to take her to Greece? Or leave her home at Girton? She pushed the thought away.

"Oh dear," she said with mock sadness. "That *is* a pity."

"What?"

"If I'm naked only in your bedchamber"—she paused, her face alight with wicked mischief—"I gather we won't make use of the bluebell wood at Girton." She smiled at him, a smile that licked his bones and made him stand harder than a piece of oak. "I know you're cured of your reluctance to be in the dark, but I thought perhaps we would need to refresh your lessons. At night."

He concentrated on taking a deep breath. "May I escort you to your chamber, Your Grace?"

She dropped a perfect curtsy. "I would be honored."

Gina tried to make her husband let go of her arm on the way up the stairs from the plunge-bath, but he ignored her.

"Stubble it, Gina," he said, amiably enough.

"We should be restrained," she said halfheartedly, as Cam pushed open the door at the top of the stairs. "I haven't informed my fiancé that I won't marry him."

"Bonnington is not an idiot. Or perhaps he is. Either way, it doesn't matter." He held open the door, and Gina walked into the corridor.

"Cam," she said, in a stiff, warning voice.

He looked over her head. "Well, if it isn't the ubiquitous Phineas Finkbottle." He pulled Gina back so she was behind his body. Then he walked slowly toward the solicitor, watching the man's hands.

Faced with a livid nobleman, Phineas began to babble. "I hope I have not misstepped—I most regretted—but Mr. Rounton's instructions—truly, Your Grace, they were quite straightforward—I couldn't think of another—the earth closet—"

Cam stopped short and tried to make sense of Finkbottle's tangled speech. The man blundered on, but nothing he said made much sense. "What the devil are you talking about? What is this talk of earth closets? And what did Rounton tell you to do?"

A nervous giggle escaped Gina. "If I understood him correctly, Mr. Finkbottle almost locked us in an earth closet instead of the plunge-bath."

Cam put an arm around his wife and pulled her tightly against his shoulder.

Finkbottle started to reply, something about keys and a gardener, but Cam brusquely interrupted. "Let's cut to the chase, shall we? Where the devil have you put the Aphrodite?"

Finkbottle visibly trembled. "The *what*?"

"The Aphrodite, you blithering idiot!"

"I merely followed Mr. Rounton's orders. He said nothing of an Aphrodite."

"Don't blame this on Rounton. He would never instruct you to steal a precious statue. The man is loyal to our family."

"I don't believe that Mr. Finkbottle has any idea what the Aphrodite is," Gina pointed out. "In fact, I would guess that the Aphrodite is safely in Esme's possession."

Finkbottle stood there, looking as buffleheaded as it was possible for a young man to look. His face was as flaming as his hair.

"Are you the duchess's illegitimate brother, then?"

Finkbottle's eyes grew large. *"What?"*

"The duchess's illegitimate brother," Cam repeated. "Are you he?"

"No!"

"I can't think how you saw any resemblance between us," Gina interjected.

"He has red hair."

"I'm not illegitimate," Phineas stammered. "I'm poor but that's not the same as being illegitimate. My father is a younger son of an earl. And my mother was a perfectly respectable woman, the daughter of a squire. And they were *married*!"

Indignation seemed to give him something of a backbone. "You have accused me of theft and of being ill-born, my lord, but all I did was lock you in the plunge-bath for a few hours."

Cam stiffened again. "Well, why the devil did you do that?" he said softly. Phineas instinctively fell back a step. "Mr. Rounton," he faltered.

"Mr. Rounton told him to do it," Gina said. "Rounton sent poor Mr. Finkbottle to the house party and told him to compromise us. I believe Rounton might have thought he was protecting the ducal line."

"Compromise us? Well, we'll see about that," said her husband in a deadly, cool voice. "Thinks he can simply arrange my life to suit himself, does he? Well, it may please you to know, Finkbottle, that absolutely no one knows that we were in the plunge-bath. It takes more than two to be compromised. You need an audience. There's nothing— absolutely nothing—to stop Her Grace from marrying that pestilent Bonnington tomorrow. And you can tell Mr. Rounton that from me!"

"Cam," Gina said.

Finkbottle nodded his head. "I will, my lord. I will tell him immediately." He edged to the side, obviously about to make a dash for it.

"On second thought, I'll tell him myself," Cam said. His voice grated with rage. "I don't believe I wish to have a solicitor who takes it upon himself to organize my sexual encounters. Rounton has gone beyond the pale."

Mr. Finkbottle turned even whiter, if that was possible. "If I might beg your indulgence, my lord," he begged. "It was entirely my misinterpretation of Mr. Rounton's directions that—"

But a clear voice interrupted them both. "Cam."

"Yes, darling," he said, turning to her.

Her eyes were dancing, and her long hair lay damp and tangled over her shoulders. She put her hands on his shoulders and smiled at him, and it was almost enough to make Cam's irritation fall away.

"I disagree with you."

"About what?" Cam asked, trying not to think about the fact that her lips were swollen and crimson from his kisses.

"I believe I *am* compromised. I am quite, quite certain that we were known to be in the plunge-bath. In fact, I believe my reputation is indisputably compromised."

She watched as his eyes cleared. "Do you, love?" He lifted her hand to his lips.

"I fear so." She sighed. "I should hate to think that you are trifling with me."

He leaned forward and spoke just for her ear. "I fully intend to trifle further, this very night."

She raised an eyebrow. "Would you feel the same had we been in an earth closet?"

"You could have sat on my lap," he said with a twinkle. She colored, and he turned back to Finkbottle. "All right.

306

Rounton's won. We're compromised. You can tell him yourself."

Finkbottle gave a shaky bow. "Please accept my humble apologies for my impertinent action in locking you in the plunge-bath."

"I am grateful to have been spared the earth closet," Gina said.

"Oh! I almost forgot," Finkbottle said. "I have these papers for you, Your Grace." He withdrew a thick folded bundle of parchment from inside his coat.

Cam took them. "Papers for the annulment?" he asked, thinking about ripping them in half.

"Oh no, that *is* your annulment," Finkbottle said, rather more cheerfully. "Mr. Rounton had no trouble at all obtaining the annulment. Under the circumstances, the Regent waived the requirement for Parliament's approval. There was no question but that—" He ground to a halt.

"—that we never consummated the marriage," Cam filled in. "And, given that the papers were signed two days ago, we never did consummate our marriage."

Gina felt a little chill. She could have been a marquess already. She moved a little closer to her former husband and tucked her hand in his arm.

Finkbottle hesitated for a moment. "I hope you understand that while I would be most honored to be your brother, my lady, I could not overlook the fact that my parents were fast married."

Gina almost laughed and caught herself. "Of course I understand, Mr. Finkbottle. Your kind wishes quite assuage my disappointment."

He bowed and left.

Cam looked at his wife. "If Finkbottle is not your brother, then who is?"

Gina began walking down the corridor. "Don't you think it's odd that there has been no follow-up letter requesting money? After all, the annulment is in hand. I could marry Sebastian by special license and the writer would have gained nothing."

"Special license!" Cam snorted. "Entirely too romantic for the wiggy marquess."

"As it happens, he has been carrying a special license in his pocket for the last month, ever since you announced your return."

"Well, he shan't have you." He opened the door to his chamber, and Gina found herself in the room without conscious thought.

"Damned if I can think of anyone who looks like you," Cam said, staring at his wife. "Red hair is surprisingly rare these days."

"There's no reason to suspect that my brother is at the house party," Gina pointed out. "Or that he has red hair, for that matter."

"If your brother isn't here, who ransacked your room looking for the Aphrodite?"

Gina wrinkled her nose. "There's no one suitable at the house party," she said with finality. "Why, the only red-haired man I can even think of is Lord Scotborough, and he's forty-five if he's a day."

But Cam was staring at the wall, obviously not listening. "When did your mother die, Gina?"

"Countess Ligny? She died in March, almost two years ago now. Although I didn't know that she had passed away for quite some time."

"Damn," Cam said in a low, vicious tone. "Damnation!" He sprang from his chair.

"What is it?" Gina asked, startled.

308

"I sent him over here myself. Careless bastard that I am."
He ran a hand through his hair.

"What are you talking about?"

"It's Wapping," Cam said. "I encountered Wapping just a month after your mother died. He must have thought we were living together. And I sent him over to you without thinking twice about it. Stupid, careless—"

"Be reasonable, Cam. Wapping can't possibly be my brother."

"Why not? He appeared in Greece at the right time."

"For one thing, he has brown hair, and for another, he has no idea that the Aphrodite—" She broke off.

"You told him," Cam guessed.

"No! But I did ask him about Aphrodite—the goddess."

Cam was at the door. "Come along, then. Do you know where he might be?"

"Upstairs. He works in the old schoolroom, if he's not asleep," Gina said, joining him. "But Cam, he *can't* be my brother! I'm certain that I would know if I met my brother. I mean, he would be my own flesh and blood, wouldn't he? Wapping is a scholar, not a thief . . ." She kept the argument up all the way to the fourth floor, stopping only when Cam rapped on the door.

"Please forgive us, Mr. Wapping," she said, as they entered the schoolroom. He was bent over a stack of books.

"Are you my wife's brother?" Cam demanded.

Wapping looked up, with his abstracted look. "If you'll excuse me a moment," he said, and returned to scratching a line of prose.

Gina sighed. She knew as well as any that Mr. Wapping, once absorbed in the intricacies of scholarship, was remarkably single-minded.

But Cam had no respect for her tutor's idiosyncrasies. He

strode over to the table and snatched the quill. Ink splattered. Wapping looked up and his mouth fell open.

"What are you doing?" he cried. "I'm working on something important! I'm just reaching the end of the fourth chapter of my Machiavelli treatise. I was at a particularly delicate moment, refuting Pindlepuss's erroneous charges, and you—"

"*Are* you the duchess's illegitimate brother?" Cam said. He leaned over and put his hands squarely on the blotched treatise and its delicate refutation of Pindlepuss's work. His words were evenly spaced, and his voice was full of danger.

"As it happens, I am," Wapping said with no apparent emotion. He rapped sharply on Cam's wrists with a ruler. Blinking, Cam straightened and took his hands off the table. Wapping began fussily blotting the inkstains, mumbling under his breath. He did not look at his sister, standing stock-still in the middle of the room.

There was a moment of silence, broken only by Wapping's mutterings as he mopped up the spilled ink.

Gina, on the other hand, had just discovered what many an elder sister could have told her about siblings: younger brothers are not necessarily a blissful addition to the family. "Why didn't you disclose yourself to me?" she said, advancing on him like a menacing angel. "Why did you go through my room? Why did you toss my belongings on the *floor*?"

Wapping glanced up. Something about her eyes seemed to alarm him more than anything had in Cam's menacing glance. He jumped to his feet and backed up. "I was looking for my mother's bequest," he said. "There's no need to be so agitated. I merely ascertained that you did not have the statue—"

"The Aphrodite?" Cam asked.

Wapping swiveled his head and looked at him. "Do *you* have it?"

310

"No. Gina had it all along. It was under a chair when you ransacked her room."

"Why didn't you just ask me for it?" she cried. "Why didn't you introduce yourself instead of sneaking around and pretending to teach me about Italian history?"

Wapping looked truly indignant. "I did not *pretend* to teach you! For your information, you have just received a truly first-class education in Machiavellian politics. In fact, if you were more diligent in your reading, you would know almost as much as I!"

Cam backed up and leaned against the wall, stifling a chuckle. Brother and sister stared at each other across the table. He was small; she was tall. Her hair was the color of a sunset, and his was the color of a brown squirrel. She was beautifully odd; he was simply odd. But the family resemblance was unmistakable. Pride and excellent workmanship must run in the family, Cam thought.

Gina chewed her lip. "Why do you want the Aphrodite?" she asked. "Cam says that it's not worth a great deal of money."

"The statue itself probably isn't worth a tremendous amount," Wapping agreed. "Although Franz Fabergé, the man who made it, is making quite a reputation in Paris with his hinged objets d'art."

"Hinged!" Cam breathed. "Of course she is hinged. That's a join down her side."

"So you wanted what was inside the statue? Jewels?" Gina snapped.

Wapping seemed unmoved by her sharpness. "I am not altogether certain what is in the statue," he admitted. "I met my—our—mother only once, on her deathbed. She informed me that her most precious possession in the world was inside the Aphrodite, and that she was sending it to you."

Gina bit her lip. "That was not very kind of her."

311

He shrugged. "I wasn't looking for kindness. However, I desperately needed a prolonged period of research in order to complete my book. Luckily, I have made remarkable progress over the last year while tutoring you."

"So you were hoping that she would leave you a bequest," Cam said.

"Would that be unusual? She *was* my mother, after all, and she seems to have spared herself any exertion in raising me."

"And you—you are my half brother?" Gina asked.

"We already agreed to that salient fact," Wapping remarked.

"You can have the Aphrodite. I don't want it."

"I don't want the statue," he said with a touch of impatience.

"You can have what's inside."

"Good," he said. "Well, in that case, would you mind if I returned to my work? I have at least an hour of writing left before I can finish this chapter. I suggest that we meet tomorrow afternoon and open the Aphrodite at that time."

Cam strode forward and grasped his wife's arm. He could see that she was struck dumb and would probably turn to stone gazing at her admittedly peculiar brother. "We will see you tomorrow, then, Wapping," he said over his shoulder.

The man didn't even grunt in reply. His head was already bent over the desk, busy retracing the splotched text onto a fresh piece of paper.

When Cam pushed Gina back into his chamber again, she didn't protest. "I can't believe he's my brother," she whispered, leaning against the door.

"He looks just like you. You're very similar, in fact."

"I look nothing like him!" Gina said, stung.

"It's your expressions," Cam said smugly. "You're two of a kind."

"Just what do you mean by that?"

"Managerial, both of you." He chuckled. "Certain that you're doing exactly the right thing, in exactly the right way."

Her lips set in a mulish line. "We have nothing in common. I shall hand over the jewels inside that wretched statue, and that will be an end to it."

Cam looked at her sympathetically. "I know it was a shock, Gina. But that's not the end to it, more's the pity. The man's your brother. And I doubt there are many jewels inside the Aphrodite," he said. "I have no difficulty believing the statue was hollowed out, but I don't believe it is stuffed with emeralds."

"What else could it be? Countess Ligny said the Aphrodite contained her most precious possession, after all."

"I wonder why she gave it to you, and not to him?"

"He probably looked at her with that condescending glance of his," Gina said. "I wouldn't leave him anything either. His father must have been a pompous bore. I'll have to think of something to do with him," Gina said, wrinkling her brow. "I wonder if—"

"*We* have to think of something," Cam corrected her.

"Of course," Gina agreed unthinkingly. "Perhaps if I asked—"

"Gina."

"What?" She was deep in thought.

He sighed. "Nothing."

"I have an idea!" she cried. "I opened a hospital at Oxford a few years ago. And I remember meeting the kindest man. I believe he was the head of Christ Church."

"Thomas Bradfellow," Cam put in.

"Yes, that was he! I shall write him a letter and *beg* him to take care of my brother. I only hope he remembers me," she added doubtfully.

"He'll remember me," Cam put in.

313

"Why?"

"Because I replaced the Winged Mercury in the central courtyard with a statue of Bradfellow. Lamentably, my statue was wearing only a wig," Cam said.

"Oh," Gina said. She started to giggle. "Was Mr. Bradford—was he as substantial then as he is now?"

"I can only imagine. He made a lovely statue. Bradfellow was a surprising good sort. He sent me down, but I heard that he put the statue in his private garden. And when I came up again the following fall, he acted as if nothing had happened."

"So I'll write—"

"*I* will write, Gina."

She looked startled. "Well, it would be wonderful if you would do so."

"As soon as we marry again, Wapping will be my brother-in-law. I am not incapable of administration, you know."

A small smile curled the edge of her mouth. "In that case, Your Grace, may I beg your help with finishing Bicksfiddle's papers tomorrow?"

He walked over to her. "I suppose," he said, standing so close to her that her nerves crackled, "I could be persuaded."

She licked her lips. "Persuaded? How so, my lord?"

"Damn it, Gina," he groaned. "I'm going to have to evict you from my chamber, or I'll have you again, right here."

Her eyes grew wide.

"Against the door," he said hoarsely. His mouth descended on hers.

He took her silence as agreement.

Chapter Twenty-Nine

Informal Dancing Followed by Private Intoxication

She had just left the ballroom when a hand caught her elbow.

"Lady Rawlings," said a harsh voice in her ear.

Esme's heart sunk. He was so tall and so—so disapproving.

"Much though I hate to interrupt you, I believe we agreed to rehearse *Much Ado*."

She opened her mouth to refuse, but he preempted her. "I realize you may have plans"—he gave Bernie Burdett a ferocious look—"but our performance is tomorrow evening. Lady Troubridge has hung a curtain in the long drawing room."

Bernie was a sportsman and a hunter. He never hesitated to put himself at risk when need be. However, he dropped his escort's arm as if it scalded. "I shall return to the ballroom," he said. "Your servant." He brushed her hand with his lips and sped to the opposite side of the room.

"I will have to fetch my copy of *Much Ado*, Lord Bonnington," Esme said.

He bowed. "I shall escort you, if I may."

They walked up the stairs without exchanging another word. She left him in the corridor and snatched her book off the dressing table. Then they walked back down the stairs. Esme was starting to wonder just how long he could walk in silence. He paced at her side like a moving portrait.

"Did you behave this way when you were young?" she asked.

"I beg your pardon," he replied with glacial emphasis.

She was unable to resist the impulse to be truly rude. "Like a walking poker. It must have been quite disconcerting for your mother. *Oh, there's my darling boy—how unfortunate that he never smiles!*" Esme smirked at him.

He declined to answer.

Annoyance spread through her whole body. What right did Sebastian have to be judgmental of her friendship with Bernie? He couldn't make it more clear that he considered her a strumpet. Of course, she told herself, I *am* a strumpet. She had never seen the reason to fool herself about the consequences of her actions.

"On the other hand," she said thoughtfully, "just imagine how my mama used to complain about me. *Look at that little daughter of mine! Only five years old and she's flirting with the gardener's boy again.*"

She glanced sideways at him. There was just a suspicion of a smile around his lips. It truly was a pity that he had such a lovely mouth.

"It's quite an interesting subject," she continued. "I have no doubt but that Gina knew how to curtsy before she could walk." They walked into a small room off the billiards room. "Oh, shall we practice here?"

By way of answer Sebastian strode over and turned up the lamps.

"And I expect that Gina's husband was always carving bits of wood in the messy way that boys have," she said. "My little brother's pockets were stuffed with fragments of wood he thought looked like ducks or boats."

Sebastian still didn't respond, so Esme kept chattering, well aware that his presence was making her into a complete ninny.

"Girton probably spent most of his time carving little statues of his nanny without her apron."

"I wasn't aware you had a brother."

He stood before the fireplace, looking so handsome that her heart skipped a beat.

"My little Benjamin," she said. "He died when he was five years old."

There was something in his expression that made her keep talking, even though she never, ever talked about Benjamin. "He got a chill. His death changed my mind about having children. For a long time I was afraid to have children of my own."

He sat down beside her on the settee. But he didn't look at her. "You don't wish to have a child? Is that why you live apart from your husband?"

"This is a very improper conversation," she said, trying vainly to draw herself together. The rehearsal—the whole performance—was a dreadful idea. All the time she was spending with Sebastian wasn't helping her ignore her ridiculous affection for him.

"In my experience, your conversation is invariably improper," he noted.

Why did he have to have such a deep voice? The truth is, Esme thought, with her usual clarity, I would rather sleep with my best friend's fiancé than with any other man I have met in my entire, misspent life. This was a repulsive thought to have about oneself, and she frowned in reaction.

He put his hand on her forehead and smoothed the frown lines with his thumb. "Are you sharing a bed with Burdett?" he asked, and his voice had a harsh edge to it.

She met his eyes steadily. "No, I am not." His shoulders relaxed imperceptibly. "But only because Bernie's mind turned out to be disappointing," she added. "I have slept with men other than my husband. Would you like to know their names?"

"Absolutely not." His hand dropped from her face.

"I thought you were indicating interest," she said, her tone tranquil. Inside her mind was screaming with tension. She folded her hands in her lap. "Shall we rehearse the play, my lord, or would you like to give me a list of *your* lovers?"

There was silence. She finally had to look at him. His eyes were the dark blue of pansies. So sober, they were.

She opened her book.

"I have not yet slept with a woman, married or unmarried." His voice was low but utterly calm.

Esme's head literally jerked in shock. "You haven't?"

"No." He didn't seem to feel the need to elaborate.

"Why on earth not?" she breathed.

"Because I am not yet married."

"I had no idea you—are you a Puritan?"

"No."

She waited.

"I have never understood the folly that leads to setting up a mistress," he remarked. "Friends of mine have broken their marriage vows and wasted their principal on opera singers. Never having met a woman who tempted me into foolish behavior, I have not followed their example."

"Oh." She could not quite think what to say next. "Shall we begin with the third act of *Much Ado*, my lord?"

He ignored her. "I would not break my marriage vows, had I made any."

"That is very appropriate of you," Esme said awkwardly.

"However, I have come to believe that Gina will stay with her husband, rather than marry me," he said, looking down at her. "I expect she will tell me so tomorrow."

318

Esme swallowed. She couldn't just sit silently. It was too treacherous, too enticing. Miles was moving back into her bed. Miles was going to father her children. She couldn't make that fact sound urgent to herself.

"Am I to understand that you have met a strumpet capable of tempting you into foolish behavior?" she managed.

"Yes."

She stood up. "Then I wish you luck in achieving the proper degree of folly. Unfortunately, it is time to retire for the night, or we could prolong this fascinating conversation. I suggest that we continue our rehearsal in the morning."

He caught her wrist just as she turned away. She refused to look. His eyes were too dangerous: his eyes and that lean beauty of his. She wasn't going to be his strumpet.

"You have slept with other men—" he began.

She jerked her wrist away from him. "The cardinal distinction is that when I have occasionally—occasionally, my lord—shared my bed with men, it was because I desired them. You seem to have ignored that important fact." She walked toward the door.

He was just behind her. He didn't touch her again, though.

"I didn't say it correctly. I should have told you how beautiful you are."

She couldn't help it: she looked over her shoulder.

He looked faintly impatient. "I was hoping that we could acknowledge our mutual attraction without attaching undue sentiment to that fact."

She took a deep breath. "I gather by *acknowledge*, you think I should invite you to my chamber?"

He nodded. "You are an extremely intelligent woman, for all you pretend to be frivolous."

"That is hardly the point."

He caught her hand and pulled her around to face him. "Then what is the point, Esme? I want you. I want you as I've

319

never wanted any woman and you are . . . available. I am not married, and I don't believe that I am truly engaged to be married either. Why shouldn't you invite me to your bed? I assure you that my brain is in far better working order than Burdett's."

"You are likely right about Gina's marriage."

He opened his mouth and she hastily interceded. "But not about mine, my lord. I am not available."

"No?"

Damn him for his beauty, for the emotion in those businesslike eyes, for the way his hands on hers made her shudder with longing. "As it happens, I am returning to my husband's bed," she said briskly. "So I am afraid that you have missed your opportunity. Strumpet today, wife tomorrow."

His eyes narrowed. "*Returning* does not imply immediate action." He paused.

She said nothing.

"Do I understand that you are not yet reconciled with the estimable Lord Rawlings?"

At her small nod, he reached behind her and locked the door. "Then I would be a fool to miss the small opportunity that I have, would I not?"

Eyes on hers, he stripped off his neck cloth and tossed it to the side.

Esme laughed unsteadily. "You've run amok, my lord. This is not like you—"

His body was large, a rider's body. Despite herself, she felt a deep, melting ache inside. *Hers*. No woman had touched that body. He threw his shirt over a chair.

"You cannot undress in Lady Troubridge's sitting room," she protested. "What if someone wishes to enter?"

"They will not." He was pulling off his right boot. Despite herself, she watched the muscles flex in his powerful back as he bent over. "The musicians were playing a last dance when you and Burdett left the ballroom. No one is at the billiards table next door, and I feel reasonably confident that the household is preparing for bed."

His hands went to his waistband, and her mouth went dry.

She made one last feeble protest. "I shouldn't—" but her mind was already made up. Every bone in her body told her to accept what had come her way. "Wouldn't you be more comfortable joining me in my chamber?"

He looked at her darkly. "I think not. I find the idea that you may have slept with other men in that bed uncomfortable. It is a foolish quibble, but I feel it none the less."

She started to protest and stopped. It was none of his business that she hadn't invited a man into her bed for years, let alone during Lady Troubridge's house party.

In a moment he was stark naked. Esme's knees felt weak; she leaned against the sitting room door.

"Aren't you going to undress?" he asked.

She cleared her throat. This was truly the strangest seduction she had ever participated in. "Will you act as my lady's maid?"

He stepped closer and she felt the blood rush to her face. He was so casual in his nakedness, so confident.

"Doesn't it bother you that this is the first time you have done this?" she asked, with some curiosity.

He paused for a second in his nimble unbuttoning. "No. The process seems simple for most men, so why would it not be so for me? The action required of me does not seem complicated or difficult." A smile played at the corner of his mouth. "I am reputed quite an athlete, Esme. I trust I shall not fail you in the field."

He gently kissed her neck, and she felt his tongue touch her skin for an instant.

The small part of her brain that hadn't slipped into heated awareness of his body noted his incredible arrogance. Had the man no lack of confidence in any area of his life?

She gently laid her gown over a chair and turned to face him. She was a great aficionado of French undergarments, and at the moment she was tricked out like a Parisian courtesan. Her chemise was naught but a few scraps of lace.

His eyes darkened to black. "You're exquisite." He put a hand on her throat. It slid to her shoulder.

She turned and walked toward the couch. Reaching up, she pulled pins from her hair until it fell in a gentle swoosh to her pantalettes. Then held out her hand.

"Will you join me, my lord?"

Esme shivered with a combination of excitement and embarrassment. She had never made love in a public room. But it didn't seem to bother the proper marquess.

He pulled off her remaining garments until she was quite naked, curling her toes into the carpet.

And he just looked at her. When he spoke, his voice made her jump.

"You're the most exquisite woman I have ever seen, Esme." He pulled her forward, into his arms.

She toppled against his chest, and he smoothed the long line of her hip and thigh, pulling her against his body.

This is the most dangerous thing I have ever done, Esme thought. But his eyes were as blue as a cloudless sky.

At some point a servant rattled the door, wishing to damp the fire for the night.

Sebastian bellowed at him.

Marquess Bonnington, widely known as the most gentlemanly gentleman of the *ton,* had lost his composure. Worse, when his companion giggled and said something very naughty in his ear, he didn't reproach her. Instead he pinned her down and said something fierce, something impolite, something that made Esme shudder and pull him, all the glorious muscled parts of him, closer.

Just because he was an athlete didn't mean that there weren't matters of finesse to learn. But great athletes are great athletes. As Esme discovered, to her great pleasure, they learn quickly. Even better, they understand that the road to perfection is a question of doing it again . . . and doing it again.

And perhaps, in the gray hours of dawn, one last time, if only to prove that innate athletic prowess is a valuable attribute in all sports.

Chapter Thirty

Courage Is Required: Lord Perwinkle's Bedchamber

Carola huddled under chilly linen sheets, safely enclosed in Tuppy's curtained bed. She had pulled the curtains so tightly together that not even a gleam of light penetrated the cloth. Everything was in place except her resolution. In fact, she was contemplating flight. She had just realized that there was one important thing wrong with Esme's plan.

She, Carola, didn't like the marital act. Didn't like it when Tuppy instigated it on their wedding night, and didn't like it any better two weeks later. Her mother's assumption that she would calm to the bridle had never taken place.

She huddled into a tighter ball and clutched her knees. The key thing to remember was that she did want to be Tuppy's wife, even if she didn't want to do *that* wifely duty. She would like to kiss him. The very thought of kissing Tuppy—of Tuppy kissing her!—sent a flush to her face.

But kissing wasn't enough. Esme had been cuttingly straightforward in her analysis. Carola had to persuade Tuppy that she wanted to be in his bed so much that she would humiliate herself to be there. To her mind, humiliation was inevitable. She was so embarrassed that she truly thought she might faint when he climbed into the bed.

The problem was that Tuppy was no good at this sort of thing. Of course, she hadn't stressed that with her friends. It wasn't a loyal thought. She was going to have to pretend to enjoy it. That was the only way she could make Tuppy believe that he wasn't a bad rider, and all the other things she said when they were first married.

She had to be congratulatory. "That's wonderful, Tuppy!" she practiced, under her breath. "What wonderful . . ." Wonderful what? Rhythm? Cadence? "What wonderful finesse you have," she decided. "What wonderful finesse you have, and how much I am enjoying this!" That sounded sophisticated. She had to avoid a tendency to sound like her mother opening a charity bazaar. She had to sound fervent. Truthful.

Just then there was a scraping noise and the door opened. Carola squeaked with panic and then buried her face in the pillow. Had he heard her gasp? She would *die* if he discovered her when he was still fully clothed. He had to come to bed unclothed and having turned down the lamp. Otherwise, he might be put off by the sight of her overgrown breasts. She was wearing her nightgown with a small corset underneath, just to keep her flesh in place. There were muffled sounds as Tuppy walked around the room, presumably undressing.

Carola's heart was beating so fast that she could hardly hear his movements over the drumroll in her ears. What was taking him so long? There was a creak, and then silence. She lay rigid. One moment. Two minutes. Surely she had waited ten minutes! He wasn't coming to bed at all. Or—perhaps it wasn't Tuppy in the room?

Carola's eyes grew wide. It was the thief! The man who rifled Gina's room had come to steal her husband's cuff links. She inched up on her knees and slowly, slowly edged toward the curtains. The thief would likely kill her as soon as look at her. Everyone knew that criminals were desperate by nature and regularly battered people on the head with heavy objects.

With the tip of a finger, she drew the curtain slightly apart. At first she couldn't see anything but the corner of the room. Then she edged to the side and saw—

Tuppy. It was no thief. It was Tuppy. Carola felt a surge of irritation. It was just like Tuppy to sit around and be idle when there was something important to do. He always wanted to sit and read a book, when she wanted to be at a play or, better, a ball.

The fire wasn't even lit. He was just sitting. His legs were outstretched and his lean face was tired. He looks lonely, Carola thought, and a pang caught her just under her heart. Maybe he's thinking about our marriage. Maybe he'll *cry*! But Tuppy had never shown any sign of tears, and Carola had to admit that he didn't look ready to succumb now. He just stared blankly at the charred logs.

Finally he stood up, stretched, and began unbuttoning his evening jacket. Carola's breath caught in her throat as he pulled his shirt over his head.

Tuppy wasn't much of an athlete, compared to some men of the *ton*. He didn't strip and box with Gentleman Jackson himself. He didn't ride to the hunt four days out of five; nor did he careen around the countryside in a racing phaeton. Nothing she knew of explained the whip-lean body he had. How could you get those chiseled muscles sitting around on a riverbank? Tuppy tossed his trousers over the chair and began looking around the room.

Carola suppressed a nervous giggle. He was looking for his nightshirt. But she had bundled it up and stuck it under the bed. She had thought that he was less likely to throw her out of the room if he were completely undressed.

After a while, he gave up the search and just readjusted his smalls in the front. Carola watched with fascination. Men were so oddly constructed. His thighs bulged with muscles as he walked across the room. She felt an odd, flickering heat all over her body.

She nervously shifted back, dropping the curtain. But nothing happened. She couldn't hear anything.

Delicately, she reached forward again and peeked out. He had apparently decided to tend to the dying fire. He was standing next to the fireplace, leaning one arm on the mantel and lackadaisically smashing the charred log with a poker.

He *does* look sad, Carola thought. Perhaps he doesn't want to leave tomorrow morning. Perhaps he cares for me.

Then Tuppy headed for the bed.

It was curtain time.

Chapter Thirty-One

Curtain Call

Tuppy opened the bed curtains and pulled at the blanket before he realized that there was already someone under that blanket. In fact, she was clutching it to her neck. Her tousled mop of curls and bright eyes were all that could be seen.

He felt an instinctive lurch in the area of his chest, instantly quelled. She was a charmer, his maddening wife. But she wasn't his. They had quarreled from their first day together, and he had come to the painful decision that it was time to end the marriage. She could marry her tidy dancer, and he would forget about her. Forget about all women.

His tone was colder than it might have been, given that last thought. "What are you doing in my bed, Carola?"

She bit her lip but didn't say anything.

"Can it be you mistook the way?" he asked. He felt anger growing in his chest. What the devil was she doing, climbing in his bed? She didn't want to be with him; she'd made that clear enough the day before. "Did you think that this was Charlton's bed? I would think that you knew the way quite well, by now."

He stared at her, willing her to blurt out the truth, but all she did was put a small hand on his arm and say, rather imploringly, "Tuppy?"

A sudden thought struck him. "You're carrying Charlton's child, and you hope to seduce me into acknowledging the

328

child as my own. It would be one of those six-month babes, I presume."

She flinched as if he had struck her. For a moment they just stared at each other in the gloomy half light cast by one oil lamp.

"The scheme is almost too clever for you to have thought of alone. Do I see Lady Rawlings's delicate handiwork?"

"Do you—do you truly think that of me?" Her voice shook.

Either Carola had become a fine actress, or she was truly stunned. "What else should I think?" His eyes searched her face. "I cannot imagine a single reason why you would frequent my bed. Unless someone has changed your mind, you consider intercourse to be a messy, utterly tedious, and rather painful task. Please let me know if I have misquoted you."

She bit her lip. Tuppy strained to see her face. Were her eyes filled with tears? A dangerous part of his heart thumped— the part of him that had seen an effortlessly joyous angel dancing and asked for her hand five days later.

He clenched his jaw. "Well, Carola? We are both older and wiser than we were. I hardly think that we need to pretend that you would initiate an activity you found so unpleasant, at least without a very good reason."

"I had better go," she said. There was a little shake in her voice that confirmed his suspicions. She began scrambling toward the other side of the bed.

Instantly he changed his mind. Did he really give a damn if she were pregnant by another man? He would never discard his wife. He grabbed her arm. "Cara." The pet name he gave her during their brief marriage fell unconsciously from his lips.

She shook her head. "Please, let me go."

He pulled on her arm. Now he was determined to find out what was going on.

"It's all right about the baby." His other hand came up, willy-nilly, and touched the little curls at the nape of her neck. He loved—he used to love the way they were so white-blond and soft, just there. "I'll take care of your child."

She still didn't look at him. He tugged gently on the curl he held. "It's just me, Cara. Your irritating old husband, remember? You can tell me about it. I didn't—I didn't expect you to remain chaste, after all. We have been apart for three years." It was almost true. Hoping was not the same thing as expecting.

She shook her head and mumbled something he couldn't hear.

"What?"

"Four years." She looked at him, and her eyes were drenched with tears. "It's been four years and two months."

He blinked. "Ah." He pushed away a tear that was snaking down her cheek. "Don't cry. It's not important, whatever the problem is. You don't have to sleep with me. I'll never, ever make you do that again."

To his dismay the tears overflowed and a sob broke from her chest. Tuppy felt a sickening pang in his stomach. He had found Cara to be one of the most incomprehensible people he'd ever met. He felt as if he'd lost the ability to understand simple English the moment he put the ring on her finger.

"I'll give you the divorce, if that's what you want," he said desperately. "There's no need to cry. You can marry Charlton, or I will acknowledge the child. And you don't have to sleep with me. I would never humiliate you that way." He wiped off the tears that were falling so hard that he couldn't stop them with his fingers.

Then, without warning, she flung herself into his arms and plastered her lips against his. They were soft and full, and it all

330

came back in a rush—his young self, so drowned in desire that he could hardly control himself every time he kissed her.

He pushed her away, embarrassed by the memory of his own foolishness. "As I said, you needn't embarrass yourself or me, Carola. I will acknowledge your child."

It was as if she didn't hear him. She just lurched forward again and actually pushed him against the bedboard. And kissed him. Tuppy had a moment of claustrophobia and gasped for air, and in that second her tongue met his and he was a drowning man. He had never felt with anyone else the rush of erotic sensation he felt with his young, obstinate wife. Certainly not with his desultory mistress of the past year or so, an older and experienced widow who admitted him to her home with a measured enthusiasm that suited them both.

Carola's tongue met his eagerly, and with a sad little pang, he thought that Neville Charlton had certainly taught his wife a thing or two. But he pushed the thought away and simply kissed her fiercely, with all the pent-up longing he felt every time he saw her.

Two things occurred to Tuppy during that long kiss: two facts slowly crystallized in a shaking wave of lust. The first was that he doubted his wife was making up her enthusiasm just to mask an unwanted pregnancy. Such a sophisticated lie wasn't in his Cara's nature. But the second was that, for some unknown reason, she had come to his bed wearing a night-gown with a corset under it, which seemed to imply that she had no intention of taking that nightdress off. In fact, it implied that she wanted to look her best—and if she never intended to undress, what the devil was she doing in his bed?

So, from the depths of his lust-fogged mind, he pushed her away and growled, "Carola, tell me what the hell you're doing in my bed."

She opened her mouth but nothing came out.

"Carola," he said, dangerously.

"I came to make—to seduce you," she said in a little, unsteady voice.

His belly throbbed, and his resolution slipped another inch. "I know that's not the truth," he said, fastening his mind on the corset. "This seems more along the lines of an old-fashioned comedy to me—the moment of the bed trick."

The flash of surprise on her face confirmed his suspicion. But anger didn't follow, just a weary sadness. "So you've arranged for people to find us together, have you? I suppose that will ensure that your child's paternity is unquestioned. *And* then you needn't go through with something as distasteful as actual intercourse."

"I don't know why you keep talking about a child, Tuppy," she said, in a steady voice. "I am not carrying a child."

He pounced. "Oh? Then why, my dear, are you wearing a corset unless it is either to prevent me from seeing your swelling belly or to look your best when we are opportunely interrupted?"

She blushed. The light was dim but there was no mistaking his Carola's blushes. Her skin was so porcelain white that she blushed as red as a peony flower. She didn't say anything, though, just wrung her hands. She was so adorable that Tuppy felt another surge of lust that almost crippled his reason.

"Well?" he asked, through clenched teeth.

"I didn't want to disgust you."

"Because of the child?" Tuppy asked awkwardly.

"There is *no baby*! This corset doesn't even cover my belly—see?" She smoothed the thin cloth of her nightgown against her body, and he could clearly see that the corset ended just above her waist. Her tummy had a gentle curve that fired him with desire but said nothing of pregnancy.

332

"Then why are you here?" His tone had all the bewildered frustration of a man who had never understood his wife since her first bout of tears on their wedding night.

She pressed her hands to her cheeks, mortified.

He tipped up her chin. "Carola?"

She took a deep breath. "You were correct when you noticed that my—my dress size has changed since we married."

"What?"

He didn't have to sound so shocked. She crossed her arms over her chest. "I made a mistake coming to your room. This is absurd!" And this time she moved so quickly that she was off the bed before he even blinked.

He slammed himself in front of the door just as she pulled a robe from behind a chair. Clearly, the corset was one of those female things that there was no point in deciphering. "Why were you in my bed?" he said, standing before the door.

"Because I wanted to seduce you!" she shrieked.

He stared at her, dumbfounded.

"But now I don't, you big oaf! And don't you dare mention that baby again. I don't have a baby, and it's unprincipled of you to even suggest that I might have—that I would do such a thing as sleep with a man not my husband!"

She stood in front of him and her golden curls turned into a fuzzy halo around her head. Tuppy could feel a heat in his chest that was so deep and so hot that he might expire. "You wanted to seduce me?"

She glared at him. "*Wanted*. I've changed my mind."

"No, you haven't," he said. He reached out and grabbed her shoulders, pulling her to him.

His kiss was just as clumsy as she remembered. There was nothing polished about Tuppy: he was direct, and fierce, and awkward. But it was different now. She melted into his clumsy

333

kisses as if he were more polished than Byron himself. When he pulled her roughly against his hard body, it didn't occur to her that he showed no finesse. Instead she trembled all over and arched back against him. He spun her quickly and backed her against the door, which was just the kind of unsophisticated thing he used to do.

He wrenched off her robe because he couldn't get the tie undone. His hands fumbled, but everywhere he touched her, she burned with liquid pleasure.

It wasn't until they were lying on the rug and Tuppy had managed to bundle her nightgown over her head that she came even slightly to her senses. She opened her eyes to find him hanging over her, braced on his elbows, and the lock of hair that was falling over his eyes was so dear that she had to brush it back and kiss him. When they emerged for air he still looked troubled.

"Cara," he said, and his voice had such a deep resonance that she almost wept to hear it. But he was talking, and so she wrenched her mind back to his words. "Would you be greatly distressed if I removed your corset?"

His big hand hovered, and she shuddered with desire to feel him—and blushed when she realized what he was saying. Shyly she pulled her hands from his shoulders and unlaced the front.

He closed his eyes for a second when she pulled the corset open and her breasts spilled free. For the first time Carola thought that she might have misunderstood him.

"You're so beautiful," he said. His voice was everything his hands were not: reverent, delicate, hushed. But she arched into his hands, his wonderful hands and then his mouth—

"You don't think I'm overfleshy," she said before she lost all capacity for thought. "You really don't, Tuppy? Because you said I was fat."

"Fat?" His voice splintered with surprise.

Carola started to smile. He never did answer her, but his mouth was on her breast, and after a while she didn't care what he might have said.

It was only when they were both undressed and he rolled on top of her that her body remembered and tensed, grew a little rigid. He stopped kissing her.

"What's the matter?" he whispered against her lips. But his hand slid down her hip—it was—surely he never touched her like this when they were first married! He eased the stiffness away, soothed the fear away.

"Would you rather be in the bed? I didn't turn the lamp down. I remember that you don't think it's proper—"

"It doesn't matter," Carola said with a little pant. And she found, to her surprise, that she meant it.

Still, she stiffened again when she felt him between her legs. It was confusing—the liquid warmth that seemed to have taken over her body, and her memories of painful intrusion. She couldn't help it. She yelped when he entered, even though he was cautious.

"Does it hurt?" he said, and his deep voice shook.

"No," she whispered. And it didn't. It felt as if molten gold spread through her legs and she moved her knees up and he fell in, a little way, and a harsh noise came out of his mouth. So she nudged against him again, and he came to her more, and more.

She never bothered to tell him how much finesse he had, because he didn't have any. And she lost the inclination to lie. Instead, she sobbed his name and clung to him as he moved in her hard and fast and without any finesse or delicacy at all. The whole experience had nothing to do with being a good rider, or any of those things her mother had said. It was about moving together in a dance so fierce and hungry that Carola

335

experienced something she had never expected or imagined. And the only thing she could do was clutch him to her as hard as she could and even—after a while—move with him.

"The French call it a *petit mort*," Tuppy told her later, lying on his side and stroking her neck. His fingers wandered downward and his eyes laughed at her.

"That's absurd," Carola managed.

But his fingers were dancing over her skin, and there really wasn't any point in arguing about terminology.

Chapter Thirty-Two

Regret Is a Morning Affair

Cam was one of those people who slept so soundly that it was as if his spirit had gone visiting. Gina had never thought about it, but now she discovered that she was the opposite type of person. When Cam rolled over, she woke up. When his large hand settled on her hip and pulled her bottom snugly against him, she stared wide-eyed into the darkness, wondering what was going to happen next. Nothing happened. He just breathed heavily into her neck, and then after a while he started snoring, although he kept her pulled tightly against him.

The stretches of darkness gave her plenty of time for luxuriating in her own foolishness. By sleeping with Cam—if one could call it sleeping!—she had discarded all her dreams of marrying the responsible, kind marquess. As the wakesome hours wound on, Sebastian grew into a larger and larger figure in her mind: a figure of fatherhood, a man who would live in England and take care of his family. A man who would love her, as opposed to calling her "love." Who would not spend his time fashioning naked women in stone, but doing responsible, organized things. She ignored her sense that Sebastian spent most of his time on horseback. Anyway, he surely didn't snore. Sebastian was far too proper for snoring.

Most of all, she kept returning to the fact that not once, not even once, had Cam said that he loved her.

When dawn broke, Gina woke from a dream in which Cam gaily introduced her to a buxom woman he called "the lovely Marissa." She pushed his hand off her hip and stared into the gray light, trying to decide whether it would be worse to marry Sebastian, who might have a mistress on the side but would never let her know about it, or Cam, who would likely parade his mistress before her. The very thought of it made her hand curl into a fist. She would *kill* the woman, she would . . . Gina was appalled at her own ferocity. What was she thinking?

It was more than likely that Cam would sail to Greece and not return for another twelve years. That meant she was going to spend the rest of her life in the sort of twilight marriage she had already experienced.

By the time morning finally came she was desperate for sleep. She was also irritable, exhausted, and incoherently anxious to let her husband know how dreadful a sleeping companion he was. And if her unspoken feeling was that he was a dreadful husband, well, she would let him know that too.

He on the other hand had the cheerful joy of a man who wakes up to find his hand on the thigh of a delectable woman.

Until he got a measure of that woman.

"You snore," she said accusingly.

Cam tried to look innocent. "I do?"

"You snore and you groped my body during the night!"

He tried harder for the innocent look. "I *do*? It's only because you're so beautiful."

She shot him a scornful look and he closed his mouth.

"I've had no sleep. None! When you weren't snoring, or groping, you were kicking, or pulling away the blanket."

"I'm sorry. Is there some way I can make you feel better?"

He started kissing her neck as she sat on the edge of the bed.

She felt nothing but acute irritation. She leaped to her feet so fast that he almost toppled off the side. "Absolutely not. I am going to dress and return to my chamber immediately. I believe we shall have to keep separate rooms, if only so that I can sleep."

"Shame on you, Gina. You who insisted that you would share a bedchamber with the marquess."

"I'm quite certain that Sebastian would not be as disruptive a sleeper as you are!" she flashed back, pulling on her gown. "Will you check the corridor, please? I would hate to be seen leaving your chamber."

Cam pulled on his trousers and thought for a moment. Then he asked, quietly, "Why?"

"What do you mean, why? I hardly think I need to detail the reasons why!"

"I would be interested in your reasoning."

"Our marriage was annulled three days ago," she pointed out. "Even if we didn't find out until yesterday, the fact remains that we are unmarried at the moment."

"You sound as if you regret the fact we consummated our marriage," Cam said.

She avoided his eyes. "Not at all. Are you?"

"Why on earth should I be?" he said in a lazy, rough tone.

Gina swallowed. Obviously he meant to carry out the plan he'd proposed in the ballroom—that they continue as they were, and simply share a bed on the few occasions when he visited England. "You won't be as free," she stated.

"Free?"

"If we are truly married, you can't return to Greece."

"No?" he asked.

"No." Her voice almost wavered but she caught it. "If we are married, we should live together."

"Greece is my home."

"So is Girton. If you insist on leaving for Greece, well"—she hurried ahead—"I shall inform Finkbottle that I am not compromised after all."

There was a moment's silence. Then: "I dislike blackmail, oh my duchess."

"I don't mean to blackmail you," Gina replied. "I simply believe—"

"You simply believe I am the sort of wastrel who would take my pleasure—and my wife's virginity—and waltz off to Greece without you as if nothing had transpired."

She swallowed.

"I consider myself compromised," he said tightly. "I am compromised by the situation and by my own lust for you. As it happens, I am not the sort of man who overlooks my responsibilities. But you don't believe that about me, do you?" There was a self-loathing to his voice that stung her heart. "After all, you easily believed that I would shape your naked body into pink marble and sell it in the public square."

"I didn't mean to insult you. I thought you would fashion me in marble because that is what you do—"

"You are quite right," he said, and his voice was full of rage now. "That *is* what I do. I sculpt naked women for a living. Moreover, I do it *in Greece*. You are a duchess, and you live in England. The two facts sound incompatible, don't they? You have no need for a husband who engages in disreputable sculpture. You see, Gina, I will not stop sculpting naked women. It is what I *do*. Stephen couldn't stop me, and neither can you."

She frowned. "I have not asked you to stop sculpting women."

He laughed. "If I am to stay at Girton and fashion bridges without nymphs, give up my house in Greece, and become a

340

philanthropic duke, when will I engage in disreputable sculpture?"

"I hadn't thought of it," she said, clenching her hands.

"You needn't think. I can see it for myself. After all, your idea of the ideal husband is the sticklike marquess. But it is impossible to fashion me into Bonnington, Gina. It won't work. Soil has never turned to gold. You might as well accept the fact, and consider whether you wish to continue in this marriage. Perhaps it was lucky that we were *not* compromised. Your wiggy marquess is still waiting in the wings."

"At least he loves me!" Gina snapped.

He stared at her.

"He loves me," she repeated shrilly. "He doesn't snore, and he lives in England." To her dismay, her tired eyes filled with tears. "You're just going to leave me here at Girton and go back to your mistress—"

"Marissa is *not* my mistress," Cam interjected.

"I'm sure you have a mistress somewhere on that island," Gina snapped back.

Cam opened his mouth, but then he remembered Bella. She couldn't exactly be called a mistress, but Gina spoke before he could articulate the distinction.

"I thought you did! Perhaps Sebastian will keep a mistress. But at least I won't know about it." The very thought of Cam sleeping with another woman sent a knifelike pain into her heart. "I just don't think I can bear it," she said jerkily. "I can't—I can't. I don't think I *want* to . . ." she trailed off.

"You don't think you want to marry me," he said. His voice was rather gentle, under the circumstances.

She bowed her head as a huge sob tore its way up her chest.

He pulled on his clothes. She kept crying. He walked over and put his hand on her hair. The caress made her weep

341

harder. "You will have to decide for yourself. If you want to marry the marquess, you needn't give me another thought. I shall return to Greece. The annulment papers are there." He nodded to the table. "You and Bonnington can be married by evening, if that's what you wish."

He pulled on an overcoat that hung by his door. "If you'll excuse me, I think I will drive to London and speak to Rounton. I do think that a solicitor so bold ought to be reprimanded, don't you?"

He wasn't even going to argue with her. He didn't even care enough to argue with her. She gritted her teeth. "I would prefer to reprimand him for Finkbottle's unaccountable delay in giving us the annulment papers."

His eyes were black and steady. "It is, of course, a question for your own moral temperament. No one knows what occurred in the plunge-bath, Gina. You should feel free to inform Bonnington that he may use his special license immediately."

She felt a pulse of terror and sorrow under her breastbone.

"Cam—"

But he was leaving.

She blinked and ran into the corridor. "Camden!" she said. But he was nearly at the end of the corridor, so she shouted: "Come back!"

He swung around. His eyes were blazing with rage. "Was there something you wished?" he said. "Something *I* could give you?"

There was no point to standing in the corridor. But Gina stood until Cam's receding footsteps on the stairs had faded from her ears.

Chapter Thirty-Three

The Following Afternoon a
Solicitor's Creativity Is Deplored

"You wrote that letter to my wife? You—my solicitor—wrote a blackmailing letter and sent it to Gina's mother? Are you absolutely cracked?"

"I do not believe so," Rounton replied. "But yes, I wrote the letter."

Cam stared at Rounton in disbelief. "I find it hard to conceive that you, a respected solicitor, my father's own solicitor, would resort to such disgraceful lengths. And all for what? So that I would have a son and continue the Girton line? What the devil do you care, anyway?"

The only sign that Rounton was at all affected by his words was the way he jiggled his pocket watch. "It seemed to me a reasonable course of action."

"Reasonable?" Cam's voice rose. "It was a bloody imposition, and you know it as well as I do! My father's despicable methods appear to have rubbed off on you. It was one thing when he forced me to marry—" He broke off. His face took on such a menacing look that Rounton actually shifted backward in his seat. "Tell me that my father instructed you to ensure that I consummate my marriage—tell me that and I'll kill you myself."

"He did not," Rounton replied. "After you left the country, he never mentioned your name again, to the best of my knowledge."

"I assumed during that excuse for a marriage ceremony that you did not agree with my father's judgment. I clearly remember when you informed my father that his decree went against the law."

Rounton nodded. "You are correct. I felt your father was making an error by forcing you to marry."

"Then why did you take the opportunity to behave precisely as my father had? At least my father's demands were straightforward. He summoned me from Oxford, demanded that I marry the girl I considered my first cousin, and threatened to kill me if I didn't. You achieved much the same result by underhanded and devious means. Writing an anonymous letter that threatened my wife with exposure! Sending Finkbottle down to compromise us! *Despicable,* Rounton."

"I would disagree," the solicitor replied coolly. "I thought my letter was an ingenious touch. Of course, I rather expected that the marquess would withdraw his suit on learning that your wife was not only illegitimate herself, but had illegitimate siblings. Bonnington's reputation is of a man rigidly concerned with propriety. It seems the duchess did not share the letter with him. Perhaps I should have sent the letter directly to him."

"How did you know of Wapping's existence?"

"I did not know his name. But your father's investigators uncovered the fact Countess Ligny had also given birth to a male child. Moreover, she had arranged to give the child to his father, a philosopher at the Sorbonne, precisely as she did with your wife. Your father could think of no practical use for the information, but I thought it interesting. I had no idea, of course, that Wapping had traveled to England after the countess died, or that he was interested in Countess Ligny's bequest to your wife."

Cam shook his head. "Why did you bother?"

Rounton answered at cross purposes. "Let me point out, my lord, that I could not force you to consummate your marriage. I simply made it possible for you to do so, if you wished."

"If my father did not make such a request, why would you bother to influence my life in such a fashion?"

The solicitor's chin set. "I doubt you will understand what I am saying, my lord. My father and my father's father served the Girtons. Your father was a remarkably difficult man to work for, yet I did not leave his employ." His eyes met Cam's. "The illegality of your marriage was only one of many such illegalities."

"If you wish me to weep over your tainted lily-white conscience, look elsewhere. You continued to work for him."

"I was brought up in the expectation that the Girtons would be the center of my livelihood. That they would be my foremost client and first point of loyalty."

"I fail to see why you think I can't understand your motives," Cam said with a cynical twist of his lips. "In order not to lose your largest client, you complied with his dishonest schemes."

"I could have all the clients that I wish," Rounton said. "I remained with your father because I was taught that loyalty was important. And *that* is what I think you will not understand."

Cam's blood chilled to the bone. "You think I have no loyalty?"

Rounton looked at him calmly. "Your father was bedridden in 1802. You did not return to England to manage your estate. Your father died in 1807. You did not return to England for another three years. When you left this country, you were a young man, but you are grown now. Yet you have shown little or no interest in the welfare of your wife or your estate.

"I judge the duchess to be an excellent manager of the estate, far better than you or your cousin is likely to be. I chose to do what was best for the Girton lineage and the Girton land. Make no mistake, my lord, I could make a great deal more money serving aristocrats who take the time to administer their own affairs, than serving a duke who fritters his time away on a Greek island."

Cam forced himself to breathe quietly through the red haze of rage that clouded his vision. Rounton had not said anything that he had not thought himself since returning to England. He *had* neglected his land and his wife. He had lost himself in the keen pleasure of creation, and forgotten that his birth entailed unpleasant responsibilities that had nothing to do with sculpting marble.

"You have a point," he finally said.

Rounton did not gloat. "I am sorry that I achieved my purpose through underhanded means."

"I need a special license," Cam said. "And someone will have to go to the isle of Nissos and close up my house."

"I can arrange that."

"I would prefer you to do it yourself. My statues will need to be packed with extreme care."

Rounton blinked. He did not usually manage such matters himself, but perhaps in this situation he should be amenable.

"I shall return to Lady Troubridge's house tomorrow," Cam said, standing up, "after I obtain a special license. If you would join me in Kent, I will give you more detailed information about my house in Greece."

"My lord, I apologize if I have offended you in any way," Rounton said.

"You haven't," Cam said. His eyes were rueful, but the anger was gone. "I'm a careless bastard, Rounton. Always have been. I would rather work with marble than think about

346

the Girton estate any day. But you are right to think that the duchess likes that sort of work. And there are marble quarries in England, after all."

The solicitor bowed.

Chapter Thirty-Four

Lady Rawlings Awaits Her Husband

Esme had slept with more men than had many ladies in the *ton*. Mind you, she had slept with fewer men than were credited to her, and yet more than she should have, as a lady who married at seventeen years old. But since her wedding night, some ten years previous, she had never invited a man into her bed unless they shared a good deal of mutual desire. In fact, for the past six years, she hadn't desired anyone enough to take the risk. Until last night, of course.

She tightened the cord around her robe. Her husband had said that he would visit tonight. She had dismissed her maid two hours ago, and still there was no sign of him.

The problem was . . . the problem was last night. With an effort she pushed away an image of her body, shaking so much that she literally trembled from head to foot. Dismissed from her memory the muscled chest, the kisses, the cries, the—

Babies, she thought. Think about babies. Last night was a fantasy, a dream. It will never happen again. She sat down before the fire. Babies were reality. A baby would love her, and stay with her. A baby wouldn't escort her back to her room without a word, and avoid her throughout the day. It wasn't that she wanted acknowledgment from Sebastian. After all, he was on the verge of marrying her best friend in the world. But a goodbye would have been nice, she thought forlornly. She clenched her teeth. She wasn't the sort of woman to whom the Sebastians of the world said goodbye. Oh, he'd enjoyed last night. She hadn't been the only one shaking. He'd enjoyed her, and enjoyed the night, and left without a word.

There was a scratch on the door, just in time to stop her from dissolving into tears. She loathed tears, despised them. Babies, she thought as she rose. Little round heads and sweet smells. Virtually every married woman said that after the third baby they vowed to become celibate. She would have so many babies that the memory of the previous night would fade into nothing.

She opened the door and smiled at her husband. "Do come in, Miles."

He tiptoed in and waited until she shut the door before he spoke. "Good evening, Esme," he whispered.

"You needn't whisper," she said. "We *are* married, after all."

Miles cleared his throat. He had an embarrassed air that she thought was terribly nice of him. "Of course. You're absolutely right. Of course." He fell into silence. His eyes slid away from hers. "What a good fire!" he said.

"This isn't very comfortable, is it?" she said, answering his demeanor.

"It isn't you," he said, meeting her eyes again. "I . . . well, you're beautiful. And here I am." He patted his stomach, which was indeed rather large. "With Lady Childe—" He ground to a halt. "Beg pardon, my dear, I meant never to mention her."

"Oh, Miles, we shouldn't pretend with each other." Against all reason, she was feeling much better. "Why don't we sit down and have a glass of wine, and talk like the sensible married couple that we are?"

They both gratefully succumbed to the little ceremony of pouring wine and seating themselves.

Then Esme looked at her husband. He truly was one of the nicest men she'd ever met. "So does Lady Childe admire your tummy, Miles?" She twinkled at him. "I think we should be quite frank with each other. After all, we are about to become lovers again, and we are already friends."

He looked startled and then enormously pleased. "We are friends, aren't we?"

She nodded. "And now that we're going to be parents, our friendship is even more important."

"True enough," Miles said. "I'm afraid that my parents were not pleasant to each other, and it made my childhood rather painful."

"Neither were mine," Esme said, and they smiled at each other with the relief of finding something in common.

"So we both value civility in parenthood," she continued, taking a sip of wine.

"Other than that, I don't know anything about parenting," Miles confessed. "My parents spent most of their time at court and left us in the country, so I never saw much of my father or my mother."

"That's why you wish us to live together," she guessed.

He nodded. "It did give me a lifelong love of the country. My hope is that we can spend time there with the children, rather than living apart from them."

"I intend to be a very motherly mother. In fact—" she looked at him challengingly—"I am going to breastfeed my own children."

Pink rose up his throat. That was obviously more detail than he had bargained for. "Whatever you wish, my dear," he spluttered.

The wish that her husband didn't have a double chin darted across Esme's mind—and then she took it back. If she started being critical, there'd be no end to it. The best thing would be to never allow herself to have negative thoughts about Miles. She swallowed the rest of her wine.

"Shall we?" She stood up and glanced at the bed, and then smiled at her husband.

He heaved himself to his feet but stood without moving. "This is damn hard," he said. "I feel like some sort of reprobate, bedding you."

"We're *married,* Miles!"

"But we're not—I'm a tub of lard, as the phrase goes." He tugged at his waistcoat. "And you're the most lovely woman in the *ton,* everyone knows that."

Esme walked over to him and put her hands flat on his chest. "Will you join me in our bed, Miles?" She leaned over and feathered a kiss across his lips. Then she stood back, untied her robe, and let it fall.

He blinked.

Esme knew precisely what she looked like: she was wearing a French creation that was designed to make any man in the vicinity ravenous with lust. In fact, when she wore it on a previous occasion, the man in her vicinity lunged in a quite gratifying way.

Miles didn't move a finger.

She started undoing his vest. "Would you like to come to bed now?"

Color surged up into his cheeks. "Yes, of course. Beg forgiveness, my dear." He removed her hands and undid his waistcoat by himself. Released from tight buttons, his stomach seemed to expand in every direction. Esme politely averted her eyes.

He began to wrestle with his cuff links.

"Would you like me to help?"

"No! No, thank you," he said.

She couldn't help but notice that his tone was rather miserable. She backed up and sat on the edge of the bed. Miles wore the kind of shirt that hung almost to his knees, so it was quite an operation hoisting it over his head. Moreover, it seemed to be a difficult business bending over to pull off his boots—obviously his valet did that for him normally—but he managed it. And finally, there he was, wearing nothing more than smalls. Esme took a deep breath. It wasn't as bad as she thought. She could do this.

The question really was: could he? He didn't appear riveted by lust. He sat down next to her on the bed, but all he did was pick up her hand and pat it, in the most paternal fashion.

She leaned over and kissed him on the cheek. But he didn't lunge at her. Perhaps she should take off her nightdress? Unlike his clothing, the French nightdress practically flew off her body, it was so easily unfastened.

He cast a glance at her but looked away, as if she had belched in public. Esme looked down at her body. As far as she could tell, it looked just as appealing as it always had. Certainly the same as when they first married, and he had been gratifyingly complimentary at the time. At least when they weren't quarreling.

"Miles, we're friends. Therefore, as a friend, please tell me what the problem is?" She tried to make her voice sound casual.

"I'm sorry," he said. "I'm not absolutely certain I can do this."

"Am I—is there something?"

"You're lovely." But she noticed he still didn't look at her. "I feel guilty," he said in a rush. His eyes were as mournful as those of a sick cow. "I don't make a very good adulterer. I feel as if I'm being unfaithful."

"To Lady Childe," Esme said.

"Yes. Isn't that foolish? You're my wife, and she's not. But—"

"She's the wife of your heart," Esme said, smiling at him. "Would you rather not do this, Miles?"

"She told me to," he said miserably. "She said that I must, that she was happy for me, that there was no choice, really."

"There *is* a choice. You could put on your clothes and go back to your room, and no one would be the wiser."

He shook his head. "I have spent an absurd amount of time in the past few years thinking about having an heir, Esme. I never believed it was a true possibility."

"You could have divorced me," she pointed out.

"No. Our marriage was a joint failure."

"You are such a *good* person, Miles," she said in a rush. "I don't deserve you."

"Nonsense!"

She bit her lip. "Here——" She stood up and walked across the room to the wine decanter. "Have some more wine." She poured it into his glass and then snuffed the candles until there was no light in the room but the glow from the fire.

Then she got herself into bed and under the covers. "Miles, will you join me?" she said, trying to sound very sensible. "I should like to make an heir now." She said it exactly as if she were requesting that he partner her at whist.

The bed groaned as he lay down. Esme drew the bed curtains so that they lay in absolute pitch darkness.

She waited a moment but he didn't move, so she gave an internal sigh and reached out. But she met his hands halfway; his slid by and rested on her shoulders.

"I'm embarrassed——"

"Miles, we're *friends*. We are not virgins either. That should make this whole thing easier."

His hand slid from her shoulder to her breast. Her hands slipped even lower on his body.

* * *

353

It was some three hours later that Esme woke up. Had Miles made a sound? No, he was breathing loudly but evenly, which was good because at some point his breath had become so labored that she thought he might be overexerting himself.

It wasn't so bad, she told herself. They had gotten through it with a modicum of grace and a good deal of humor. She could certainly do it again, if need be. Well, it likely took a while to become pregnant. Perhaps even four or five times.

She did hear something! She rose up on her elbow but the bed curtains were still drawn and she couldn't see anything. Yes—there was definitely someone in the room. She could hear a shuffling noise.

Then, with an awful lurch to her stomach, she remembered the statue that Gina had given her for safekeeping. It stood on her bedside table, in clear view of the intruder.

She put her mouth to Miles's ear. "Wake up! There is a thief in our room!"

He woke up without a sound and pushed her back. The bed creaked when he sat up, but the thief didn't seem to have noticed. She didn't hear the door open. Perhaps he thought that she made the noise turning in her sleep. Soundlessly she slid to the other side of the bed, off the side and under the bed curtain.

Grabbing the Aphrodite, she started to tiptoe around the bed when there was a muffled scrambling sound. She ran around the end of the bed to see that Miles had lunged from the bed and seized the intruder. The fire was quite out by now, so all she could see was two black forms grappling in the darkness. She could hear Miles grunting with exertion.

Suddenly she found her voice. "Help! Help!" she screamed, darting to the bell cord and pulling it with all her might. "Someone help us. There's a thief in the room!"

A second later she heard a confused noise up and down the hall. But it all happened so fast that afterward she had great difficulty describing the scene. The two men struggling before her separated, and the larger one swayed and went to his knees, clutching his chest.

"Miles!" she shrieked, running to him.

Oddly enough, the thief didn't immediately flee. She waved the Aphrodite at him. "I'll brain you with this if you approach!" Then she cast a closer look at her husband and dropped the statue, which fell to the ground with a dull thump. "Miles, are you all right?" He was oddly slumped with his head on his chest. He made a gargling noise.

With one swift movement the thief crouched at her side and reached out his hand to prop up Miles's head.

"Oh my God, Sebastian!"

Chapter Thirty-Five

Just Before Dawn

The door burst open and a crowd of people exploded into the room, but Esme paid no attention. When the door opened, light flooded in from the candles people held. Miles's face was an odd grayish-green color. She tried to push him backward so that he could lie down but she couldn't move him from his knees.

"Someone help me," she said hoarsely. "Miles, please. Speak to me."

Strong hands pushed her to the side. Lady Childe pulled Miles forward so that his head lay against her chest. Esme saw with a sickening thump of her heart how limply his body collapsed. She scrambled to straighten his knees.

"Miles," Lady Childe said in her deep voice. "Open your eyes, Miles."

There was a hushed silence around them. And then Esme heard, as if from a distance, Helene ordering everyone from the room. Vaguely she wondered about Sebastian, but her husband had opened his eyes. He looked up at Lady Childe for a moment and the breath caught in Esme's throat at the look in his eyes.

Lady Childe put a hand on his cheek. "Don't speak, dearest."

Esme saw that all the color was gone from his face now.

"Make sure they've sent for a doctor," Lady Childe whispered.

Esme jumped up and threw open the door. Sebastian was standing just outside, looking as grim as a sentinel. She recoiled. "What are you doing here?" she hissed.

"Waiting to see if Lord Rawlings will recover." His face was absolutely white.

"We need a doctor!" she said furiously. "Go get one!"

"A curricle has already been sent for the doctor," Sebastian said. "May I—"

But she couldn't bear to listen to him. She shut the door with a quiet rap.

Miles was looking at Lady Childe again. The room was so quiet that Esme started counting his breaths. They came slowly and with visible effort.

"William," he said in a harsh whisper.

"William? William who?" Esme asked.

"The babe," Lady Childe said. Her hand cupped his cheek. "We'll name your babe William. Don't worry about it, sweetheart. Just stay with us until the doctor arrives."

Esme's eyes filled with tears. "He's not—he's not—"

Miles had turned his face against Lady Childe's bosom. She stroked his face and dropped a kiss on his forehead. "It's all right, darling," she said, and her voice was as soft as water falling. "I love you."

He seemed to be struggling to say something. She hushed him. "I know you love me, Miles. I know, I know. And I love you." She pulled him tighter against her chest. "We'll name him William, and I will make sure he knows you, darling. I will tell him all about you."

Esme clutched the hand she held. "I won't ever leave William alone in the country and go to London, Miles. I'll take him with me everywhere."

She couldn't tell if he heard her and it didn't feel right to sit with the two of them, so she rose after a few moments and went to the window. She pulled the heavy drape and looked out, her back to the couple on the ground. She could hear a confused clamor from the household, footsteps and raised voices.

Why had Sebastian entered her chamber? She closed her eyes. Obviously, he thought to surprise her in bed. Humiliation, anguish, and pain beat an alternating rhythm in her chest. Her lover had come into her room and her husband was dead as a result.

It was early, early morning. White fogs danced over Lady Troubridge's lawn, swept over the rose bushes as they waited to be evaporated by the sun.

The sky was just turning a delicate pearly rose color when Lady Childe rose and stood beside her.

Esme cast a quick look over her shoulder. Miles looked as if he were sleeping, except that he was lying on the floor. "I'm not sure that I *have* a child," she said. Her throat was rough with tears. "I think it takes more than one night."

"Very likely. But Miles knew little of reproductive matters. He was comforted by the thought."

"Yes, well." Esme put her hand on her tummy and wished with all her heart that a small William was nestled there.

"Last night . . ." she said stumblingly.

"It doesn't matter," Lady Childe said. Her face was utterly calm and she didn't appear to have shed a tear, unlike Esme, whose eyes were swollen.

"It mattered to Miles," Esme insisted. "It wasn't a simple thing. He felt adulterous . . . he couldn't . . . we had to be in the dark." Tears rolled down her cheeks. "He loved you so much."

"Yes he did," Lady Childe said, and Esme saw the first crack in her composure. "And I . . . and I too—"

She was smaller than Esme, so Esme pulled her husband's mistress against her shoulder and wept with her, for the sweetness of Miles, for the love of Miles, for Miles.

It was sometime later, after Lady Childe and she had managed to put Miles's shirt and trousers back on, that there was a scratch on the door. Lady Childe was sitting on the floor, stroking Miles's hair. Esme walked to the door and opened it slightly. Sebastian was still there. He looked at her without speaking. Lady Troubridge and an elderly gentleman stood beside her.

"This is Dr. Wells," Lady Troubridge said in a low voice.

"I'm afraid it's too late."

She nodded. "May I speak to Lucy?"

With a start, Esme realized that she didn't even know Lady Childe's first name. Lady Troubridge must be a close friend to address her as Lucy. She moved back silently.

The doctor bent over Miles for a second, talked briefly to Esme and Lady Childe, and then left. Esme stepped into the hallway and faced Sebastian. "Do you . . . did everyone see you?"

"Yes. How would you like to proceed, Lady Rawlings?"

"Proceed? What do you mean?"

"I realize this is not a propitious time for a marriage proposal, but—"

"Are you deranged? You think I would marry *you*? The man who killed my husband?" She spoke out of the depths of her fury and self-hatred.

He went completely still. "I apologize from the bottom of my heart," he said. "I can only offer—"

"Your hand!" she spat. "I wouldn't take your hand in marriage even if you weren't a stodgy—boring—*virgin*!"

She wouldn't have thought it was possible for him to grow

whiter, but he did. "I am afraid that your reputation will be damaged—"

Again she cut him off. "Leave. I want you to leave. The one thing you can grant me is the promise I will never see you again. Ever. Have I made myself clear?"

His eyes searched hers. "Quite clear," he said.

She stepped back and waited for him to go, and after a moment he did. She went back into her bedchamber and sat next to her dead husband. But she didn't belong there. Lady Childe belonged there.

Still, she sat. It was the least she could do for Miles, even though it was too little, too late. She sat, twisting her hands in her lap, her stomach knotted in self-loathing.

After an hour or so, Lady Troubridge looked at Esme and said, "Would you mind asking a footman to summon my maid, my dear?"

Esme walked back into the corridor and almost collided with Helene. "Does everyone know?" she asked, without ceremony. She had to force the words out past lips grown stiff.

Helene was known in the *ton* as a woman of utmost composure. Faced with her husband's worst depravities, she had never showed a twinge of emotion. But her face was condemning now. "Bonnington was partially dressed," she said. "He had taken off his shirt when Miles attacked him. Apparently he thought to steal into your bed."

"Does Gina know?" Esme whispered.

Helene drew her across the hallway and into her room. "How could you? How could you do that to Gina?"

"I didn't until night before last. Not until it was clear that Gina was going to remain with her husband. Sebastian knew I was reconciling with Miles. But he left before I could tell him it was happening immediately."

360

"You shouldn't have done it," Helene said. "And Bonnington—the fool—men are such fools!"

"It's all my fault," Esme said dully. "I killed my husband. I killed Miles because I'm a trollop."

"Bonnington is protecting your reputation," Helene said. "He has announced that he mistook the room."

"What? Whose room did he say it was?"

"He said that he meant to visit his wife."

"His *wife*?" Esme's voice rose.

Helene nodded. "He has told the entire house party that he and Gina were married yesterday afternoon, by special license, and that he was visiting his wife's room. Except that he miscounted the number of doors and ended up in your room by accident. Esme! You're not going to faint, are you?"

"I never faint," she muttered. But she did sit down. "Did you say that he told the house party that he and Gina were *married*?"

Helene sat down as well. "Yes."

"That's impossible! Gina is still married to her husband."

"In fact, I gather that the annulment was finalized a few days ago."

"But she is in love with her husband."

"I have no idea about her feelings." Helene's voice had regained its customary dispassionate ring. "She has not yet denied Bonnington's account. There is, naturally, a good deal of speculation regarding the presence of your husband in your bedchamber."

Esme made an impatient gesture. "Let the vultures think as they will. Where is Gina?"

"I haven't seen her. I assume that she is downstairs accepting congratulations on her marriage. Naturally, everyone is horrified by your husband's death. Most people are leaving the house party immediately, out of respect."

There was a noise at the door and Gina slipped through.

Esme rose to her feet. "I'm sorry," she said haltingly, "I know there is nothing I can say, but I'm so *sorry*. I shouldn't ever have—" Her voice cracked.

For a moment Esme and Gina just stared at each other. "I cannot say that it doesn't matter," Gina finally said. "It does. Do you wish to marry Sebastian?"

A revolted look crossed Esme's face. "Absolutely not," she said. "I must have been crazed to sleep with him in the first place."

Gina sank into a chair. "Everyone thinks I'm married to him now," she said, her tone stark. "So I gather I'll be the one sleeping with him next."

"You don't have to acquiesce in that story," Helene stated.

"If I don't, Esme's reputation will be ruined," Gina said. "If people even suspect that Sebastian intended to visit her bedchamber, she will be thrown out of society."

"Esme's reputation is hardly untarnished now," Helene pointed out.

"And I don't care!" Esme put in. "I betrayed your trust, and slept with your fiancé. Why are you even *thinking* about my reputation?"

Gina's eyes were strained and bleak. "Most husbands keep a mistress," she said. "I suppose I shall become accustomed to sharing Sebastian."

Esme swallowed. "He isn't that kind of—" she started, but Helene put a hand on her arm.

"Where is the duke?"

"He's in London although he'll likely return soon, because he thinks we're performing the play tonight. We did not part on the best of terms. In fact, I told him that I was planning to marry Sebastian." Then Gina added, rather miserably, "and he didn't argue with me."

"This is my fault," Esme cried. "It was I. I killed Miles, and—"

"Nonsense," Helene said in a quelling voice. "Miles died of a spasm of the heart. Lady Troubridge told me that he had had two episodes just this week. She had urged him to send for a doctor from London. He could have gone at any time. He was not well."

"I didn't know that. I'm his wife, and I didn't even know he was ill." Tears were falling down Esme's face again and her voice was raw. "No one thinks I loved him, but I *did*. He was so good, and true, and I should never have made him leave. I should have stayed with him, and by now we would have had children. He wanted a baby but I don't have it—" She broke down into convulsive sobs. "If only I hadn't been so stupid!"

Helene patted her shoulder. Gina reached over and took her hand.

Esme's face was blotchy and swollen. At that moment, she was far from being London's most beautiful woman. "Sebastian must tell the truth," she said. "I shall do so myself, as soon as I go downstairs. I don't care a bean for my reputation. I'm going to retire to the country."

"And do what?" Helene said fondly. "Grow beans?"

"I shall be in deep mourning. Please, Gina, tell Sebastian to be truthful. I intend to leave the house immediately. It is of no consequence what people think of me."

Gina swallowed. "The *ton* will crucify you, Esme. There has to be another way."

"There isn't. I don't give a hang what people think of me. I will never, ever sleep with another man, so help me God. All I want is to be left in peace. You and Sebastian have my blessings." She hesitated. "I just want you to know, Gina, that I never would have done it, except that I believed you wanted to remain married to Girton."

"That's just it," Gina cried. "I don't know what I want! One moment, I want to be married to Sebastian, and the next, I want to be married to Cam."

There was a noise in the hall. Esme wrenched open the door just in time to see four footmen carry her husband from the bedchamber. She stood in the doorway, hand on her heart. Helene came up behind her.

"Do they know where to take him?" Esme asked. "Miles has to go home to the country. He would want to go home."

"There's time," Helene said soothingly. "They'll put him in the chapel for the moment. The coach will leave this afternoon."

"The coach . . ." She stumbled to a halt.

"You will follow your husband's coach. I expect that Lady Troubridge has already ordered it hung with black. Do you have a black gown?"

Esme didn't answer.

"I will accompany you, if you wish."

"That would be kind of you," she said dully. She walked across the hall into the empty room. Her foot kicked something as she walked forward. "The Aphrodite." She picked it up. "It's fallen into pieces. It must have cracked when I threw it down. I broke this too. I'm sorry. I broke the Aphrodite. It's ruined. I ruin everything I touch."

"Hush," Gina said. "It's simply hinged, that's all. I meant to ask you for it. I must give my brother whatever is inside."

"Your brother!"

Gina met the startled eyes of her two friends. "Mr. Wapping," she said with an unsteady smile. She took the Aphrodite from Esme's hands. "Didn't I tell you that Mr. Wapping is yet another child of Countess Ligny?"

"Mr. Wapping is your *brother*?" Esme asked.

Gina pulled a roll of paper from the hollowed center of the Aphrodite. "He's my half brother, actually. There's only paper here," she said. "Just paper. No jewels."

"Mr. Wapping?" Helene repeated, stunned. "Your tutor? Did he give you that statue?"

"No, the statue is a bequest from Countess Ligny," Gina said as she undid the ribbon holding the roll of paper. "Why, why, how very peculiar!"

They both looked a question.

"It's my letters. The letters I wrote her. Here's the first one, and the second. The last letter I wrote before she died. Why did the countess send back my letters?"

"Is there a message from her?"

Gina shook her head, looking through the little sheaf of papers once more.

"Perhaps she forgot the letters were inside," Helene suggested.

"Mr. Wapping will be disappointed," Gina said. "He was hoping for emeralds."

"How on earth did your tutor—your brother—know about the Aphrodite?" Helene asked.

"The countess told him that the Aphrodite held her most precious possession," Gina answered, cutting herself short with a little gasp.

A smile crossed Esme's face. "Her most precious possession," she said softly, reaching out and touching the letters. "That's lovely."

Gina bit her lip. "She can't have meant it."

"She did," Helene stated.

"Then why didn't she write to me herself?"

"Who knows?" Esme said. "But your letters were the most precious thing she owned." Her eyes filled with tears again.

"I never thought." Gina fit the Aphrodite back together and looked at it. "I thought she sent me a naked statue because she believed I was a strumpet like—"

"She sent you the statue because it was beautiful and she wanted you to know that your letters were precious," Esme said.

Gina's mouth wobbled. "I thought she was just like Cam."

"What about Cam?" Helene asked.

"He sent me a naked statue too. When I turned twenty-one, he sent me a naked Cupid. At first I was grateful, but then I felt angry. It was so unlike me."

"I expect the Cupid is very beautiful, isn't it?" Esme put in. "The Aphrodite certainly is."

They all looked at the Aphrodite. Gina's fingers had been clenched around her middle. Now she uncurled her hand and propped the goddess up with her other hand.

"She is beautiful, isn't she?"

The Aphrodite stood with her arm thrown over her head, looking backward in fear, in shame, in sorrow, or with love.

Each woman saw something different in her face.

Chapter Thirty-Six

Sometimes a Wife Cannot Be Found

"Is my wife below?"

Gina's maid was packing a trunk. She looked up. "I beg your pardon, Your Grace?"

"I am looking for my wife. Your mistress, the duchess."

Annie gaped, and then said, "No, she has gone to the village with—with her—"

"With whom?"

"With her husband!" the little maid blurted out.

Cam froze in the bedchamber door. His voice was as smooth as honey and fifty times more barbed. "Am I to understand that my—that your mistress married Marquess Bonnington?"

"They married by special license, sir," Annie said a bit shrilly. This was the most thrilling thing that had happened to her in weeks.

"He put me in mind of a viper," she confided later to the assembled upper servants. "A viper! My mistress is better off without him, great hulking Greek that he is."

"The Duke of Girton isn't Greek. He just lives there," said an upper housemaid. And she added, showing that she was an avid reader of the gossip columns, "His mother was one of Lord Fairley's daughters."

"Living in Greece is good enough, isn't it? A murderous lot, foreigners. Why, the duke looked as if he'd murder me, just for telling him that my mistress married another man. Everyone knew his marriage was annulled. So why was he so surprised? Why, I've know this fortnight."

"Fortnight? They have been married a *fortnight*?" the housemaid gasped.

"Not married, but engaged at least that long," Annie said, nodding at the circle of faces around the butler's table. She was hugely enjoying her newfound power as the personal maid to the notorious Duchess of Girton, now the notorious Marchioness Bonnington. Previously, she had hardly been noticed by Lady Troubridge's sniffy butler, and here she was, seated to the right of the butler himself.

"The duke has a right to look murderous," the house-keeper, Mrs. Massey, put in. "Lady Bonnington *was* his wife, after all. Common decency should have made her tell him that she was remarrying."

"I think he didn't want to end the marriage," Annie said.

"Well, his valet is packing his things as we speak," the butler remarked. "I gather that the duke is returning to Greece immediately. I've set the outdoor men to taking down that stage, what with the duke gone and Lady Rawlings in mourning."

In fact, Cam was watching Phillipos throw the last of his belongings into a trunk.

"What shall I do with these papers, sir? You know charcoal doesn't travel well." Phillipos held up sketches of Gina.

Cam methodically tore the paper into small pieces without comment.

"And the marble?" Phillipos nodded toward the untouched block in the corner.

"Convey our regrets to the butler for the inconvenience, and ask him to dispose of it as Lady Troubridge wishes."

The valet placed a last neck cloth in a small valise.

Cam looked cursorily about the chamber. "The sooner we're in Dover and preparing to sail, the better. I shall say a brief farewell to Lady Troubridge and beg the use of one of her carriages."

"What of Mr. Rounton?" Phillipos asked.

The duke didn't seem to hear him. He was staring at a fragment of paper in his hand, a sketch of the duchess's hand.

Phillipos cleared his throat. "Mr. Rounton is waiting for you in the library, my lord."

"Oh yes," Cam said absently. He thrust the paper into his pocket and walked out the door without another word.

In the library, Rounton was pacing the floor and giving himself a silent lecture. Girtons were trouble. Look at the illegalities in which the old duke involved himself. The new Girton was as much trouble as the old.

Of course, the duke was right to say that he had stepped out of bounds. But devil take it, he had only instructed that ass Finkbottle to nudge events in the proper direction. Not to overturn the whole apple cart. Devil take it, you couldn't trust anyone these days.

He pressed the heel of his hand hard to the burning spot in his stomach. Perhaps he should take the doctor's advice. Take a trip, the doctor had said. Go to a warm country. And now Girton wanted him to go to Greece and close up his house. It was almost providential. Rounton twiddled with his pocket watch. Given young Finkbottle's skills, he would have no clients when he returned home. Which might be all to the best.

He swung about as the door opened. "Your Grace," he acknowledged, bowing. "I am prepared—"

But Girton cut him off. "I am catching the first available boat from Dover to Greece. I'm fear your little scheme has failed. Apparently the duchess married Bonnington yesterday by special license."

Rounton was struck dumb with surprise.

"She must have rushed to the altar after I left the house," Girton went on.

"Impossible! Marquess Bonnington married in such a harum-scarum fashion?"

"Lady Troubridge just confirmed it. Apparently the marquess blundered into another guest's room in the middle of the night, trying to find his new wife's chamber. Caused a death with his marital enthusiasm."

"What?"

"He tussled with Miles Rawlings in the dark, and Rawlings had an attack of some sort," Girton said impatiently. "I am told that the wedded couple has taken a short drive to the village. I trust that you can convey my farewell and congratulations, Rounton."

The solicitor pursed his lips. There was something fishy here. "I find it difficult to believe that Her Grace would make such a rash decision," he said, a vision of the eminently practical duchess flitting through his mind.

"There's nothing rash about it," the duke snapped. "She has been engaged to the man for months."

"I am disappointed," Rounton remarked. "I won't deny it."

There was a heartbeat's silence in the room. "Not as much as I am," Girton admitted, a rueful twist in his voice. For the first time, solicitor and duke looked at each other as man to man rather than employer to client. But Rounton looked away. It wasn't proper, what he saw in Girton's eyes.

"I'd like you to contact Thomas Bradfellow of Christ Church. Endow a chair in Italian studies and make him put Wapping in it." The duke walked to the door. "Settle the estate on Stephen as soon as possible," he added.

"Yes, my lord," Rounton murmured. He was hardly in a position to offer advice.

The wide vestibule outside the library was crowded with gentlefolk alternately shrieking at the misuse of their luggage and kissing one another goodbye with shrill enthusiasm. Lady Troubridge's house party had, perhaps, been slightly shorter than it was wont to be, but it had been even more thrilling than anyone expected.

Cam was making his way toward the door when he felt a hand on his shoulder. He turned to find Tuppy Perwinkle just behind him.

"Good afternoon," Cam said, bowing. "I'm afraid that I'm returning to Greece immediately. Otherwise I would be—"

"My wife," Tuppy interrupted, "says that the duchess loves *you*."

Cam's stomach instinctively clenched. "I fail to see why you have chosen to share your wife's musings on the subject with me."

Tuppy frowned at him. "I wrote my wife off as a lost cause. I didn't want you to make the same mistake."

"Given that my *former* wife remarried yesterday, I believe the matter is out of my hands," Cam replied icily. "Now, if you will excuse me." He jerked his head at Phillipos, standing in the corner of the vestibule with his luggage, and bid a firm farewell to Lord Perwinkle.

The trip to the coast was uneventful, if slow. Several days later, Cam gripped the rail of a sweet little sailing ship called *The Molly* and tried to force himself to look away from the dock. It was absurd to think that this cloud of dust, or that carriage, might disguise his errant wife—no, Bonnington's wife now. Worse than absurd to think that his wife might have followed him, might have changed her mind. It was imbecilic to hope that this was a black dream, and he would wake to find himself being accused of snoring in her ear, and groping her body in his sleep.

And yet he couldn't stop hoping. A large carriage drew up that might hold a duchess. Straining his eyes, he saw a fat parson lumber out of a carriage and haul out an even larger woman. Even from this distance, he could hear the woman shrieking, calling the parson an oaf and a nincompoop.

Gina had made her choice—and chosen well. Bonnington was a good man, a solid man, besides being infernally handsome. Moreover, he lived in England. So Bonnington looked at Esme Rawlings the way a starving dog eyes a bone? He would be discreet. Presumably he wouldn't set up his wife's closest friend as a mistress.

I wouldn't have been respectable, Cam thought. At times during the trip to the shore, he had tried to picture himself living in the English countryside, building flat bridges and supervising harvest dinners. His thoughts always ended with an image of himself hoisting his wife onto a plank table amidst the marrows and beans and—

He wrenched his mind away again and went down into his cabin. Three passengers, the captain had said. It didn't take a genius to realize that he was about to spend two to three months in close proximity with a hymn singer and his bad-tempered shrew of a wife. He refused to watch the fat parson board the ship. It might look as if he were waiting for someone.

Phillipos looked into the cabin around an hour after the ship had set sail. "The captain reports that we are clear of the shore, sir. He would like the passengers to join him for sherry."

Cam looked up with a frown. He had just recovered from a fit of the sulks, as he'd taken to labeling his black moods, and he was making rapid sketches in charcoal, rather jagged but not terrible. He knew from experience that it took several hours before he gained complete hand control while on board ship.

"Goodness' sakes," Phillipos said with relish. He had picked up several English idioms and meant to use them regularly. "That's a stern-looking woman."

"Medusa," Cam said briefly, putting the snake-haired goddess to the side and washing his hands in the basin. "Do you suppose I have to dress for dinner?"

"Undoubtedly, my lord. Captain Brackit appears to be a rather formal man. His valet told me that he has a boy whose sole work is starching the captain's clothing."

Cam responded with a grunt as he stripped off his comfortable cambric shirt and began to wash. Ten minutes later, Phillipos wrestled his gloomy master into a black coat and declared himself satisfied.

Cam walked into the captain's cabin in a mood of savage despair. Intellectually, he knew it would pass. He would find peace in the heady pleasure of shaping marble.

Someday he would find another woman, and push his onetime wife to the back of his mind. Someday he wouldn't mind the fact that he would never again read a letter from Gina, never again hold—

Someday.

He shoved open the captain's door and slammed it straight into the back of the plump parson.

"I beg pardon, sir," Cam exclaimed, stooping to lend the man a hand. The parson had gone heavily down on his knees. Bracing his legs, Cam hauled him to his feet.

"That's all right, Your Grace," the parson said, beaming at Cam with the delight of a plain Englishman who has just discovered that he's in close quarters with aristocracy. "I was just telling your lovely wife that . . ."

The parson kept talking but his voice faded from Cam's mind.

She was smiling at him as if nothing had happened. As if he hadn't fled helter-skelter across the countryside, running like a coward from the knowledge of her wedding. As if she hadn't married the better man.

"Ah," Cam said, cutting into the parson's conversation. He bowed and raised her hand to his lips. "My last duchess."

"And your next," she replied.

She was exquisitely dressed and groomed, from her darkened eyelashes to her curled hair. Every inch of her was duchesslike.

He could only grin.

She turned to the parson and tapped him lightly on the arm. "You see the duke struck dumb with surprise, Parson Quibble."

"My sister was the same at parting," Quibble said promptly. "Cried as if I were going to the Antipodes. Are you making a long visit to Greece, Your Grace?"

Gina looked pensively over her glass of sherry. "The duke sculpts marble in the islands," she said to the parson. "We shall likely live there for several years, at least."

Cam drank weak sherry and tried to contain the singing joy in his body. Apparently, she was still his wife, every practical, managing inch of her. Or she would be his wife again, to be exact.

"A sacrifice indeed!" Parson Quibble said with a shudder.

"For a delicate lady such as yourself, the islands are a dreadful place. The mainland is bad enough." He tossed back his sherry. "My dear sister has asked a hundred times if she's asked once whether she might come live with me and soothe my travail. I have had to be firm. The harsh life is not for a rosebud such as you, I tell her. She would likely wilt in the fearsome heat, but even worse, she would be offended to the bone by the natives. Ali Pasha has no refinement, no manners, no culture. The court at Tepeleni has not even one ballroom!"

The duchess looked precisely as Quibble thought a duchess should look: exquisite and expensive. She would certainly wilt in the heat. No island could be home to an English lady. Several years indeed! He'd warrant that the duke would accompany his wife back to England in a week or so.

He erred by a matter of months.

Chapter Thirty-Seven

In Which a Duchess Dances for Joy

Twilight on the isle of Nissos has a strangely blue quality, a crystalline pearly glow that dances along the skin and shakes pure gold from hair like that of Gina Serrard, Duchess of Girton. She and her husband were leading the harvest dance. She laughed, holding her white frock up to her ankles as she skipped around the fire. And he danced after her, faster and faster, satyrlike, dark to her white.

When he caught her up in his arms, nodded to the assembled villagers, and began climbing the stone steps to the great house on the hill, there were many who wondered what he whispered so tenderly in her ear. Love poetry, perhaps. The Englishman was a fool in love. Anyone could see that.

Gina blinked. "What?"

"Rounton should arrive sometime this week or next," her husband repeated.

"The solicitor?" Her voice ended in a little squeak.

"He will arrange to sell the house and ship my statues to England."

"Why?"

"We are returning," he said calmly. "We'll take *The Starlight* back to London next month." He looked down at her with an expression of extreme innocence. "Thought I couldn't arrange an ocean voyage, did you?"

"But why . . . what . . ."

"What do you think I was doing in the quarries every day?"

Gina smiled up at her husband. "Lifting stone? You're hoisting me as if I were a featherweight."

"You are a featherweight," he said. They reached the top of the steps and he put her deftly on her feet. "Rounton will ship tons of marble home to Girton. Enough to keep me in naked Dianas for the rest of my natural life, should I so choose."

"Oh," Gina breathed.

He tipped up her chin and brushed a kiss on her lips. "First thing, I'm placing marble Marissas all over the formal gardens, just to keep my hand in."

Gina grinned. She'd come to like his indolent, sweet-hearted former mistress. "But Sebastian thought it best if we stayed out of England for a while, given the scandal."

"The scandal is Bonnington's, not ours," Cam said firmly. "*He* chose to play the gallant idiot, sacrificing his reputation to save Esme's. That was his choice. The story he wove about using a false special license to fool his way into your bed— well, it boggles the mind that anyone could believe it. But believe it they did. Bonnington, poor sod, is exiled to the continent and reviled as a disgusting reprobate who tried to bed a duchess without the benefit of marriage. His unhappy fate shouldn't affect our decisions, however."

"Well, Sebastian said that if we stayed away, it would—"

"His ploy worked, Gina. He's an exile; you're considered lucky to have escaped his evil scheme; Esme's reputation is saved. And you belong in England, duchess that you are. Bicksfiddle is probably buried in a stack of inquiries. Certainly he has chopped our hedges down to their bare stubs. Your brother is languishing in Oxford for lack of a family." She made a face. "It's been months," he pointed out. "Bessie

Mittins is likely in the family way again, and in need of hardship funds. Who knows if Bicksfiddle will be as understanding of her fondness for the men of Lower Girton as you are."

"But I like it in Greece, Cam."

He stopped just inside the door and cupped her face to his. "I don't need to live on an island anymore, love. I can walk in the dark now." He gave her a swift, hard kiss.

Gina caught her breath. Surely he was saying that he loved her?

"You are my light," he said, towing her toward their bedchamber.

Chapter Thirty-Eight

The Grand Staircase, Girton House

They had quarreled, as they did occasionally. Cam said she should have asked his advice before she told Bicksfiddle to regrade the sewers in Lower Girton. He would have allocated some of the money to building stone banisters in the arboretum. Gina said he never thought about the future. Cam retorted that sewers were tedious, but that if she had asked, he had an idea about stone sewers, like those built by the Romans.

Gina walked away, up the stairs. She knew what he really meant. She made a tedious duchess. She looked down at her gloved hand as it lightly rested on the stair rail. Of course she always held onto the railing as she walked up the stairs. What if she fell? What if she teetered and fell? What then?

Nothing. She had spent entirely too much time in her life avoiding risks.

A small sound caught her attention and she paused and turned around.

He was still there, staring up at her.

"What are you doing?" she asked, taking her hand off the railing.

"Waiting," he replied, his voice gentle.

Still looking at him, she started unbuttoning her left glove. "Waiting for what?"

"You might change your mind."

She pulled off the glove and tossed it down the stairs. It missed three or four stairs and flapped down. Together they stared at the small pile of crumpled cloth. She looked up to find her husband's eyes dancing with laughter.

She pulled at the buttons on her right hand.

A large male hand came over hers. "You once told me that gloves are difficult to remove. I could help. Would you like me to help you?"

"Help?"

He nodded. "The thing you never ask for. So well trained you were by my dear papa. Have you ever asked for help, Gina?"

"Of course I have!"

"With something that mattered? Why didn't you write me when I lived in Greece, and tell me how much work the estate was? Why didn't you ask me to return? Why don't you ever ask me for help?"

"I am used to being independent," she said mulishly.

He was drawing off her glove, finger by finger. He put a finger on the base of her hand, just over her pulse. "Ask me, Gina."

She saw the crinkles at the corners of his eyes as he smiled . . . uncertainty behind his rakish smile. She knew him now, knew that his smiles hid—hid what? Need? Need for her? Her blood was racing from the simple touch of his finger on her wrist.

"I . . . I would like—" but she broke off. It was too hard, after years of silent wishes and the letters she didn't write.

After the unspoken fears that she would never have a family of her own. Asking for help meant discarding the idea that if she were a perfect duchess, she would be rewarded with a perfect duke. Because he was a perfect duke—for her.

He helped her then. "They tell me I have a wife," he whispered. "Do you know where I might find her?" Gina saw the hint of something behind his laughter. Something less certain than joy.

"Would you like some help locating her?" she replied.

"The woman I love is here." He tipped up her chin. "Will you marry me, Ambrogina? Will you be mine, for better and for worse, in good times and in bad?"

She swallowed, hard. "I will." Her voice cracked. "Will you marry me, Camden William Serrard, and live with me, forsaking all others, till death do us part?"

He cleared his throat and said, "I will," rather huskily. Then he bent his head and gently, so gently, brushed her lips.

"I need help," she said, looking straight into his eyes.

"Anything."

She turned around, not bothering to hold the railing, teetering on the little heels of her dress slippers. "I would like to undress."

"Undress!" He looked around. Girton's vast arched stairway stretched above them, the newel posts wrenched from their places, to be replaced by statues. No one stirred; it was late at night. But there was nothing to stop Rundles from entering the hallway on a late night errand. True, the butler was more likely to use the servants' stair.

He laughed and protested: "Gina!"

She said nothing, just stood with her back to him, neck curved gently so that the long line of elegant buttons that ran down her gown were in evidence. He kissed her neck . . . it smelled like apple blossoms. Then despite himself, his fingers started undoing the buttons, one by one, right there on the palatial stairs of his home.

A memory leaped into his mind: his father poised on the stairs like a feudal lord, shouting furiously at the servants in mid-step because he couldn't wait until he reached the bottom of the stairs. Cam's fingers faltered.

Gina began pulling pins from her hair and tossing them heedlessly to the side. They pinged lightly against polished walnut railings, fell to the marble, fell in all directions. His fingers were covered with a rush of sunlit-rosy hair, sleek and smooth and smelling of apples. His hands steadied and he began unbuttoning in a frenzy.

When he reached the last button, he pulled the dress forward. She helped, wriggling out of the arms. The cloth pooled and fell. Gina stepped away and kicked the garment to the side. Then she turned, dressed only in a frail chemise laced with blue ribbon. Eyes on his, she untied the little bow and the chemise fell open.

"I still need help," his wife said, throatily. "I need—"

"I'm here, Gina." Something ripped as he pulled the chemise down, down over creamy shoulders and beautiful breasts, half hidden by a sweep of red hair.

There she was, naked but for delicate silk stockings, her garters and slippers. He knelt down in front of her because worship seemed to be called for, but more because he couldn't stop himself. The skin just under the rise of her breasts was as sleek as the side of a peach. She giggled as his tongue wandered around her belly, and he said, "Quiet, wench," and let his hands settle down on the luscious curve of her bottom.

Then he discovered that if he shifted down one stair . . . well, that put his mouth just at the juncture of her legs. He ignored her protests and after a while she stopped wiggling. She forgot to be a duchess and leaned back against the banister like someone accustomed to nudity in public places. He kissed her until little puffing moaning shrieks escaped into the dim twilight that surrounded the stairs. And then, just when he could feel her trembling all down her legs, he stopped. Pulled away and gave her a little bite in the thigh. Explored that interesting hollow in her hip. Listened to her coming back to herself, regaining a sense of propriety—"No, you can't! Cam, we're on the *stairs*!"—and then settled back into an exhibition of mastery. Settled back in the juncture of those lovely thighs and drove her into a shivering, shrieking wife. *His* wife.

When she finally melted into his arms, gasping for air, crying for mercy, he just grinned.

Until she gave him a sultry smile that promised retribution, and wiggled against his groin. He sucked in his breath.

"Hmm," Gina purred. Her tone reeked with revenge. "My chair is most uncomfortable. There's something *protruding* from it."

He was too late. She slipped from his hands and hopped up two stairs, with a grin that was half lustful and half a giggle. Looking at his wife, Cam felt a burn in his chest that would never go away, no matter how many times he held her in his arms, no matter how many nights she slept beside him, no matter how many times she asked him for help.

He wrenched his shirt off as she watched with that frank and hungry gaze that never suited the prim Duchess of Girton. "You would have made a terrible marchioness," he said. "Terrible!"

Gina was not interested. She leaned back against the railing and enjoyed the way her husband's fingers fumbled with his boots when her breasts rose in the air. When she ran a lazy finger over her breast and down her tummy, he wrenched off a boot and accidentally dropped it right down the stairs.

"I feel a wave of embarrassment," she drawled, lounging against the railing, as much the bold courtesan as she ever envisioned her French *maman*.

He raised an eyebrow. "Really?" He was almost ungarbed.

"Indeed. I should like you to put out the candles, Cam."

He laughed. "My little duchess . . . you already cured me of my fear of the dark, don't you know that?" He moved to stand just before her. They were both naked now.

He kissed her, but without touching her body. She pulled back from the heat and desire and said, "Cam," in a shaky little voice.

Naked, he had a beauty such as she could never have imagined. One never looked at his body when he was dressed. His personality was too vivid, too explosive, too engaging. But without clothes, one saw the long line of thigh, the taut beauty of his arse, the leashed strength in his arms as he cupped the candles leading up the stairs.

One by one the shadows grew, casting the stairs into darkness. He skipped the candle just before her and continued up the stairs. When he looked from the top of the stairs, there was a dim candle glow halfway up the stairs, and there, to the side of it, a beautiful creamy shape that he knew to be silky from top to bottom: a body that laughed with a breathless chuckle, kissed with a lustful glee, *loved* . . . Gina loved with a fierce strength.

He snuffed the last candle with no more ado than one steps on an ant.

And then, finally, he did what he had wanted to do for the last hour. He sat down on a stair and held out his arms.

But she couldn't see him. The high mullioned windows let in little light when the moon was full, and tonight there was no moon at all.

"Gina," he said, and his voice was full of husky promise. "Come here."

She sounded uncertain. "Where are you?"

"Across from you. Don't worry; I won't let you fall." And he reached out and found a slender ankle. Walked his fingers up that ankle, pulled gently on her leg. And then he had her

384

sitting on his lap, those gorgeous long legs slung around his hips. He leaned back against cool marble and ran a deliberate thumb over one nipple.

The tiny strangled noise in the back of her throat was everything he wanted in life.

She traced her fingers down his cheekbones. "No jokes?" she whispered. His fingers moved and she cried against his mouth.

"My pulse is steady," he said.

She put her lips to his neck and pressed forward into his hands. She could feel him stir under her. His pulse thundered under her lips. "No, it isn't," she said.

"It's not the dark, it's you," he said. His voice was as quiet as velvet and not at all joke-filled. "You are my wife, my prim duchess, my naked love." His hands molded her body to his. "I don't need to tell jokes . . . holding you is joy enough."

"Oh, Cam——" Her voice broke on a sob that turned to a gasp, and then to a moan.

He forgot it was dark. All that mattered was the silky touch and rounded curves, the fiery heat and gasps of his own, his very own duchess.

And Gina forgot that *Duchess is as Duchess does.* Her husband lifted her, held her poised over him, let her fall; delicious weight. She cried out. There was nothing poised about her now, nothing neat, nothing proper. She rode him with a clear fierce joy and an exuberant pleasure that disregarded convention. She laughed, rubbing her breasts against his chest, glorying in the sensation. He laughed when she tickled him, until her fingers trailed lower.

At some point Gina reached over and snatched her gown so that Cam could stuff it behind his back, since he swore the marble was crippling him for life. But she refused to leave the stairs, and he couldn't even think of standing without her.

She needed him to anchor her to the ground, just as he needed her to light the darkness.

Finally they stopped laughing, and her breath grew shorter, came only in gasps. He could feel every inch of her silky skin, her softness, her forgiveness. He held her tight, thrust up hard, harder. She cried out with every thrust, kissed him again and again, kisses and cries melting against his face.

He thrust harder, just to hear her shuddering cry. "I love you," he said fiercely. "I think I've always loved you."

He wasn't certain that she heard him. She was trying to go somewhere that only he could take her. So he gripped her hips and pumped into her so hard that he actually rose off the steps. She screamed and clutched his shoulders and screamed again . . .

They were together, in a tempest in the darkness, in the heat.

And in the shuddering darkness that wasn't lonely, Cam picked up his wife and without sparing a thought for the clothing strewn over the stairs, walked to their room. Her head lay on his shoulder, as peaceful as a babe's.

He put her on the ancestral bed. On his father's bed, his grandfather's bed. On the bed where his own child would be born. Many of them, if he had his way. He lit candles, only so he could watch her.

She opened her eyes, a lazy smile and the hint of shyness that was his duchess. "Come here, Your Grace," she said sleepily.

"Thank you," he said. "I believe I shall."

And he did.

Epilogue

The Lawn, Girton House

There was no denying the fact that the duchess was kissing the baby too much. Whenever he looked at that poor mite, all wrapped up in lace and fribblededoos, Cam felt a pang of sympathy. Even now, his wife and her friend Helene were hanging over the little bundle, balanced on the duchess's knees. As he watched, a small waving fist managed to grab a few strands of red hair and pull vigorously.

That's my son, Cam thought with satisfaction as his wife squealed and kissed the babe in appreciation of his infant violence.

Helene rose as he strolled over.

"Maximillian is very beautiful," she said, smiling at him.

He grinned back. He'd grown very fond of his wife's friends, with their sharp tongues and disastrous marriages.

Not that Esme was married at the moment. Her reputation was indeed saved by Sebastian's announcement that he had attempted to trick Gina into his bed, using a false wedding certificate. But Esme retired into the country anyway. And these days she swore that she needed no one other than her little baby.

Helene touched Gina's shoulder. "I will return in a moment with Max's blanket." She walked toward the house, a willowy, lonely figure.

"He doesn't need a blanket," Cam said. "Come here, you little scrap." Max gurgled with laughter and reached his arms toward him. Cam's heart bounded.

"Isn't he the most intelligent baby you ever saw?" Gina said, hanging on his arm so she could see her son's face. "He knows his daddy."

"Mmmammmmamm," Max said intelligently.

"And he's speaking! He already knows my name. Nanny told me that he wouldn't speak until he was over a year. Here he is, talking at only four months. She just didn't know how wonderful you were, did she, Buttercup? She thought you were like other babies."

Gina took the babe back into her arms and lavished kisses on his sweet smooth skin and the wild black ringlets that covered his little head.

Cam's vision blurred. He reached out and cupped his son's head in his hand.

Gina leaned against him and they watched as Max yawned, a wide, toothless yawn. He curled his finger around his father's large one and turned his face inquiringly toward his mother.

"I think he'd like some milk," Cam observed, demonstrating that all the family intelligence was not in its offspring.

"My little Buttercup," Max's mother cooed, demonstrating the possibility that family intelligence lay only on the male side. She seemed to be unable to stop kissing the poor scrap of a boy. Not that he was complaining, exactly.

"Do you remember telling me about my mother's diary?" Cam asked. He was winding Max's ringlets around his fingers and letting them spring free.

"Of course," Gina said absentmindedly. She had sat down and was rearranging her nursing gown to give the baby a bit of luncheon.

"The part where she writes about my black curls?"

"Mm-hmm," she said. "Just like our little Max."

He knelt down before the child and tipped up his wife's chin. "I was bald, sweetheart," he said. "Bald for two years. I'm the hairless child depicted in the schoolroom. Who says that I'm the only one with imagination in this family?"

She bit her lip.

He kissed her. It was only the ten thousandth kiss the duke had given his duchess in the past two years. But he seemed to be unable to stop kissing her, even in the broad daylight, and with a mildly interested audience of one Maximillian Camden Serrard, future Duke of Girton.

A Note on the Rarest of Marital Surprises:
Of Recognition and Annulment

In the late 1590s, the Earl of Essex returned to England after a trip to the continent that lasted many years. Entering a ball-room, he saw an extremely beautiful woman dancing. Turning to a bystander, he asked her name. It was his wife.

Most husbands in 1810 did recognize their wives, and most did not seek annulment. Yet annulment did occur, especially among the aristocracy. For example, the Essexes later annulled their marriage. In 1785 the Fifth Earl of Berkeley married and later annulled the marriage, remarrying the same lady in 1796.

The nullification of Gina's marriage to Cam would have hinged on two facts: Gina's illegitimacy, and the age of consent for girls. Gina married before age twelve. The law at this time provided that if a couple disagreed once they both reached the age of majority, they could marry again to others. Moreover, because she was an illegitimate child, the name on Gina's marriage certificate was assumed rather than accredited. The name Lady Cranborne gave her adopted daughter was not legally valid, and marriages were invalidated for precisely this reason.

I have taken a fictional liberty in giving Peter Fabergé, who immigrated to the Baltic province of Livonia in 1800, a brother Franz, who remained in Paris. The Fabergés were a family of goldsmiths. In my reconstruction, the art of hinging beautiful objects was a family passion, and Franz created hinged alabaster statues while his brother Peter dreamed of hinged alabaster eggs. Peter's grandson Carl would perfect that most precious of hinged objects, the Fabergé egg.

About the Author

Author of four award-winning romances, ELOISA JAMES is a professor of English literature who lives with her family in New Jersey. All her books must have been written in her sleep, because her days are taken up by caring for two children with advanced degrees in whining, a demanding guinea pig, a smelly frog, and a tumbledown house. Letters from readers provide a great escape! Write Eloisa at eloisa@eloisajames.com or visit her web site at: www.eloisajames.com.

Do you love historical fiction?

Want the chance to hear news about your favourite authors (and the chance to win free books)?

Mary Balogh

Charlotte Betts

Jessica Blair

Frances Brody

Gaelen Foley

Elizabeth Hoyt

Eloisa James

Lisa Kleypas

Stephanie Laurens

Claire Lorrimer

Amanda Quick

Julia Quinn

Then visit the Piatkus website and blog
www.piatkus.co.uk | www.piatkusbooks.net

And follow us on Facebook and Twitter
www.facebook.com/piatkusfiction | www.twitter.com/piatkusbooks

piatkus